P9-CCW-067

"What's a few million dollars between enemies? Read *BAGMAN* and find out."
—*Colin Harrison*

"Audacious, twisted, and ultimately unstoppable. . . . Brace yourself."
—Carsten Stroud, author of *Cobraville*

DEAD ON DELIVERY

Simon extracted the money pack, purposely brushing the edge of his jacket to one side, exposing the Mauser. El Pato leaped forward, shockingly fast, pinning Simon against the rail and ripping the gun from his belt. "What you do with this, Bagman?"

"Protection," Simon snapped. "I'm toting a bit of money here."

El Pato stepped back, looked at the gun, and slipped it into his belt. "No more *dinero*. No more need."

"Hey, that thing cost me over four hundred dollars."

"You pay too much. It cost El Pato *nada*."

"What, you can't afford it?" Simon glanced at the money pack. "Seven million isn't enough?"

El Pato leaned down and picked up the pack.

"Adios, *gringo*."

The finality of the words confirmed the ominous feeling. A gun seemed to materialize in El Pato's right hand. Not the Mauser loaded with blanks, but something big and black with a thick extrusion attached to the barrel.

"Wait!"

The man smiled, exposing his gold tooth in a ghoulish grin, and pulled the trigger. . . .

Also by Jay MacLarty

The Courier

Now available from Pocket Books

BAGMAN

JAY MacLARTY

POCKET STAR BOOKS
New York London Toronto Sydney

An *Original* Publication of POCKET BOOKS

 A Pocket Star Book published by
POCKET BOOKS, a division of Simon & Schuster, Inc.
1230 Avenue of the Americas, New York, NY 10020

ISBN: 0-7434-6490-7

First Pocket Books printing August 2004

10 9 8 7 6 5 4 3 2 1

POCKET STAR BOOKS and colophon are registered trademarks of Simon & Schuster, Inc.

Cover art and design by Carlos Beltran

Manufactured in the United States of America

For information regarding special discounts for bulk purchases, please contact Simon & Schuster Special Sales at 1-800-456-6798 or business@simonandschuster.com

This book is dedicated to:
My sister and brother-in-law,
for always being there.

Mimi & Jim
*fifty years together
best friends and lovers*

Acknowledgments

The author wishes to thank the following people for their help:

Larry Wagner and James Blackmon for their invaluable insights into the gas and oil industry.

Dr. Roger Bartels and Lewis Nelson for their advice with all things aeronautical, both of whom will cringe at my literary shortcuts, for which I take full responsibility.

Elaine Nelson and Lisa MacLarty, who read the manuscript with a fresh eye and didn't hesitate to offer suggestions.

Deny Howeth and Jiselle Crawford for their artistic contribution.

Ed Miller for questions regarding Colombia and Ecuador.

And always, my literary compatriots: Liz Crain, Gene Munger, and Louise Crawford, who never fail to spot my wrong turns and nudge me back on course.

BAGMAN

PROLOGUE

Galápagos Islands

Saturday, 1 November 16:02:59 GMT −0600

Once clear of San Cristobal, Kyra disengaged her autopilot and banked toward the southern tip of Santa Cruz, gradually reducing altitude. Her butt felt like petrified wood, as if all the blood had drained into her legs. *Long day. Long, long day.* From Bogotá, where she spent the night, to Guayaquil, where she topped off her tanks, to this Pacific archipelago—twelve total hours when you counted the flying, the filing, the fueling, and the fussing with customs. She silently added one last *F* to the list, then reminded herself it was for a good cause, and had given her time to think, to work on *the problem.*

It was getting late, the sun low on the horizon, nearly blinding her view of the island. It had been four years since her last visit and she wanted to see for herself just how much Puerto Ayora, the largest settlement on Santa Cruz, had grown. She had read the latest studies and analyzed the statistics, but wanted to see for herself just how much impact the population growth was having on the island's unique ecosystem. That, of course, was her *excuse* for being there—to address the issue, rally the donors, and help raise a fresh pile of money for the Charles Darwin Research Station, the *Center,* to all current and previous employees—but the *reason* she was there, the only reason she had agreed to interrupt her life at such an awkward moment, was to honor her old friend and mentor, Dr. Elsworth Marshall, who was being forced into retirement at the youthful age of seventy, despite his enthusiasm, undiminished energy, and thirty-four years of dedicated service.

No one needed a zoologist from Washington to tell them what everyone already knew about the expanding population and the effects it was having on the biogeochemistry of the island. They had plenty of experts to sing that tune. Her voice would add little to an already overcrowded chorus, but what they *really wanted* was Dr. Kyra Rynerson-Saladino, daughter to one of the world's richest men, and her ability to raise money. And of course they hoped she might contribute just a bit of her own. She would. But what they *truly wanted,* at the very top of their fantasy list, was that her father, Big Jake Rynerson, *businessman and billionaire*—God, how she hated that overused tabloid description—might become a benefactor. He wouldn't. Not that her father was insensitive toward a good cause, but they rarely spoke and she would never ask.

Never ask—Never take.

It was a pledge she had made to herself years before, on the very day Big Jake dumped her mother for trophy wife Number One, a sin Kyra would never forgive, in sharp contrast to her mother, who seemed to harbor no ill feelings toward her former husband—something Kyra had never been able to understand. It was an old argument, but the familiar words never seemed to change.

"Kyra, great men have great appetites; you can't expect a man like your father to be satisfied with one of anything. Especially when it comes to women."

"Hardly an endorsement for Husband-of-the-Year, Mother."

"Get past it, dear, I have. He misses you."

But she couldn't, though she never really tried. Why should she? She hated everything about him: his money, his lifestyle, his wife—he was now on trophy wife Number Three. "I can't stand to be around that woman; she's younger than I am."

Her mother laughed and groaned at the same time. "Kyra, for God's sake, Tammi was in diapers when your father and I divorced. You can't blame her. I've spoken to her a number of times and she seems very nice."

Yes, very nice, and for some reason that made Kyra dislike the woman all the more. "She's twenty-six years old. It's obscene!"

"Yes, it is. You should feel sorry for your father."

"Sorry!"

"He keeps getting older and his wives keep getting younger. Trying to keep up"—she chuckled, the wrinkles around her eyes crinkling with mischievous humor—*"must be a terrible burden."*

Her mother's none-too-subtle double entendre was enough to make Kyra grimace; the thought of her father with an erection was way beyond anything she cared to imagine. "Mother!"

"You need to forgive him. You need to move on."

"Move on? How can you tell me to move on? You're the one who never remarried."

"Your father's a hard man to replace."

"I don't understand how you can say that."

"Kyra dear, your father has made my life very easy. We've not exchanged one cross word since the day I left. And remember, I'm the one who walked out."

"You talk about him like he's a saint or something. For God's sake, Mom, you caught the son of a bitch in bed with another woman."

"Well, he at least had the decency to marry her."

"Yeah, like that lasted a long time."

"And how's your marriage, young lady?"

The memory of that question stung, enough to jolt Kyra back to the here and now. She reached down and touched her stomach—still flat—but it wouldn't remain that way for long. She needed to make a decision. *Soon*.

She leveled off at twenty-five hundred feet, eye-level with the Cerro Crocker volcano and the upper reaches of the Highland rain forest, the most significant patch of green on the island's scorched lava-scape. The beauty, at least for her, were the things she couldn't see from that altitude: the unique animal species that inhabited the Galápagos, and that she had studied for two years as a neophyte zoologist. *Good years. The best.* Freedom from home and school and parental authority. Freedom from Big Jake Rynerson.

Her mother's voice renewed its niggling mantra: *"You need to forgive him, Kyra. You need to move on."*

"I don't want anything to do with him."

"Really? I don't remember you refusing that two-million-dollar trust he gave you on your thirtieth birthday."

"I've never touched it." But that wasn't *exactly* true. She had used it as security to buy the only thing she really wanted: a 1983 vintage Beechcraft Baron B-55. *Babe.* The only *baby* she wanted. Kyra Rynerson-Saladino was not going to be one of those idiot women who tried to save their marriage with a kid.

Her mother cocked her head, a doubtful, slightly amused expression on her face. "You haven't?"

"Absolutely not." *Absolutely* might be a bit of an overstatement, but taking advantage of her trust to finance Babe wasn't the same as *using* it. She made the payments with her own money. And it wasn't as if *Babe* was a toy; as a traveling ambassador for the National Zoo, having her own plane was an absolute necessity. The fact that she loved to fly was just a perk, something she had been doing since the age of sixteen, when Big Jake gave her flying lessons for her birthday. Instantly, it had become both her passion and her escape. "You can't buy love, Mother."

"Kyra, don't be such a self-righteous bitch; it doesn't become you. Your father didn't give you that trust in an at-

tempt to buy your love and you know it. If anything, he was showing his support for the choices you've made."

"Bullshit, I'm nothing but a disappointment to him. He's always hated what I do."

"It wasn't his first choice, I agree. He wanted you to help him in the business, but despite that he never turned his back on you."

Help! Big Jake Rynerson needed her help about as much as she needed a cracker crumbler.

When she reached the southern tip of the island, she dipped *Babe*'s right wing for a better view and slowly circled the town. No longer a sleepy little harbor village, Puerto Ayora had grown significantly since her last visit. Every year an increasing number of tourists were finding their way to the islands; wanting to see and photograph the unique wildlife, to walk where Charles Darwin once walked and where he began to formulate his *Origin of Species*. More visitors meant more jobs, and more jobs meant more workers, all of which endangered the very existence of what everyone came to see. *Catch-22.*

Kyra banked *Babe* toward the north and tuned her VOR receiver to the Baltra frequency. The airport's Morse code identifier came back instantly, followed by a recorded weather report: clear, 28° Celsius, winds ENE 5 mph. *Normal,* Kyra thought, remembering her time on the island. Only twenty miles out, she contacted the tower and requested landing instructions.

Thirty minutes later *Babe* was on the ground, tied down in a cordoned-off area reserved for private aircraft, chocks under the wheels. A Customs officer arrived five minutes later, wrote Kyra's name on a clipboard and departed without giving *Babe* so much as a perfunctory look-through. It was 4:45, thirty minutes prior to her ETA and the time Elsworth promised to have someone pick her up. Hoping to get a significant part of her next preflight out of the way before the driver arrived, Kyra popped the cowling on both engines and began checking fluid levels. It was going to be a long flight back and she wanted to make a quick escape the minute her give-me-your-money spiel at tomorrow's fund-raiser was over. She needed to settle things with Anthony once and for all. *No more procrastination.*

The fuel truck had come and gone and she had just removed her carryall and garment bag from the luggage compartment when an open Jeep with no doors came barreling across the tarmac and skidded to a stop no more than three inches from *Babe*'s right wing. "Dr. Rynerson?"

Kyra suppressed her irritation. "You found me."

"I'm Kelly Anderson, your driver." He was young, obviously American, dressed in a T-shirt and cutoffs, with an Angels baseball cap and RayBans. He looked like a California surfer on a good day: not more than twenty-two or -three, golden tan, dazzling white teeth, big smile.

Fresh out of college, Kyra thought, serving his internship at the Research Station, just as she had done. "Hello, Kelly. Mind grabbing my bags?"

"You bet." He came around the back of the Jeep in an exuberant rush. "Sorry I wasn't here to meet you. I thought—"

"I'm early, don't worry about it."

He snatched up the canvas carryall and nylon garment bag. "Nice plane. Yours?"

"Someday. Right now the bank owns most of it." He gave her a look, a mixture of surprise and disbelief, something she had seen a million times. Why would the daughter of Big Jake Rynerson owe money to a bank? Not about to explain, she retrieved her laptop from the cockpit, locked the cabin door, and climbed into the passenger seat as Kelly strapped her bags onto the Jeep's open bed.

"Ready?" he asked, his eyes making a quick, admiring tour over the contours of her body. "Seat belt on, tray table in its upright position?"

Okay, she wasn't too old to enjoy a little flirtation from a younger man. "All set, Captain Kelly."

"It's going be a little breezy. You want a hat? I brought an extra."

"No thanks." She dug a hair band out of her purse—making an effort to ignore her wedding ring lying at the bottom—and pulled her hair back into a ponytail. "I'm fine."

The ferry between Baltra and Santa Cruz took fifteen minutes and Captain Kelly never stopped chattering, obviously having older-woman-away-from-home seduction fantasies and trying to impress her. "How was your flight over?"

"Long. I spent the night in Bogotá."

"Oh yeah, Bogotá, interesting city. I came through there on my way to the Center. Been piloting your own plane long?"

"Awhile."

"I've been meaning to take lessons, just haven't had the time. I'll get around to it one of these days."

Kyra nodded, hoping he wasn't going to play twenty questions all the way to Puerto Ayora, an hour drive. "You should, it's a great way to escape."

"That's what everyone says. You live in Washington, right?"

"Close. Just outside the city."

"Your father's Big Jake Rynerson?"

Good for you, Captain Kelly, that was the question most people asked first. "Sure is."

Kelly nodded, as if this confirmed the stories he'd heard. "Must be nice."

She was tempted to ask *why,* but knew exactly what he meant: your father's a billionaire; your life is nothing but champagne and caviar. When she was young and foolish she had tried to correct the misconception, but no matter what she said, everyone had their own fantasy about what it would be like to have a billionaire father, so she learned to let it go. If anything, life as the daughter of Big Jake Rynerson was nothing more than a bloody curse. Along with the name came the expectations and celebrity-by-association, something she didn't ask for and didn't want. "Yeah, real peachy." *Peachy!* Did she actually say *peachy?*

"When did you work at the Center?"

Good way to learn her age, Kyra thought, though the question seemed part of his inquisitive patter and without guile. "About fifteen years ago."

His pupils popped and she could see the wheels turning behind them. "Thirty-five," she said, providing the answer to his unspoken question.

"Oh." He seemed to deflate, his fantasy balloon leaking air. "You don't look that old."

She laughed. "Well, I don't know how old you *think* I look, but until this moment I didn't exactly consider myself long in the tooth."

His cheeks flushed, his eyes darting back and forth between her and the road. "I didn't mean you were old. I meant—" He glanced back at the road, as if searching for a cliff to drive over. "You look so young. I mean you are young, but—"

She held up a hand, cutting him off before he fumbled his way into adolescent purgatory. "I understand. Thanks. I'll consider that a compliment."

"You bet. You should. Yes, ma'am."

BOOM!—her own balloon exploded—nothing like the word *ma'am* to make a woman feel ancient.

Thankfully, the remainder of the trip passed in relative silence, normal conversation precluded by the wind howling through the open Jeep. "You'll love this place," Kelly said, as he pulled up to the Red Mangrove Adventure Inn.

Though Kyra knew exactly where she was, barely a stone's throw from the Research Station, the hotel was new and unfamiliar—a pleasant surprise. Surrounded by wild red mangrove trees and perched at the edge of the sea, the shell-pink structure reminded her of La Valencia in La Jolla, where she once vacationed as a child with her mother and father, in those wonderful days before Big Jake had gone and ruined their family. "I'm sure. It looks wonderful."

She signed in using her entire name—Kyra Rynerson-Saladino—the name on her passport. Lately, she had been dropping Saladino—the marriage was over—she knew it and Anthony should have known, though he continued to resist the reality. Being pregnant was only going to make the problem more difficult. He wanted a child, desperately, and would not willingly accept her plan to end the pregnancy.

Kelly started to pick up her bags but she caught his arm. "I can take it from here, thanks." She didn't want to have to push him out of her room, in case he might still be harboring fantasies about seducing an *older* woman.

"Oh sure, okay." He took a hesitant step back. "Dr. Marshall said to remind you about the reception."

Ugh, just what she needed, smiling and chatting and acting bubbly to a roomful of potential donors. "Looking forward to it. Seven-thirty, right?"

"You got it. Want me to pick you up?" he asked, eyes shiny with anticipation.

She saw no reason to torture the boy with false hope. "Thanks, but an old friend asked me to call when I got in. I'm sure he'll drop me."

"Oh, sure. Great." He backed toward the door, then gave her a jaunty little salute, finger to eyebrow. "See you there."

"Absolutely. Thanks for the ride."

Her room was large, overlooking Pelican Bay, with white adobe walls and a great hammock for lounging, but most important it had a private bath—an oddity for that part of the world—and a bed. Hoping to squeeze in a power nap before the reception, she stripped down and turned on the shower. Waiting for the water to heat, she took a hard look at herself in the mirror, something she hadn't done for a while, and tried to imagine herself through the eyes of Kelly Anderson. Was he just another horny graduate student, marooned on Santa Cruz without female companionship, or could she still attract men, something she might have to face sooner rather than later? *Ugh, dating.* It was something she always hated—did they really like *her,* or were they attracted to the Rynerson name and wealth?

Tall and slim, she could see no sign of that foreign object growing inside; she didn't want to think of it as human, a baby boy or girl; that would make things too difficult. Her breasts were still firm. *Small,* but that was something that had never bothered her—*Better than big and saggy*—and her skin was still smooth and unblemished, though darkened by the sun to an unfashionable golden brown. Her shoulder-length blond hair, solar streaked in shades ranging from platinum to dark honey, looked like she had just stepped out of a tornado. But overall—*not bad.*

She stepped into the shower. *Not bad at all—for a ma'am!* Oh well, she could live with that, as long as she didn't become *matronly.* That was the ultimate curse—a place she never intended to go. *The ultimate ma'am.*

She waited until 7:45, putting off the inevitable as long as possible, then took a taxi to the reception. The Research Station was only a short distance, one she could easily have walked, but thought she might look a bit odd traipsing down Charles Darwin Avenue in heels and a long cocktail dress.

The reception was already in high gear, the locals clearly determined not to miss any part of the festivities, social events being somewhat rare on the island. A small lecture hall had been converted into party central: the walls decorated with poster-size pictures of the island's unique animal species; the ceiling awash with lanterns made of mulberry paper and imbedded with natural leaves and petals, casting a warm glow over the partygoers. An impressive hors d'oeuvre buffet had been laid out down the center of the room, with drink stations strategically located throughout. Kyra was barely in the door when Elsworth Marshall swept down upon her. A man of average height and unremarkable features, his expression was wide and friendly, with Santa Claus eyes that made a person feel good just to be included in their twinkling gaze. "Kyra, my dear, you're more beautiful every time I see you."

At least she wasn't a *ma'am* to older men. "No wonder they're putting you out to pasture, Elsworth, you've become senile."

He laughed heartily, a booming HEHHH, HEHHH, HEHHH, from deep inside. "No, it's true, it's true, you look fabulous." He took her by the shoulders, holding her at arm's length, admiring the view. "Or maybe it's because I've never seen you in a dress."

She had to admit, she didn't look half bad in the dress: a simple black sheath with matching sling-back heels. "Dr. Marshall, that sounds positively risqué!"

"I mean—" He laughed again. "Oh, you know what I mean."

"You probably didn't even notice I was a female when I was your A-Number-One pupil."

His emerald eyes sparkled, the lecherous twinkle of an old man who had not yet lost his memory or appreciation for a younger woman. "Oh, I knew."

"You better be careful, Elsworth, I might just take you up on that unspoken offer."

The sparkle faded from his eyes. "Things are not well between you and Anthony?"

She smiled, hiding the truth, glad she remembered to wear her ring. "Everything's fine."

"And your father?" He leaned forward, his voice a confidential whisper. "How are things between the two of you?"

She shrugged. "The same."

He shook his head, slowly and sadly. "I'm very sorry to hear that, my dear. I had hoped things might improve between you. And your mother, she is well?"

"She's great. Busy, busy, busy."

"Charity work?"

"Oh no, she refuses to put her foot in that trap. She's been writing—children's stories. She's actually had a couple of them published."

"That's wonderful! Very inspiring for one about to enter the queue of the unemployed." He reached down and took her hand. "Come my dear, there are many people I want you to meet."

The partygoers were exactly as Kyra expected—academics, alumni, previous donors, and new pigeons—most of them gathered in small coveys, everyone eating and drinking and talking at once. Elsworth guided her from one group to another, introducing her as: "Doctor Kyra Rynerson-Saladino from the National Zoological Park in Washington. A former resident here at the Center."

The response was always the same, the questions familiar. Kyra offered up her best smile and did her duty, avoiding the personal questions with long-established answers, schmoozing the pigeons, and sipping white wine to help her get through.

"Oh, you're the Rynerson girl. I just love your father."

All the world, it seemed, knew Big Jake Rynerson, and everyone always spoke as if they knew him personally. It wasn't his fault, Kyra told herself—Big Jake was news, always good for a memorable quote or a spicy story, and the press was always there to record it—but for some reason she still blamed him. "He's a classic."

"Do you live in Las Vegas, in that fabulous new resort your father built?"

"No, I live in Washington. That's where I work."

"Oh, I thought maybe you just . . ."

Just what? But she knew exactly what most people thought. She gritted her teeth and forced a smile. "No, I *really* work."

"I so admire your independence." This from a woman who had never had an independent thought in her life and began every sentence with: "My husband thinks—"

"My work is very rewarding," Kyra answered, "as I'm sure your contribution to the Center is rewarding for you."

The woman beamed. "We do what we can."

The most popular question, and the one that irritated Kyra the most because of its disingenuous nature, was the *contrived realization.* "Rynerson? You wouldn't be related to Big Jake Rynerson by chance?"

By chance, as if they didn't know.

As if she didn't realize she was that evening's celebrity.

As if she couldn't hear the buzz of conversation as Elsworth escorted her around the room. The real celebrity, of course, was her father—Big Jake Rynerson, *Billionaire*—but it hung around her like a net, trapping her in its web, refusing to let her go no matter how hard she struggled to escape.

They had pretty much worked the crowd, up one side and down the other, when Elsworth introduced her to a man standing alone near one of the drink stations. "Kyra, I'd like you to meet Señor Luis Acosta, one of our newest benefactors. Señor Acosta, Dr. Kyra Rynerson-Saladino."

Kyra flashed her best smile. Though she could tell by the change in tone that this was someone Elsworth wanted to impress, there was something about the man that didn't quite fit the mold of *benefactor.* Short and stocky, mid-forties, small dark eyes, with skin the color and texture of wet sandpaper, he was wearing a tan Panama suit that didn't quite fit his body—or more accurately, Luis Acosta didn't quite fit the suit. Though his nails had been filed and cleaned, there remained a thin, dark line around the edge of his cuticles, the kind of dirt that builds up over years of labor and couldn't be scrubbed away with a boxcar of borax. "Señor Acosta, I'm very pleased to meet you."

The man bowed, his movements somewhat stiff. "My pleasure, Doctor." Though his English was clear enough, he had a heavy Spanish accent and a slight slur, as if he'd learned the language on the street and not in school.

Elsworth clasped an arm around Acosta's shoulders. "Luis has just pledged twenty-five thousand dollars to our Save the Island fund."

"That's wonderful," Kyra said, working hard to sound enthused, the long day and the wine beginning to take its toll. "The work is so important and so few people understand the problem."

Acosta shifted his weight from one foot to the other. "It is only a small thing." He grinned awkwardly, is if embarrassed, showing a gold tooth.

"Well, I can assure you, it's a very big thing for the Center. What kind of business are you in, Señor Acosta?"

"Agriculture."

That made sense, and would explain the dirt around his nails—a man not afraid to work with his hands—something to be admired, but for some reason he made her uncomfortable. Some undefined, unreasonable prejudice, she was sure, and that made her angry—at herself. "Really? What kind of agriculture?"

"Corn and potatoes," Elsworth answered quickly, as though wishing to show his interest in the affairs of such an important contributor. "Luis has a plantation along the Mantaro."

"In Peru?"

"Sí."

"I love your country. It's beautiful."

For the next five minutes they talked about the Center and the work being done. Kyra let Elsworth carry the conversation as she struggled to keep her eyelids above avalanche level. Just when she thought she couldn't last another minute, Captain Kelly swooped in for a landing. He bobbed his head toward Kyra and Señor Acosta before turning to Elsworth Marshall. "Sorry to intrude, Professor, but I was about to leave and remembered that I promised Dr. Saladino a ride back to the hotel."

Escape, nothing could have sounded better, but Kyra still didn't want to mislead Kelly into thinking she might be interested in anything more. Elsworth misread her hesitation and supplied the push she needed. "Kyra, you've done enough. Let Kelly take you back to the hotel."

It was true, she had done her duty: promulgated, proclaimed, and publicized all the fine work done by the Center, and all the wonderful things it had done for her—she had oiled the pigeons' wallets, and if she could get some sleep, would clean their nests in the morning. What more could they expect? "It has been a long day." She turned to the South American. "Señor Acosta, if you wouldn't mind . . . ?"

He reached out and took her hand. "It has been a great pleasure, Doctor." He bowed, his lips lightly brushing her hand. "I look forward to your lecture."

Though a common gesture in South American society, Kyra sensed an awkwardness in the man's movements, like an actor rehearsing an unfamiliar scene. "Thank you," she said, forcing out one last smile. "I promise not to make it overly long."

Thankful for the rescue, but determined not to mislead her savior, Kyra turned on Kelly the minute they were outside. "I hope you don't think—"

He interrupted her with a big flashy grin. "Don't worry, Doc, I got the message this afternoon."

"Then why . . . ?"

"I thought you were about to take a swan dive off those heels. Someone had to save you."

"Oh no." She couldn't suppress a groan. "That obvious?"

Kelly shook his head. "Nah, don't worry about it, I'm probably the only one who noticed. Anyway, so what? You had a right."

"And why would you be the only one to notice, may I ask?"

"I said I got the message, that doesn't mean I can't admire the messenger."

She laughed, surprised that a young man's words could make her feel so good—so attractive. "Well, thank you for the rescue, Captain Kelly. *And* the compliment."

"No sweat." He gave her a wink. "My pleasure."

Despite her exhaustion, Kyra was up at 5 A.M.—daybreak—a habit that had stayed with her since college and a three-month internship into the Amazon rain forest to study the effects of deforestation on the indigenous wildlife. A place where you worked as long as you could see, then crawled into your tent and slept until the sun came up.

She made a quick sprint through the shower—in and out, three minutes—pulled on a T-shirt and shorts, and was ready to hit the day running, though she had no intention of doing anything so literal. Setting up her laptop on the terrace and using her cellular to make the connection, she logged into her office network, downloaded both her voice and email messages, then disconnected. Below the balcony, four young men with kayaks and fishing rigs pushed away from the shore and began paddling toward deeper water, their soft voices trailing behind in a melodious murmur. Kyra sucked in a lungful of the damp tropical air and took a moment to enjoy the view—the sun breaking over the horizon, the light shimmering off the water like diamond chips—then went to work. It took an hour just to answer her email and fill out her expense vouchers for September, something she hated and always avoided until the last moment.

At 6 A.M. she called the restaurant located directly beneath her room, The Bay Café, and ordered breakfast: whole-grain cereal, fresh papaya, and a large carafe of *strong* coffee. *Another long day,* she was sure of that.

She had finished breakfast and was making a sizable dent in the coffee when someone began rapping on her door, insistent and hard. "Kyra! Kyra!"

She recognized the voice immediately and pulled open the door. "Elsworth, what's the problem?" He was panting, cheeks flushed. "You okay?"

He took a quick breath. "The stairs—" He waved a hand, indicating it was nothing. "But we do have a problem."

"Come in. Let me get you some coffee."

He sank down into one of the rattan chairs, across the table from her spot on the terrace. "Thank you." He took a large gulp, then winced as the hot liquid hit his throat.

"What's wrong?"

He ignored her question. "When are you leaving?"

She hedged, not wanting to sound like she couldn't wait to rush off the moment she finished her speech. "Well, I'm not sure exactly." *True.* "Once my part is done and they've given you the golden boot, I guess. Why?"

He stared back at her with a bemused, knowing expression. "Can't wait to go wheels-up in that little bird of yours, right?"

"It's not that, it's just that—" But she couldn't explain, couldn't tell him she was pregnant and her marriage was about to go up in flames.

He held up a hand. "No need to explain. I understand."

He didn't of course, but it didn't matter, he was a good

friend, and good friends didn't require an explanation. "What's on your mind, Elsworth?"

"There was a man I introduced you to last night . . ."

For some reason she knew exactly who he was referring to. "You introduced me to a lot of men last night."

"Yes, of course. He was alone. And uh—"

"And he had just made a *significant* pledge."

"Yes. Luis Acosta. You remember him?"

"Of course. He didn't seem—"

Elsworth nodded, as if he understood precisely what she meant. "The right type."

"Exactly. What about him?"

"He came to my house just a short time ago. Quite frantic. His four-year-old daughter was bitten by a bushmaster."

"Oh my God, that's terrible!" With proper treatment an adult might survive a bushmaster's attack, but she knew it was nearly impossible for a child to overcome the snake's deadly venom. "When did this happen?"

"It's only been a couple hours. She's been stabilized for the moment, but—" He spread his hands in a helpless gesture.

"That's terrible, but why are you telling me?" Not that she didn't have a good idea.

"Well, of course Luis wants to get home immediately. He can make connections in Guayaquil, but there's no flight off the island until late afternoon. He tried to charter a plane but there was nothing available." Elsworth shook his head slowly, squeezing out the words like the final breath of air from a balloon. "She's not expected to survive the day."

Kyra didn't like it, but wasn't sure why. Luis Acosta was clearly a good man—had proven it with his concern and contribution. So why hesitate? Some prejudice because he didn't fit the mold of dilettante benefactor? It was only a four-hour flight to Guayaquil, and not out of her way. Had he said anything wrong? Anything offensive? *No.* It was more what he hadn't said that bothered her. He was the type of person who would usually drop her father's name in the first two minutes of conversation, but the name Rynerson had never once crossed his lips.

Elsworth leaned forward, reading her trepidation. "You don't have to do it, Kyra. He doesn't even know you have a plane."

That too surprised her. "He doesn't?"

"I never mentioned it. Told him I might be able to arrange something and would have to make some calls."

"It's not that I don't want to help. It's just that there was something about him that made me uncomfortable."

Elsworth bobbed his head. "I know. I understand. He's not the type we're used to."

Not the type we're used to. That made her feel even worse, as if she had looked at the outside of Luis Acosta and judged what was inside the man. That was *not* the type of person she wanted to be. "You said he made a pledge. He hasn't actually given you the money?"

"No, but I too had reservations so I had someone in the office make a few discreet calls."

"And . . . ?"

"He's the biggest landowner in the Mantaro Valley. A very rich man."

So there it was—a well-known businessman, perfectly legitimate—how could she even consider not helping? His daughter was dying. She stood up. "Give me a few minutes to get my stuff together. Have him meet me downstairs."

Elsworth put a hand on his knee and levered himself to his feet. "I'll have him there. Kelly will drive you."

"Looks like you're going to miss my open-your-wallets-and-do-the-right-thing speech."

"Aaah." He exhaled through puffed cheeks, making an

exaggerated sound of relief. "That I can live without."

"Me too. But I do hate missing your big sendoff."

"And I'll miss having you there." He reached out and gave her a hug. "You were always my favorite."

"You say that to all the girls."

"True, but with you I mean it."

"You'll make my apologies?"

"Of course. I'll make you a hero. By the time I'm through telling everyone the story, the money will be pouring out of their wallets and into our Save the Island fund."

"I'll send you a check."

He started toward the door. "Not necessary. You did your duty."

"We didn't really get a chance to talk. Now that you're going to be a free man you can visit me in Washington."

"I will." He blew her a kiss. "Promise."

She packed quickly, then dashed off a quick email to her husband, explaining her change of plans. The marriage might be over, at least in her mind, but Anthony worried and she felt an obligation. Then she grabbed her bags and headed for the lobby. At least she wouldn't need to wear another dress and give another one of her funky speeches. *Thank you, God.* She still didn't have the best feelings about Luis Acosta, but realized she was being silly. It wasn't like she was going off with a complete stranger—Elsworth had checked the man out, and would know who she was with and where she was going.

Kelly was waiting with his Jeep outside the hotel, Luis Acosta pacing nervously alongside. The man rushed forward to take her bags, his hurried, waddling gate reminding her of a duck. "Doctor, I feel so terrible about this, taking you away from the conference. Your work here is so important."

"Señor Acosta, I'm nothing more than frosting on Dr.

Marshall's retirement cake. Getting you home to see your daughter is more important than my presence here."

"I told Elsworth that I could wait for the afternoon flight but he was most insistent that I leave now."

"And he's right. Let's go."

The trip to Baltra was made in silence, Luis Acosta obviously thinking about his daughter, and Kelly having the good sense not to shout over the wind. Kyra closed her eyes and tried to reconcile her misgivings about Luis Acosta. She had been around the rich and successful all her life and had come to recognize certain characteristics—the nouveau riche, never missing an opportunity to let everyone know how much they had; or the inheritors of old money, exuding a confidence that only great wealth could bestow—but new money or old, they all seemed to share one common characteristic, whether real or imagined, that most people lacked: an aura of superiority. A trait alien to Luis Acosta. *Why?* She couldn't explain it, not beyond the *exceptions-to-every-rule* rule.

A customs official—having received a heads-up call from the Center—was waiting when Kelly pulled alongside *Babe*. While Kyra completed her preflight walkaround and filed her flight plan, the man stamped their passports and cleared them for departure without looking at their bags.

Kyra leaned forward, gave Kelly a sisterly peck on the cheek, and whispered, "Thanks, Captain Kelly, I do appreciate your dash to the rescue last night."

"Any time, Doc. Come back and see us."

"I will," though she had a feeling that with Elsworth gone she would not be returning to the Galápagos anytime soon.

"Ready?" she asked, as she fired up *Babe*'s dual Continental 300 hp engines. Sitting beside her in the copilot's seat, clutching his briefcase like a parachute, Luis Acosta nodded. "Want me to stow that in back?" she asked, indicating his briefcase.

He shook his head, as if afraid to open his mouth for fear of what might come out.

Conversation, she decided, was not to be encouraged.

It wasn't until Kyra began her descent into Guayaquil, over four hours later, that Luis Acosta finally spoke. "There's a small landing strip four nautical miles south of Milagro. We will refuel there. Please adjust your heading to 071 degrees."

Stunned, Kyra could only stare at the man, who suddenly appeared completely at ease, his expression one of arrogant self-confidence. Smiling, he snapped the locks on his briefcase—*CLICK-CLICK*—and pulled open the top. It was empty except for two items: a pilot's aeronautical map, and a steel-blue automatic pistol.

That was the moment Kyra knew she was in trouble. *Serious trouble.*

CHAPTER ONE

New York, New York

Tuesday, 4 November 23:02:59 GMT –0500

Momentarily alone at his two-stool bar, Simon took the opportunity to kick back and enjoy the party. The guests were losing steam, the crowd beginning to thin. Never, he thought, had his little home seen so many people. *Home*, of course, could only be whispered silently to himself, the word enough to send Lara into one of her get-a-life speeches. She had never been able to reconcile herself to the fact that her brother lived in a hotel. But it suited his needs, and he liked the lifestyle. He didn't need much space: a small kitchen—he ate out most of the time—a cozy dining room, a comfy bedroom, and a spacious living area with a tremendous view of Central Park. That was the thing he liked most about his suite, every room had a view of the Park. A thousand square feet, with an eight-hundred-and-forty acre front yard—what more could a man want?

And despite her misgiving about his domestic lifestyle, Lara seemed to be having a wonderful time, inflicting a bit of family history on an unsuspecting group gathered near a collage of family portraits. "That's me, of course." She pointed to herself, not more than a few months old, in the arms of their mother. "The cute one." Her finger moved to the left, stopping over Simon, a pudgy eight-year-old, standing next to their father. "And that's the birthday boy, Boris Leonidovich Pasternak Simon."

Harry Kessler, Lara's date, gave a howling hoot,

"Oooooooweeeeee, Boris Leonidovich Pasternak Simon! Now that's a mouthful."

Lara grinned, more than happy to explicate and embarrass her older brother with the story of how Boris Leonidovich Pasternak Simon eventually became Simon Leonidovich. "Old mom was crazy as a hatter, but we loved her."

Victoria Halle, looking lean and luscious in a leather outfit that made her legs look about four miles long, glanced over her shoulder and gave Simon a wink. Typical of someone who never had to worry about weight, she held up a cracker loaded with cream cheese and Nova salmon, and mouthed the words, "Want one?"

He shook his head, that was all he needed, a load of cream cheese to thoroughly wreck his diet. What he wanted was a set of earplugs to block out Lara's tale of accessorial humiliation: the Russian writer who might have been, and the drunken father who was. He gave up the fantasy and settled for a third glass of Krug champagne—a fine compromise.

A few minutes later, having finished her story, Lara slipped up beside him. "What are you smiling about, Birthday Boy?"

"Nothing special, just enjoying myself."

"Good, I was afraid you might be depressed about your advancing age."

"Forty-one is *not* old."

"If you say so, Boris. It just sounds ancient to someone of my tender years."

"No one likes a smart-ass, Sissie. Especially a thirty-something smart-ass."

She fluttered her eyelashes. "Thirty-three to be exact."

"Thanks for the reminder, I'll try to forget."

"Okay, tell the truth, were you really surprised?"

"Really truly, cross my little black heart, I didn't have a

clue. It's the only time a surprise party actually caught me by surprise. I thought you forgot."

"Have I ever?"

He slipped an arm around her waist and gave her a squeeze. "Not yet, Sissie. Not yet."

She grinned, clearly pleased with herself. "I think everyone had a really good time."

Simon glanced around at the remaining guests, the ones who wouldn't leave until the last grape had been stomped and sucked dry. "Some of them still are. This keeps up I may have to open the guest room."

She looked up at him, her face a mixture of disgust and exasperation, a common expression whenever he slipped into the area of *home* heresy. "You don't *have* a guest room."

"Of course I do. Four hundred and twenty-three to be exact."

"It's not the same, Simon."

"You're right, it's better." He gestured toward the Park and the panorama of lights. "You have to admit, it's not so bad."

"A hotel is no place for a wife and children."

"Neither of which I have."

She nodded, a small grin of satisfaction. "My point exactly."

"Some people just aren't destined for domestic bliss, Sissie."

Lara nodded toward Victoria Halle, standing with her date near a table of appetizers. "What about Vic? What's wrong with her?"

"There's nothing wrong with her and you know it. She's one of my best friends."

"Friends." She spit out the word like it was a piece of bitter lemon. "It could have been more and you know it."

No, he didn't know. After Pilár he wasn't sure there could ever be *more*—or anyone else. "It wasn't meant to be. The timing was wrong." Lara opened her mouth to argue but he cut her off. "It was *too soon.*" Her mouth snapped shut, his subtle reminder of Pilár Montez enough to silence her. "Besides, you're the one who should be dating, Sissie."

"I have a date."

"Don't give me that bull. Harry's nothing more than a friendly escort and you know it. You need more than that. And what about Allie and Jack Jr.? Don't you think they'd like to have a father around?"

She fixed him with a glare hot enough to melt the enamel off his pearly whites. "They have a father! Jack will always be their father."

Oh crap, he could never mention Lara's late husband without getting into trouble. "Of course he will. I meant—" *Damn.* "You know what I meant."

She backed off a step, crossing her index fingers as if to ward off the Cupid vampire. "You stay out of my love life, I'll stay out of yours."

He knew better. Women—his sister in particular—had some kind of natural affinity for matchmaking. "Right. It's okay to pick on me but you can't take the heat yourself."

She flashed her teeth. "Female prerogative. I was simply trying to point out that no self-respecting woman is going to have anything to do with a man who lives in a hotel."

"That's bull, but let's say it's true. What's *your* excuse for a life of celibacy?" *Bad question,* he knew it the minute he spoke the words. It had been less than a year since Eth Jäger and that ordeal, and he couldn't blame her for not venturing too quickly back into the world of men. He gritted his teeth, ready for her attack, but was saved when her beeper began to chirp. "I thought we agreed to use the answering service at night."

She read the numbers pulsing across the display. "It *is* the answering service. Must be important."

Simon nodded toward his bedroom. "Use the phone in there, away from the madding crowd."

She was back before he finished opening a fresh bottle for the last of the grape stompers. "Who was it?"

"A woman by the name of Caitlin Wells. Says she works for B. J. Rynerson."

"Big Jake Rynerson?"

"Only B. J. Rynerson I know."

"What's the job?"

"Wouldn't say. Insists on talking to *Mr. Simon Leonidovich.*"

"See, I'm a very popular guy with the ladies." He handed her the bottle and corkscrew. "Big Jake probably wants to wish me a happy birthday."

She snorted a laugh. "Yeah, right, you're both in the same club. From what I've read he's another guy who lives in a hotel and can't keep a wife."

Holy Mary, Joseph and Jesus, the woman never gave up. He closed the bedroom door behind him, sat down on the bed, and picked up the phone. "This is Simon Leonidovich." He made a point to pronounce his name distinctly, the way he always did when speaking to someone the first time—Le-on-o-vich—letting them know the *d* was silent.

"Mr. Leonidovich, my name is Caitlin Wells. I'm the executive administrative assistant to B. J. Rynerson. We would like to retain your services."

Nice voice, feminine but strong, very direct. *A powerhouse,* he suspected, if she was really *the* executive administrative assistant to Big Jake Rynerson. "Okay, why don't you give me a few details. The what, when, and where stuff." He opened the notepad on his night table, ready to write.

"Mr. Rynerson would prefer to discuss the specifics personally."

"Okay." Big Jake Rynerson was obviously the type of man who expected to do things his own way. "Why don't we start with your timetable then?" He pulled his PDA from his pocket, a tiny Rex that offered none of the fancy features of the Palm or BlackBerry, but suited his needs and didn't add a pound of weight and a bulge to his pocket. He had enough extra lumps.

"That would be now. Immediately."

Now, immediately—couldn't be more specific than that. His calendar showed nothing for the next four days. "That's possible, but I'll need an idea of how long the assignment might take?"

"You'd have to discuss those details with Mr. Rynerson."

Until that moment Simon hadn't considered that the job might be anything other than normal and ordinary; he did lots of work for important people, and important people dealt with important documents, and important documents often required special and immediate handling, that was his job—*the man who could deliver anything, anywhere*—but he suddenly had a feeling this was not about anything *normal* or *ordinary*. He could insist on more information, or refuse the job, but working for one of the wealthier and more colorful characters in the country had a certain appeal. And he was curious. He decided to give Ms. Caitlin Wells one last chance before turning down the job. "It's impossible for me to accept an assignment if I don't know the timetable. It might conflict with other commitments."

"Just meet with Mr. Rynerson. If the assignment conflicts with other obligations and you're unable to accept the job, we'll be more than happy to pay your minimum just for the opportunity to discuss it. *Please*, we really do need your assistance."

The way she said please, it almost sounded like begging, and Simon had the distinct feeling this was not a woman who did that easily or often. "Fair enough, where would Mr. Rynerson like to meet?"

"In Las Vegas."

For ten thousand dollars—his minimum—a trip to Vegas didn't sound too unpleasant. "The address?"

"I'll have a car meet your plane."

"Okay, I'll check on flights and get back to you with my arrival time."

"I've taken the liberty of making those arrangements. A driver will pick you up at your hotel. He should be there by the time you're ready."

Damn, the woman was just like Lara, give either one of them a set of balls and she'd be running the world within a week. He glanced at his watch—11:22—the early morning flight he had in mind had just gotten earlier. "I can be ready in thirty minutes."

"Excellent. I look forward to meeting you."

"Likewise."

"And happy forty-one, Mr. Leonidovich. I apologize if I interrupted a celebration."

There was a soft click and the line went silent. When Simon looked up Lara was standing in the door. "So? What's the job?"

"She wouldn't say. Rynerson wants to handle everything himself."

"Sounds like him." She said it as if they were a couple of old bridge partners.

That, Simon thought, was the problem with celebrity; everyone assumed they knew a person because of their public persona. "You must have said something about my birthday."

Her eyes flashed. *"Of course not,* you know I would never mention anything personal to a client."

"Potential client," he emphasized. "I haven't agreed to take the job."

"Okay, *potential.* So what did she say about your birthday?"

"She not only knew I was forty-one, she knew I lived

in a hotel. That's a woman who does her homework."

"That's what we *executive* administrative assistants do."

"So now you're my *executive* administrative assistant? Last time I checked you were my office manager."

"That too," she answered, with that special inflection that straddled the line between serious and droll. "Guess you should give me a raise."

"Yeah, right. Remind me to discuss that when I get back."

"Oh happy days! I'll be sure to circle the date on my calendar with a smiley face. Back? What you mean *back*, Birthday Boy?"

"I agreed to meet Rynerson to discuss the job."

"When?"

"Now. There's a driver downstairs waiting to take me to the airport."

"And where is this little powwow to take place?"

"Vegas."

"Well, happy birthday to you. A free trip to Sin City. Some people have all the luck."

But he remembered the previous year—trapped in a plane on a three-day trip to hell—and hoped he wasn't stuck in some birthday version of *Groundhog Day*. "Yeah, lucky me."

CHAPTER TWO

Somewhere in South America

Tuesday, 4 November 23:31:06 GMT −0500

Kyra woke with a start, her body damp with sweat. She forced herself not to move, to breathe slowly and evenly, straining to hear anything out of the ordinary. The air was heavy and still, the tiny room like a steam bath, though the rain had finally stopped. She tried to judge the time, but there were no clues, the darkness so pure she could have grown old and never seen the wrinkles. That was the way of the jungle: the night fell like a black sledgehammer, the rain in a rush, as if God had opened a spigot. How many days?

Three. Somehow she needed to mark them, before she lost track. *Three days, three nights.*

The first, that had been the worst, realizing she was once again being punished for her father's wealth, being held for ransom, not sure what was going to happen, if she would live or die. Acosta answered all her questions exactly the same, with a cold, threatening look, and she stopped asking. They had flown west, crossing the Andes just north of Chunchi, then turning northeast toward Colombia. By midafternoon they were somewhere near the border—she wasn't sure if they were still over Ecuador or had crossed into Colombia. Acosta directed her to a dirt airstrip, a bald slash of land cut out of the jungle. The surrounding trees were so tall and the strip so short she had to make a full-flaps, diving approach, and hard-flare landing to get Babe stopped before they ran out of runway.

Acosta popped the door and the jungle air rushed in, hot and sticky. By the time Kyra shut down and climbed to the ground, her blouse had glued itself to her body. Less than fifty meters away, parked back in the trees where it couldn't be seen from above, sat a rusted-out Volkswagen van, hippie vintage.

"Keep your mouth shut," Acosta warned as a young man, not more than twenty, stepped out from behind the VW and started toward them.

In contrast to his rusty wreck of transportation, the boy was shiny and handsome, and full of native swagger, enhanced significantly by the sawback machete strapped to his right leg. Based on his inquisitive expression, he hadn't expected a woman. He gave Kyra a big smile, his teeth gleaming against his dusky skin, his dark eyes caressing her body before they moved on to Acosta. *"El Pato, mi amigo."* His tone was friendly and confident, though perhaps a little affected—a boy trying to be a man.

Kyra translated the name in her mind. *El Pato: The Duck.* How appropriate, he waddled like a duck, and she already suspected he had *borrowed* the name Acosta, which would explain the glowing background report; either that, or Elsworth was in on the kidnapping, and that was something she would never believe.

El Pato nodded toward the plane. The boy smiled and redirected his attention to Babe, carefully checking the wings and ailerons, the rudder and elevators, the landing gear and both engines. Apparently satisfied, he pulled a wad of American bills from his pocket and quickly counted out eight stacks of ten bills each, all hundreds.

It wasn't until that moment Kyra realized what the inspection was all about: *Drugs.* The young man was a pilot—which would explain his overconfident swagger—a boy-pilot who intended to steal her plane for a measly eight thousand dollars and turn it into a mule for coca powder, the area's number one export. *Eight thousand dol-*

lars!—she had paid nearly four-hundred thousand for *Babe* and still owed a quarter million. *Ugh!*

El Pato shook his head. "We agreed on ten thousand. *Diez mil.*"

The boy grinned and motioned toward Kyra. *"Inclusivo piloto."*

El Pato flashed his gold tooth and Kyra held her breath, wondering if he might actually make the deal—*including pilot*—but then, faster than she could focus, before the boy-pilot could even twitch, El Pato had his gun out and leveled. The man might waddle like a duck, but his hands were quicker than a cat.

The boy shrugged good-naturedly, as if to say, "I was only making a small joke, amigo. No harm done." He dropped the last of his money alongside the other bills. *"Si. Diez."*

El Pato, the smile still curling the edge of his lips, lowered his gun, but only a little, and *BANGBANG*, discharged two quick rounds into the boy's stomach. *"Gracias, mi amigo."* He spit the words, as if clearing his tongue of a disgusting bug.

Kyra felt like the wounded boy looked, an expression of complete and utter disbelief as he stared at the red flower blossoming across the front of his shirt. El Pato calmly scooped up the money, stuffed it into his pocket, and turned. "I think this *puerco* would like to see you naked before he dies."

She could have argued—made the case that this boy, pig or otherwise, who had just collapsed into a fetal heap, was not really concerned with her naked body—but she didn't. She didn't even hesitate. El Pato was clearly a psychopath, as pure as God made them, and she wasn't about to test his patience—not after what she had just seen. He watched her strip, seemingly without sexual emotion, but with intense interest, his eyes following every movement and every piece of clothing until it hit the ground—her blouse and bra, then her shorts and panties—until she was bare except for her shoes.

"Those too."

Despite her intense fear, that scared her even more. *Why the shoes?* She added them, along with her socks, to the pile. He circled around her, up close, scrutinizing every inch of her body, like an animal marking its territory. She stood there, stiff as a soldier, skin covered in sweat, staring straight ahead, ignoring his eyes, determined not to let him touch her—not where it mattered, in her mind. Finally, he reached out and ran his hand over her pubic mound, slowly sifting the hair between his fingers, but he didn't probe and the gesture seemed more curious than sexual. Then he stepped back and extended his hand, palm up. *"Sus pendientes."*

She quickly removed her diamond studs—a gift from her father when she received her pilot's license—and dropped them into the man's outstretched hand.

"Su anillo."

She didn't argue—her wedding band should have come off long before—so if nothing else, it gave her an excuse to do the right thing. But, to her surprise, taking it off seemed to strip away her last bit of personal identity. Though she had always rejected her father and his way of life, she now realized there was a measure of security and confidence that went along with being the daughter of Big Jake Rynerson, never more than a phone call away from his power and wealth. It was a luxury she had never before considered, but now felt the loss of—distinctly. She was standing naked, on a bare swath of land in the middle of a jungle, a tiny bug caught in the web of a spider. Whether by intention or not, El Pato had stripped her of everything—including her identity.

What happened next was beyond anything she cared to remember, but far beyond anything she would ever forget. El Pato stepped in close, his dark eyes boring into hers, his sour breath washing over her face. "You will not move. You will not close your eyes."

She nodded, somehow knowing her life depended on it.

Then he turned and walked over to the boy, still clutching his midsection, still hanging on to life. El Pato reached down, rifled through his pockets, taking everything he found, then stripped off his boots—he wore no socks—pulled the boy's machete, glanced toward Kyra, as if to assure himself of her full attention, then raised the blade over his head and brought it down. She closed her eyes, she couldn't help herself, but only for an instant—the time it took for the blade to slice through the boy's ankle, severing his foot. Though close to death, the boy managed one long, bone-chilling scream before passing out.

El Pato reached down and picked up the foot, holding it by the big toe, and extended it toward Kyra. "You want to run?"

She tried to speak past the cloying smell of blood that clogged her throat, but failed, and could only shake her head to indicate she understood.

El Pato smiled, a small grin of satisfaction, then turned and with another slicing move took off the boy's head. Kyra gagged, but managed to hold back the flood, afraid that any show of revulsion might get her killed. The next thirty minutes passed in a blur as El Pato stuffed the boy's body—including his foot, but not his head—into the plane. Her clothes followed, everything, including both her earrings and wedding band, which he threw in last, before taking her cellular phone and closing the door. Next he opened the fuel cocks on both the auxiliary and main tanks, letting the gas drain onto the ground, below the wings. Finally he picked up the boy's head—the eyes locked in perpetual surprise—and started toward the van, casually swinging his trophy by the hair. "We go."

She followed—what else could she do?—naked and

trapped and mentally beaten down, but *still alive*, she reminded herself. And that, she decided, was how she intended to stay. *Somehow.* Whatever it took, she would take. Whatever she had to do, she would do it. But she was *not* going to die. *Not like this.*

El Pato opened the van's passenger door, tossed the boy's head onto the floor, then pointed toward the back, which had been stripped to the metal, all the windows painted black. She climbed in and he followed. She realized he might rape her, but the thought didn't frighten her, she was beyond that—the only thing that mattered was staying alive—but if he had any interest in her body, he was saving it for later. Using a piece of wire he tied her wrists to a metal floor strut, then climbed into the driver's seat, pulled his automatic, leaned out the window, and fired one shot.

There was a loud *WHOMP*, and *Babe* burst into flames. Squatting, her arms down between her legs, Kyra watched through the windshield as her pride and treasure, her bird of freedom, disintegrated into a metal skeleton. When the cockpit was fully engulfed, the air thick with the smell of gas and smoke and the sound of flesh popping like bacon in a skillet, El Pato started the engine and began to drive, the road little more than a trench cut through the jungle. He stopped only once, only a few kilometers from the airstrip, where he literally bowled the boy's head into the underbrush.

That was the moment Kyra understood the puzzle, why he had taken her shoes and wedding ring. If the plane was found, which seemed unlikely, they would find the cremated remains of one body, maybe her wedding ring, but no dental records. The obvious assumption would be made. Did that mean he intended to kill her, or was he only covering up a murder? What frightened her most was that killing the boy had not been premeditated, that he would still be alive had he not acted so youthfully

arrogant. El Pato had simply exploded, then improvised a
plan as events dictated. The man was not only a psychopath with a hair-trigger temper, he was a *clever* psychopath with a hair-trigger temper, and that made him
infinitely more dangerous.

After an hour of bumping and lurching through the
jungle they reached some kind of dirt road, not much
wider, but smoother, and El Pato increased speed. Kyra
tried to measure the distance and time against the location of the sun, but at some point exhaustion over-
whelmed her and she fell asleep. When she woke it was
dark—black as a deep pit, beneath a canopy of trees no
star could penetrate—and El Pato was dragging her out of
the van. He retied her wrists with a six-foot length of
rope, then started down some indistinguishable path,
yanking her along like a disobedient pet. Every few steps
something would cut into her bare feet but she was too
numb to care and too determined to cry out. After what
seemed forever, but couldn't have been more than fifteen
or twenty minutes, they broke through into a small clearing with a tiny dwelling. It looked like a gaucho hut, old
and abandoned and misplaced in the middle of the jungle.
She caught only a glimpse of the main room—a table with
one chair, a narrow bed, a crude kitchen—before he
pushed her into a tiny, dark room and bolted the door behind her. She collapsed onto the dirt floor, cut and bruised
and naked, but still breathing.

That had been the worst, the first day.

Three. Somehow she needed to mark them, before she
lost track. *Three days, three nights.*

CHAPTER THREE

Via Las Vegas

As promised, the driver was waiting when Simon reached the lobby, his Mercedes S600 parked at the curb. Simon climbed into the rear seat, leaned back into the soft leather, and closed his eyes.

"Mr. Leonidovich, we're there."

He came awake with a jerk and it took a moment to realize where he was, or more accurately, where he wasn't. *Not LaGuardia. Not Kennedy.* "Where are we?"

The driver twisted around in his seat. "I'm sorry, I thought you knew. We're at the Republic Airport in Farmingdale."

Simon glanced at his watch—12:44—then at the snow-white Lear parked not ten feet away. Ms. Wells, he decided, could handle his travel arrangements anytime. "That was quick."

The man nodded as he bent to open the door. "Yessir, not much traffic this time of night."

An attractive young woman, dressed in a well-tailored burgundy uniform with an Executive Air pocket-insignia and three stripes on the sleeve, hurried down the ramp to welcome him aboard. "Good morning, sir. I'm Jenny Thompson, your copilot."

Damn, being called *sir* by any woman was bad enough, but hearing it from a young, beautiful aviator made him feel absolutely prehistoric. "Don't remind me."

He meant his age, she assumed the time. "Yes, it is early, isn't it?" She reached for his luggage.

He let her take his travel bag—an expensive but scarred carryall, meant to look worthless—but kept his security case, empty except for his laptop. "I'll keep this with me." He dug out his wallet and pulled a twenty for the driver, but the man waved him off. "Thank you, sir, but that was taken care of. Have a good flight."

The pilot—another young woman, four stripes on the sleeve—met Simon at the top of the steps. "Good morning, sir, I'm Captain Salvo. Any time you're ready, we're ready."

Damn, she looked about sixteen, but he resisted the temptation to ask if she was old enough to drive. *A brave new world.* "Thank you." He glanced around at the cabin, an executive configuration with a four-chair conference table and an assortment of leather recliners. "Assigned seats?"

She indulged him with a gracious smile. "Your choice, sir."

The copilot, temporarily playing the role of flight attendant, motioned toward a compact but well-designed workstation toward the back, complete with computer, fax machine, scanner, printer, and phone. "If you need to work, I think you'll find anything you need right here."

He didn't *need* to work, but felt strangely obligated, as if needing to justify his exalted presence with the illusion of doing something important. "Looks good." He dropped into the leather chair, a plush, swivel recliner with a sleep adjustment in case the drudgery of such important work should suddenly overwhelm him.

The young woman smiled. "I'll check back when we reach cruising altitude."

He spent most of the five-hour flight surfing the Web, researching the life and times of Big Jake Rynerson. After his conversation with Caitlin Wells, Simon had the feeling this was not going to be any typical *Pick and Drop* assignment, nothing so mundane as moving money or gold. Not that many of his jobs were *typical*, there was usually something of real value involved, and the things of *real* value—art, medicine, human organs—were beyond monetary value. That's what made his job so fascinating. Even so, being picked up and transported by private jet was not exactly an everyday experience.

The research proved both easy and interesting, Rynerson's life well chronicled by the press. The man was colorful and quotable, an easy target for reporters. He had grown up in west Texas, in Odessa—at the very center of the Permian Basin, with nothing to break the landscape but drilling rigs and mesquite stretching from one horizon to the next—a place of tumbleweeds and wind, where no sane person would live unless he had a small piece of a big well. His father, a roustabout driller and drunk, had died when Jake was nine. His mother scratched out a living cleaning the homes of the affluent, most of whom lived in Midland, twenty miles east and one giant step above the blue-collar residents of Odessa, home to the Drillers, the Pushers, and the Derrick Men: the men who actually worked the wells.

After his father's death, Jake worked after school at a pipe yard to help feed his three brothers and four sisters. He caught on quick, learning about the rigs: how to build them, and how to repair the equipment when it broke down. When he was sixteen, his mother became bedridden with acute arthritis and Jake quit school to work the fields and support the family. Tall and gangly, he quickly bulked up from the hard work, and when he came to work, few men could match the tenacity of "that Rynerson kid." Stepped on and abused by his father, teased at school because of his poverty, Jake was on a mission to prove himself, and it didn't take long. Not only big, he was brighter than the average roughneck, and in later years would prove himself brighter than most corporate executives sitting around board tables. But in those early years, it was the work that set Jake Rynerson apart; he had both a talent and desire, and like most things in life, when you're good at something, you excel at it.

He progressed quickly from Rig Man, to Derrick Man, to Driller. In later years he'd be quoted as saying his progression was not so much a reward for skill, but a result of *sticking his nose in and gettin' in the way*. Every time somebody turned around there was "that Rynerson kid." At the age of twenty he became a Tool Pusher: in charge of his own rig and all three tower crews. But it wasn't until the age of thirty-two, that Big Jake—as he was now referred to by most of the Permian Basin roughnecks and roustabouts—got his first real break in life. A biographical story about billionaires—*How They Made It*—told it best:

Big Jake was in the logging trailer—a combination office, bunkhouse, and kitchen—comparing seismic charts to the latest core samples when he happened to overhear a phone conversation that would change his life. William Clamore, the owner of the well, was on the phone looking for investors, a constant battle for small- to medium-size Wildcatters and Independents. It was the opportunity Jake had been waiting for and he didn't hesitate. "I might know of some available cash, Mr. Clamore."

Clamore's head jerked up. "Yeah?"

Jake nodded, not wanting to say too much too quickly. "Possible. How much you lookin' for?"

"Thirty grand. Gotta have thirty grand to finish that hole."

"What kind of interest would thirty grand buy a man?"

"Five percent."

The answer came too quick and Jake realized instantly that Clamore was willing to give up more than five percent. "We're talking WI, right?" Of course he knew they were talking Working Interest, but thought he needed to drop the hint, to get Clamore thinking about what other kind of interest might be on the table.

Clamore smiled knowingly. "That's right, and one-percent ORI to you if you close the deal."

He couldn't argue with that—a one-percent Overriding Royalty Interest was standard for this kind of deal—but he needed more than a five-percent Working Interest if he was going to risk every dime he had in the world, especially now that he had a wife and daughter. "I appreciate that. I'll see what I can do."

"Don't take too long," Clamore warned, "someone else might jump in and grab the deal."

Jake doubted that. They were down seventy-one hundred feet—deeper than they had ever intended to drill, and below the level of any producing wells in the area—a hard sell. But he also knew his chance of being offered a stake in anything more promising was virtually nonexistent. "Yessir, I'll get right on it."

He intended to wait a couple days, not to appear over-anxious, but Clamore pulled him off the rig floor early the next morning. "Any luck finding me an investor, Jake?"

Jake shook his head. "I talked to a couple guys. Everyone thinks we're too deep. That we missed the pay zone." Clamore's shoulders drooped slightly and Jake let the disappointment sink in before adding, "But I might be interested in takin' a little piece for myself."

"You got some money, Jake?"

"Yup." One consequence of all the extra shifts and days, of vacations not taken and holidays not celebrated, was a lack of time to spend what he earned. "I got a little saved up."

"Sorry, Jake, but I couldn't consider anything less than thirty thousand."

"I could do that, but I'd need at least a ten percent Working Interest plus the ORI for that kind of money. Thirty thousand dollars about all I got in the world."

Clamore laughed, the sound forced. "Jake, Jake, Jake. I

couldn't give you a ten percent Working Interest for a measly thirty thousand."

"Yessir, I understand. Sure do. But if it comes to that, you need it, you get back to me. I'd do it for ten percent."

Clamore smiled as if it were nothing, but his eyes dulled with disappointment.

Three days later he called Jake into the logging trailer. "You still got that thirty thousand, Jake?"

"Yessir, sure do."

"Thirty thousand for a ten percent WI, right?"

Jake grimaced; he didn't want to take advantage of the man, but they were about as likely to find oil at that depth as they were to run a pipe up the backside of some China-man. "I'm sorry, Mr. Clamore, but things are looking real bad out there. We're down almost eight thousand feet now—could just as likely hit chert as a good zone. I'm afraid I'd need fifteen percent plus the ORI to take that kind of chance."

Clamore laughed, without humor. "You're a gutsy one, Big Jake."

"You know and I know I'll probably lose my money, Mr. Clamore. No offense, sir, but if you don't take it you're probably gonna have to plug that well."

Clamore had no choice but to make the deal. Jake handed over his money with no regrets, knowing he'd just have to work harder to make up for what he expected to lose. In the meantime, he started working two-a-day, ten-hour shifts to cut payroll and give themselves a few extra hours of drilling before the money ran out.

Eight days later—July 17, 1982—the money was gone and payroll was due. And that was the day the Gods of Serendipity and Chance decided to smile on Jake Ryner-son. But it didn't come in the way of oil, they were much too deep for that. At nine thousand, four hundred and forty-two feet they tapped into a reservoir of natural gas—enough gas to keep the lights burning in Chicago until the

Cubs won a pennant. "Just a roll of the dice," Jake would say later, "and I was lucky enough to throw a seven."

From that day forward, *luck* played a very minor role in the life and success of Big Jake Rynerson. The man had an innate sense for business. A pragmatic risk taker with vision, he knew when to get in, and more importantly, when to get out. He dumped his oil and gas properties in '87, when oil was still selling for thirty dollars a barrel, and put his twenty million into the stock market immediately after the November crash, when everything had bottomed out. He rode his investments into Tech Nirvana, saw that things were overinflated, and bailed out with more than three-hundred million. That's when he went to Vegas. It seemed to surprise everyone, but to Simon it made perfect sense. Las Vegas offered the ultimate outlet for Big Jake's gambling spirit, though it wasn't gambling that drew him to the city. He sensed the boom, recognized what the need would be, and began to build homes. Thousands of homes.

Affordable homes for the workers.

Custom homes for the executives.

Palatial homes for the kings of gaming.

Condos for the upwardly mobile, and patio homes for the downwardly retiring.

In two short years Big Jake had turned his millions into billions. "That's when I got into the resort business," he was quoted as saying, "just for the fun of it."

But Jake Rynerson, Simon realized, did very little *just for the fun of it.* He now had one of the best resort hotels in North America—the Sand Castle—spread over two-hundred and forty-three acres between the elaborate theme extravagances that lined The Strip and the seedy bet-your-last-buck casinos that languished "downtown."

By the time the plane touched down at the Signature Terminal in Vegas, Simon knew a great deal about Big Jake Rynerson, a man he couldn't wait to meet.

CHAPTER FOUR

Somewhere in South America

Wednesday, 5 November 00:12:52 GMT −0500

Three days, three nights, she needed to mark them somewhere—someplace El Pato wouldn't notice. She closed her eyes, as if that would help her see through the darkness, and for some reason it did, allowing her to picture the little room in her mind: the tin galvanized roof, which the rain hammered constantly; the plank walls, the gaps caulked with mud and grass; the one small window, barred with bamboo; the narrow cot bolted to the outside wall; and one thin wool blanket, as filthy and black as the dirt floor. *A dungeon.* The air muggy and still, the light so choked by trees she couldn't have read a newspaper at midday. The door was the only thing that looked newly constructed, with a plank slide about halfway up, so he could sit and watch her without having to open it. And he did watch, like some demented kid who had just ripped the wings off a bird, then watches with fascination as it struggles.

When she asked to go to the bathroom, he pointed to a rusty bucket in the corner and laughed. He watched that too.

She ran her hands down below her belly. *Was it there? Still growing?* For some stupid reason she couldn't get it out of her mind, as if the circumstances had shoved her into a new dimension: mother-protector. No psychopath known by his waddling gait was going to kill her baby. There, she said it, if only silently to herself: *her baby.*

What about food? Could it survive on the same tedious diet? Both days, both meals, exactly the same: flat bread and a gelatinous mound of black beans, a small helping of shredded pork and a slice of papaya. Everything tasted the same, the flavors mingling into one unappetizing glob, but she ate it anyway, all of it, determined to maintain her strength. A little salsa would have helped, but she wasn't about to ask.

Never ask—Never take.

CHAPTER FIVE

Las Vegas

Wednesday, 5 November 02:29:17 GMT −0800

As promised, Caitlin Wells had a car waiting when the Lear rolled to a stop not fifty yards from Las Vegas Boulevard and The Strip. Simon pressed the zone button on his watch, adjusting the time from 5:29 to 2:29 A.M., but the illusion of time recovered seemed to have no effect on his brain, which felt stuck somewhere over Kansas. The co-pilot popped the door and he stepped from one luxury vehicle to another, a cream-colored limousine with a small Sand Castle crest on its door. *Happy birthday to me . . .*

Ten minutes later the driver passed the resort's main tower—fifty-one floors of tan and beige glass, the colors of the desert—and turned into the underground parking garage. Unlike the Bellagio with its lake and fountains, the Mirage with its volcanic eruptions, Paris with its faux Eiffel Tower, or the Venetian with its concrete canals, the Sand Castle offered no manufactured diversions or attractions. The resort was designed around an idea, not a theme, offering only one enticement to its guests—*the best.*

The best rooms—all suites.

The best food.

The best liquor.

The best golf—eighteen holes of white sand, blue water, and green fairways.

The best gaming.

The best service.

A haven for relaxation, rejuvenation, and reward. *The best of everything.*

As the limo approached one end of the immense garage, the driver reached up and touched a small button on the visor. A section of wall immediately began to move upward, exposing a private parking area that could easily accommodate a dozen vehicles, but at that moment contained only seven: a white Jeep Grand Cherokee, a cinnamon colored BMW Alpina Roadster, a black Cadillac limousine, a silver Mercedes SL55 AMG Roadster, a gray GMC Sonoma pickup, a blue Ford Taurus, and a green H2 Hummer. *Perfect,* what every red-blooded American billionaire needed—*a car for every occasion, a color for every mood.*

The driver pulled up next to an elevator, complete with uniformed attendant, who opened Simon's door. "Just leave your bags, sir. We'll take care of them." Short hair, built like a tank, with a slight bulge beneath the left armpit of his blue blazer—it didn't take a genius to guess the man's *real* job.

"Thanks." Simon stood up, then reached back and grabbed his security case. "This one I'll take with me."

The man nodded. "Of course. But I will need to check it." He motioned toward a small table and a large EDS luggage scanner, similar to the type used in airports.

Being careful not to expose exactly what he was doing, Simon placed his case on the table and quickly ran through the unlocking sequence—right latch toward the handle, foot-lock one-half turn clockwise, left latch outward—and snapped open the case. "There you go."

The man pulled the laptop, ran his hand around the lining, then placed both the laptop and empty case into the scanner. A moment later the machine gave a warning *BEEP* and the man was suddenly all business, any pretension of cordial attendant gone. "I'm getting an explosive warning. Don't suppose you can explain that?"

Though surprised—most airport sniffers and scanners were not sophisticated enough to pick up his security measures—Simon could indeed explain, and tried. "I frequently transport important documents. The case contains a small dye bomb, guaranteed to turn anyone who tries to steal the goodies a very bright shade of pink." He saw no need to mention the ear-splitting siren—a disconcerting surprise for unsuspecting thieves—or the homing transmitter. "Not enough powder in there to give your pacemaker a hiccup."

The man's face revealed nothing beyond a polite, well-practiced rigidity. "Doesn't matter, sir, you can't take the case with you."

"Look, I understand your position, but—"

"You're not taking it." His words and granite-like expression more than said it—*No way, José*—but he was clearly a man disinclined to ambiguity and felt the need to add: "And that's final."

"Dale." A woman's voice, which Simon recognized immediately as that of Caitlin Wells, reverberated from a small speaker over the elevator door. "It's okay. Mr. Leonidovich may bring his briefcase."

The guard turned his head, facing the security camera adjacent to the speaker. "Yes, ma'am." Though he clearly didn't like the order, he didn't hesitate or argue. He extended a key attached to a retractable chain and inserted it into the elevator's lock. The door slid open, and Simon, security case in hand, stepped inside. The carpet was thick and plush, the walls covered in a grayish mauve silk, providing a neutral background for three dramatically colorful paintings by Peter Max. *Originals.* The control plate had only three buttons: START, STOP, and CALL. *Simple enough.* Simon punched the top button, confident that wherever START stopped, it would be the *right* floor—and very near the top.

When the door opened Cinderella was waiting; or perhaps Cinderella's mother, but a princess nonetheless. A tall princess, five-ten at least, with short taffy-blond hair styled in a boyish cut that somehow heightened her sexuality. "Mr. Leonidovich, thank you for coming on such short notice." She extended her hand. "I'm Caitlin Wells."

Of course you are. She had a firm grip and soft blue-gray eyes that seemed to absorb the light—to absorb him. No one, he thought, should look that good at 2:57 in the morning. He gave her his best smile, the one his sister referred to as boyish. "My pleasure." *Very much my pleasure.*

"I hope we didn't ruin a celebration." She extended a small package, wrapped in green-and-gold foil. "Happy birthday."

The gesture surprised him, though he assumed it was no more than one of those token gifts given to special hotel guests. "That wasn't necessary."

"Of course not. But appropriate."

"Thank you."

"You're welcome." She motioned for him to follow. "Mr. Rynerson is waiting."

She led him on a circuitous route, skirting a large central room overlooking The Strip, where more than half a dozen people were gathered in a tight group. Despite the time, their tense body language suggested the meeting to be anything but social. Simon had the sudden and very uncomfortable feeling he was not going to enjoy the assignment about to be offered. *Happy birthday to me.*

Ms. Wells pushed open a large teakwood door—a panoramic relief of a thousand-derrick oil field carved into its surface—and there he was, Big Jake Rynerson, standing behind a big desk in a big office, looking bigger than life. He rounded the desk with a couple of equally big strides, a very large and very old Labrador retriever at the heels of his scruffy cowboy boots. "Welcome to the Sand Castle. Mind if I call you Simon?"

For a moment Simon thought his hand might be

crushed in Rynerson's massive meatgrinder, but his handshake matched his business reputation: powerful, assertive, take no prisoners, but no bone crusher. Everything about the man was BIG, including the pain that dulled his blue eyes. "Please do."

Rynerson reached down and gave the dog a pat on the head. "This here's Brownie, and I'm Jake. Not Big Jake, I hate that pissant name."

"I'll remember that."

Rynerson stepped back, giving Simon a serious head to toe. "So you're the fella who blew the lid off Mira-loss? That was one helluva nice piece of work and I just wanna take this opportunity to thank y'all personal. My wife was taking that crap."

"Thanks, but my role was highly exaggerated by the papers."

"Now there's something I know about," Rynerson howled good-naturedly, "surely do. But don't knock the publicity, Simon. That's why I called you. I need a man I can trust. Appreciate very much you coming out so quick-like."

"Ms. Wells was quite persuasive."

Rynerson barked a one-note laugh. "Ha, and don't I know it. Most men go weak at the knees and piddle their pants in this gal's presence."

Caitlin Wells rolled her eyes. "Pay no attention to him, Mr. Leonidovich. I don't."

"See there, Simon, damn woman doesn't even pretend I'm the boss. Disgusting!" Then he smiled and leveled his sad eyes on the object of his feigned disgust. "Caity honey, will you ask Hos and that other fella, what's his name . . . ?"

"Leo Geske." Her voice took on a slight edge. "You did read my brief?"

"I read it, dammit. He's supposed to be good."

"No, Jake, he's supposed to be the best. You need to give the guy a chance."

"I understand. Now will you get off my horse and ask them to join us, please?"

She turned to Simon, seemingly ignoring Rynerson's benevolent command. "Mr. Leonidovich, may I take your coat? We're pretty casual around here."

Damn, forty-one years old and he still felt like Porky the Pig in the presence of a beautiful woman. And he wasn't *fat,* not really—so what if his gut bulged a little? But it mattered—enough to keep his sports coat on and the extra poundage hidden. "I'm good, thanks."

"Coffee? A person gets used to these ridiculous hours living in Vegas, but I'm sure you're exhausted."

"Actually, my batteries adjust pretty quick—have to in my line of work. But a little caffeine charge wouldn't hurt. If it's not inconvenient."

"Hell no," Ryernson boomed, "ain't no problem a'tall."

Of course not, Simon thought, they were in one of the best twenty-four-hour coffee shops in the world—one phone call and they'd probably have their own personal barista grinding the beans; but to his surprise Rynerson took over the assignment himself, stepping behind a four-stool bar—complete with its own massive espresso machine. Big Jake was clearly not the type to order people around for little things just to appease his ego, nor did he expect Caitlin Wells to play the role of lackey. Simon liked the man immediately.

"So, how you take your espresso, Simon? Single, double, or Texas-size?"

Simon glanced at his watch—6:07 eastern time—and decided to go for the gusto. "Texas size sounds good to me, Jake." He already felt like Rynerson was a friend.

"Good choice. Caity?"

"I'll pass." She crossed the room to a cluster of chairs circling a low cocktail-style table and picked up the phone. "Security, please."

Simon took the opportunity to check out the rest of

Rynerson's office. Like the man, it was big: the outside wall entirely of glass, providing a panoramic view of Las Vegas Boulevard, with an eight-chair conference table along the adjacent wall. Rynerson's desk, an L-shaped behemoth of gray wood, was gouged and scarred and covered with stacks of paper—a desk where serious work got done. Though beautifully appointed, there was a lack of symmetry to the placement of pictures, plaques, books, and mementos that lined the walls—as if Rynerson just stuck them up wherever he liked them. Everything was warm and real, a clear reflection of its inhabitant, and not the work of a professional decorator. Big Jake Rynerson was just a "good ol' Texas boy," who knew exactly who he was, and saw no reason to gussy up the package.

The big man finished his manipulations at the espresso machine, a task he seemed to thoroughly enjoy, then transported two Texas-size mugs together with accoutrements—cream, sugar, cinnamon sticks, and biscotti— to the small table where Caitlin Wells had just finished her call. She smiled at Simon, as if reading his mind. "Jake's a very good host."

"Never hurts to be prepared," Rynerson said, as he pushed a mug toward Simon. "If things go bad I can always get a job waitin' tables."

A moment later two men entered the room. Caitlin Wells made the introductions: "Mr. Leonidovich, this is Charles Case, Head of Security here at the Castle." Case looked the part—Tiger Woods at forty—tall, wide shoulders, lean frame, with sharply chiseled features, dark chocolate skin, and intelligent eyes. His tailored suit fit impeccably, hiding his shoulder rig to the casual observer, the tan color contrasting perfectly with his dark skin. Strong handshake. Simon smiled to himself. *Hos:* Head of Security.

"And Leo Geske. Leo represents our insurance underwriter." Geske didn't seem to fit any part, everything about him common and unremarkable: average height, slight frame, mid-sixties, milky-white skin, milquetoast handshake.

Everyone pulled up a chair and settled in, including Brownie, who collapsed beside Jake's feet, dropped his head onto his front paws, and sighed. Simon studied the two newcomers, wondering about their roles. In the business of transporting valuables, insurance was always a factor, and the presence of a security officer was not uncommon, but it was now past 3 A.M. and nothing about anything felt *common*. Maybe that was the way they did business in Vegas, the city that never slept, but he had the uncomfortable feeling it was more than that.

Rynerson leaned forward on his elbows, his melancholy eyes fixed on Simon. "I just want to say how pleased I am that you've agreed to help us."

Though tempted to clarify his position, to make it clear he hadn't agreed to anything *yet*, Simon decided to let it go, to first hear what the big man had to say. "What exactly do you need delivered?"

Rynerson glanced at the others, then back to Simon. "This is a very private matter." There was a slight edge to his voice, a warning just beneath the surface.

"Mr. Rynerson—"

"Jake."

"Jake, your business is your business, no one will ever hear about it from me."

"Simon, I truly do apologize if I offended you in any way. It's just that—"

Simon held up a hand, not wanting to embarrass the man. "I understand." Rynerson was accustomed to reading about his life in the tabloids—had probably been stung a thousand times by misquotes, erroneous stories, and unsubstantiated leaks from unattributed sources—and he didn't need to apologize for wanting to keep some things private. "As long as I'm not subpoenaed," Simon added, "in which case I would tell the truth, you have complete confidentiality."

"Understood. Fair enough."

Still feeling a little uneasy, Simon added one more condition. "And I won't break the law."

This statement seemed to cause an uncomfortable exchange of glances. Rynerson's eyes settled on Charles Case. "We askin' this man to break the law, Hos?"

Case didn't hesitate. "Directly, no. Technically, yes."

Rynerson rocked back in his chair, considering the answer, then turned back to Simon. "Maybe you better tell us how you stand on technicalities, Simon."

"I think you need to spit it out, Jake. Tell me what you want. Then I'll tell you whether or not I'll do it." He felt better—there it was, on the table—the possibility he might not take the job.

"Fair enough. I need for you to deliver a bit of money."

Simon waited, knowing there was more.

"Four million dollars. Cash. It's possible there's a tad bit of danger involved."

A bit of money—four million smackers—no big deal, he once delivered forty million for a Saudi sheik who wanted to keep his accumulation of gold out of the papers. *A bit of danger*—there was always some danger in his work. So what was the *technicality?* He waited.

Rynerson made eye contact with the others, as if giving each a chance to speak up before he continued. "My daughter's been kidnapped."

Simon didn't know what to expect, but that wasn't it. It did, however, explain the sadness in the big man's eyes. "Kyra?"

"You know my daughter?"

"No. Of course not. But on the flight I did some research on—" He threw up some quote marks with his fingers. " '—Big Jake Rynerson.' So, when did this happen?"

Rynerson glanced at his watch, a silver and turquoise

Native American creation that looked heavy enough to break the arm of most men. "We received the ransom demand about twelve hours ago."

"And you want me to deliver the money?"

"And bring back my daughter."

Charles Case leaned in, as if trying to clock the speed of Simon's synapses. "You understand the technicality?"

Of course he understood; the place wasn't exactly swarming with law enforcement. "Having knowledge of a crime and not reporting it, you mean?"

Case nodded, one deliberate drop of the chin.

"That's not a technicality I'd worry about. The government isn't stupid enough to prosecute a father, or anyone else trying to help get his daughter back."

"I just wanted to be sure you understood."

"I understand perfectly, I just don't agree."

Case narrowed his eyes. "Don't agree with what?"

Simon kept his eyes on Case, though he knew Rynerson would be the one calling the shots. "No offense, Mr. Case, I'm sure you're good at your job, but I don't think you should be handling this on your own. This is a job for the FBI."

Case sat back in his chair, and though Simon couldn't read much in the man's closed-off expression, he had the distinct feeling Case agreed with him. Caitlin Wells made it clear that she did not. "The message was very explicit, if we contact the authorities Kyra would be killed immediately. No negotiations. No appeal. No exceptions."

And *no good,* Simon thought, all kidnappers say that, but he decided to withhold his decision until he'd heard the entire story. "You better tell me everything."

Charles Case glanced at Rynerson, got the nod, and proceeded to do exactly that. He talked for twenty minutes, his narration direct and precise, sticking to the facts and not speculating. When he finished, Simon had a clear picture of what had happened and where things stood. He also knew that some federal agency had lost their "best and brightest" to the charm and money of Big Jake Rynerson. "So that's it, at this point you're just waiting for instructions?"

"Pretty much," Case acknowledged. "Except for the calls I mentioned, to confirm that she was actually taken. Jake doesn't want me to do anything that might set them off, make them think we've contacted the police."

"So it's possible this Dr. Elsworth Marshall could be involved?"

"Possible, but I doubt it. The man sounded absolutely shocked when I told him—could hardly talk. Felt like he was responsible. Kyra's husband confirmed that Marshall was an old friend. A mentor to Kyra when she was doing her postgraduate work in the Galápagos."

Husband? That was the first mention of a husband. Why wasn't he involved in this little get-together? Something in the eyes of Caitlin Wells warned him not to ask. "And Luis Acosta, you're sure about him?"

Case nodded. "Talked to the man myself. Doesn't like planes—hasn't been out of Peru in twenty years. I checked with the local authorities, they confirmed his story."

Nothing Simon had heard had changed his thinking. "Jake, you don't need me. This is a job for professionals."

"That's why we have Mr. Geske. According to EDK, he's the very best." Though not unkind, it was clear by his tone that Rynerson had some misgivings about *the very best*.

Everyone looked at Leo Geske, who until that moment hadn't opened his mouth. He seemed to shrink under the sudden attention. Caitlin Wells jumped in to explain. "We carry kidnapping insurance on all our executives, as well as family members. EDK, that's our carrier, has sent Mr. Geske to handle the negotiations. He's their top K and R specialist."

Simon nodded, trying but failing to juxtapose the image of such a timid little man with that of a kidnap and ransom specialist. "So, you do this a lot, Mr. Geske?"

"Oh yessir." The man's falsetto voice expanded with pride. "Last year my company handled over forty cases. Most of those in South America. Our success rate is very high."

"Very high isn't good enough," Rynerson snapped. "We ain't drilling for oil here."

Geske melted deeper into his chair. "I understand, sir. Yessir, I do. We're going to do our best, you can be very sure of that."

Before Rynerson could tear into the man about *best not being good enough,* Simon asked his next question. "I assume you have some kind of established procedure for handling this type of thing?"

"Oh, yessir. Our response formula is very well established."

Big Jake looked ready to explode, his voice one decibel below bellow. "I can tell you right now how we're gonna respond. Tell us when and where and I'll pay—simple as that."

Geske looked ready to melt into the carpet and Simon gave Rynerson a back-off look. *Screw it,* so what if the big man got pissed—it wasn't going to help if he turned the one person who had experience in these situations into a mute. "Is that right, Leo—" He used the man's first name, trying to soften the mood. "Mr. Rynerson agrees to pay, simple as that?"

"No sir, that may be the worst thing you could do."

"Why's that, Leo? Explain that, will you?"

"There are over six thousand kidnappings a year in South America. Colombia mostly, and that's the direction her plane was heading before it dropped off the radar. It's a business down there, and the rules of business have been pretty well established. The various factions are well known and we know their MOs."

"Factions? What do you mean by factions, Leo?"

"There's a few. FARC, they're the biggest. That's the Revolutionary Armed Forces of Colombia. And the ELN, the National Liberation Army. They're not as big, but they're active. There's a bunch of smaller ones—gangs, really."

"So they have a political agenda?"

"No. Most of them started that way, left-wing mostly, but now it's just business. The commerce of kidnapping. All they care about is the money."

"That sounds good for us."

Geske bobbed his bald head. "Yessir, Mr. Leonidovich, sure is. Absolutely. They don't care if Mr. Rynerson is the biggest, meanest imperialist in the Western World. All they want is his money."

"Okay, Leo, I get the picture. So what do we do?"

"We need to establish who we're dealing with, then we divide the abduction into one of two categories: Pay or Extraction. Most abductions fall into the first category. You pay, you get the abductee back. But there are a few—" He glanced at Rynerson. "The vast minority, I assure you, that fall into the Extraction category."

Case was now leaning forward, notepad open, pen poised—full-on investigator. "Meaning?"

"We attempt to extract the victim rather than pay."

"And why would you do that?"

Geske stole another quick glance at Rynerson. "Certain factions will kill the abductee whether you pay or not."

Case nodded, as if that confirmed his own thoughts. "In which case the faster you pay, the quicker the victim ends up dead?"

"Yessir, Mr. Case, that's it precisely. And that's the reason we need to find out who the kidnappers are—if they're part of a known faction."

"And how do we find that out?"

"Usually they'll tell us. If they won't, they're much more likely to kill the abductee."

Rynerson stood up and began to pace. Geske followed the big man with his eyes, then continued. "Once we've established who we're dealing with, we'll know how to proceed."

"Pay or extraction, you mean?"

"Right."

Case looked up from his pad, nailing Geske with his dark eyes. "And how successful have you been with extractions?"

"Not very," Geske admitted, "it's always difficult to identify where the abductee is being held. Extraction is always our last choice." He leaned forward and tapped a bony finger on the table. "But either way, we negotiate."

"Even if the party is willing to pay, no questions asked?"

Geske nodded emphatically. "Absolutely. If we agree to an amount too quickly, they'll just up the price."

"Which only delays the process."

"Yessir."

"And the longer we negotiate, the higher the probability that we'll be able to locate where Kyra is being held?"

"Exactly."

"Okay, Mr. Geske, bottom line. How long do these things normally take. Typically?"

Geske threw up his small, white hands. "Weeks. Usually months."

Case closed his notepad and turned to Rynerson, who was stalking the office like a lion, not knowing who or what to attack. "Jake, this man knows what he's talking about. He makes sense."

"Yeah, Hos, I hear that." But it was obvious he didn't like it. Geske was offering no easy way out, no way for the big man to just plunk down his money and take control—

not easy for someone accustomed to grabbing the world by its axis and giving it a little personal spin.

Simon didn't like it either, for a number of reasons. Geske might know his stuff, but could a man like that, so fearful and timid, be *the very best* when it came to negotiating with killers and kidnappers? *Not likely.* And he was the only expert they had, so of course he sounded credible, but how would they know unless they talked to other experts. *The FBI.* Charles Case would certainly recognize these same things and point them out to Rynerson the minute Geske left the room; but what bothered Simon was how he fit into the picture—how he could help? The process could take weeks. *Usually months.*

Rynerson dropped back into his chair, his eyes directly on Simon. "What do you think?"

"Call the FBI."

Rynerson shook his head. "Can't trust those peckerheads to keep quiet. They like publicity too damn much."

"Come on, Jake, you're an important guy. Go at them through the back door. Call the President."

Rynerson smiled, a strained effort. "I'm not the most popular fella with the current administration."

Caitlin Wells stood up and began circling the table, as if the movement helped her think. "Jake's right, he's too high profile, someone would leak it to the tabloids." She stopped, her blue-gray eyes fixed on Charles Case. "Charles, you worked there for more than ten years, you know I'm right."

"No, Caitlin, I don't know that. There's a lot of good people in the Bureau and I wouldn't mind speaking to some of them right now." He turned to Geske. "You ever work with the FBI?"

"No, sir, not really. They can't do much outside the country. But I wouldn't be offended if you talked to them, Mr. Case. No, sir, that would be fine with me."

That made the vote 3–2, in a democratic society enough

to carry the day, but this was no democracy—it was Jake Rynerson's daughter and Jake Rynerson's fiefdom—and he wasn't changing his vote. "I can't take the chance. I'd never forgive myself if something happened to Kyra."

Simon couldn't blame the man; it wasn't an easy decision—not for any father, billionaire or otherwise. "Jake, I feel terrible about your daughter, I wish I could help, but it's obvious you don't need me." He started to stand but Rynerson stopped him.

"Whoa, hold on there, partner, just a minute." He turned to Leo Geske. "Mr. Geske, I heard everything you said. I didn't like it none." The words hit like a hammer, pounding the man deeper into his chair. "But I'm sure you're right. Problem is, I can't leave my little girl out there all alone for weeks or months. Can't do it. I wanna pay the money. Those bastards up the price, I'll just pay it, no questions asked. I just can't—"

Charles Case interrupted. "But Jake, what if we find out it's one of those splinter groups holding Kyra. The ones who—" He paused, searching for some euphemism to soften the blow.

Not the kind to back away from bad news, Big Jake supplied the word himself. "Kill the hostage, you mean? Whether we pay or not."

Case nodded.

"Well then, we'll just have to play things different. If we can't identify who we're dealing with, then you'll have to call some of those *good men* over at the Bureau." His voice took on an edge. "And hope they're smart enough to keep their mouths shut. My daughter's life depends on it." He turned to Simon. "So, whataya say, you gonna help me out here? I need someone I can count on to make the payment and bring my little girl home."

Simon knew it wasn't that simple. Big Jake assumed it would be an exchange, Kyra for the money, but few kidnappings worked that way and no one had agreed to it.

"I'm really not the best man for the job, Jake. You need a professional, someone who would notice things I wouldn't think to look for, who's been trained to deal with these kind of situations."

"Is that a no?"

"Reluctantly. But still a no. I'm afraid I would only jeopardize your daughter's life. I can't take that responsibility."

"Nothing I can say to change your mind?"

Simon realized the man was talking money—probably a huge amount of money—but was smart enough not to say it. "No. Sorry."

Rynerson nodded slowly, reluctantly. "Would you do me one favor?"

"If I can."

"Will you at least think about it for a day or two? What the hell, it's Vegas, have some fun. My treat."

Though Simon didn't like it—he preferred to face difficult decisions immediately and get them over with—he couldn't deny the man such a simple request, there was too much sadness in those big eyes. "I don't need any special treatment, you're already paying my minimum, but I'll tell you what, I'll consider taking the job if you consider bringing in the FBI. At least to consult."

Rynerson smiled, just a little. "Fair enough. I'll consider it." He turned to Caitlin Wells. "Caity, honey, would you see that Simon gets a decent room?"

A day or two. So why did he have the feeling Big Jake had just slipped a fast ball by his gut? "Did your boss just snooker me?"

Caitlin Wells smiled, an amused flash, and shook her head, as if he'd just suggested something naughty, and turned back to the elevator. "Are you a billiards player, Mr. Leonidovich? We should play. I'm not too bad—" She gave him a wink. "For a girl."

The thought of *playing* with Ms. Wells gave him a surprising jolt—the first in almost a year. Maybe because she reminded him of Pilár, her teasing sense of humor. "You're avoiding my question."

"I am?" The door slid open, barely a whisper of sound, and she stepped inside. "I must be having one of those senior moments." She inserted a magnetic key-card into a slot beneath the panel, opening a small door and exposing the full array of floor buttons. "I can't even remember the question."

Or didn't want to. "Ms. Wells, if you're a senior I can't wait till I hit old age."

She laughed softly, a woman accustomed to compliments. "Actually, we're the same age." She punched the button for the forty-ninth floor, two down from the top and one below the Rynerson domain. "My birthday was just last month."

He liked that, a beautiful woman not afraid to admit her age. "So you're *actually* older than me."

"True."

"I've always been attracted to older women."

She gave him a sidelong glance. "That's unusual. A teacher fetish, I assume."

"Not really. I didn't realize it until about ten seconds ago."

She grinned, a 1000-watt blinder that made his heart go giddyup. "Mr. Leonidovich, are you flirting with me?"

"It's Simon."

"You're avoiding my question."

"Touché."

She started to laugh, then stopped abruptly as the elevator door slid open. "Do you feel guilty laughing at a time like this?"

He fell in beside her as she started down a spacious corridor. "A bit, but I learned long ago it's the ability to laugh that gets you through this kind of shit."

She gave him a look, her expression caught somewhere between amused and sad. "It is shit, isn't it? Kyra's a wonderful woman, she doesn't deserve this."

It was the opening he'd been hoping for. "So where's her husband?"

She didn't hesitate, as if she'd been expecting the question. "Let's leave that until after you've decided whether or not to take the job."

"Fair enough. What about those other people? In the living room."

"Family. Close friends." She stopped in front of a wide door, a Cairo street scene carved into its surface. There was no room number, only a gold nameplate on the wall:

> # PALACE WALK

One of his favorite novels, written by one of his favorite authors: Naguib Mahfouz. "You named the room after a book?"

"Yes, this is one of the Literary Suites. Jake thought it would be a fun way to decorate some of the suites, recreating images from his favorite books."

"Interesting concept."

"And very popular. We even have a Sand Castle Book Club. The members receive a passport and whenever they stay in one of the suites they receive a commemorative stamp. We literally have thousands of people working their way through the list." She turned, absorbing him with those warm blue-gray eyes. "Are you a reader? I'd be glad to enroll you in the Club."

He could smell her, the faint scent of lemon and soap, and see the green flecks that made her eyes flash when she turned into the light, and damn near forgot her question. "I am. Sign me up."

"Consider it done." She inserted a magnetic pass-key into the lock, waited for the green light to flash, then pushed open the door. *Voilà!*—an Egyptian palace—or at least a corner of one, plus a few modern-day enhancements: computer, plasma-screen television, Jacuzzi for four, bed for two, and a view of the world, Vegas-style: New York, Paris, Venice, and the great pyramid itself, the Luxor. His bag was on a luggage rack next to the walk-in closet. No question about it, *a decent room.* "Ms. Wells, is your boss trying to bribe me?"

"Is it working?"

"Absolutely."

She laughed and handed him the passkey. "As I said, Jake's a very good host. See you in the morning?"

"It's after four. What do you people consider morning around here?"

"How about eleven o'clock? Breakfast?"

Five hours of beauty sleep, what more could a man want? "Sounds good. Where?"

"My room. It's private, we won't have to worry about anyone overhearing our conversation."

"You live in the hotel?" He couldn't keep the surprise out of his voice.

"No, I have a place in Summerlin, but one or two nights a week I get stuck working late and stay here. I'm in the Shogun Suite, right down the hall."

He showered and was about to crawl between the sheets when he remembered the birthday gift sitting next to his security case. He picked it up, sat down on the edge of the bed, and ripped off the foil wrap. What looked to be an old-fashioned, round pillbox turned out to be an antique compass when he popped the gold lid. Though thin, it felt solid and substantial in his hand, with fine scrolling over the top and around the edges. The back was plain and smooth, except for the newly engraved initials: $S£.

A small gift card was included:

Caitlin Wells

Simon, may you never lose your way. Thanks for interrupting your birthday celebration. Jake paid, I picked—I hope it's right.

C.W.

Very right. Not many people surprised him—Caitlin Wells did.

CHAPTER SIX

Somewhere in South America

Wednesday, 5 November 07:22:26 GMT −0500

Fourth day. The sun had been up at least an hour, but Kyra knew El Pato was still asleep by the sound of his rattling snore that vibrated through the wall. She had learned the rhythm of his slumber, the snotty gurgle of air as it passed back and forth through his clogged nasal passages for two or three minutes, then silence, complete and dead. *Sleep apnea.* At times, during the hush, she found herself holding her own breath, afraid he would die and she would be left to starve; but after thirty or forty seconds, there would always be an abrupt snort as his body struggled for air, and then the cycle would repeat. She rolled over, bracing her body against the bruises and sores. The ride in the van had bruised and scraped nearly every inch of her body, and she still felt like a piece of tenderized meat.

Need a plan. She could explain the situation with her father, that she had rejected his wealth, and pretend to be sympathetic toward El Pato and his cause—à la Patty Hearst and the Stockholm Syndrome—but he had no *cause,* other than greed, and she knew it would never work. She could feign some physical attraction, but that would never work either; not even Meryl Streep could play that role. Besides, he didn't seem the least interested in her body. He watched her the way a kid watches a pair of dogs copulate, with morbid curiosity. She had a feeling that was the way he saw her, as an animal, to be controlled and broken—the reason he didn't give her clothes or eating utensils.

Beaten and helpless, that was a role she could play—an animal trapped in a small room. She glanced up at the small window, at the gray light sifting between the thick bamboo bars, and tried to estimate the time. *Seven. Maybe seven-thirty. Same as Washington.*

She closed her eyes. *Seven-thirty,* breakfast over, sipping the last of her coffee while Anthony cleared the plates and cleaned up. He was good about things like that. The memory tugged at her cracked lips, the first time she'd smiled in four days. But where would he be now, this minute? *Vegas,* they would all be in Vegas, drawn like iron dust to the magnetic power of Big Jake Rynerson. *Earlier there—five-thirty.* Would they still be up, trying to negotiate her release, wrangling over the value of her life?

Anthony and her father, that would be interesting. *No, that would be nasty.*

Her mother and father and trophy wife Number Three. *A three-ring circus, worth the price of admission—every penny.*

And Caitlin Wells, her secret confidante and only link into the Rynerson fortress. *Putting out the fires.*

El Pato gave a sudden, unfamiliar snort and she held her breath, listening. . . .

Then he grunted, expelled a long sputtering fart, and rolled over. A moment later the air vibrated once again with his familiar, gurgling snore. *Four days,* she needed to mark them now, before he woke up. She reached out, found the two-inch sliver of wood she had stripped off the wall, then waited for him to begin a new cycle. The moment he snorted, she rolled silently off the cot and onto her knees. The room was narrow, not more than a body stretch—and wide, about twelve feet. Staying on all fours, she edged up close to the door, then using the frame as a starting point, ran her hand over the hard-packed dirt until she found a smooth patch along the wall, a spot that would be hidden behind the door. It took only a minute to scratch the first two marks and test them with her fingers. *Perfect.* She leaned down, trying to see them in the dim light when a sharp *BEEP-BEEP-BEEP* erupted from beneath the door. Startled, she could barely contain a squeal from escaping her throat before realizing it was only a beeper, the alien sound magnified by the silence. El Pato grunted and sat up, the sound so clear she could almost see him on the edge of his bed, reading whatever number or message had been received.

Was this it—*Ransom Paid*—the message that would set her free? But for some reason she didn't believe it. The message could just as easily be a death sentence—that once they had their money, El Pato would kill her. A wave of nausea welled up from the pit of her stomach—not that he might kill her, she had known that from the start—but how he would kill her. He liked to watch. He would turn it into an event—some gruesome entertainment. The thought of it paralyzed her, the screams of the boy-pilot echoing in her ears, his youthful eyes dark and dull as his head dangled from El Pato's fingers. *Don't pay him, Daddy! Please don't pay!*

But she knew he would. How many times had Caitlin said it? *"Your father always tries to do the right thing, Kyra."*

"You sound like my mother."

"You should think about that."

But she didn't. Didn't want to think about it. Didn't want to forgive him. But deep down she knew it was true—her father was a good man, perhaps a great man, and that was the very thing that made her so angry. Anything less and she wouldn't have cared so much that he had ripped their family apart. *Don't do it, Daddy—don't pay. Come find me—me and my baby. Your grandchild.*

Suddenly a sound broke through her thoughts and she realized El Pato was up and moving toward the door. It couldn't have taken more than a heartbeat to unlock her paralyzed legs and scramble back to the cot, but it felt like a lifetime, as if her feet were digging through sand. She lowered herself quietly onto the rough canvas and closed her eyes just as he pushed open the slide. She could feel his eyes, like a cockroach crawling over her skin, and forced herself to breathe slowly, afraid he would see her heart pounding against her chest, but almost immediately there was another scrape of wood and then he was gone. She took a deep breath and let it go, the relief so overwhelming she could hardly stop herself from laughing.

A few minutes later he was outside, close enough to her window that she could hear the splatter of urine as he relieved himself into the vegetation. He finished, walked away a few steps, then stopped. "What is urgent?"

The sound of his voice and the realization that there could be someone else out there, nearly stopped her heart. She sat up, careful not to make the slightest noise, and crouched beneath the window.

"*Sí.*"

She then realized he was on cellular, responding to the page. Was this it, the judgment call? Liberation or execution?

"FBI." He seemed to spit the words, his voice low and sharp. "This you said would never happen."

She could hear him moving, pacing like someone with a bad tooth, then his angry response: "Assurance! El Pato has heard enough of your assurance. How long you think it would take the FBI to put the real face on Luis Acosta? A day? You want to assure me that?"

So intent on not missing anything, it took Kyra a moment to recognize the implication of his words. Payment or not, he would never release her, never give her the chance to identify him. She laid her head against the wall and closed her eyes. She needed to do more than survive—she needed to escape.

"El Pato knows how to convince this rich *yanqui.*" He started to walk toward the front of the hut, his voice fading. "I give him . . ."

She didn't like the sound of that. *Convince how? Give him what?*

The conversation continued, but she could no longer make out the words, only the impatient anger in his voice. Who was he talking to? Someone who obviously knew exactly what was happening. Someone inside the FBI? Someone in Vegas? She laid down, playing the conversation back through her mind, trying to fill in the other side.

Suddenly the door burst open and El Pato was standing over her, his face burning with rage. Bare-chested and covered with sour sweat, his body stench seemed to make the room smaller and darker. "Your padre is not so smart!"

The fear and anxiety finally overcame her, not in a cowering way, but by opening the dam to her anger. "Smart enough to find you, you filthy pig!"

His hands were too fast, she saw the blur, coming at her from the left side of her head, but by then it was too late. The pain bloomed quick and bright, her brain exploding with a thousand brilliant colors, then slowly fading into darkness.

CHAPTER SEVEN

Las Vegas, Nevada

Wednesday, 5 November 11:03:41 GMT −0800

The wide hall was deserted and silent, not so much as a maid to break the plush landscape of silk and Berber. *Typical Vegas,* Simon thought, gamble all night, sleep till noon. He glanced at one of the floor-to-ceiling mirrors as he went past, wondering again if he was underdressed. What did one wear to breakfast at the Sand Castle, in a private suite with the beautiful Caitlin Wells? *Khakis and a sweater,* that's what he had, that's what he was wearing. Despite the long night, he felt good. Perhaps there was some truth behind all those rumors about Vegas resorts blasting negative ions into the air.

The battle scene carved into the door of Caitlin's suite was no less than a work of art: Captain Blackthorne and Lady Miriko caught between two worlds and a thousand samurai warriors, the great Lord Toranaga hovering over them like a puppet master. *Big Jake Rynerson, give or take a few centuries?* He reached over and pushed the gold button beneath the gold nameplate:

SHŌGUN

The door opened almost immediately. "You found me." She was wearing tailored blue jeans that accentuated her narrow hips and long legs, and a tweed jacket over a black, ribbed cashmere turtleneck that went perfectly with her crown of taffy-blond hair.

Damn, five hours sleep and she looked fresh as a spring flower, and smelled even better. "Of course, I'm well equipped." He held out his hand, exposing the compass. "Thank you. I love it."

"Good, I thought it might be something you'd like."

"Very much." He pointed to the tiny figure of Lord Toranaga. "Your boss?"

Her gray eyes crinkled with amusement. "I've had that same thought, but no, Jake wouldn't know a scheme from a scam."

He stepped inside and she closed the door behind him. Unlike his Egyptian palace, her suite was decorated with Oriental carpets, black walnut antique furniture, and colorful Japanese art. "You're saying he's naive?"

"No. I'm saying he's straightforward. What you see is what you get."

"And what exactly is that?"

"Jake's just a good ol' boy who managed to punch a hole in the ground at exactly the right spot and make himself a few bucks. A simple story of boy makes good."

"I don't believe it's quite so simple or so few."

She laughed. "You're sure right about that. Jake may be straightforward but there's nothing simple about that man, though plenty of people get fooled by that good ol' boy persona." She motioned toward two tables near the window, facing east, overlooking the golf course: one set for dining, the other covered with a multitude of platters and chafing dishes.

Damn, the woman must have thought *el Porko the Pig* was coming to breakfast. "You sure we'll have enough to eat?"

"I didn't know what you liked, so I ordered an assortment."

"So much for my diet."

"Really, you don't look heavy."

He tried to read her face for some lack of sincerity, but found none. Maybe she was beautiful and blind—his dream date. "Are you kidding? Dieting with me is a lifestyle."

"That's something I've never had to worry about."

That he believed. "So you're one of those skinny broads with a hollow leg that the rest of us mortals are always trying to emulate?"

She cocked her head, eyes appraising. "So you think I'm a broad, uh? Should I be offended, or are you just testing the waters to see what it takes to ring my bell?"

Hallelujah, let the angels sing, a trifecta of Bs: Beautiful, Blind, and Brilliant—what more could a man want? "And did I?"

"Ha, are you kidding? I've been accused of having balls bigger than most men."

That was the fourth B—one he had no intention of adding to his fantasy list. "That's an image I don't care to explore."

She laughed, a rib-scraping, full-of-pleasure staccato. "You're funny, Leonidovich. I like you."

He smiled to himself, not really surprised. Women always *liked* him—the cuddly brother-type that made them feel fuzzy and safe. What he needed was a dark and dangerous side. "Why do women always go for bad guys with motorcycles?"

"Oh?" Her eyes widened. "You have a motorcycle?"

"Forget it, that was purely academic. My mouth momentarily got away from my brain."

"Sounds painful. Maybe we should feed it before it escapes altogether."

Right, stuff the damn thing before he blurted out something totally inane. Caitlin filled her plate and poured coffee while he struggled to decide what to try and how miserable he wanted to make himself. He finally settled for a conservative portion of Eggs Benedict made with quail eggs and topped with hollandaise sprinkled with black caviar, and a small ration of potatoes roasted with garlic and rosemary. "That should be enough to stop my heart."

She slid a fruit tart filled with kiwi and assorted berries onto his plate. "A little fruit shouldn't hurt your diet."

"Absolutely not, fruit is good, especially if you don't count the four thousand calories in the pastry, the custard, and that nice sugary glaze."

She smiled and sat down. "I promise not to count."

He took the chair opposite, facing the golf course. "That's what they all say."

"Who are *they*?"

"Skinny broads with hollow legs."

"If it makes you feel better, I guarantee to eat more than you."

And she did, over the next twenty minutes polishing off twice as much food, a large tomato juice, half a bottle of sparkling water, and two cups of coffee. Finally satisfied, she poured herself a third cup of coffee, and leaned back. "So, Simon Leonidovich, what do you think of our desert oasis?"

"All I see are lakes and fairways. No desert."

"That's what Vegas is all about—illusion."

He was starting to wonder about Caitlin Wells, was she an illusion—a bit too perfect? "So, what's the deal here? You're the designated closer, the one who's supposed to bring me onboard?"

"Something like that." Her eyes glowed with amusement. "How am I doing?"

At least she was honest. "I have some questions."

"I thought you would. That's why I suggested we get together."

"Jake kept talking about an exchange . . ."

She shook her head. "Wishful thinking. We've only had the one message."

"Which I'd like to see."

"I thought you would." She reached over and pulled a sheet of paper off a stack of documents piled on a nearby chair. "All calls are transcribed directly into a computer, which fills in the time, date, and The Point operator taking the call. In this particular case the operator had to translate from Spanish to English as she typed."

Phone Message
Tuesday, 4 November 12:41 p.m.

For:	JR	
From:	Unknown	___Please return call
Company:	Unknown	___Will call again
Phone #:	Unknown	

We have your daughter.

The price for her return is four million American dollars.

If you notify the police or FBI we will know and your daughter will be dismembered and sent to you in pieces. No second chances.

You will be contacted.

PO:JV

He didn't want to become emotionally involved and tried not to feel anything as he read the words, but it was impossible to read *dismembered* and not empathize with Jake Rynerson and fear for his daughter. "Sick."

She nodded and poured herself a fourth cup of coffee. "Yes."

"You mentioned something called The Point, what's that?"

"All calls to my office or the Fishbowl get routed through a senior operator, a position we refer to as The Point. They screen the calls and direct them to the appropriate party. The woman who took this call has been with us eight years. Judy Vasquez. Her Spanish is perfect. If she missed anything, it wasn't important."

"And she won't say anything?"

"Absolutely not. You could cut out her tongue before she would say anything that could hurt Jake."

"He's that good a boss?"

"No, he's that good a man. He takes care of his employees and they take care of him."

"Okay. And what's the Fishbowl?"

"Jake's office."

Of course. "Why is everyone so satisfied to believe it's one of the factions Geske talked about?"

"I wouldn't say satisfied. But Jake does have oil interests in Arauca, one of the most dangerous regions of Colombia, so they know the Rynerson name and they know he's rich. It makes sense."

He nodded, as if satisfied, but something didn't feel right. The note and the semipolitical faction didn't seem to mesh, but something might have been lost in the translation. That, or his imagination had taken a zig when it should have zagged. "So the insurance company . . . what's the name?"

"EDK."

"You make a claim and EDK just lays out four million? No questions asked?"

"Two million. There's a fifty-percent deductible. Jake will have to throw in two million of his own."

"A percentage deductible? Never heard of that."

"It's not unusual for this type of insurance. The amount of a kidnapping claim is rarely finite, it's negotiated. So naturally—"

"The insurance company wants there to be some incentive not to offer up the farm."

"Exactly."

"And Leo Geske is their best man? The one they want to negotiate the deal?"

"So do I."

That surprised him, but his opinion seemed irrelevant so he didn't bother to debate the point. "And Jake wants me to make the payment to avoid a conflict of interest."

"You catch on quick."

"It doesn't take a genius. EDK would prefer to catch the bad guys than cough up a couple million."

She nodded. "And that's one of the reasons Jake doesn't want to use the FBI. They look like losers unless they catch someone. Rescuing the victim is secondary, whether they admit it or not."

"So it's not just the fear of a leak he's worried about?"

"We're afraid of that too."

"And he doesn't care if they're caught?"

"Not if Kyra's released unharmed."

"Two million, that's a lot not to care about."

"Jake's a billionaire, Simon. Do you have any concept of how much that is?"

He understood the math just fine, but the concept of having that much money did stretch his imagination a little beyond focus. "I don't suppose you'd have to worry much about retirement."

"Not unless you wanted to buy Hawaii. Just think about it, one million dollars, *multiplied* by one thousand! Trust me, he won't notice the dent."

"I get the picture."

"Good. I think it's important to—" The chirp of her cell phone interrupted. She frowned, glanced at the number on the display, then pressed the tiny unit to her ear. "What's up?" She listened for thirty seconds, not saying a word, then finished with a three word response: "Okay, ten minutes." She dropped the phone into the pocket of her jacket and turned back to Simon. "Sorry, that was Charles. My presence has been requested."

"News?"

"No. Jake is trying to decide about the FBI. They want my input."

"So, he is considering calling them in?"

"Of course, he gave you his word." An odd expression burned across her face, there and gone in less than an eyeblink, some memory or thought momentarily caught and exposed between axon and neuron. "And Jake *always* tries to do the right thing."

Sarcasm? Bitterness? Or was he now hearing inflections that didn't exist? "That's good to hear."

She stared into his eyes, like an optometrist searching for problems. "And you? Do you always do the right thing, Simon Leonidovich? You did promise to consider taking the job."

Something he now regretted. "And I will."

She leaned forward, reading his hesitancy. "But—"

"But I don't think you're going to like my answer. Anyone on your security staff is better equipped to do the job."

"That's not the way Jake sees it. You've been through this kind of thing before, and because of you everything worked out."

But that wasn't true, if everything had worked out

Pilár Montez would still be alive. He couldn't do it again—couldn't take the responsibility for another woman's life.

Though indistinct, Caitlin could hear Jake's voice booming over the whine of vacuums as she stepped out of the elevator. The friends-and-family group had momentarily abandoned their vigil, probably to catch a few hours' sleep and give the housekeeping staff a chance to do their job. As she expected, Jake was pacing and rattling on about the pros and cons of bringing in the FBI, attempting to honor his promise to at least consider the idea. Charles Case, sitting at the bar with a Texas-size espresso, had gotten stuck with the unfortunate task of defending the idea—an assignment destined to failure—with Big Jake arguing against the very thing he was trying so righteously to consider. *So typical,* Caitlin thought, always trying to do the right thing. Something the big man failed at frequently, as often as any other mortal, but there was a difference—Big Jake *always* tried. And, as always, he tried to assuage his guilt by soliciting her support. "Caity, honey, you know I'm right."

"Yes, Jake, you're right." At least she could say that with a clear conscience.

Case fixed her with a stare hot enough to melt chrome. "I hope to hell you are, because if we need their help later, it won't be easy."

Impossible, she assumed, but that didn't matter; if the FBI got involved everything would go to hell in an instant. She circled the desk and dropped into Jake's chair, a behemoth that made her feel like a dwarf. "Where's Geske?"

Jake frowned, like he suddenly remembered a bad dream. "In his room, calling all his contacts in South America. For a minute there last night I thought that little pissant was going to pee on my chair. Can't believe he's any good at his job."

"That's a piss and a pee in one sentence, Jake. That's a new record for you."

"Now, Caity, honey, don't you go getting on me about my language. This is not a good time."

But he grinned, just a little, the first time since getting the news, so she'd accomplished at least a part of her job: *keep the big man positive.* "He's supposed to be the best."

"I know what you said. I just don't see how someone like that can talk to those sonsobitches took my little girl."

She was tempted to remind him that his daughter was thirty-five years old and hardly a *little girl*, but Kyra hadn't really been in his life since she was twelve, and that's the way Jake would always think of her. "He's done it enough times, he knows what he's doing."

He snorted and turned back to the window. "Well, I don't believe it. That boy's as nervous as a long-tailed cat in a room full of rockin' chairs. You find someone better."

Impossible, there was no *better* than the *best,* and the best would never be good enough when it came to his daughter—not his son-in-law, and certainly not someone as meek as Leo Geske. She gave Charles a beseeching look, hoping for a little support.

He gave her a nod, pushed his mug away, and stood up. "She's right, Jake. I made a couple of calls myself. Everyone agrees, Geske's very good when it comes to negotiating with these bastards. It's actually because he's so timid that he's so successful."

"You better explain that to me, Hos."

"Kidnappers generally assume whatever he says is true—that he's too afraid not to play it straight with them."

"That doesn't make much sense."

"No, Jake, it does. It makes perfect sense. You send some hard-nosed negotiator up against these bastards and all you've got is a pissing contest between a couple of schoolyard bullies. That wouldn't help us. We don't care if they win, all we care about is getting Kyra home."

"You got that straight."

"So what we need is someone who can get them to the bottom line. Someone they'll believe when they're told there's a limit. That someone is Leo Geske."

"Okay, Hos, I'll go along. For now." His voice dropped to a growl, cold enough to freeze alcohol. "He better not screw up." He turned to Caitlin. "What about Leonidovich?"

"I'm working on him."

"And?"

"He's stalling, hoping something good will happen and we won't need him."

"Push him."

"I did. He promised me an answer one way or the other by tomorrow morning. But I don't think he'll do it."

"Why?"

A question she'd been asking herself all morning. "I'm not sure, probably for the same reason you're not going to call in the FBI. You don't trust them—he doesn't trust you."

There was a dead beat of silence, as though the great Jake Rynerson couldn't believe someone would actually question his integrity. "He tell you that?"

"No, but that was my impression. He thinks you're a cowboy, just wanting to go down there and blow those bad boys off the planet and save your little girl."

He smiled, just a little. "I told ya that boy was smart."

"Very smart. Smart enough to know if this isn't handled right both Kyra and the person who delivers the money end up on a cold slab."

Jake shook his head, clearly not wanting to face that possibility. "No. You heard what that little peckerhead Geske said, that's not the way these people work."

"*Most* of the time, Jake. But we're not even sure who we're dealing with. These might be the type of people who think it's safer to kill whoever delivers the money and run. Leonidovich knows that."

"I've read about this guy. He doesn't scare easy."

"Well, if he's not worried about himself, then he's afraid of getting Kyra killed. I think we need to find ourselves another bagman."

"Absolutely not! Leonidovich is smart and he's been through this shit before. Where you going to find someone with those qualifications? He's the guy I want. Convince him."

"And how do you suggest I do that?"

"You like the guy, don't you?"

She hesitated, and realized that she did. He was smart, funny, and real, not like most of those flashy, full-of-themselves Vegas yahoos who asked her out. "So?"

"I saw the way he looked at you. You won't have any problem convincing him."

"I hope you're not suggesting—"

"Now, Caity honey, you know me better than that. Use some of that famous Caitlin Wells charm."

"I don't feel very charming right now."

"We need him."

She pushed herself out of the chair and started toward the door. "I'll be in my office. Someone's got to run this joint."

Jake fell in beside her, wrapping an arm around her shoulders. "Good idea, you take care of things. I need to catch myself a couple hours' bunk time."

She gave him a hard look, her pay-attention look. "Don't get mixed up on *which bunk*, Jake. I saw you giving Kyra's mother the eye."

He grinned sheepishly, like a schoolboy caught reading *Playboy*. "Billie does look good doesn't she? I mean for a woman her age. Damn good."

"Yes, she looks good, but you already have a wife, Jake. A very young wife who feels intimidated enough around

Billie. Don't go making things any more complicated than they already are."

He gave her shoulders a little squeeze. "Yes, ma'am. I'll keep my pistol holstered."

"I'm serious, Jake."

"Me too, honey. I'm not feelin' too frisky right now."

"I know, but when you're worried you like to nuzzle up to something soft and warm and sympathetic." Something she knew much too much about.

Embarrassed, he glanced a look toward Charles as he steered her out the door. "Now don't you worry none about ol' Jake, you just take care of Leonidovich. We need him."

"Prepare yourself, I don't think it's going to happen."

His head tilted down, his expression serious and dark. "I want that boy. Whatever it takes."

Whatever it takes. Of all the words, those were the three she hated most.

CHAPTER EIGHT

Somewhere in South America

Thursday, 6 November 07:26:15 GMT –0500

Fifth day. Despite the dimness, Kyra could barely open her eyes against the light. Her head felt like a hammered drum, with a booming echo that never stopped. She touched the left side of her face, trying to assess the damage, but the moment her fingers found the wound a burst of hot light filled her head and she abandoned the effort. At least he hadn't used her body as a punching bag. She reached down, probing the area beneath her belly. *You okay?* She tried to concentrate, to reason through her options, but the effort only increased the thunder. She closed her eyes and waited until the reverberations faded to a dull rumble, then tried again, sneaking up on one thought at a time, trying to hide the effort from her brain so it wouldn't realize it was being called on to exert itself.

She needed some way to defend herself. But how? A kick to the scrotum always worked in the movies, but she suspected that was Hollywood hyperbole and it would take more than that to incapacitate the man. She needed a weapon, but had nothing to use or no way to make one. The best she could do was peel a three- or four-inch sliver of wood from the wall, but what good would that do unless she got close enough and lucky enough to get him in the eye? The chance of that seemed remote, and if she tried and failed he would kill her without thought, just as he had the pilot. *Too much risk,* unless it became her only option.

She could do nothing and hope to be rescued, but that seemed unlikely. There had been no human sounds beyond the tiny structure. Twice, shortly before sundown, a small plane had flown directly overhead, low, just above the canopy of trees, but she could tell it was landing, not searching. *Drug smugglers,* she assumed, the occupation of choice for this part of the world.

No defense. No offense. No rescue. That left only one option—*escape.* But how? The hard-packed floor was like concrete, the bamboo bars as thick as her wrist and hard as steel. *Excuse me, Mr. Duckman, you wouldn't happen to have an extra jackhammer available? No. Perhaps a saw— just a little one? No.* That left the door.

Somehow she needed to get past him—if he ran like a duck, he would never catch her—but how? The man was careful, very careful, and the routine never varied. Twice a day he would open his little window and growl, "Pail," then wait until she placed her waste bucket next to the door and returned to the cot before he opened the door; and then only long enough to reach in, drop one bucket, pick up the used one, and close the door. That done, he would slide a plate of food through the window slot. It was all very structured and base—the exchange of food for waste. *Turds for tots.*

She thought about it for hours, but could think of no way to avoid his quick hands and hard fists. But there had to be a way, and she intended to be ready when the opportunity presented itself. It might only come once, for only a moment, and she couldn't hesitate, couldn't even think about it. Just run—fast, before he could pull his gun—out the door, a quick cut around the side of the hut and into the jungle. Then what? She had no clothes, tools, or weapons—no food, or water, or map. She didn't know where she was, or even what country—Ecuador or Colombia—but she knew the jungle, and if three months in the rain forest had taught her anything, it was how to survive under similar conditions. At least for a short time. Do nothing and he would kill her, she had no doubt about that.

Need to be ready. Need to be strong. She could exercise at night and sleep during the heat of the day. She could do sit-ups and push-ups, and run in place during El Pato's snore cycle. During the silence she could do squats to keep her heart pumping and build her stamina. A hundred mini-jogs.

She felt better. She had a plan.

CHAPTER NINE

The Fishbowl

Thursday, 6 November 04:38:19 GMT −0800

It took a few seconds for Simon to extricate the pulsating buzz from his dream and realize it was the phone. He rolled over, groping the night table as he tried to shift his brain from REM to reality. Typical of most Las Vegas hotels, the room was designed for nightcrawlers, the blackout curtains obliterating any distinction between night and day and all he could see were the glowing red numbers on the bedside clock. 4:38. Groggy or not, he hadn't slept sixteen hours, he was sure of that, and equally sure no one called at that time of the morning with good news. He found the receiver, cleared his throat, and tried to sound human. "Hello." Despite the effort, he sounded like a wounded frog.

"You awake?"

The tightness in Caitlin's voice swept away the last cloud of fog. "I am now."

"I need to see you. May I come to your room?"

He had one of those fleeting, nasty-but-nice visions of her popping into his room wearing some silky, thigh-teasing teddy, but knew from her tone this was not a social visit. "Sure. Give me five minutes."

He made a quick dash through the bathroom, managing to wash his face, brush his teeth, and pull on one of the suite's fine Egyptian robes before she arrived. Though not dressed in anything provocative, she still looked amazingly appealing in a burgundy blazer, black slacks, and pink turtleneck. She smiled but there was no hiding the concern in her eyes. "Sorry to wake you."

"Not a problem." He motioned toward a chair.

She shook her head. "There's been a development. About thirty minutes ago—"

He held up a hand, stopping her. "Don't. You shouldn't say any more. I've decided not to take the job."

She sighed, just a little, letting her disappointment bleed into her voice. "I suspected as much. But before you make a final decision—"

He interrupted her a second time. "That *is* a final decision."

"I understand. I really do. But I think you should talk to Jake before you leave."

He didn't want to. Not because he didn't like the man, but because he did. It was hard enough to say no to a man like Jake Rynerson, but doubly hard with someone so damn likable. But how could he refuse? The man had paid ten thousand dollars, he deserved to hear it firsthand. "I assume you mean now?"

She nodded. "Please, he's waiting in the Fishbowl."

"Okay, give me a few minutes. I'll meet you there."

Leo Geske was pacing back and forth in front of Rynerson's private elevator when Simon arrived. Dressed in a dark blue three-piece suit, a starched white shirt, and a tightly knotted paisley tie with matching pocket handkerchief, the little man looked nervous as a bridegroom having second thoughts. "Oh, Mr. Leonidovich, good morning. How are you today? Get enough sleep? What's going on?"

Simon answered the last question, the only one the man really cared about. "Not a clue."

Geske bobbed his head, as if to confirm the mystery. "Ms. Wells called about ten minutes ago. Said there's been some kind of development."

Development, every time he heard the word it sounded more like *catastrophe.* "That's what she told me too."

"Good news, I hope."

Simon knew better. Nothing good happened between four and five in the morning. It was a law of the cosmos.

Charles Case was waiting when they reached Rynerson's fiftieth-floor domain. "Good morning, gentlemen." He tried to add a smile, but it congealed in the middle of his face, confirming what Simon already suspected—there was nothing *good* about it. Neither Caitlin Wells or Big Jake attempted to put a smiley face on the day when they entered the Fishbowl. Rynerson motioned them toward his desk, which looked relatively bare compared to its previous condition. "Thank you for coming."

Geske shifted his weight from one foot to the next, two tiny beads of sweat glistening at the corners of his nose. "Ms. Wells said there'd been a development." His voice came out high and squeaky.

Rynerson nodded. "Take a seat."

It was then Simon noticed the white plastic box, no larger than a cigarette pack, sitting on an unfolded piece of brown wrapping paper, squarely in the middle of Big Jake's massive desk. It could have been anything, but for some reason it looked ominous. His foreboding intensified when Charles Case pulled on a pair of latex gloves. "This was delivered to the front desk about an hour ago."

Even before Caitlin Wells turned her head, Simon knew he wasn't going to like whatever Case was about to reveal, but like watching the space shuttle disintegrate over Texas, he couldn't turn away. Case lifted the lid off the box and lying there on a bed of white cotton, glistening like a display pastry dipped in glaze, was someone's left ear, a round diamond stud sparkling from the lobe.

Geske covered his mouth and turned away. Simon forced himself to take a breath. "You're sure . . . ?"

Big Jake nodded. "I gave her the earrings myself. When

she got her pilot's license." He glanced toward Caitlin. "Caity picked them out."

Case replaced the lid, then held up a business card, holding it by the edges between two fingers. "This was included."

Kyra Rynerson-Saladino, PhD, DSc

3001 Connecticut Avenue NW
Washington, DC 20008   202 673-4800

He turned the card over, being careful not to touch either side.

---

call the FBI
you get her tongue

Simon felt the words as much as read them, one thought after another scrambling for attention. "You can't believe . . ." His words trailed away as he considered the possibility.

Case nodded. "Somebody talked."

"Like we should be surprised?" Caitlin snapped. "Someone always talks. It's the world we live in. We should have anticipated the possibility."

But it wasn't that simple, and Simon realized it instantly. "Are you saying one of us? We were the only ones who knew."

She shook her head, a distasteful look that melted into sadness. "You remember that group in the living room?"

"Family and friends, you said."

"Right, family and friends." Her lips curled slightly, a smile that was neither happy or amused, but somehow deprecating. "After we left, Jake brought them up to date. He mentioned the possibility of bringing in the FBI."

"Even so, I can't believe—"

"Plus the house staff," she added in what sounded like a major understatement. "There were people in and out of here all night. No one is supposed to say anything, but you know how that goes."

Jake leaned forward in his chair, elbows on knees, his head drooping in utter defeat. "It's my fault. I never should have considered it."

The words cut into Simon like a dull knife, and he knew he was really the one at fault, the one who forced Rynerson to consider calling the Bureau. Even so, it didn't make sense; there was some out-of-sync vibration he couldn't bring into balance. There had been nothing in the papers, not so much as a whisper about Kyra, so how could some group of South American bad guys hear about something that hadn't made the news? *Unless . . .*

Case seemed to read his thoughts. "We sweep this office for bugs on a regular basis. We checked yesterday, the place is clean." He gave everyone a pay-attention look. "Someone opened their mouth."

Big Jake jerked upright, like someone had just shoved a cattle prod up his backside. "No, I can't believe that! No one here"—he thumped a finger on the desk to emphasize his point—"including the staff, would divulge that kind of information."

Caitlin gave her boss an annoyed glare. "Oh for God's sake, Jake, wake up and smell the manure. How many times have you been stung by an employee showing off to friends by telling a 'Big Jake Rynerson' story? By the time it gets to the *National Enquirer* it's twice as juicy and ninety percent horseshit."

A momentary silence enveloped the room, everyone

dispirited, while Simon tried to work through the math. *Twenty-four hours. Four thousand miles.* Was it even possible? *Assuming* someone had inadvertently opened their mouth, and *assuming* the wrong person had overheard the slip, and *assuming* the information had somehow gotten to the kidnappers—would they have enough time to react and return their little warning? *Yes,* but the elements of chance seemed to overstretch the laws of probability. *Unless?*

Unless Kyra was closer, not in South America at all.

Unless the leak had not been inadvertent.

Charles Case was apparently thinking along the same lines. "From now on we've got to limit the flow of information."

Big Jake straightened in his chair, making a visible effort to recover his strength and push forward. "Right, need-to-know only." He began defining the group, counting off the names on the fingers of his massive right hand. "Charles, Caity, Mr. Geske—" He turned his tormented eyes on Simon. "I hope you understand why I can't talk to the FBI. Not now. You have to admit they have a different agenda. They want to catch bad guys. I just want my daughter back." He took a deep breath and charged ahead, as if needing to justify his actions to himself. "Not that I don't wanna see those bastards burn in hell, but I'm willing to pay the money. Why should I have to risk my daughter's life?" Tears crept into the corners of his eyes and he blinked them away. "Any chance you might reconsider? Give us a hand here?" His voice welled up. "The sonsobitches are cutting up my little girl."

Holy mother, what could he say to that? The guy wasn't playing Big Boy Billionaire—he was just being a father, frightened to death for his daughter, and probably felt worse because he *was* a billionaire, the very reason she had been kidnapped. He didn't sound like some rich guy trying to buy a service, but just a man asking a friend for help. And that's what made it impossible to turn the man down, because that was exactly how Simon felt—like a friend. "Count me in."

Big Jake nodded, a momentary look of relief, and Simon had the uncomfortable feeling his life had just been thrown into animated suspension, subordinate to the macrocosm of Big Jake Rynerson, who extended another finger. "That's four. Who else?"

"Billie," Caitlin answered.

Big Jake grimaced and leaned back in his chair. "We couldn't tell her—" He glanced at the white box. "About that. It would kill her."

Still wearing his latex gloves, Charles reached over and carefully began to refold the brown paper around the box. "No reason she has to know. It won't help anything."

"Okay," Jake said, "that's five. That's our need-to-know group."

"What about Anthony Saladino?" Geske asked, his gaze moving anxiously from one person to the next. "Doesn't he have a right to know what's going on?"

"No," Jake snapped. "Absolutely not."

Caitlin Wells didn't hesitate an instant to contradict her boss. "Jake, you can't cut Tony out of the loop. He's Kyra's husband, for God's sake."

Big Jake opened his mouth to respond, then reconsidered, pushed himself out of his chair and began to pace, tromping back and forth in his scruffy cowboy boots. Simon felt like a late arrival at a three-act play; he understood the main drama but none of the subplots: Big Jake and Anthony Saladino; Big Jake and Caitlin Wells. He looked at Caitlin and wondered if he wanted to know. A real ballbuster, no doubt about that, but smart, funny, and oh so good to look at. Big Jake suddenly stopped, made a pirouette off the heel of one boot, and dropped back into his leather chair. "You're right. But nothing about this." He pointed to his ear. "No telling what he might do."

Simon expected an argument—it didn't seem right to keep a secret like that from Kyra's husband—but Caitlin simply nodded, apparently satisfied with the decision, and moved on. "What about Tammi?"

"This has nothing to do with her."

"It doesn't matter to me, Jake, she's your wife, but eventually she'll find out you were telling things to your ex-wife you weren't telling her. That could be a problem."

He leaned over, right in her face, going eyeball to eyeball like a big-league manager about to tear into one of his ballplayers. "My problem, pussycat." He spoke softly, barely above a whisper, but loud enough to hear the warning in his muscular voice: *That's enough.*

"I'll remember that when—" She stopped herself. "Fine. Your problem."

He nodded and sat back, the polite but pissy exchange over as quick as it started. Apparently Caitlin could push the big man only so far—which he allowed with a kind of innocent humor—but there came a point when Big Jake would dig in the heels of those old boots and that was the end of it. It was undoubtedly his charm with women— and his downfall.

"That's seven," Charles said, making an obvious effort to fill the unnatural silence. "Counting you, Jake."

Everyone seemed to take a breath, an intermission between acts, and Simon wondered how long it would take for him to move from spectator to actor. He turned to Leo Geske, who seemed lost in some kind of mind fog, his eyes on the small package containing Kyra Rynerson's left ear. "So what's the next step, Leo?"

The little man blinked, coming back from whatever remote galaxy his mind had wandered into. "What?" He glanced around, suddenly conscious that all eyes were on him.

Simon repeated his question. "Is there something we should be doing?"

Geske looked at Charles Case. "Are the phones ready?"

"Everything's set. Every call to and from this floor is being monitored and recorded." Charles paused, his gaze circling the group. "If you don't want someone listening in on your calls, I suggest you use a cellular."

Geske bobbed his head. "Good. Excellent. And what about the tracing equipment?"

"Automatic tracing begins the minute a call gets routed to this office. The trace is terminated once the call is determined immaterial." Charles leaned back in his chair, crossing his arms over his chest. "They'll be expecting this, I'm sure. It's highly unlikely we'll be able to keep them on the line long enough to get a trace."

"The first call," Geske corrected. "Once we've opened a dialogue and they become comfortable, they may get careless. It happens."

It was obvious to Simon that most of this had already been discussed. "What makes you think there will be more than one call?"

"Experience," Geske answered. "It's a process. Give and take, one step at a time. The objective of every call is to close the gap between us and the victim."

"How do you do that?"

"We have a specific set of goals," Geske answered, his voice gaining confidence as he moved into his area of expertise. "We try to accomplish at least one with every call."

"What kind of goals?"

Geske extended one of his bony fingers. "Proof-of-life. That's a must. We don't agree to anything until we know Ms. Saladino is still alive." He extended a second finger. "The amount. That's a tough one, and usually the thing that takes the longest to agree on, but since Mr. Rynerson doesn't want to attempt any knockdown on the four million, we're hoping that won't be an issue."

Though not sure, Simon thought he detected a burr of

disapproval in Geske's tone. "Unless they up the ante."

Geske nodded, a deliberate one-stroke drop of the chin, as if to say: *I warned you.* He extended a third finger. "Goal number three: simultaneous exchange. Ms. Saladino for the money. I doubt very much if they'll agree to that."

Simon understood why, but asked anyway, hoping to dampen Big Jake's fantasy to a realistic level. "Why?"

"Because once we have Ms. Saladino there would be nothing to stop us from grabbing whoever takes the money. They know that and they're not going to take the risk." He extended a fourth finger, pointing all four at Simon. "This is where you come in. Time and place. They'll insist on picking both and we won't have much say in the matter. So our goal here is simple: get them to at least agree on a public location. Someplace that provides maximum safety."

Simon forced a smile, trying to look confident. "Okay, I get the idea. Sounds good." He just didn't believe it; especially if Kyra was being held in Colombia, where *maximum safety* was located somewhere between Wishful Thinking and Fantasyland. "So what now, we just sit and wait for the call?"

"Not much we can do," Geske answered. "I'm in contact with all my sources in South America—nobody's heard anything. Whoever did this is—"

There was a sudden loud *WHAP* and the door burst open, followed by a woman Simon didn't recognize: midfifties, slender and fair with strong features, dressed in a khaki shirt and pants, stylish in a casual way, typical of so many European women. Big Jake jumped to his feet. "Billie, what the hell? What's going on?"

She advanced on him like a bad storm coming over the mountains. "That's what I came to ask you, Jake Rynerson." Her speech vibrated with a slight West Texas twang.

"I don't understand."

"I just got a call from your wife—crying her eyes out."

He stood there in trancelike bewilderment. "I . . . I—"

"Stop stuttering, you ol' fool. Poor little thing, wakes up and finds you gone. Now why that would upset a woman I have no earthly idea. Sounds like a reason to celebrate if you ask me."

"I—"

"Oh shut up, Jake, and sit down." She reached out and gave him a shove, hard, and he toppled back into his chair, looking bewildered and helpless as Billie continued her harangue. "Calls me at five-thirty in the morning, thinking she's gonna find you in *my* bed. Now why would she think that, Jake?"

"I—"

"I—I—I, is that all you can say for yourself? As if I'd want your baggy old ass between my sheets." She glanced around, as if noticing for the first time there were other people in the room. "What's going on here?"

Simon couldn't decide whether to laugh or duck for cover. Billie Rynerson was a tornado, a wipe-out-anything-in-her-path type gal. Everyone else seemed equally stunned at her abrupt arrival and equally disinclined to offer up an explanation. Big Jake foolishly tried to regain command. "Now, Billie, if you'll just settle down for a—" She stopped him with a subzero look, then turned and leveled her ice-blue snake charmers on Caitlin. "Caity dear, why don't you tell me."

Caitlin smiled and stood up, clearly not intimidated by the woman. "Good morning, Billie. You know everyone here," her gaze shifted to Simon, "except for Mr. Leonidovich. He's going to help us get Kyra back. Simon, this is Billie Rynerson, Kyra's mother."

Simon leaped to his feet, taking the hand that was suddenly thrust in front of him, her handshake firm and confident. The woman studied his face, closely, as if reading a road map. "Mr. Leonidovich, what exactly is your role in this? And what exactly is going on here?"

When this woman said *exactly*, he had a feeling she meant *exactly*. He also noticed that the box containing Kyra's ear had disappeared from the desk, and wondered *exactly* how little he could say without lying, something he had no intention of doing. "Mrs. Rynerson—"

"Billie," she interrupted. "Please call me—" She paused, as if some internal lightbulb had just blinked to life. "Simon did you say? Simon Leonidovich? I recognize that name. Aren't you the one who discovered Mira-loss was killing people?"

"Not really. I—" He wanted to say *didn't do that much,* but after all the publicity that would sound like disingenuous humility. "—just helped get the information to the right people."

She smiled, as if she knew it was more than that, then turned to her ex-husband. "You always get the best, Jake, I have to give you that." He opened his mouth but before he could say anything she had refocused her attention on Caitlin. "Okay, Caity, what are y'all doing here at dark-thirty in the morning? Have you heard something?"

Caitlin didn't hesitate, not for an instant. "Yes, Billie, we have. We received a second message, warning us against bringing in the FBI."

"May I see it, please?"

"It came through the switchboard, just like the last one." The lie came off her tongue like honey, sweet and smooth. "We're afraid inside information may have somehow gotten back to the kidnappers. That's why we're meeting."

Big Jake pushed a chair up behind his ex-wife and she sat, the movement robotic and natural, without thought. "Are you saying the warning was in reaction to the discussions we've been having?"

"It's possible," Caitlin answered, "or it might have just been a reminder. But we can't take any chances. We've decided to limit the number of people in the information loop."

Billie nodded, her eyes suspicious as they circled the group and stopped on Big Jake. "I hope to hell you're not trying to cut me out of this information loop, Jake Rynerson."

"Oh, Billie, of course not. I just didn't want to wake you so early. Isn't that right, Caity?"

"That's the truth, Billie. Jake asked me to give you a call no later than seven."

Billie looked over at Caitlin and smiled, just a little, letting her know she wasn't fooled. "Caity dear, I love ya, you know that, but don't think for a minute I don't know you'd lie for this man."

Caitlin stared straight back at the woman, not backing down, but not defending herself against the accusation either. Simon couldn't decide if they were just trying to protect Billie from the fact that Kyra had been maimed, or there were other things going on—*had gone on*—that he didn't understand. *Act Two*, and the subplots were getting more confusing by the minute.

Jake reached over and put an arm around Billie's shoulders. "Now, Billie honey, don't you go pickin' on Caity just because I made a mistake."

"And don't you try and sweet-talk me, Jake Rynerson. If I blamed Caitlin for all your mistakes she'd have more bruises than a Georgia peach. So where's Tony? I hope you don't think you can keep him in the dark."

Big Jake held up his massive hands, as if to ward off this unfair and unwarranted attack. "Absolutely not! Wouldn't dream of it."

Billie snorted with sarcastic amusement. "I'm sure glad you're an honest man, Jake, 'cause you don't lie worth shit."

"Billie honey, do you have to embarrass me in front of all these nice people?"

"No, but I sure do enjoy it. What about your wife, is she included in this little club?"

He shook his head, an empathic left, then right, and you could almost see the heels of his boots digging into the carpet. "There's no reason for her to be involved."

"No reason at all," Billie snapped back, "except she's in the bedroom cryin' her pretty little eyes out and thinkin' you're with me. For God's sake, Jake, haven't you learned anything about women? You've damn well had enough practice."

"Now, Billie, don't you go gettin' on me about women. I ain't perfect."

"Perfect! Ha, you ain't even close, Jake Rynerson." She turned, laying the crosshairs of her steely blues directly on Caitlin. "Am I right, or am I right?"

Caitlin failed to suppress a grin. "You're right, Billie. When it comes to women, the man doesn't have a clue."

The information loop, Simon realized, had just gone from seven to eight. *Too many.* A quick glance at Charles confirmed the thought.

Big Jake grunted and scrunched down into his chair. "Well, ain't that just a doodle, now I got the two of ya pissin' in my sandbox."

Billie reached over and patted the big man's shoulder, a feline expression of satisfaction on her face. "It's okay, Jake, we still love ya."

"Well, that's good to know. If things get any better around here, I'll have to hire someone to help me enjoy it."

"What you gotta do is get your ass up out of that chair and go fix things with your wife." She turned to Caitlin. "Caity, you call Tony. Tell him we're going to meet here at"—she glanced at her watch, a gold, wafer-thin Gondolo by Patek Philippe with a crocodile strap—"nine o'clock." Her gaze moved around the circle, pausing just long enough to let everyone know she meant business. "Then you're going to tell us how things stand and what y'all are gonna do to get my daughter back."

CHAPTER TEN

Las Vegas

Simon followed Caitlin into the elevator. He waited until the door closed before speaking. "What the hell was that?"

She smiled, just a little. "That was the best damn thing that ever happened to Jake Rynerson and he lost it."

Simon wondered if she might be a bit jealous of her own description of Billie Rynerson. "Does he know it?"

"Oh yeah, they're cut from the same cloth, those two. Maybe I should say the same West Texas dirt, though I guess you picked that up from the accent."

"Hard to miss. They sound just alike."

The door opened and she stepped into the corridor. "They share some history, that's for sure."

"And a daughter."

She grimaced, as if he'd just poked her in the ribs. "I hated to lie, but I don't know what else we could have done."

He nodded, as if he understood, but it wasn't the lie that bothered him, it was the way she lied—so easy and natural.

"We agreed not to tell her," she added quickly, as if to justify her position. "I really don't believe she could handle the thought of Kyra being mutilated. It would have broken her heart."

He didn't say anything, not wanting to make an issue of something he didn't fully understand. Maybe it was true, maybe Billie couldn't handle the truth. They knew her, he didn't, but she seemed the type who could handle just about anything, and keeping it from her didn't seem right. Caitlin stopped at the door to his suite and pulled a key card from her pocket. "This is for the elevator. It's been programmed to give you access to the fiftieth floor."

Her confidence—the fact that she had programmed the card before he accepted the job—bothered him. "You always so prepared?"

She smiled, most of it conveyed in her soft blue-gray eyes. "Let's just say I was hopeful."

He suddenly felt awkward, standing outside the door of his room, trapped in some kind of gender reversal. "You want to come in? I could order breakfast."

"Thanks, but I've got an important call I need to make."

He nodded, he had one of his own to make—something he wasn't looking forward to.

"WorldWide SD, how may I help you?"

Though it had only been a couple days, it felt longer, and it was good to hear Lara's voice. "How you doing, Sissie?"

"Ahhh, the prodigal brother. How's life in the city of sin?"

"I asked first."

"Nothing much happening, but you knew that, I emailed you the calendar yesterday. So, what's the deal? Did you take the job? What is it? What's Big Jake like? Tell me about the Sand Castle. Is it as fabulous as they say? When are you coming ho—"

"Whoa-whoa-whoa. Take a breath, kid, the air is free."

"No stalling, Simon, I mean it. I might get another call. Tell me everything."

"Yes, I took the job. I can't tell you what it is. Yes, the—"

Her voice came snapping back over the line. "Wait, hold it right there, Boris. What do you mean you can't tell me what it is?"

"Sorry. I had to take a blood oath and swear on your life never to reveal—"

"My life! Ha! I'm the irreplaceable one in this company."

"The last I checked you were my Executive Administrative Assistant and my Office Manager. You now want to add *Irreplaceable One* to your unending string of titles?"

"Damn right, and I want a raise to go with it. Now stop stalling. What's the job?"

"I'm serious, no can do."

She *humphed* in response, the sound of defeat. "Okay, so tell me about Big Jake."

"Typical billionaire. Met one, you've met 'em all."

"Well, I've never met one. You like him?"

"Yeah, I do. Very interesting guy."

"Interesting! I want more than interesting."

But he didn't want to say more. For all he knew Charles Case had everyone's phone on the tap. "Sorry, we'll have to talk later. I just called to tell you we're going to have to refer the work out for a while."

"Tell me you're kidding."

"Sorry."

"For how long?"

Good question. "I'm not sure. You better not plan on having me around for a couple weeks."

"A couple weeks! How much are we getting for this job?"

"I didn't ask."

"Oh boy. I smell trouble."

"Don't worry, Jake's a fair guy. He'll do what's right."

"Jake. So now you're on a first name basis with the guy?"

"Gotta run, Sissie. I'll call you tomorrow."

"I hate you, Boris."

"Okay, I'll give you one little tidbit about the infamous B. J. Rynerson."

"Oh, goodie."

"He doesn't like to be called Big Jake."

"Swell. I'll remember that the next time I run into him at Starbucks."

CHAPTER ELEVEN

Las Vegas

Thursday, 6 November 08:58:13 GMT –0800

Caitlin was waiting when the elevator opened on Ryner-son's fiftieth floor domain. Simon was starting to believe that *omniscient* could be added to her list of qualities. "What are you, psychic?"

"Hardly." She pointed to a small bull's-eye camera lens located at the top, back corner of the elevator. "The door won't open on this floor until you've been identified, announced, and cleared."

"Impressive. And fast."

"Charles runs a tight ship." She turned in the opposite direction of the Fishbowl. "We're meeting in the kitchen."

He fell in beside her, checking out the other rooms as they passed. Though the walls were painted in a variety of soft pastels, each room furnished and decorated in a somewhat different style, it all seemed to blend, everything warm and comfortable. Much, Simon thought, like Big Jake himself. "So, what's the deal with Anthony Saladino? I get the feeling Jake doesn't like the guy."

"Tony's a good guy. It's just that—" She paused outside a wide door. "Ask me later, I'll try to explain. Remember, you can't say anything about—" She touched her ear.

"Doesn't he have a right to know?"

"Trust me on this—" She pushed open the door. "That would not be a good idea."

Big Jake—standing in the middle of an industrial-size kitchen, behind an industrial-size island grill, wearing a bib apron and floppy chef's cap—looked up from whatever he was cooking. "What's not a good idea?"

"Refusing," Caitlin answered, "to eat your world famous Megas."

Big Jake looked at Simon as if that was the greatest foolishness he ever heard. "What, you don't like Mexican chow?"

"No-no, it's not that," Simon answered quickly, determined to match Caitlin Wells' mental dexterity. "I just didn't want you to go to any special trouble on my account."

"No trouble. Charles gave the boot to all my good helpers, so I'm making him do the heavy lifting."

Charles, dressed in a shirt and tie with a Beretta hanging beneath his armpit, was stooped over a stainless steel pot sink. He glanced over and rolled his eyes. "Don't laugh, I'm the highest paid dishwasher you ever saw."

"Wouldn't think of it," Simon answered, "my mama taught me never to laugh at any man who wears a 9mm automatic to wash dishes."

Charles glanced down at his shoulder rig, as if he'd forgotten it was there. "Damn smart woman, your mama."

Nutty as a Snickers bar, Simon thought, as he took a moment to check out the room—a masterpiece of modern culinary design disguised as a country kitchen, with pickled white oak cabinets, an immense fieldstone fireplace, and a dining table overlooking the golf course. It seemed ridiculously large to have such a huge facility in a hotel with more than a dozen restaurants and nearly as many different cuisines, but he had the feeling this is where Big Jake came to find relief, the place where he could momentarily forget. *Busy hands.* "Need any help?"

Jake shook his head. "Relax. We'll eat as soon as the others get here."

"Coffee?" Caitlin asked, motioning toward an array of

dispensers on a cart near the dining table. "I recommend the Jamaican Blue Mountain."

"Don't listen to Caity," Jake warned in the tone of an old argument, "that ain't nothing but snob coffee. Have some of that stuff marked Jake's Juice, it's my own special blend. Guaranteed to get your heart a-thumpin'."

"Yeah, really great," Caitlin whispered sarcastically, "if you don't mind flossing coffee grounds out of your teeth."

Simon decided to take the diplomatic route—it was, after all, Ms. Caitlin Wells who really made his heart do the double thump—and filled a mug with his own favorite, the Hawaiian Kona. A moment later Billie Rynerson made her entrance, flanked by Leo Geske and a man Simon assumed to be Anthony Saladino: mid-thirties, olive skin, dark eyes, dazzling white teeth, and thick wavy hair, dressed in a tab-collared white shirt and blue jeans. The minute he made eye contact with Big Jake the air in the room seemed to thicken. In an obvious attempt to keep things amicable, Billie steered her two escorts toward the coffee cart. "We're going to have a nice breakfast"—she smiled, in contrast to her warning tone—"*then* we'll talk. Anthony, this is the man I told you about, Simon Leonidovich. Simon, this is my son-in-law, Anthony Saladino."

The next ten minutes seemed to last forever as everyone conspicuously tried to avoid the subject of Kyra, which hovered over them like an enormous storm cloud. Big Jake finally finished his culinary manipulations and began lining platters along the front of his cooking island. "Okay, Billie, you lead the way. Show these people how we eat in Texas."

He talked like they were still married, a realization not lost on his ex. "Where's your wife, Jake?" She gave him a look so hard and straight you could almost hear it twang through the air. "You were supposed to fix things. I don't want Tammi thinking I've still got eyes for your flabby old ass."

"I did, dammit," his voice rising with indignation. "Everything's copacetic. She went to the gym—should be here any minute."

Simon stared at all the food and immediately felt his stomach swell. In addition to Big Jake's famous Megas—a spicy combination of sausage and onions, jalapeño peppers and salsa, cheese and eggs—there was ham and hash browns and grits, pancakes and French toast, English muffins and poppy-seed bagels. "The gym doesn't sound like such a bad idea."

Billie nodded knowingly. "Jake used to cook for all the boys when he worked the rigs."

"Damn straight. They loved my cookin', that's a fact."

"Any of those boys still alive," Simon asked, "or did they all die of clogged arteries and cholesterol poisoning? Just curious."

"Now don't you go getting all prissy on me, Simon. Fill up that plate."

Caitlin gave Simon a friendly little poke in the ribs. "Stick with the Megas, you'll die happy."

Advice he fully intended to follow, but good intentions didn't get a person very far on Big Jake's buffet line. The man watched over his gastronomic creation like a proud papa, making sure everyone took enough, and heaping more on their plates when he determined they hadn't. Just when everyone got settled at the table, the current Mrs. Rynerson made her appearance. About thirty, with blond hair, green eyes, fair skin, and perfect teeth, she had obviously come straight from the gym, a gauzy white pullover draped around her bodysuit—a shiny-gold spandex number that matched her sneakers and hid nothing. In a nutshell, she was perfect—long and lean with a NordicTrak ass—like she'd been airbrushed into the world. She buzzed through the kitchen at mach speed, grabbed a yogurt out of the Sub-Zero, and descended on the table like a honeybee looking for a place to land. She plopped down next to Big Jake and turned her green eyes on Simon. "Hi, I'm Tammi. Who are you?"

"Simon Leonidovich, I'm doing some work for your—" Holy Christ, he almost said *father*. "—husband."

She nodded and turned away, dismissing him as unimportant. In her world, everyone worked for Big Jake. "What's happening? Have we heard something about Kyra?"

"Apparently so," Tony answered, his voice thick with anger, "though no one bothered to call me."

Big Jake's booming baritone overrode Billie's attempt to intervene. "You're right, Tony, I shoulda called you immediately. I apologize." He glanced around, letting everyone know he meant it. "Now let's eat. Then we'll talk about things." His sad eyes brightened slightly when they reached his wife. "Is that all you're eatin' there, sweetie?"

Miss Honeybee bobbed her pretty little head. "It's my new diet, Jakey. I told you about it."

Big Jake smiled, as if he remembered, though it was obvious from his cloudy expression his thoughts were absorbed with more important issues. Feeling like a voyeur staring into the exposed guts of a typical, slightly dysfunctional family, Simon concentrated on his mountain of food, though he couldn't help fantasize about what area of Miss Honeybee's zero-fat body needed dietary attention. Big Jake clearly had a talent for attracting beautiful women—his problem seemed to be in the area of long-term custody, a malady apparently common to billionaires.

Twenty minutes later, with everyone approaching critical mass, Billie raised her juice glass. "Jake, you haven't lost your magic touch."

There was a general chorus of agreement followed immediately by a shuffle of chairs as everyone, in an eager attempt to move, helped clear the table. Five minutes later, dishes stacked and coffee cups refilled, the ugly business of Kyra Rynerson began. "Okay, here's the deal," Jake said, standing at the head of the table. "We've received a second warning against bringing in the FBI."

Tony interrupted. "What kind of warning?"

Jake shuffled from one foot to the other, avoiding eye contact. "Same as last time—came through the switchboard." Unlike Caitlin, Big Jake wasn't good at deception; but Tony merely nodded, oblivious to his father-in-law's uncharacteristic discomfort.

"Can I see the transcript?"

"Of course," Caitlin answered, not the slightest hesitation or evasion in her voice. "I left it in my office, but I'll get you a copy after the meeting."

Right after she created one, Simon thought. As much as he liked the woman, and understood her reasons for lying, the ease with which she avoided the truth made him uncomfortable. Very uncomfortable.

"The problem," Big Jake went on, "is that the warning may have been in response to our most recent discussions."

Tony frowned, perplexed. "What do you mean by that? What discussions?"

"Discussions about whether or not we should notify the FBI."

"I thought we settled all that. No police. No FBI."

Big Jake nodded thoughtfully, his gaze wandering off. "Well, that's true enough, we did, but Mr. Leonidovich asked us to reconsider—"

Tony turned on Simon. "Who the hell do you think you are? What gives you the right to stick your nose in our business?"

Before Simon could formulate a response, Big Jake was all over his son-in-law. "Now you hold on there, boy! It wasn't but a few hours ago *you were the one* telling me we needed the FBI."

In no mood to reason, Tony was suddenly on his feet,

going eye to chin with Big Jake. "Yeah, well isn't that typical? You listen to a complete stranger before you take my advice."

Billie jumped up and literally forced her way between them. "Okay, that's enough!" She gave them each a warning poke in the chest. "Sit! Both of you." They reluctantly backed down, growling at each other like a couple of mad dogs itching for blood. Billie turned to Caitlin. "Caity, you take over. I've got the stink of testosterone up my nose and I'm too damn old to enjoy it."

Despite the underlying tension, it took an effort for Simon not to laugh. Even Charles lowered his impenetrable shield and let his lips curl into an amused grin, as if to say "can you believe that broad?" The current Mrs. Rynerson obviously couldn't; she stared at the former Mrs. Rynerson with a look of utter disbelief—the sight of someone sticking a finger into the chest of *her* husband, the great and mighty Big Jake Rynerson, and telling him to *sit*, like some disobedient pet—was clearly beyond her level of comprehension. In contrast, Leo Geske, who hadn't uttered a word since arriving, merely glanced at his watch, as if he couldn't wait to escape the drama.

Caitlin Wells, smart enough to recognize real power, stood up. "Yes, there have been additional discussions about bringing in the FBI." She looked right at Tony Saladino. "And yes, you were kept out of the loop, Tony. That was a mistake. Jake apologized. Get over it." He opened his mouth but she held up a finger, warning him off. "We all want the same thing—to bring Kyra home. Safe. But we're concerned that some things we discussed might, and I emphasize the word *might*, have somehow gotten back to the kidnappers. We can't take any chances." She paused, giving everyone a meaningful look. "Kyra is not to be mentioned outside of this group. Not even to her coworkers and friends, Tony. We can't control who they might whisper to."

He nodded in the affirmative, but slowly, as if thinking through the ramifications. "We'll need to invent some kind of cover story. People are going to start asking questions."

"Good point," she agreed. "Why don't you come up with something plausible? Something that fits Kyra's lifestyle. Whatever you decide, we'll go along."

Slick, Simon thought. In one simple move Ms. Wells had turned Tony Saladino from adversary to ally.

"But *nobody,*" she emphasized the word with a vengeance. "Nobody-nobody-nobody, says anything to anyone outside of this group. That's final. Absolute."

Despite his mellowing, Tony the Pit Bull hadn't forgotten how the argument started. "What about the FBI?"

"First of all," Caitlin answered, "they can't do much in South America. At best the Bureau could provide support. Offer advice." She looked over at the insurance man. "Isn't that right, Mr. Geske?"

The little man bobbed his bald head. "Yes, ma'am, that's correct. Sure is."

"We're not like most families in this position. We can afford whatever we need logistically, and Charles, through his contacts at the Bureau, will attempt to pick the brains of a specialist or two." She turned to Charles. "Right?"

It occurred to Simon that she was spreading the responsibility around—for whatever happened, success or failure. And if they failed there would to be plenty of finger-pointing and second-guessing. *Lots of blame.* Charles apparently recognized it and was smart enough not to take a full swan-dive into the shit pile. "You said it—*attempt.*"

She gave him a quick little smile, then leveled the power of her blue-gray eyes on Tony. "Given all that, we don't think calling in the Bureau or any other law enforcement agency would justify the additional risk to Kyra. I hope you agree."

It was rightfully his decision to make, but Simon

doubted if anyone—husband or not—had veto power over Big Jake Rynerson. Whether Tony recognized that or not, he didn't argue. "Sounds right to me."

Caitlin dipped her chin. "Okay. Good. Now we should—" She suddenly gave a jerk, like she'd just gotten a zap of static electricity. "Damn." She pulled her cellular—apparently set to VIBRATE—out of her pocket and read the number on the display. "What the hell—" She held a finger to her lips, indicating everyone should be quiet, then answered the call, her voice tentative. "This is Caitlin Wells."

She listened for a second, her pupils expanding like a pair of umbrellas opening at slo-mo speed. "Yes. Okay. Uh—" She looked confused, not quite sure what to say. "Just a moment." She pressed the Mute button, then held out the phone, as if it had suddenly turned radioactive. "It's them. Some man. He wants to talk to Jake."

No one needed to ask who she meant by *them*. Big Jake reached for the phone but Charles caught his arm. "No." He turned to Caitlin. "Stall, we need to record this. Tell him you're looking for Jake, it should only take a minute." Before she could answer he was out the door.

Caitlin turned to Jake, who was still sitting there, his hand inches away from the phone and some connection to his daughter—a connection he clearly wanted to make. "I don't think we should wait. I better—"

Leo Geske interrupted, his tone uncharacteristically confident. "Mr. Case is right. We're not set up to trace a cellular call. We should at least try to record it."

Big Jake grimaced, struggling to make up his mind, when Billie made the decision. "Do it, Caity. Try to stall him."

Caitlin nodded, took a deep breath, hit the MUTE button, and pressed the phone to her ear. "I've paged Mr. Rynerson. He should be here any minute." Her face stiffened noticeably, her expression caught somewhere between embarrassment and outrage, then she slowly lowered the phone. "He hung up."

Big Jake's arm, still stretched out like the limb of a giant redwood, dropped to the table with a lifeless thud. "He didn't say anything? Didn't mention Kyra?"

"Oh yeah, he said something, all right. Something about me and an overendowed, oversexed baboon. The rest I'll leave to your imagination."

There was a dead beat of silence, then Charles came bursting through the door, dictating into a microrecorder as he crossed the room. "Thursday, November sixth." He glanced at the chronometer on the back wall. "10:02 Pacific standard time." Then he looked up, saw their faces, and stopped. "You lost him?"

"No, *you* lost him," Jake snapped back. "You can't fool with these people."

Little Miss Honeybee patted her husband's hand. "Now don't get upset, Jakey. You know what the doctor said about your blood pressure."

He ignored his wife and turned his anger on Caitlin. "You never take calls during a meeting. How'd you know to take that one?"

"I recognized the number." She smiled, uneasily, like someone waiting to see the dentist. "It was Kyra's."

Tony straightened, from the look on his face, one might have thought she'd injected hot lead into his veins. "What are you saying, the call came from Kyra's cell phone?"

"Yes. I guess that's how he got my number. It was probab—"

"Wait a minute," Jake interrupted, "you hold on right there. Kyra had your number on her cell phone?"

"Yes."

"Why?"

Caitlin took a breath and released it. "We talk occasionally."

"You talk to my daughter?"

Simon studied their faces, trying to read what he couldn't understand. Why shouldn't Kyra have the number of her father's top executive? Why shouldn't they talk?

"Yes," Caitlin answered, her voice taking on a stubborn tone. "We're friends."

Jake stared at her as if she had just snapped into existence from another dimension. "You're friends?"

"Yes."

He nodded, very slowly, like a volcano about to erupt but struggling to hold back the lava. "We'll talk about this later."

More secrets, Simon thought, and from the look on everyone's face he was the only one flying through the darkness. It probably wasn't important, and he probably didn't need to know—but he sure was curious.

Billie took a deep breath, as if to gather herself. "Now what?"

Leo Geske, who seemed to have found some new reservoir of courage, didn't hesitate to speak up. "Don't worry, Mrs. Rynerson, he was just sending us a message. He'll call back."

"Really?" Her face brightened. "You think so?"

"Within minutes. I'm sure."

"Oh God, I hope you're right. I do hope you're right."

Second that, Simon thought. He really didn't want to be around when the next gift box of body parts arrived. "You sound awfully confident, Leo."

"Yessir, Mr. Leonidovich, I'm quite sure it's going to happen. And when it does I'm going to send that man a message of my own."

Big Jake leaned forward over the table, his eyes burning laser shots into Geske's forehead. "A message? What kind of message?"

The little man looked the big man straight back in the eyes. "Tell you what, Mr. Rynerson. We get that call within five minutes, you let me try things my way. If he doesn't call back—" He held out his hands, palms up, and raised his shoulders. "Well then, you call the shots."

Big Jake sat back, thinking about it, seemed ready to speak, then changed his mind and turned to his ex-wife. "Whataya think, kid?"

Billie nodded, a single decisive drop of the chin.

Jake looked at his watch, then leveled his eyes on Leo Geske. "Okay, you've got yourself a deal there, Mr. Geske. Five minutes, starting now."

"Fair enough." Geske turned to Charles. "You ready, Mr. Case?"

"Almost." Using a suction-cup attachment, he finished linking the second of two jumper wires between Caitlin's phone and a microrecorder. "Okay, we're good to go."

Geske nodded and turned to Caitlin. "Ms. Wells, would you please activate the ringer?"

Caitlin did as instructed. She had barely laid the phone back on the table when it started to chirp. Charles leaned forward, pressed the RECORD button on the microrecorder, and dictated the time. "Thursday, November sixth, 10:08 Pacific standard time."

Geske picked up the phone and leaned back in his chair, like he was about to have a casual conversation with an old friend. "This is Leo Geske. Who's calling, please?" There was a momentary pause as he listened to the response. "Mr. Rynerson is not the person you want to speak to right now. He's a very unstable and emotional man who only wants to hunt you down and feed you to a tankful of sharks in the grand ballroom of his hotel." In contrast to the words, he spoke in a very nonconfrontational tone, almost as if he were sharing a secret and sympathizing with the man. "Whereas I only want to negotiate the safe return of Ms. Saladino. Shall we talk?"

There was another pause and Simon had the distinct feeling he would be leaving for South America much sooner than he originally thought. In his own way, Leo Geske went straight for the jugular.

"No," Geske continued, "I believe I made myself perfectly clear on that point. It would not be in your best interests to speak with Mr. Rynerson. If you don't wish to speak with me I'll just say good-bye. Have a nice day." Then he smiled, a wicked little grin, and terminated the connection.

Have a nice day! A new low, Simon thought, for the most overused and overabused idiom in the world.

Big Jake stared at Geske like he was a bug—a bug he wanted desperately to squash. "Have a nice day! You told the man who—"

Simon held his breath, could almost hear the words: *cut off my daughter's ear.*

"—kidnapped my daughter, to have a nice day?"

"Yessir," Geske answered without apology, "I sure did."

"And you hung up on him?"

Geske made no attempt to mask a satisfied smirk. "Mission accomplished."

"What the hell is that supposed to mean?"

"Remember our conversation about goals?"

"That was the goal?"

"Yessir. I needed to let him know there are rules. Break the rules, you don't get what you want."

"What rules?"

"Well, for one, never ever ever ever verbally abuse a man who's trying to give you money. He'll think about it for a while, realize I have no way to call him, so he'll be forced to call me. He won't like that—it'll make him feel like he lost." He flashed another wicked grin. "It's a little game of Chicken I like to play—with a predetermined winner." He glanced at his watch. "Ten minutes—max."

Big Jake shook his head in cold disbelief. "Caity, that sonofabitch calls back within ten minutes you're fired."

She seemed unfazed by the threat. "And Mr. Geske gets my job?"

"Bingo."

"Good, now I have two reasons to hope he calls."

Billie gave them a disgusted look. "Will you two cut the horseshit."

Tony reached over and clutched Geske's arm. "You're going to ask about Kyra, aren't you?"

"Yessir, I sure will. You wouldn't happen to know the name of her favorite movie, would you?"

"Yes, it's—"

Geske held up a hand. "Don't tell me. Don't tell anyone. Not yet."

"Good idea," Charles said, as if he understood exactly what Geske intended. "So, what's your impression?"

"South American," Geske answered. "No question about that. Somewhere in the north. Colombia or Venezuela, most likely. Heavy accent, but his English is good. He's definitely had some education."

"How old?"

Geske rolled his hands in a gesture of uncertainty. "Forty to sixty. After I've talked to him again I should be able to narrow that down a bit." He turned to Big Jake. "Mr. Rynerson, I know your feelings on this, but I want to warn you one last time. If we don't try to negotiate a lower price, the price is probably going to go up."

Big Jake waved a hand, as if batting away a bothersome fly. "I don't care about the damn money. Those idiots should have asked for more. I'd have paid anything."

Geske grimaced noticeably. "That's not the kind of thing you want to be saying, sir. They get wind of that attitude and we'll never get your daughter back. We need to make a stronger stand. We need to negotiate."

Big Jake shook his head—had been shaking it from the moment Geske started to talk. "Whatever they ask, I'll pay."

Not good, Simon thought—Geske was right and Big Jake determined. *The immovable object.* "What about offering them more money before they ask?" He ignored the have-you-gone-crazy looks and hurried to explain before anyone could express the thought. "Tie the additional money to conditions, like a quick release and simultaneous exchange. Make it seem like a negotiation, a little give and take. I know it sounds crazy and probably won't work, but it might, and they sure as hell won't be expecting it."

No one said a word, everyone looking at everyone else, as if searching for some confirmation to their own opinion—some consensus on the craziness scale: a little, a lot, or over the top. Leo Geske was the first to find his voice. "My company would never agree. Insurance companies don't make a habit of paying out more than—"

"Oh, to hell with your company," Jake interrupted. "That sounds like a pretty clever idea to me. Let's offer an extra million, I'll pick up the tab myself."

Geske shrugged good naturedly. "In that case I like the idea just fine."

Everyone agreed, what harm would it do to try—it wasn't their money and Big Jake could well afford it. The next couple of minutes passed in edgy silence, like they were hunkered down in a bomb shelter, holding their breath, listening and waiting for the next detonation. Finally the little phone chirped, and Charles once again dictated the date and time before Geske answered. "This is Leo Geske."

He listened and nodded. "Yes, I understand perfectly." He listened some more and nodded again. "This may be hard to believe, but I'm on your side. I have no interest in the money, it's not mine. All I care about is the safe return of Ms. Saladino." He looked apathetic, like he'd said the words a thousand times, but sounded sincere.

"I don't know, that's so very much money." He looked confident but sounded pessimistic.

"Oh dear, that would be terrible." He looked bored but sounded shocked. "Under those circumstances I might be able to convince Mr. Rynerson to pay an additional million. But only if I could assure him the quick release of his daughter." He made it sound like the thought came straight off the top of his head.

A long pause, then another nod. "Really? Okay then, if you could do a couple of things for me, I could try to make that happen for you." He looked hopeful but sounded skeptical. "Of course we would expect Ms. Saladino to be released at the time of payment."

This set off some kind of lengthy response. As Geske listened, he leaned forward and stirred his coffee, setting up a tiny whirlpool that kept growing until it spilled over into the saucer. "Uh-huh. Yes. Uh-huh." Weary of playing with his coffee, he began to push a crumb around the tablecloth with his bony forefinger. "I understand. No, that would be difficult. I don't think so, but I'll need proof Ms. Saladino is alive and well. The name of her favorite movie, written in her own handwriting would be acceptable."

He nodded again and sat back in his chair. "Mr. Rynerson would have to make that decision." Holding the phone with his chin, he interlaced his fingers and leaned back, placing his hands behind his head, elbows winging out to the side. "Uh-huh. Okay. Thirty minutes." He lowered the phone and pressed the END button.

Everyone tried to speak at once but Geske held up a hand, cutting off the clamor. "Please—" He gave them a smug, derisive smile, the kind that women do so well. "Let me tell you where things stand." He paused—the expression of a man who treasures big moments—especially those of his own making. "Then you have a decision to make."

CHAPTER TWELVE

Somewhere in South America

Thursday, 6 November 17:51:46 GMT –0500

The light was starting to fade, the day almost over, but Kyra could still hear El Pato pounding away in the other room: *THUNK-THUNK-THUNK*. It had been going on for at least an hour. Was he building something? She tried to imagine what, but the only images that came to mind were medieval contraptions of torture, and she abandoned the effort, preferring not to know.

The constant pounding only added to her misery. The open wound on the left side of her head continued to throb, and she felt nauseated, unable to keep her heart from fluttering. She had felt that way most of the day, ever since the first call. There had been five. She hadn't heard much—El Pato listening more than talking—but something was happening. Something dramatic. Something that would set her free or end her life.

Need to be ready. She worked her fingers into the crack behind the cot and pulled out the three-inch sliver of wood she had managed to peel off one of the planks. Not much of a weapon, not unless she got him in the eye, but better than nothing. She glanced around, frantically searching the shadows for anything she might have missed. But there was nothing to find, nothing to over-look. Besides the waste bucket and blanket, he had given her nothing—forgotten nothing.

Kick-Gouge-Bite, that's what it would come to. She didn't intend to go quietly, whimpering into the abyss like some beaten dog. Absorbed in the thought, she didn't realize the pounding had stopped until El Pato opened the pass-through—the scraping sound like a cold finger tracing a path down the middle of her back.

He extended a pencil stub and single sheet of paper through the slot. "Here. You must write."

She slid off the cot, trying not to aggravate the drumechoes that continued to ricochet through her skull. "Write what?"

"Your favorite *film*."

She understood the implication immediately; that someone she knew—someone who knew the answer and would recognize her handwriting—would see what she wrote and would know she was still alive. *Anthony*.

And then her father would pay.

And then she would die.

Was there some way to send a message? A wrong answer? A coded answer? *Stalag 17. The Great Escape.* What kind of message would that send?

El Pato watched her closely, his dark eyes never seeming to blink.

A made-up movie? *You Pay, I Die.*

"Write!"

"I'm trying to remember." What if she was wrong? What if he intended to release her? *No way.* Unless she hadn't thought of something. Unless-unless-unless . . .

Unless her father insisted on a trade. A simultaneous trade: her for the money. Was it possible?

"Write!"

She smoothed the paper over the dirt, then pressed the pencil down hard, purposely breaking the lead. "Damn!" She held up the pencil, so he could see. "I need something smooth to write on."

He hesitated, then slammed the cover over the pass-through.

Think, but the door to her brain seemed stuck, the answer locked away in the endless maze of cerebral fissures. Right answer? Wrong answer? What movie title would send the best message? The harder she tried the more hopeless it seemed, and then before she could make a decision El Pato was back.

He dropped a small tablet and another pencil through the opening, his eyes dark and impatient. It was a look she remembered well, that moment before he smiled and shot the boy-pilot. A look she cared not to test. She picked up the pad—purposely smearing a bit of dirt across the bottom with her thumb—and in large cursive letters scrawled her favorite romantic comedy across the center of the page.

Annie Hall

Anthony, who shared her passion for Woody Allen, would remember. Maybe some hotshot investigator would analyze the dirt, realize it could have come from only one place on earth, and call the Marines. A girl could dream.

El Pato stared intently at the words, as if challenged by the language or her distinctive script. "Who is this person?"

Kyra could have told him everything about that wacky, wonderful woman—who she was and what she represented, the lines she spoke and the looks Diane Keaton gave her—but could think of no good reason to waste the breath. "It's the name of my favorite movie. I thought that's what you wanted. It won the Academy Award for Best Picture in 1977."

For a moment he stared hard into her eyes, as if he could read the truth off the back of her brain, then he slammed the window-slot closed, apparently satisfied. She immediately felt herself going soft inside, a sense of fail-

ure enveloping her body. *Idiot!* Her one opportunity and
she fluffed it, unable to come up with a single idea, some
way to send a message. *Idiot-Idiot-Idiot!* She reached
down and picked up the four-inch pencil stub. At least she
had gotten that, though for what she had no idea.

The light had completely disappeared from the sky
when El Pato suddenly yanked open the door, the glow of
his lantern turning her skin as yellow as old candle wax.
Though determined not to show any fear, she could feel
herself shrink beneath his cold eyes. He placed a shallow
wooden box on the floor and without saying a word
closed the door. Before the light faded, she caught a
glimpse of papaya and mango, some pint-size plastic containers, and a number of water bottles. She sat there, still
afraid to move, trying to make some sense of it. A moment
later, when she heard him close and bolt the outside door,
it began to make sense. Off to deliver her movie-question
answer. Enough food to last . . . ?

She crawled over to the box and with her fingers began
to inventory the contents: three plastic containers with
lids, six water bottles, two small papayas, two mangoes,
and four bananas. *Not much,* barely enough water for two
days. She suddenly had a new appreciation for how Gar-
funkel, her tiger-striped tabby, must have felt when they
left her alone for a long weekend.

Two days, alone, without him watching. Without him
there to hear what she was doing. What could she accomplish in two days?

CHAPTER THIRTEEN

The Fishbowl

Friday, 7 November 00:22:55 GMT –0800

Sitting at the small conference table with Leo Geske, Simon tried to block out the argument swirling around Big Jake's desk, and concentrate on the transcript. Something in the back-and-forth dialogue between Geske and the man identified as KID—an oddly benevolent abbreviation for *kidnapper*—didn't feel right. Perhaps it was the written form that made everything seem so stilted, almost rehearsed. He needed, he decided, to listen to the recording as he read the transcript—hopefully that would help put things in context.

The voices around the desk suddenly became louder. Things were starting to get ugly, everyone's temper growing shorter with each passing hour. Even Caitlin, who always seemed to sparkle, had lost a bit of her fresh-out-of-the-shower luster. Big Jake shook his head. "Dammit, Tony, stop blaming me. You read the list of demands. No family."

"But I'll stay on the plane," Tony argued. "No one would know."

"Well, she's your wife, you put up the money and I guess you can do any damn thing you want."

That was the first unkind thing Simon had heard Jake Rynerson say. Tony didn't have that kind of money, and even if he did, Big Jake wasn't about to *let anyone do anything* that might endanger his daughter's life. Tony recognized it, knew he was beaten, and slumped down into his chair.

Billie reached over and squeezed his hand. "Of course you want to go, we understand that. I want to be there myself, but we can't take any chances. Not now. Not when we're this close."

"But I'm her husband, I should be there when she's released."

"Caitlin will be there." She gave him one of those meaningful, please-don't-ask-me-to-spell-it-out looks that women do so well. "Kyra may need a woman."

There it was, Simon thought, the *female* thing, the ultimate male-slayer. No man in history knew how to argue against *that*. It had become obvious that sometime over the last twelve hours Billie and Jake had set aside old wounds and pulled together as a team—a formidable duo determined to save their daughter. If the current Mrs. Rynerson noticed, she didn't show it, her role confined to an occasional pat of sympathy and reminder that *Jakey* needed to watch his blood pressure, a warning the big man seemed to ignore.

"But don't you worry," Billie continued. "Mr. Leonidovich is going to give those men exactly what they want and bring Kyra home."

Damn, they were all doing it, talking like her release was nothing more than a formality, as if they'd forgotten the kidnappers had *not* agreed to a simultaneous trade. Simon leaned close to the negotiator, keeping his voice low. "You okay with everything?"

A worried ditch formed down the center of Geske's forehead. "What do you mean?"

"Things are moving awfully fast." *Too fast,* but he hesitated to say that much. "Not exactly the way you described how most of these South American kidnappings progressed."

"Can't disagree with you there," the man answered, his worried expression melting into relief. " 'Course, I've never been in a situation where we offered *more* than the ransom demand. That's a first."

"Yeah, I'll bet."

The little man lowered his voice to a conspiratorial whisper. "Though we once had a wife offer to pay *us* if we'd just forget about her husband."

Simon nodded, a common enough sentiment if his observations about marriage were accurate. "That must have been a fun reunion."

"Actually, it worked out fine." He flashed that wicked little grin that popped up at the most unusual times. "We paid, but all she got back was his head."

"Are you serious?"

Geske hunched his narrow shoulders. "Guess the old broad had a better relationship with God than her husband." If he felt any remorse about the outcome, he didn't show it.

Simon tapped his finger on the transcript, keeping his voice to a whisper. "Do you believe this guy? You really think if we pay they'll release Kyra within twelve hours?"

Geske shrugged again. "Pay and pray."

Before Simon could respond to what seemed a rather naive approach, Charles Case arrived with the ransom demand. As everyone gathered around, he opened a sealed plastic container and began stacking the contents onto the table: 100 packets of hundred-dollar bills, totaling one million dollars; and fifty packets of thousand-franc Swiss notes, totaling four million dollars. The band on each packet had been initialed by Charles and by Arnel Dittmar, the Sand Castle's head cashier and controller of the casino's twenty-million-dollar float.

"What about Arnel," Caitlin asked, "any questions?"

Charles shook his head. "Nope. All he cared about was that debit receipt with your signature. A real bean counter, that guy. As long as all the columns add up, he's happy."

When all the packs had been stacked, straightened, and lumped together, it made a tidy little five-million-dollar mountain, approximately eleven inches square and twelve inches high. "A little over thirty-four pounds," Charles said, answering the question before Simon could ask it. "Plus the nylon duffel. Think you can handle that okay?"

"As long as I don't have to climb any mountains," Simon answered.

Charles reached into the box, pulled out a sheet of paper, and slid it across the table. "All yours. Just sign on the dotted line."

Simon read the short paragraph—making sure he was only signing a "chain of evidence" record and not taking responsibility should the money be lost, which was, of course, the object of the exercise—then signed his name.

"They'll run you around," Geske warned, as Simon began packing the money into the nylon pack. "They'll want to make sure you're alone before making contact."

Something Simon had already surmised. "I picked up a good pair of walkers this afternoon." He squeezed the last bundle of hundred-dollar bills into the pack, sealed the zipper with a plastic zip tie, squeezed the blue duffel into his security case, attached his titanium wrist-strap, and turned to Caitlin. "Ready?"

She nodded. "The pilots are standing by."

Billie Rynerson reached over and squeezed Simon's arm. "You bring our girl home, ya hear?"

"Yes, ma'am, I sure will." He didn't miss her use of the word *our*, or the sadness reflected in her ex-husband's eyes. "I promise." He wanted to make them feel better, and the *I promise* slipped out without thought—which he regretted instantly. Something inside told him it would not be an easy promise to keep.

CHAPTER FOURTEEN

Somewhere in South America

Friday, 7 November 06:44:37 GMT –0500

As soon as she could see, and before she forgot, Kyra made her calendar mark in the dirt. *Sixth day*. It felt like a month.

She pulled the food box over below the window, then carefully opened each of the three plastic containers. Though El Pato hadn't left her with any gruesome, crawling surprises, it wasn't exactly gourmet fare: the first two containing the normal mush of black beans, and the third a single chunk of cooked pork. The thought of downing another mouthful of the same crud was enough to make her gag, but she ate it anyway—*for the baby*—washing down each swallow with a big gulp of water. The realization—that she could drink as much as she wanted—was enough to make her grin like a monkey with its first banana. It hit her during the night, when the rain started and it suddenly occurred to her that she could refill the water bottles. A person could live a long time on water. *And wash!* Just the thought of such an indulgence made her giddy with anticipation.

She forced herself to eat most of the pork, which would quickly turn rancid in the heat, then ripped a small corner off the thin blanket and began to wash herself. She started with the wound on the left side of her head—sometime during the night, the pounding had given way to a dull ache—carefully cleaning away the dried blood, then slowly began to work her way down. She spent at least thirty minutes cleaning the dirt from beneath her nails, and used three full bottles of water, but felt like a new person when she finished. Revived and energized, she sat back, trying to see everything with a fresh eye.

The roof was too high, unless she could dismantle the cot and use it as a ladder, but it was bolted to the outside wall and she dismissed the possibility immediately. The floor was like concrete, and would take a year and a shovel to dig through. *No time. No shovel.* The plank walls were even more impenetrable. She could possibly scrape through some of the mud-and-grass caulking, but where would that get her? That left the window and door. She had studied every inch of both and could see no way to break through. *Has to be a way.*

She started over, staring up at the tin roof. That was the weak point. *Nine, maybe ten feet.* How to get there? She circled the room, checking the spacing between the planks, and found a few spots along the inside wall where the space felt wide enough for a toehold if she could dig out the caulking. Just the thought of it, the possibility of escaping, made her heart gallop and she had to rein in her excitement. *Time to dig.*

She spent more than an hour trying to locate the best spots and mapping a route upward, before finally starting to dig with the only tools she had: the sliver of wood she had saved as a weapon, and the four-inch pencil. The mud around the first location, about thirty inches up from the floor, was like rock, and she realized immediately the pencil wouldn't last, so she moved to a spot higher up, near eye level where the weight and pressure would be less. The pack seemed equally hard, but she could now see tiny little cracks and fissures where the mud had dried and contracted. She wedged the tip of her wood sliver nearly an inch into one of the cracks before it snapped, dislodging a chunk of dried mud. The cavity was small, barely big enough for a finger, but surprisingly deep, and even more surprising, deep enough to open a tiny peephole into the room beyond. The pinprick of light came as such a surprise it actually frightened her, the thought of what El Pato would do if he discovered it. *No,* that was foolish, she couldn't see the spot from more than a foot away. Her next thoughts were much more exciting—the realization that she could do it. Given enough time—*three, maybe four days*—she could peel off enough slivers of wood and chip away enough toeholds to reach the roof. And if she could reach the roof . . .

She took a deep breath and stepped in close, eye to the hole. She could see only part of the room: a narrow cot along the wall, a rough plank table, one chair, and a crude makeshift kitchen. The table was cluttered with food and supplies, including an outdoor stove and two kerosene lamps. Using the pencil, she drilled the hole a bit larger and looked again. It took a second, barely a hiccup in time, before the realization hit—and then it struck like a hard blow to the solar plexus. *Oh Jesus God!*

El Pato would be back, that was clear, but not to release her. *THUNK-THUNK-THUNK,* the sound reverberated through her head like a bad dream—the pickax, the shovel, the shape—how often did one see their own grave?

CHAPTER FIFTEEN

Somewhere over the Pacific

Friday, 7 November 09:04:52 GMT −0500

Simon reached over and lifted the window screen—nothing but blue, the sky and water so similar in color he couldn't tell where one began and the other left off. Not from thirty-five thousand feet. Without thought, the habit so familiar, he pressed the zone button on his watch, adjusting the time from 6:04 to 9:04 A.M., then reached over and rewound the audio tape. The fourth time.

Two things continued to bother him. The back and forth between Geske and the South American still seemed . . . *awkward,* in a way he couldn't identify. It was, he finally decided, nothing more than that stutter in time that sometimes occurred with international calls and gave the conversation its out-of-sync tone. The second problem was not so easily dismissed. Caitlin's transcription had been perfect, not a single word missing or misinterpreted between the spoken and written, but something had been *added* to the text. A demand—a demand not made by the kidnappers. Simon glanced down at his own summarized checklist.

- ✓ 1 million in unmarked, nonsequential US hundred dollar bills
- ✓ 4 million in unmarked, nonsequential Swiss thousand Franc notes
- ✓ Pack in a grey nylon backpack
- ✓ No tracking devices

✓ One person to make delivery
✓ No video or audio surveillance
✓ No law enforcement
   No family
✓ Hotel Inter-Continental in Cali
✓ Wait for instructions

Two extra words: *No family*. He remembered the argument between Big Jake and Tony, and had a good idea who ordered the change. But why? Absorbed in the thought, he didn't hear Caitlin approach until she tapped him on the shoulder. He swiveled around, pulling off his headphones. "Good morning." No lipstick, no makeup, no magic wand and she looked fresh as the Energizer Bunny, complete in a pink-and-gray jogging suit. "Get some sleep?"

"Three solid hours." She settled into a leather lounge on the opposite side of the small table, folding her bare feet up beneath her like a schoolgirl. "How about you?"

"Not really. I don't sleep that well on planes."

She did a little Groucho thing with her eyebrows. "This is *not* your typical plane."

Actually, except for the paint and Sand Castle logo, the exterior of the plane was about as *typical* as they came—a BBJ-2, which was nothing more than a converted Boeing 737, the most common jetliner in the world—but there was nothing typical or common about the interior of Big Jake's flying penthouse, which in addition to the main cabin, offered a full galley, exercise room, private office, conference area, and master suite. "You're right about that."

She glanced at the recorder. "What are you doing?"

"I've been trying to make some sense of that last conversation between Geske and the bad guy."

"Oh, I didn't realize—" Her composure slipped for a nanosecond. "I didn't know you had the tape."

He looked her straight in the eyes, wanting to see if she

would offer an explanation before he asked the question. "Charles gave me a copy."

"I guess—" Embarrassment tangled her tongue. She took a breath and started over. "I guess you realize something was added?"

At least she didn't deny it. He nodded, waiting.

"Jake didn't want Tony to make the trip."

"That was clear enough. But why? It seems to me he should be here."

"You need to understand, some people could benefit if Kyra *isn't* rescued."

Though obvious, now that it was pointed out, it was a factor he hadn't considered. "Tony, you mean?"

She nodded. "Kyra's an only child. Jake's already placed a considerable amount for her in trust, and that's nothing compared to what she'll someday inherit. And since she and Tony have no children, that makes Tony her primary beneficiary."

"Okay, but—"

"Being super rich has its downside." She motioned with her hand from one end of the cabin to the other. "Sure, this is nice, but Jake doesn't care much about material things—he likes people. And one of the lessons he's had to learn is that a whole bunch of those people only care about his money. It's been a tough lesson. He likes to take people at their word and it's made him overly suspicious. He believes the marriage is nothing but a sham and the money is the only reason Tony is hanging around."

"I understand." In fact, he was starting to understand a lot of things. "I'm curious about this demand for the ransom to be divided between U.S. and Swiss currency. That strikes me as awfully peculiar."

"I thought so too, but the Castle does carry a significant inventory in Swiss currency."

"Is that a common practice with big casinos?"

"No," she answered, "we do it as a special accommodation for our international players, many of whom prefer to be paid in Swiss francs."

"Is that common knowledge?"

"No, but it's the type of thing someone with a little initiative could find out."

But not, Simon had a feeling, some Colombian kidnapping faction. "Anything else I should know?"

"Yes. Adding that extra demand was my idea. I was trying to prevent a fight between Jake and Tony. Jake knows nothing about it."

He had to admire her honesty. Or was it loyalty, and this just another lie? He leaned over the table, until they were eyeball to eyeball. "I need to know this stuff. You've asked me to do something potentially dangerous and—"

"Don't worry," she interrupted, "Jake will take care of you."

He wasn't about to let her get away with that kind of evasive temporizing that women always used against men. "Don't twist this around," he snapped. "You know damn well I wasn't talking about my fee."

"I didn't think you were," she fired back. "I just thought I should say it."

Exchanging verbal bullets with Sniper Wells was not getting him the information he needed, and he softened his tone. "It's not the risk that bothers me. There's always an element of danger in my work. But I like to know the facts so I can minimize those risks. I think that's fair. What do you think?"

She stared at him for a long moment, then sat back in her chair, a slow smile passing over her lips. "Well, since you put it that way—"

He held up a hand, cutting her off as the flight hostess approached. She stopped at the end of the small table, glancing back and forth between them. "Can I get you anything? Breakfast?"

"Not me," Caitlin answered, "I want to get in a workout, then take a shower." She looked at Simon.

Breakfast sounded great; he'd been drinking coffee all night and his stomach needed something to quell the battery acid, but it also felt a little large in the company of Skinny the Sniper. "Thanks, Vicki, but I was actually planning to put in a few miles on the bike myself."

She smiled and nodded. "Okay, just ring if you need anything. I'll be in the crew cabin."

Caitlin gave Simon a suspicious look, but waited until Vicki had disappeared before speaking. "Planning on it, were you?"

"You know what they say, *'El camino al infierno se pavimenta con buenas intenciones.'*"

She stared at him, incomprehension in her eyes. "I don't speak Spanish."

Which answered one of his questions. "Me neither. Not fluently, anyway. It's just one of those sayings I picked up along the way."

"Meaning?"

"The road to Hell is paved with good intentions."

She smiled, their spat apparently forgotten. "Ahh, so you're one of those." She stood up, took his hand, and gave him a jerk. "Come on. Let's work up a sweat."

Ahh, now that was an enticing thought, working up a sweat with the beautiful Ms. Wells, but he had a feeling her intentions were not so erotically inclined. "Now that I think about it, I forgot to pack my workout gear."

She pulled him along, surprisingly strong for her size, toward the exercise room, located just behind the master suite. The room wasn't really a room at all, but an open area partitioned and hidden from the main cabin by a wall of rosewood cabinets, containing weights, towels, and a full assortment of exercise outfits—all colors, all sizes. "No excuses, Leonidovich, you're going to sweat if you want me to answer any more of your damn questions."

"Yea, team. Do we share the same shower?"

She rolled her eyes heavenward as if to say *men!*

He changed into a bulky sweatshirt, which he hoped would hide a few pounds, and some cotton workout shorts. *Might as well market the assets,* he didn't have any fat on the wheels. By the time he changed, Caitlin was pumping hard on the StairMaster and had stripped off her jogging suit, revealing a white spandex bodysuit that left little to the imagination but didn't stop him from taking a short voyeuristic excursion down fantasy lane. He climbed onto the stationary bike and sat there, dazzled by all the options, which included a small computer and screen that displayed all the pertinent data: heart rate, miles traveled, calories burned, and a dozen other bits of minutiae, including a formula for calculating life expectancy. Thankfully, for those who didn't care to know their drop-dead date, there was a movie-option mode and a link to the internet. It was clearly the ultimate in exercise equipment, designed with one thought it mind: to disguise the *work* in *workout.* "Man, this is some sweet machine. Where's the starter?"

She gave him a sidelong glance and it was obvious from the way her eyes danced that she was having a grand time, a fitness dominatrix glowing with anticipation. "You want breakfast aboard this ship you've gotta earn it, Leonidovich. Pump those legs!"

He selected the Fat Burn mode—it sounded good, whatever it was—and did as ordered, building up to a steady eighty rpms—eight calories per minute according to the numbers on the monitor. Twenty minutes, 160 calories. *Breakfast!* Not much of one, but something. Then the machine began throwing up roadblocks, disguised on the screen as a rolling landscape of gentle, green hills. Not so gentle on the legs, but not so tough either. Pump-pump-pump—up and over. *No sweat.* Up and over—up and over. *Oh yeah, feel the pain!* He was now burning through fourteen calories a minute and breakfast was sounding bigger and better with each revolution. Then the machine turned sadistic, he could see it coming, gliding across the screen like some giant, avenging glacier, out to flatten the world and anyone stupid enough to be in its path—namely, Simple Simon Leonidovich. He glanced over at Caitlin, who showed no sign of give-up, her tan legs pumping away like pistons, her bodysuit nearly transparent with sweat. *Oh, mama*, what a fine looking woman, equal to any *Playboy* centerfold, except her breasts were small and firm and real. *Better*. He took a deep breath, trying not to sound winded. "You look tuckered out, Wells. Ready for a little breakfast?"

She flashed her pearly whites, not fooled for a second. "You make it over that—" She reached over and tapped the great ice mountain, which now looked about twenty seconds shy of turning his legs into molasses. "And we'll take that shower together."

Oooooooweeeeee, he was tempted to try—*reeeeally tempted*—but he still hadn't made up his mind about the gorgeous Caitlin Wells, and wasn't about to go swimming in Big Jake's pool before he knew if the water was safe. "Sorry, I couldn't do that to you, Wells. You see me naked you'd never be satisfied with another man." *Probably turn gay*. He reached down and pressed the mode button—switching from FAT BURN to CARDIO—about two seconds before the Great Glacier met the Great Leonidovich. She stared at him—*Puzzled? Disappointed? Intrigued?*—he couldn't decide. "What's the matter, Wells? No one ever turn you down before?"

"You knew I was teasing."

I did? "Of course I did." *Damn!* "Any fool could tell that." Time to change the subject. "You know, I'm having trouble picturing Big Jake without his boots. Does he actually use this equipment?"

"Are you kidding? Jake considers exercise an unnatural act. He doesn't even use the plane, let alone the equipment."

Now that surprised him. "Jake doesn't strike me as the type who would buy something just to show off."

"Oh hell no, it's not that. We use this thing to transport whales."

He knew there was a missing link in the logic of what she just said—some "Save the Whales" benevolent fund Big Jake supported—but couldn't imagine how this luxurious flying penthouse could be used to transport giant, rubbery mammals. "The whales?"

"High rollers. People who can afford to drop a few million at the tables without worrying about how they're going to feed the kids." She paused, taking a second to catch her breath as she finished a hard-pumping cycle. "A lot of our players come from the Orient. This is just transportation."

"Oh." He nodded, trying to think of some way to segue the conversation toward the questions he needed to ask. *"Those* whales. Nice taxi."

She gave him a wink. "Something you could use in your business, right?"

Right, he couldn't imagine how many hours a year he could save by avoiding airport terminals. On the other hand, if he was rich enough to have a private plane it wasn't likely he would be playing bagman to the rich and famous—*the whales.* "So tell me, speaking of *my business—*" He paused, reminding her that she was the one who opened the door. "What did you mean when you said you were trying to encourage Kyra to resolve things with her father?"

Her legs slowed slightly as she considered the question, then resumed their pistonlike movement. "Kyra has never forgiven her father for divorcing Billie."

"I'm not stupid, girl. I got that."

"Yes, I'm sure you did, but it's worse than you think."

He hated it when someone assumed they knew what he thought, but resisted the temptation to throw a hard strike and lobbed another softball instead. "Oh?"

"Kyra doesn't want anything to do with Jake. Won't even speak to him if she can avoid it."

"Ahh. Which is why every time he talks about bringing his little girl *home* a big white elephant floats through the room."

She nodded, sweat dripping off her chin. "Kyra has never crossed the threshold of the Castle."

Interesting, but nothing he didn't already suspect. Time now, while he had her chatting and back on her heels, to toss a change-up. "And what makes you think Jake won't go ballistic when he finds out you altered the transcript?"

"I can handle Jake."

Exactly the answer he hoped for, and the lead-in to his fastball, the one question he didn't really expect her to answer. "Okay, what makes you so confident you can *handle* him?"

She looked like a woman sifting through a dozen possible responses for the most favorable one, then apparently gave up and decided to take the Fifth. "You'll have to ask me that when you know me better."

Count on it—that was one question he wouldn't forget to ask.

CHAPTER SIXTEEN

Hotel Intercontinental—
Cali, Colombia

Friday, 7 November 10:53:42 GMT –0500

"Señor Ramon Baca?"

Though he had repeated the name to himself a thousand times, it still sounded foreign to his ear. He had been El Pato, The Duck, for so long even his birth name had faded from memory. *"Sí.* I am Ramon Baca."

The bellman—a baby-faced teenager, with a thin mustache that ran along his upper lip—affected a small bow and extended a silver plate containing a single white envelope. El Pato snatched up the envelope, tore it open, and read the one-line message below what he knew to be a contrived fax header.

Everything is in order. Proceed as planned.

Everything is in order, the words danced through his head. *One more day*—he could almost feel the money in his hands. When he looked up the young bellman was still there, the plate still extended. *What did this fool . . . ?* Then he remembered, dug a five-hundred peso coin from his pocket, and dropped it onto the tray. The young man stared at the coin for a long moment, then smiled stiffly and withdrew. Five-hundred pesos, was this not enough? He glanced around to see if anyone had noticed the exchange. At least two dozen people were lounging around the huge lobby, mostly in small groups, mostly men, everyone absorbed in their own affairs.

El Pato took a deep breath and forced himself to relax. Hotels made him uncomfortable, especially big, expensive hotels with people who acted *grande*. But that was something he needed to learn. One more day and he would have enough money to stay anywhere, go anywhere. Now, more than ever he hated the thought of going back to the jungle—the *gringa princesa* would die with or without his help—but the *norteamericano* had insisted: *"No evidencia."* Once the snotty bitch was in the ground with the *cabaña* burning over her head, then it would be over.

He pretended to read the paper, trying to dissolve into the background, but it felt like people were staring, though every time he looked up no one seemed interested in his presence. Why should they? He glanced down at his suit—his Luis Acosta suit—then at the other men in the room, but could perceive no difference. In some ways the jungle was better, where he understood the rhythms of the landscape, everything measured by the comings and goings of the sun and rain. He would not live in the city, he decided, a small village in the Caribbean would be better. A *cabaña* on some beach, lobster and steak every day, a different woman every night.

A few minutes past midday, the copilot and flight attendant—both women, easily identified by the Sand Castle insignia on their uniforms—appeared at the front desk. The two remaining members of the flight crew, the pilot and navigator, both men, had apparently gotten stuck with the first onboard rotation. Exactly as the *norteamericano* had predicted. Caitlin Wells came through the door next, followed closely by Simon Leonidovich, the one they called the courier. El Pato lowered his paper. No need to hide his interest—every man in the lobby seemed to have his eyes on Caitlin Wells, which made no sense. She was slim like the Rynerson *princesa,* with no meat—a boy with breasts. She seemed not to notice the attention, but he knew better, women always knew. He turned his attention to the courier and his travel bag—one of those black rectangular cases with a fold-over top that pilots typically carry—but this one, El Pato knew, contained *five million dólares!* Just the thought of it made his mouth go dry.

He forced himself to look away, to concentrate on the other people in the lobby, to see if anyone else had an interest in the new arrivals. More important, if anyone appeared to have an interest in him. Despite the *norte-americano's* assurances, El Pato knew he needed to be careful, that he was the one most at risk. But once the men had mentally ravished the Wells woman, no one seemed to pay him or the Rynerson group any special attention. Suddenly he felt invisible—his power without limits.

Simon waited until they were alone in the suite before speaking. "Did you notice that man sitting on the far side of the lobby?"

Caitlin raised an eyebrow. "There were quite a number of men in the lobby."

"Near the restaurant. Sitting alone."

She poked her head into one bedroom, then the other. "No, not really. Why?"

Good question, he wasn't entirely sure himself, though the man did seem to match the description of the Luis Acosta impostor. "There was something about him. He didn't seem to fit."

"What do you mean, *fit?*"

"I'm sure you've seen them around the Castle. People out of their element. He didn't look the type who would normally stay here."

She paused in her inspection tour. "That's awfully observant, there were quite a few people down there. "

"People don't hire me to deliver the mail. Being observant is part of my job."

"I think you're paranoid."

"You're probably right." Still, he would have felt better if she hadn't dismissed the possibility so quickly.

"You have a preference on bedrooms?"

He purposely ignored the question. "You sure this is a good idea?"

"What's the matter, you afraid of me?"

Absolutely, beautiful women scared the bejesus out of him. "I just know how irresistible I can be."

She gave him a heavy-lidded, vampy look. "You are rather cute."

Cute! Cute never got the Homecoming Queen into bed. "I prefer irresistible."

"Don't press your luck, Leonidovich." She narrowed her eyes, as if trying to read his thoughts. "Look, if you're uncomfortable with the situation I can bunk with the flight crew. But this is Colombia and I'm not about to stay in a room by myself."

Was that it, or was she just looking for an excuse to keep an eye on him? And if so, why? "Take whatever room you want." He rolled the numbers on his wrist lock into position and unsnapped the security cable. "But don't complain later that I didn't warn you."

She opened her mouth to respond, but was interrupted by a sharp, double rap at the door. Simon pulled the cable up through his sleeve and set his case down next to a chair, as if it contained nothing valuable, and opened the door. A young bellman, his upper lip containing the shadow of a want-to-be mustache, smiled obsequiously. *"Señor Le—"* He glanced down at the padded manila envelope in his hand. "Le-on-do-vitch, *por favor.*"

Simon nodded and took the envelope, being careful to touch only one corner. "Did someone give you this, or was it left at the front desk?"

The bellman shook his head. *"Lo siento. No inglés."*

Simon nodded again, to indicate he understood, and

gave the young man a ten thousand peso tip, equal to about three American dollars. The bellman smiled and bowed slightly as he backed away. "*Gracias,* Señor Le-on-do-vitch."

"That didn't take long," Caitlin said, as Simon carried the package into the suite's kitchen and gently laid it on the counter. "I suppose you think that means it came from your Mr. Didn't-fit?"

"Not necessarily," but it wouldn't have surprised him. What did surprise him was the package itself—he expected written instructions, but the padded envelope had some weight and thickness. The thought of a bomb came to mind—it was, after all, Cali, Colombia, where people got blown up on a daily basis—but what he feared most was another body part. "You better stand back."

Caitlin stared at him, in trancelike bewilderment as he retrieved a razor blade and a pair of the latex gloves from his bag. "You certainly don't think . . ." Her words trailing away as she considered the possibility. "But that doesn't make sense. Why would—"

"It makes perfect sense. If we go *BOOM,* the bad guys could just waltz in and pick up the money. No complications."

"Ohhhhyeah, you're right. You want me to do it?"

It wasn't a flip remark, he could see she meant it, but he would never consider letting her take the risk. "No thanks. I get very prickly about people opening my mail."

"I'm serious. Kyra's my friend."

"And I'm serious. Back away. And don't stand in front of the windows."

She didn't move. "Is this some kind of macho thing, Leonidovich?"

Now that was a stupid question—of course it was a macho thing—did she actually think he liked the thought of having his face turned into Kibbles 'N Bits? "Absolutely not. It's a hero kind of thing. Now get back."

She smiled in an understanding sort of way. "Well that's different. I wouldn't want to deprive you the opportunity." She glanced around. "Where do you suggest—"

"Behind the couch. No. On second thought, get in the bathtub."

"In the bathtub! Are you serious?"

"I saw it in a movie once. It worked great."

She shook her head, as if that was the greatest foolishness she had ever heard, but picked up his security case and disappeared into the bathroom. A true pragmatist, Simon thought, as he slowly turned the envelope over, looking for some clue to the contents. Nothing. He leaned down, putting his nose up close to the sealed flap, hoping *not* to smell anything—and didn't.

Okay, Leonidovich—Showtime!

Thinking the flap would be the most obvious place for a trip wire, he carefully cut an opening along one edge, then with even more caution, leaned down and peeked inside. No bomb, no body parts, only a single sheet of paper and a small cellular phone. He carefully removed the phone—an Ericsson i888, a cheap and popular model available throughout the world—which was charged, on, and wiped clean of fingerprints. He took a deep breath, waited a moment for his pulse to drop below prestroke level, then quietly tiptoed over to the bathroom. Caitlin was in the bathtub, on her back, eyes closed, hugging his security case to her chest. Too much to resist. *"BOOM!"*

She squealed and nearly jumped out of the tub. "Damn you, Leonidovich!" Then she laughed, full of relief. "I about peed my pants!"

He reached down and helped her up. "That'll teach you to take a bath with your clothes on. What were you doing in there, Wells?"

"You told me—" She stopped mid-sentence, her eyes suspicious. "You didn't . . . ?"

"What? You thought I was serious?"

"I'll get you for this, Simon Leonidovich, I swear I will."

The way she said it, used his full name, reminded him of Pilár Montez, one of many appealing similarities he had noticed over the last couple of days—attractive and smart, with a good sense of humor, but there was another part of Caitlin Wells he couldn't read and couldn't decide how to deal with. "Promises, promises."

"You can count on it." Her dark eyes glinted with mischief. "So what was in the package?"

"Let's have a look."

She watched as he carefully extracted the paper from the package. "Is that her handwriting?"

Annie Hall

"Thank God." She released a relieved sigh, like someone slaking a thirst. "No doubt about it. And that's the answer Tony said she would give."

"So we know she was alive as recently as yesterday."

"I'll call Jake and give him the good news."

He caught her arm. "Just a sec. You see this?" He pointed to a smear of dirt across the bottom of the paper. "What do you think?

She leaned down. "You think Kyra did that? On purpose?"

"It's possible. Call Jake, then call Charles and give him a heads-up. Have him line up some kind of . . ." He couldn't think of the right word.

She cocked an eyebrow. "Dirt expert?"

"Right, a dirt expert. While you're making the calls I'll seal everything up and then you can get it on the next plane to Vegas."

"I can have Vicki do it."

He anticipated she might say that, but he had an idea and needed some time alone. "We don't want to screw up the chain of evidence. I'd do it myself, but—" He held up the phone. "I'm supposed to wait here for instructions."

She hesitated, appeared ready to argue, then changed her mind and disappeared into one of the bedrooms to make the calls. She was back ten minutes later, just as he finished placing the letter flat—containing the envelope and note—into a transparent WorldWide security pouch. He removed the safety strip—its control number corresponding to the one on the bag—and folded the flap over onto the quick-drying glue, making it impossible to open without cutting, then signed and time-dated both the strip and bag. Satisfied he hadn't contaminated the evidence—something Charles had stressed repeatedly—he removed the latex gloves. "So how'd they take the news?"

"Jake and Billie are ecstatic. They're probably doing cartwheels down Las Vegas Boulevard about now."

"Uh-oh."

"What do you mean by that?"

He hated to lie, wasn't good at it, but this was not a subject he cared to discuss with Caitlin Wells. "I mean I hope they don't get careless. We don't need another leak." That, of course, was not at all what he was worried about. More and more it was becoming the Jake & Billie Show—which was understandable, considering the circumstances—but Little Miss Honeybee wasn't completely stupid and things could get complicated. And if that happened, he had a feeling the Kyra genie would be out of the bottle.

Caitlin gave him the fisheye. "Don't give me that bullshit, Leonidovich. You meant Jake and Billie, and that's *not* going to happen."

What was that—a prediction . . . a hope . . . a threat? "I don't know what you're talking about, Wells."

"Jake might try, but Billie's not about to go down that road again."

He believed that, Billie wasn't the type to *willingly* jump into bed with another woman's husband—former or not—but Jake Rynerson had a way of making things happen. "What did Charles say?"

She shook her head in mock disgust, like a schoolteacher who had finally given up on a disobedient but likable child. "Typical male, you don't lie worth a damn so you change the subject."

"That's one of the first things you learn in male school. We call it dissociative denial."

"I call it bullshit."

"Yeah, we call it that too. Now what about Charles?"

"He asked twice if you remembered to wear gloves. I told him you didn't, but that I reminded you."

"Thanks for the support. What about the dirt guy?"

"He promised to have a forensic geologist standing by."

Forensic geologist, that sounded a bit like calling the garbage man a sanitation engineer. "I think *dirt guy* sounds better."

"Me too, but I don't think it pays as well."

"I'm sure you're right." He knew the answer to his next question without asking. "Did you check on flights?"

"Of course. No direct flights to Vegas. But if I get out of here"—she glanced at her watch—"now. I should be able to get it on the afternoon flight to L.A. Charles can pick it up there."

She was gone in less than a minute, and a minute after that Simon was on the phone to Victoria Halle. "Hi there, VicTheQuick."

"Bagman! Where are you? Sounds like you're in a well."

He had a feeling she might already know. When it came to monitoring phone calls, no one did it better than the National Security Agency, though she had always avoided saying exactly what she did. "I'm in South America." *Specific enough.* "Can you talk?"

She hesitated for just a moment. "Do I have time? Or privately?"

"Both."

"The answer to the first is yes. The second doesn't exist."

That was clear enough, but he had to take the chance. "I need a favor. A big one. Life and death and all that sort of thing."

"Sounds familiar. I hope you're not talking about thirty-three million lives this time."

"No, just one." *And Simon makes two.* "Maybe two."

"And I suppose it's foolish to ask for details."

"Can't do it. Client confidentiality."

There was another slight hesitation, then, "Hold on." He could hear her lay down the phone, silence, then the sound of a door being closed. "Okay, Bagman, what is it you need?"

It was the answer he expected—Vic didn't turn her back on friends, and he considered her one of his best. "I've got a cellular phone. I need anything you can get me on where it came from, who it's registered to, the complete record of any calls. In or out. Is that asking the impossible?"

"You're in Colombia, right?"

Damn, he didn't even want to think about the ramifications of that—that the government could track him like some rat in a maze—but ironically, that was exactly the kind of power he hoped she would have. "Yes."

She didn't hesitate. "That shouldn't be a problem. We have some assets down there."

He had a feeling *some assets* meant *mucho plenty*—the government had been in Colombia for years, tracking narcotraffickers and trying to break the cartels. "It gets harder."

"When did you ever ask for anything easy?"

"I give the easy ones to Lara."

"Whom I talked to yesterday. She said you were in Vegas. Had been since your birthday party."

"You know me, every day a different continent."

"You'll never find a woman that way, Simon."

Uh-oh, she was now sounding like Lara. He was tempted to defend himself, tell her he was with someone—a very beautiful and smart someone—but what woman wanted to hear that about another? And it would have been a lie—Caitlin wasn't really *with* him. *Not yet.*

"I'm a domestic failure, what can I say?"

"You can say you're going to hire someone so you can stay home once in a while. But I know, you don't want to hear it. So what's the complication?"

"Do you have the ability to monitor any calls I receive on the phone?"

"What do you mean by monitor?"

"Record. Track the source."

The line hummed with silence for a long moment before her voice reverberated back. "It could be done. Legally it's a little touchy, but you are out of the country and you are giving us permission."

Was there a question in there? "I'm giving *you* permission."

"I can't guarantee confidentiality. We monitor a lot of calls in that area."

What choice did he have? "What do you need to know?"

"Is it the phone you're using? The number I'm looking at?"

Damn, he'd think twice the next time he needed to make a private call. Did such a thing even exist? "No, I'm calling from my room. Give me a sec." He picked up the Ericsson cellular, pressed the power button, and read the number as it flashed onto the screen.

"Okay, Bagman, I'll do my best."

The best from Victoria Halle had once saved his life—he couldn't ask for more than that. "Thanks, Vic. I'll call you tomorrow."

He sat back, feeling for the first time that he actually had a chance to help Kyra Rynerson.

CHAPTER SEVENTEEN

Somewhere in South America

Friday, 7 November 17:24:26 GMT –0500

Kyra leaned in close, her nose almost touching the wall, searching for one last crack in the mud caulking before it got too dark, but the shadows were too deep. She stepped back, trying to measure the distance to the ceiling against her progress. *Halfway*—the easy half. It was one thing to stand on terra firma and gouge out a few toeholds, but would be twice as hard when she had to hang off the wall and try to dig over her head. The finger holes would have to be bigger and deeper. *Two more days.*

She collapsed onto the cot, exhausted. She had stopped only once—to finish off the pork and eat a mango—and should have been hungry, but the thought of more black-bean mush made her nauseated. *Lamb chops,* that's what she wanted. Nobody did lamb chops better than Anthony. Lamb chops and his special "poppers"—red potatoes dipped in olive oil and rolled in course-ground salt and cracked pepper—cooked over an open fire until they were crispy and ready to explode. *Oh God, that was the best.* A small vinaigrette salad, lamb chops, red-potato poppers, spring asparagus, and a good bottle of Cabernet. *Bring it on!*

She leaned back against the wall and closed her eyes, enjoying the fantasy. Anthony at the grill, a glass of wine in one hand, his long BBQ tongs in the other, a half-smile curling the edge of his lips. *Contented,* when he had her to himself, something that didn't happen often in their lives.

Something she avoided. The intimacy made her uncomfortable, knowing how much he loved her and wanted a baby. And now she was pregnant, Anthony's dream come true, and he didn't even know it. Might never know.

Poor Anthony, he deserved better—deserved the child he always wanted. Anthony Saladino *Jr.* And it *was* a boy, she could feel it, the testosterone pumping through her veins. Maybe that was her redemption. Save the baby—save herself.

CHAPTER EIGHTEEN

Cali, Colombia

There was a soft tap on the door, followed by Caitlin's muted voice. "Simon, you awake?"

Waking up to the soft whisper of Caitlin Wells had a rather voyeuristic appeal, something he could get used to in a hurry. "I am now." He rolled over, snapped on the light, and sat up. "Come in." His head felt like a giant fuzzball. "I'm dressed."

She pushed open the door. "You said to wake you at five-thirty."

"Sometimes I say stupid things. You should ignore them."

"I'll remember that. You always sleep with your clothes on?"

"I wasn't sleeping. Anything less than three hours is a nap." He stood up and made a slow turn. "So how do I look?"

"Like you slept with your clothes on."

Perfect. "Like a middle-aged traveler with a scarred-up old travel case and no money?"

She nodded slowly, a look of comprehension coming into her eyes. "Very good."

"I hope it's enough. I'm not real excited about walking around Cali with five million in currency attached to my wrist." He didn't want to even think about how many people would cut off his hand for that kind of money.

"You still think they'll call tonight?"

"Maybe, maybe not." He sat down on the edge of the bed and pulled on his new walkers, which now looked old and scruffy after he'd torn away some of the trim and stained them with a few well-placed streaks of brown shoe polish. "Either way, I want to be ready."

"They could just show up here."

"Not likely, they wouldn't have bothered with the phone. I think they'll run me around until they're sure I'm alone, then move in quick before someone else decides to relieve the stupid foreigner of his property."

Her dark eyes glinted with amusement. "How will they know you're stupid?"

Ha-ha. "Anyone who walks around this city at night without a team of bodyguards is certifiable."

The humor disappeared from her eyes, her expression suddenly serious. "You think it's that dangerous?"

"Absolutely." He reached down, picked up the shopping bag from his afternoon excursion, and dumped the contents on the bed. "So I did a little shopping while you were at the airport."

"Is that what I think it is?"

"I have no idea what you think, Wells." *Ain't that the truth!* "But what you're looking at is a Kevlar S45 upperbody vest. The latest and greatest in body armor."

"You think that's necessary?"

He didn't, but figured it was like wearing clean underwear in case of a car crash—it never hurt to be prepared. "Probably not."

She nodded, confirming that was exactly what she thought, but her eyes had focused on his second purchase. "And that?"

He unplugged the watch from the video Walkman and handed it to her. "What's it look like?"

She turned it over in her hand. "It looks like a diver's watch."

"It is. *And* a camera. Check out the zero in the number ten, it's actually a tiny lens."

She leaned in close, found it, then shook her head. "This is not a good idea. You may be searched. They could see the wire and—"

"Forget the wire, that stays here. Afterward we plug the watch into the video player, and bingbangboom, we've got pictures."

She continued to shake her head. "I can see the lens. They specifically said no video or audio surveillance."

"The only reason you can see the lens is because I told you where it was."

"But why take the risk? You heard what Leo said, they'll pay someone to pick up the money. He won't know anything." With an expression of finality she finally stopped shaking her head, as if the decision were hers and she'd made up her mind—no more discussion, no appeal. "Forget it. It's too big a risk."

"And I'm the one taking it."

"What about Kyra?"

"Whatever happens to Kyra has already been decided."

"You don't know that."

"Think about it, she's already seen the guy masquerading as Luis Acosta. We have his description." Similar to the man he'd seen in the lobby. "A picture isn't going to affect her situation, but it might help us."

She hesitated a moment, as if considering his argument. "Okay, for the sake of discussion, let's say it doesn't change things for Kyra. What about you? They find the camera they might just decide to put a bullet in your head."

"That may be their plan anyway. That's one of the reasons I think this is so important, at least you'll know who to look for."

"Assuming they *don't* find the camera."

"I'll take my chances."

"No," she said firmly, "it's an unnecessary risk. I can't let you do it."

Damn, why did she have to put it that way? "I'm sorry, Caitlin, but with all due respect I don't work for you."

Her face went tight and the air between them seemed to thicken. "Okay, fine, let's call Jake. It's his daughter, it should be his decision."

"I don't think we should do that."

"And why not?"

"Because I don't work for Jake either. I'm an independent contractor, hired to do a job. And I'll do it. But I'll do it my way, the best way I know how."

"And if he doesn't agree?"

"Then you'll need to find another bagman. Let's not back him into that corner."

Her gray eyes sparked with anger. "That's blackmail."

It was also an idle threat—he had made a promise to Billie and would never walk away from that—but he needed to make Caitlin believe otherwise. "I'm sorry you see it that way. You've asked me to step into the lion's den, and I'll do it, but I'm tired of sitting around while everyone tries to convince each other that if the money gets paid, Kyra comes home. You believe that because you want to believe it, Kyra's your friend. Jake believes it because he can't accept the possibility he might never get a chance to make things right with his daughter. Billie believes it because she can't face the alternative. But I don't know Kyra, and I'm not so emotionally blind I can't see the risk of pay and pray. God doesn't work that way—He expects us to do a bit of the heavy lifting ourselves."

The fire in her eyes dampened to a simmer. "So now you're an expert on God?"

"Nope, but I don't believe 'Okay, God, we paid the money, now give us our daughter back,' will impress Him much."

The last of her anger dissolved into a look of indecision. "You should have made that argument to Jake. It's his daughter, you can't ask me not to tell him."

He couldn't argue with that and was saved from having to try by the phone—*the Kyra phone,* as he now thought of it. He took a moment to clear his mind, flashed Caitlin a confident smile—a confidence he didn't feel—and pressed the TALK button. "Hello."

"Leonidovich?"

He immediately recognized the voice, the same as on the taped conversation with Leo Geske, and in that moment he realized two things—two very bad things. Despite the man's heavy accent, he pronounced *Leonidovich* perfectly, something no one ever did without hearing it first. On the tape, Leo had always referred to him as *the courier,* and had spelled his name, but never pronounced it. This seemed to confirm the kidnappers had someone working on the inside. Close to the inner circle. And if that was true, this was not some typical South American kidnapping where the established rules would be followed. "Speaking." He hoped Vic was listening.

"You have the package?"

"Yes." That should make Vic's ears jump to attention; in Colombia everyone assumed a *package* contained either a bomb or drugs.

"As ordered?"

"Exactly."

"You are alone?"

Simon almost said *yes,* then realized the foolishness of a lie—the man could know everything. "No. Mr. Rynerson's administrative assistant is with me." He wanted to pull back the words as soon as they crossed his tongue, but it was too late. It would take Vic no more than ten seconds to put Rynerson and Las Vegas together and come up with Big Jake. *You idiot, Leonidovich!*

"She is to remain at the hotel."

She. Did he assume or did he know? "Of course."

"You will be watched. Anyone follows the woman will be returned in *pedacitos. Comprende?*"

Yes, he understood very well—*small pieces.* The threat was not unexpected, but Simon knew it would bring Vic to the edge of her seat. "I understand."

"You will follow my directives *exactamente.*"

"I'll do my best."

"You will now go to the *céntrico estación de ferrocarril.*"

It took a moment for Simon to translate the words in his mind: *central railway station.* "Where exactly?" But the man was already gone.

From his spot in the lobby, El Pato watched the courier exit the elevator and cross the lobby. Dressed in wrinkled slacks and a baggy shirt, he no longer looked the type to be staying at the Inter-Continental. With his backpack and *Deportiva Cali* baseball cap, he would easily fade into the city's diverse population. Perhaps the man was not so simple as the *norteamericano* had indicated. This became more apparent when Leonidovich insisted on taking the last of three taxis waiting in line outside the door. An argument immediately erupted between Leonidovich and the drivers of the first two taxis, but the courier quickly solved the problem with a round of tips.

El Pato watched the taxi disappear into the flow of traffic but made no move to follow. No reason to hurry, he had Leonidovich on a string and could reel him in at will. He waited ten minutes—saw no signs of unusual activity and no signs that anyone else had tried to follow Leonidovich—then pulled his cellular and made the second call.

Leonidovich answered immediately, his voice impatient. "I'm listening."

Beyond the man's voice El Pato could hear the clamorous sound of commuters. Many commuters, just as he planned. "And I am watching." He could imagine the courier glancing around, looking for someone with a phone, finding many, and wondering: *Which one?* "Listen carefully."

As Simon took down the directions, he listened hard for any background sounds, but heard nothing and suspected the man was nowhere near the busy terminal. It didn't surprise him, the picture was slowly coming into focus, and none of it looked good. He had, he now realized, been ignoring too many small coincidences. And he knew why: *Caitlin Wells.* If he accepted the circumstances as they now appeared, he had to accept the fact that she could be involved. That was not something he wanted to believe, but not something he could ignore either. *Too many coincidences.* Colombian kidnappings were typically acts of opportunity, taking advantage of foreign travelers within the country; but that was hardly the case in Kyra's abduction, which had been well planned and well executed. It meant the kidnappers had prior knowledge of her schedule, which Tony insisted no one knew outside of a select circle of coworkers and friends—including, Simon suspected, her secret confidante: Caitlin Wells. Was it simply a coincidence the ransom demand specified American dollars and Swiss francs, both of which were readily available at the Sand Castle, and could be retrieved without attracting unwanted attention? *Unlikely, but possible.*

A coincidence the man in Cali would know how to pronounce Leonidovich? *Possible, but unlikely.*

No matter how much he resisted the thought, a Las Vegas connection seemed more than just a possibility. And now, despite the efforts to make it look otherwise, he could identify the involvement of only one person outside of Vegas—*Mr. Didn't-fit*—hardly the modus operandi of a Colombian faction. The same man he saw in the window as the taxi pulled away from the hotel. A man who closely resembled Elsworth Marshall's description of Luis Acosta. The same man, Simon assumed, he was now listening to.

"*Comprende?*"

Yes, he understood perfectly—the map and all the prominent locations of the city were fused into his brain—but he wanted to keep the man on the phone as long as possible, to give Vic time to track and trace the call. At least that's what he hoped she was doing. "No. You better repeat that last part."

"Maybe you would like another ear, eh?"

Something Mr. Didn't-fit wouldn't hesitate to do—it was there in his voice, an undertone of pleasure at the thought. Not a man to aggravate. "I'll find the place."

Finding *the place* began what seemed to be an endless cycle of telephone calls and instructions as the man ran Simon from one location to another: all public areas, all within walking distance, all crowded with a mixture of locals and tourists. Despite a light breeze, the air was hot and muggy and within minutes the T-shirt beneath his Kevlar was soaked with sweat, the forty-pound case like a lead ball attached to his wrist. Typical for that part of the world, the restaurants were just starting to open, the smells of roasted chicken and peppers and guinea pig wafting into the street and mixing with the sounds of salsa music from the cantinas. Twice, though he was careful not to show any sign of recognition, Simon thought he caught a glimpse of Mr. Didn't-fit before he melted into the Friday-night crowd.

Finally, apparently satisfied with his game of direction and misdirection, the man turned Simon down a narrow side street to a small cantina: El Gusano—The Worm—a name that didn't exactly stimulate the appetite. No windows. Though he tried to ignore it, Simon couldn't shake the thought that once he stepped through the door he might never come out.

It's possible there's a tad bit of danger involved. Thanks, Jake, I'll remember that *tad bit* when it comes time to submit my bill. *Holy Mother,* there were times when a man had to question his chosen line of work. He took a deep breath, let it gradually slip away, then shoved open the door with what he hoped was a look of confidence.

The room was long and narrow, the odor of sweat and tobacco and stale beer thick enough to choke an elephant, and so dark if it hadn't been for a small television behind the bar, Simon would have thought he had just gone blind. The camera watch—though he had opened the aperture to its maximum setting—would be useless in such an environment. The bartender, a mountain of flesh with leathery skin and beefy shoulders, glanced up, then went back to drawing a beer for one of his six customers: all men, all sitting at the bar beneath a cloud of cigarette smoke, all apparently engrossed in the soccer match on television. Simon waited for his eyes to adjust, then as instructed, took a seat at the last table at the very back of the room, next to a door marked *baño,* which, judging from the stench of disinfectant and urine and worse, had to be the most god-awful toilet facility in Cali. Simon could almost feel the germs sneaking out from below the door, searching for victims.

The bartender arrived with a look that matched the establishment—dirty and dark—and a glass of beer already in hand. Apparently *choice* was not high on the list of attractions at El Gusano. The beer looked wonderful—liquid gold topped with a perfect layer of white suds—the glass about the last thing Simon ever intended to let touch his lips. He laid a ten thousand peso note on the table, then watched the money disappear into the man's pocket as he returned to the bar. Some things were the same all over the world.

Searching his memory for past encounters, Simon studied the six profiles at the bar—men beyond their youth, their faces hard with the effort of living—and was certain he had never seen any of them before. And none of them seemed to have the slightest interest in his presence. Perhaps that was the way of Cali: mind your own business, live another day. But what if they knew some idiot foreigner had five million in unmarked, untraceable bills sitting virtually unprotected on a chair in the back of *their* bar?

It's possible there's a tad bit of danger involved.

A good time, he decided, to take a chance and see if he could even up the odds—*just a tad*. He pulled a hundred-dollar bill from his pocket, tore it in half, then tapped his beer glass on the table to get the bartender's attention.

Hidden in the darkness between two buildings, El Pato methodically scanned each side of the narrow street. *Nothing.* As expected. As the *norteamericano* promised. Even so, this was the moment and he needed to be careful. *Paciente. Very* patient. If Leonidovich had been followed, they would have to show themselves soon: a drunk that did or did not stumble at the right moment, a car or van with too many antennas. If they came, he would see them, he had picked a good spot. Still . . .

He turned back to the cantina. El Gusano might not have been the perfect choice. No back exit—his main reason for picking the place—now seemed more like a trap than a cage. If something went bad he would be cornered. Perhaps he should have greased the palm of the bartender, but that had its own risks and could have drawn attention. He waited another five minutes, saw not so much as a stray cat, then quickly crossed the street. He paused outside the door, made one final check in each direction, then closed his eyes for thirty seconds, giving his pupils time to adjust, then opened the door and stepped inside.

Simon recognized the man instantly—Mr. Didn't-fit—who seemed to fit perfectly alongside the other men at the bar where he pulled out a stool and sat down. The minute he saw the man's waddling gait, Simon was sure of it; this was not some didn't-know-anything dummy hired by FARC or the ELN or any other arm of the Colombian kidnapping machine. Luis Acosta, Mr. Didn't-fit, Duckman, whatever you wanted to call him, they were all one and the same. He was *the man*: the one who had passed himself off as Luis Acosta, had abducted Kyra, and very possibly the one holding her. She had seen his face, perhaps overheard conversations with his contact in Las Vegas. Once he had the money, what motivation did he have to release her? Not a single one that Simon could think of. What could he say to make the man realize that harming Kyra would not be the smart move? But the harder he tried find the words, the slower his brain seemed to function, and for a few minutes seemed to stop completely, stuck in muck, like recess time in hell, then some unheard bell rang and his brain jumped into overdrive as the man suddenly stood up and started toward the back of the room. Simon forced himself to stare straight back into the man's small, dark eyes. Then, just before he reached the table, Simon cut a glance toward the bar.

El Pato caught the look and followed it. The bartender was watching, his expression closed and unreadable, but attentive. Very attentive. *Mierda,* what was this about? He turned back to Leonidovich. And why was this asshole *yanqui* so calm? *A trap?* He still had time, could still turn and walk away, but why, he had already dumped the phone, and as long as he kept to his story—*Some imbécil gave me a hundred thousand pesos to pick up a package*—what more could anyone prove? *Nada.* All this passed through his mind in a flash, between one step forward and the next, then his eyes shifted to the black case and he made up his mind. "I am told you would have something for me." A slow smile passed over the *gringo's* lips, as if the question amused him.

"Really, who told you that?"

It took all the self control El Pato could tap not to draw his knife and gut the man, and had there been a back door he would have done it, taken the money and the *gringo's* hand with it, but too many things felt wrong, there were too many men behind him. He took a breath and forced back his temper. "Perhaps I was wrong."

Leonidovich shrugged. "Maybe so, maybe no. What is this something?"

Did this *gringo* asshole have a recorder, did he think El Pato was stupid? "This I was not told."

Leonidovich nodded slowly. "I have to be cautious. I wouldn't want to give *something* to the wrong person."

"I was told only that a Señor Leonidovich would have something for me. That is all I know."

And all that Simon was waiting to hear—*Leonidovich,* as clear and perfect as the great Boris Leonidovich Pasternak could have pronounced his own name, a confirmation of what he heard earlier, and a confirmation of his worst suspicions—that the man was working with someone in Vegas. He smiled, as if this verbal interplay had all been a misunderstanding. "You should have mentioned that. I'm Leonidovich. Please sit down, I have a message for you."

"I was told only to pick up a package and return *inmediatamente.* Nothing about a message. My *inglés* is not so good."

"Your English is very good. And my instructions were very specific—not to turn over the package until I delivered the message." He reached down, being careful to touch only the base of the glass, and pushed his untouched beer across the table. "I ordered you a beer."

The man hesitated, glanced toward the bar, then pulled back a chair. "What is this message?"

Simon leaned forward and casually crossed his hands, aiming his watch directly at the man's face. "The message is—" He stopped as the bartender caught the signal and started toward them. The Duckman turned sideways in his chair—the look of a cornered cat ready to leap—but the bartender merely passed by, opened the door to the *baño* and stepped inside. As the dim light momentarily flooded the table, Simon snapped three quick shots, but they were all in profile and not what he wanted. Then the stench of the toilet hit and it was all he could do not to gag. "Sheesh." He waved a hand in front of his nose.

The Duckman nodded and seemed to relax, a gold tooth peeking out from between his thick lips. *"Mucho mierda."* He reached down, picked up the beer, and drained it in one long swallow.

Simon smiled—as if he found the image of Crap Mountain to be amusing, though that was certainly not the reason—and tried again, keeping his voice to a low whisper in an attempt to draw the man closer. "The message—" The Duckman leaned forward just as the door to the toilet popped open and Simon got two full-on face shots before the light disappeared. He waited a moment for the bartender to pass, then continued, "The message is from Mr. Rynerson."

The Duckman cocked his head to one side. "Runderson?"

No, but he didn't bother to correct the man's hapless attempt to play the innocent fool. "Right. He has kept his end of the bargain. Now he expects to receive *his* property. *Comprende?*"

The Duckman hunched his shoulders, his eyes as dark and uncaring as the ocean floor. *"Sí,* I will deliver your message."

"But," Simon continued, "if the property is *not* returned—" He paused to let the impact of his words sink in. "He has pledged his entire fortune and the army it will buy to find those responsible and execute them one by one. No trial. No appeal."

Though he showed no reaction, there was a distinct pause in the raspy back-and-forth of the man's breathing. *"Sí,* I will remember."

Enough, Simon hoped, to make him reconsider any plan he might have to kill Kyra. "It's important you do."

El Pato studied the courier's face, trying to read the meaning behind the words. They felt personal, as if the *gringo* suspected El Pato might be more than just a messenger. It didn't seem possible, but . . . ? The solution was simple and tempting: two quick slashes of his knife—one to the throat, one to the wrist—but to get out of El Gusano, that might not be so simple. Was it worth the risk? He considered the bartender and the other six men between his position and the door. *No,* not for five million. *Your lucky day, Leonidovich.* "And the package?"

Simon realized he had just dodged a bullet, it was written there, in the Duckman's dark eyes. Being careful not to expose what he was doing, Simon picked up his case, ran through the unlocking sequence, snapped open the top, and extracted the blue nylon duffel. "Don't get mugged." He cut a glance toward the bar, a subtle warning. "Lots of nasty people around."

El Pato pulled the duffel into his lap. "Perhaps I would take your case."

Simon looked toward the bar, this time not so quick or subtle. "I don't think so."

The moment the Duckman was out the door, Simon reached over and picked up the empty beer glass, being careful to touch only the base, and slipped it into his security case. A few seconds later the bartender was hovering over the table. "Eh?"

Simon nodded and handed the man the second half of the torn bill. Getting paid a hundred American dollars to take a piss might have been the easiest money the man ever earned. And it might, Simon had a feeling, have been the best money he ever spent.

CHAPTER NINETEEN

Cali, Colombia

Friday, 7 November 22:12:33 GMT –0500

Simon took a deep breath of the cool night air, sucking it in through his pores. Getting out of El Gusano with all his body parts had been a victory and he felt slightly light-headed, almost giddy. *Thank you, God.* He quickly retraced his steps back to the Plaza de Caicedo, then made his way north until he found a quiet corner in a small bar overlooking the Río Cali. He ordered a Costena beer—"in the bottle, *por favor*"—and began making calls, the first to Victoria Halle.

She answered before he heard the first ring. "I was getting worried, Bagman. You okay?"

"I'm fine. Tell me you got something."

"You need to tell me what this is about."

"I can't, you know that."

"Come on, Simon, I'm not stupid. Rynerson . . . Las Vegas . . . a package . . . the woman will be returned in little pieces . . . some nasty sounding Latino running you all over Cali. I have a pretty good idea what's happening and who it's happening to."

That he didn't doubt, in fact expected it—VicThe-Quick was too smart not to catch on. "Maybe," he said, "but I can't confirm it and you don't want me to."

"Oh? And why is that?"

"Because you work for the government. If I confirm what *you think*, you'll have a legal obligation to act on that information. If I don't confirm it, it's pure speculation on your part. Trust me, you do not want to be involved."

"Damn you, I am involved. You're one helluva smart guy, Simon, but this is way beyond your level of expertise. You need help."

"That's why I called you, sweetheart."

"Don't try and play me, Simon. You know what I mean."

"You're going to have to trust me on this, Vic. As much as I'd like to get some of that help you're talking about, I can't. Any inkling of outside involvement and things are going to end badly, if you get my meaning. Now are you going to help me or not?"

"Like you have to ask? I just hope to hell you're right."

Me too. "What did you get?"

"I got it all. Which wasn't much. Both phones, the one you were using and the one he was using, were purchased from a street vendor this morning. I've already traced the billing name. Bogus, of course."

"What about calls to or from Vegas?"

"No. No incoming calls at all. And until an hour ago the only other calls were between the two phones."

"Until an hour ago?" He tried to contain his excitement but his heart went into overdrive, thumping away like the Energizer Bunny beneath his Kevlar. "So he's still making calls and you're tracking it?"

"I'm tracking it, but it's not going to do you any good. He must have handed it off to a gang of teenagers. In the last hour at least six different people have used it, just having a grand old time making free calls to their friends. Whoever he is, he's no dummy, Simon."

Damn. No, the guy wasn't a dummy, but he wasn't a rocket scientist either—someone a lot smarter than the Duckman was calling the shots. "So that's it? We've got nothing?"

"I'll review the tapes, make sure I didn't miss something, but I doubt if there's anything we could use to find or identify the guy."

"Thanks, I appreciate it."

"I could also have the voice analyzed, come up with some kind of a profile if that would help."

He knew it wouldn't. He had looked the guy in the eyes, he didn't need some psychologist to tell him what he already knew: approximate age, Latin-American ancestry, screwed-up childhood, antisocial behavior—*dangerous*. "No, I don't think that would do any good."

"Okay—your call." She hesitated, her voice dropping to a conspiratorial whisper. "I shouldn't be asking, but what else can I do?"

"So glad you asked. How are you with fingerprints and mug shots?"

"You got both?"

"I did."

"Well, aren't you the clever one! Maybe you're not so far out of your league after all, Bagman."

"Thanks. Can you help?"

"I could probably get the stuff into the right hands."

A *probably* from Vic was worth more than a *promise* from anyone else. "I'll send what I've got first thing in the morning."

"What are you going to do?"

Good question. He was wondering the same thing. "You know me—adapt, improvise, overcome."

"You're not a marine, Simon."

"I'm wearing a Kevlar vest."

"Oh, Christ. Now I am worried."

"Don't. I'll be fine. I really appreciate the help, Vic, I really do."

"By the way . . . ?"

Uh-oh, when a woman hit you with a casual "by the way," it was time to duck and run. "Yeah?"

"Who's this administrative assistant you're with?"

Did he detect a bit of jealousy? *Nah,* they were strictly friends. "I'm not *with* her, if that's what you mean."

"Does she have a name?"

Maybe that was it: Vic was just trying to confirm her suspicions about the Rynerson connection. "Sorry, that falls under the umbrella of confidentiality."

"Yeah, sure it does. Just remember to keep your own head out of the rain, Simon."

He wasn't sure how to interpret that and knew better than to ask. *Women,* they were so damn complicated and mysterious, God must have been in some kind of schizophrenic mood the day he conjured up the species. "Thanks, Vic. I appreciate the help."

"Sorry I couldn't do more. Watch your back, Bagman."

Exactly what he intended to do. He took a long swallow of beer, then dialed Lara's home number. "You ready to do some work, Sissie?"

Both her voice and smart-ass attitude came snapping back. "I live for the opportunity to serve you, Master."

"It's about time you understood how things are supposed to work. Keep that up and you might get that raise."

"Oh goodie, another one of those might-get, remind-me-later, we'll-see-about-that promises I can add to the list."

Sheesh, did all women keep a list? "You got a pen?"

"Fire away, Master."

"First thing—burn the list."

"Oh, Simon, I'm so disappointed. Do you actually believe we're dumb enough to write this stuff down? The list is imbedded within the female brain—inviolable, indestructible, invisible to the vagaries of man."

He almost believed it. "Okay, okay, you win, close the *Thesaurus.* I need you to check out some people."

"What do you mean, *check out?*"

"Anything and everything, drugs, gambling, financial problems, whatever you can get, complete background."

"My specialty."

"Here are the names. Charles Case, he's head of security for Rynerson. Leo Geske, he works for EDK Insurance. Anthony Saladino, that's Kyra Rynerson's husband. Goes by Tony. I especially want to know if he screws around. And if so, if he's involved with someone."

"That's it, those three?"

"Tammi Rynerson, she's—"

"I know. Wife Number Four."

"And Caitlin Wells. You know who she is."

"Right. Superwoman. Same job I've got."

Super-pain-in-the-butt was more like it, but he resisted the temptation. "How long? Day or two?"

"At least. I'm still running a business back here, Boris, referring *your* jobs to other companies. Please tell me we're getting paid lots of money for whatever it is you're doing."

"Bunches."

"You haven't even discussed the fee, have you?"

"I'll get to it."

"Good to hear. I'd hate to think we were giving away the farm just so you could live an *Ocean's 11* lifestyle and hang out with Big Jake Rynerson."

"Gotta run, Sissie. Tell the kids their Uncle Simon loves 'em. I'll call tomorrow." He hit the disconnect before she could ask about Vegas and he'd be forced to tell her he was in Colombia, hanging out with kidnappers, narcotraffickers, and Superwoman Wells. All of whom seemed equally dangerous.

He finished off the Costena and signaled the waiter for another. Despite the cool breeze off the river, he was still sweating like a longshoreman beneath the Kevlar. *One more call,* the one he should have made first—Billie and Jake would be climbing the walls by now—but he couldn't decide how much to say, or more important, how much *not* to say. Someone in Vegas was involved, he was almost positive of that, but he didn't want to set off any alarms that would make finding him—*or her*—more difficult.

The big man answered on the first ring, as if he'd been waiting with his hand on the receiver. "Hello."

"It's Simon."

"Thank God! You okay, boy?"

"I'm fine." Under the circumstances he was touched Jake could think of anyone besides his daughter. "Thanks."

"And what about—"

"Sorry, Jake, the guy pretended he was hired to pick up a package. That he didn't know anything."

The line hummed with silence while Jake absorbed the news. When he finally spoke his voice had lost a bit of its familiar strength. "Why don't you tell me everything that happened?"

For the next five minutes Simon did exactly that, and though he softened the edges, he tried not to raise any false hope. "Keep in mind they've already got your five mil. They don't have much incentive to let Kyra go."

Another few moments of silence followed before Jake's voice reverberated back over the miles. "But that's the way Leo says these Colombian groups work." He sounded like a man trying to convince himself.

"Right." *If* it was a Colombian group, and *if* it was one of those predictable factions who did this sort of thing as a matter of business, and *if* they could be relied on to *follow the rules*, but he didn't believe it. "And I'm hoping that's exactly the case. But I'm positive this was the same person who passed himself off as Luis Acosta, and he's the same guy on the tape with Leo. I'm guessing he's also the one holding Kyra."

"That's not much of a group."

"Exactly. But if the guy has a record, we may be able to trace him."

"You got a picture?"

"Yes." He wasn't surprised Jake knew about the camera, he expected Caitlin to tell him—it was her job and he couldn't blame her for doing it. "And his fingerprints."

"How the hell did you manage that?"

"I bought the guy a beer. He was dumb enough to drink it."

"That's terrific work." His voice echoed with renewed confidence. "I knew you were the right boy for this job."

"Thanks, but unless the guy has a record we don't have zip. I'm going to ship everything overnight to a friend who works for the government. We should know something pretty quick."

"Oh." The big man wasn't pleased, it was obvious from his tone. "Wouldn't it be better if Charles—"

"Trust me, Jake, this person knows how to keep a secret." He hated to stick the man in the eye, but he didn't want to lose control of the only solid clues they had, not before Lara had a chance to check out Charles Case. "We can't afford another leak."

"Okay, but I don't see how anything could slip out. We've got this place buttoned up tighter than a bull's ass at fly time."

Not an opinion Simon shared or an image he cared to envision. "Let's pretend otherwise—for Kyra's sake."

"Okay, as long as you're sure this person can be trusted. Now what?"

"Now we wait, hope they keep their end of the bargain, and release Kyra within twelve hours."

"Pay and pray, as Leo says."

"Right." But Simon had no intention of sitting on his duff waiting for God to do the right thing. The Almighty had a rather odd, irrational way of choosing who to help. Perhaps *He* was a *She*—that would explain everything.

CHAPTER TWENTY

Somewhere in South America

Saturday, 8 November 11:51:41 GMT –0500

Hanging off the wall like Spider Woman and digging holes into cementlike dirt was not exactly white-collar employment. And not fast. After a day and a half, her uppermost toehold was no more than thirty inches above the dirt. Even with her height and long reach, she still had a good eighteen inches to go before she could touch the roof, and would need to get higher for enough leverage to push her way through the tin sheets. Still, if she started at daybreak she could make it by nightfall. One more day—*Freedom!*

By the time the light gave out she could hardly move her arms. She stared at the wall, measuring how much she had left, then down at her hands. Every finger was raw, every nail broken from trying to peel slivers of wood off the planks. She collapsed onto the cot, letting them dangle between her legs, and eyed the last of her food: two small papayas, one mango, two bananas. *Ugh.* She picked up the mango, lay back, and began to peel away the skin with her teeth.

The rain woke her sometime during the night, the half-eaten mango still in her hand. *Day eight.* She needed to get up, to refill the water bottles, but something held her back. Then she heard it, hidden beneath the pounding crush of rain, that soft, snotty gurgle of breath she knew so well. He was back—staring at her through the darkness.

• • •

The drive from Lago Agrio had been long and tedious and he had spent the time reviewing all that happened, down to the smallest detail. *One mistake,* but so *insignificante* he was sure it had gone unnoticed. So *insignificante* he didn't think of it for hours—the fact that he had left his finger-prints on a beer glass at El Gusano—but the more he thought about it, the more confident he became that Leonidovich would not have noticed. The man was a *mensajero*—a messenger boy—who would never notice such a small thing. Satisfied that the woman was asleep, he slid the pass-through closed and set the bolt.

Kyra heard the bolt slide into place but waited until she heard him move away from the door before cracking a lid. *The Duckman Returneth.* It was like a horror movie coming to life, and she couldn't even scream. *One more day!*—six, maybe seven hours of digging and poking and scratching and she could have been free. She memorized exactly how she was lying, then tried to sit up but couldn't muster the energy. Her feet, her arms, her hands, they all felt numb, paralyzed by a sense of foreboding and hopelessness. Struggling to compose herself, she took a deep breath and fought back the tears. *One little break,* was that too much to ask?

Maybe it was. Maybe she deserved it for the way she had treated Anthony and her father. She lay there, allow-ing herself to wallow in self-pity for a good two minutes, then mentally pushed away the woe-is-me bullshit. Sure, she could have done better, but she didn't deserve to die in the middle of some godforsaken jungle, in some godfor-saken shack, at the hands of some psychotic fuck who didn't deserve to share the planet with the rest of human-ity. *No,* she didn't deserve that. And she wasn't going to accept it—not without a fight.

She sat up, listening hard for any movement, then silently stepped across the room and placed her right eye over the pinprick of light seeping through the wall. He was standing over the table, busily moving all the food and supplies to the floor. Clothes soaked by the rain, he looked pale and tired, but there was something manic in his movements, his eyes blazing like some pipehead junkie. He pushed the lantern to one side and with a grunt hoisted what looked like a large pet carrier onto the table. Gray, with a wire-grid door on one end and grid windows on the sides, it was big enough to accommodate a large-breed dog, which it apparently did, judging from the low-humming growl that suddenly rose up over the sound of the rain. When El Pato stepped away, Kyra got a good, full-on look at the animal's face: a pit bull, his head wide and thick with uncropped ears tucked in tight like a bat's, his eyes feral and dark, his lips peeled back to reveal a full complement of yellow teeth. Contrary to common belief, the breed was not naturally mean; it took an abusive human to turn one into a killer, which this one had obviously been trained to do. A sudden chill traced a finger down the middle of her back. How could she defend herself against that? She couldn't.

El Pato came back into view, vigorously shaking a half-liter bottle of water, which he then proceeded to pour through the mesh as the dog snapped and snarled and tried to eat its way through the thick wire. The moment El Pato turned away the dog lapped up the water. El Pato smiled and began to peel off his wet clothes, first his shirt, then his pants and underwear. Thick and scarred, he looked like a wrestler slightly beyond his prime: big shoulders, broad chest, a hard belly and muscular legs. Everything big and beefy except his sexual organ, a dwarf penis barely visible in its nest of black hair. Undoubtedly the victim of many sexual failures, it probably explained much of his voyeuristic behavior.

By the time he was naked the dog was on its side, either dead or comatose. Though animals were her life's work, she fervently hoped this one had taken its last breath. Using the handle end of a long wooden spoon, El Pato gave the animal a hard poke. Twice. Once to the nose, once to the top of its wide skull. It never moved. He opened the cage, reached inside, grabbed the dog by the scruff, yanked it through the opening, and dropped him onto the floor. It landed with a dull *THUNK*, like a heavy bag of flour. Apparently not dead, El Pato looped a chain around the dog's neck and unceremoniously dragged the unconscious beast across the floor and staked him near what Kyra thought of as her burial plot.

Moving at an increasingly frenetic pace, El Pato returned to the table and using a short-handled screwdriver began removing a number of tiny lockscrews from around the inside perimeter of the carrier. In less than a minute he had separated the cage area from the base, which exposed looked unusually thick, about five inches in depth. He set the cage aside and began removing additional screws circling the base. The floor plate came away with the last screw, revealing a hidden compartment packed tight with bundles of money. Kyra felt a sudden sinking sensation; it was over and done, ransom paid, release or kill her, and she had no illusions about which of the two El Pato would choose.

He turned the base over and with a vicious shake dumped the money onto the table. The sight of so much money seemed to have some kind of catatonic effect. He stood there, transfixed, like Ali Baba staring at the thieves' treasure and not believing his eyes. Finally he sat down, sweaty and naked, and began to assemble the money into some kind of order. When he finished dividing and stacking, he fanned each packet, making sure it was all real, then broke the band and carefully began counting and inspecting each bill. The job quickly became repetitious and tedious, but Kyra continued to watch, afraid she might miss something—some clue to what he intended to do. With her. To her.

For more than an hour, he continued to inspect his treasure, until every bill had been counted and stacked. By the time he finished the rain had stopped, the sky had gone from black to gray, and the pit bull had started to twitch and squirm, slowly coming back from its narcotized nap. Obviously tired, El Pato leaned back in his chair and smiled, a lazy, wolflike grin. Then he suddenly pitched forward and buried his face in the mountain of money.

It had, El Pato thought, the most wonderful smell in the world. *Five million dólares!* It smelled like . . . like *libertad!* Freedom from cold frijoles and hot beer. Freedom from all the *grande aristócratas* who thought they were better. Freedom from all the cheap *prostitutas,* who took his money and laughed behind his back. Freedom even from the arrogant *norteamericano,* though once again everything had gone exactly as predicted. The money was all *perfecto,* unmarked, no more than three serial numbers in sequence. No electronic transmitters. No *policía.* Everything *perfecto.* Except for the glass, but that was *nada,* Leonidovich would never have noticed such a small detail. Why would he even care, a delivery boy, hired only to deliver the money?

El Pato took another deep breath, filling his head with the wonderful scent. He wanted to scoop it up, kill the *grande princesa* and disappear into his new life, but the *norteamericano* had insisted: *Wait for my call. Follow the plan.* He was sick of these words. *Wait for my call. Follow the plan.* But he would wait—it was only a small thing.

Almost over. Then he thought of the courier's message and wondered.

He has pledged his entire fortune and the army it will buy to find those responsible and execute them one by one. No trial. No appeal.

Would the capitalist *gringo* try, or was this only a *grande* threat, a desperate attempt to save his little *princesa?*

A threat, most certainly a threat. Why would the man spend more of his *dólares* if he thought his *princesa* was dead? That would be *estúpido;* and according to the *norteamericano,* Señor Rynerson was not a stupid man. But El Pato was not stupid either, this they would understand soon enough. By tomorrow he would be in Rio de Janeiro, at the best hotel on the beach, lying between silk sheets. New identity. New life. He was ready, ready to do it now. Just the thought of it—the look on her face when she came face-to-face with El Diablo—made his lizard squirm for attention.

Kyra watched, disgusted but also transfixed, wondering what had suddenly gotten El Pato so aroused. The money? No, he was past that. Not sex, the expression on his face exceeded sexual fantasy. He looked . . . ? And then she remembered—he had the same expression when he killed the boy-pilot—and she knew exactly what he was thinking. The only question was how he would do it. Something ghoulish. Some entertainment to satisfy his voyeuristic appetite. She looked at the pit bull, now lying on its side, its tongue hanging in the dirt, its eyes unfocused but open, its tiny brain struggling to regain chemical equilibrium. One more hour, two at the most, and it would be back to normal. Only meaner. Was that El Pato's plan, to watch some bruised and abused animal turn her into Dog Chow?

She retreated to her cot, watching as the darkness faded and the soft contours of her cell regained their hard edges. Was this it, her last dawn? Without conscious thought she curled into a protective ball, some long-repressed maternal gene asserting itself, driving her to protect her baby. *Had to be a way*—all she had to do was find it. She let her mind drift, hoping that if she didn't try so hard some clever scheme would suddenly spew forth from her subconscious, but like a Gordian knot every idea seemed to twist back on itself, leading nowhere. Her thoughts were interrupted by the now familiar chirp of El Pato's beeper. She knew the routine, first the beeper, then the call, and it took no acrobatics of logic to figure out that this was *the call,* that some unknown person—someone close to her father and the one issuing orders—was about to give her life a thumbs-up or a thumbs-down.

Though careful not to make a sound, she nearly flew off the cot and across the tiny room. With a grunt and what appeared to be a grin of anticipation, El Pato pushed himself up from the table. He momentarily disappeared from view, then reappeared with both his satellite phone and beeper, reading the message as he waddled back toward the table. He suddenly stopped, the anticipatory grin reforming itself into an expression of disbelief and anger.

Ironically, Kyra felt only a sense of relief. He was angry because something had gone wrong, which could only mean something had gone right for her. If not a pardon, at least a temporary stay of execution.

CHAPTER TWENTY-ONE

Cali, Colombia

Sunday, 9 November 13:17:51 GMT −0500

Simon glanced at his watch, something he found himself doing with ever increasing frequency, mentally added the hours—*thirty-nine*—and turned back to his laptop. The progress bar seemed stuck, the download speed excruciatingly slow. He had set up his work space in the suite's small dining room, where the light was good and the large windows offered a panoramic view of the city. Despite its reputation for indiscriminate bombings, Cali was remarkably beautiful, the river cutting a huge green swath directly through the heart of the central area, where most of the hotels, boutiques, and cantinas were located. The tourists—mostly South Americans—continued to crowd the streets in spite of a light rain, apparently confident the inconvenience was only temporary, a typical afternoon shower.

Though it was past midday and he knew she was up, Caitlin had yet to emerge from her bedroom, where she had spent most of the last two days—on the phone. The calls from the Sand Castle never seemed to stop—the hotel manager, the casino manager, the executive chef, the head of hospitality, the entertainment director, and the head of housekeeping—they all called with their departmental crises and interdepartmental disputes, big fires and small fires, and despite the circumstances of location and the pressure of waiting for Kyra to be released, Caitlin seemed to handle each matter with surgical skill: analyzing, dissecting, and excising each problem. She was not only powerful, but decisive and fair, and Simon was starting to believe his lack of trust to be nothing more than cautionary paranoia.

Charles Case called only once—to hear Simon's account of his meeting with the Duckman—so either the Head of Security had his own fiefdom under control, or was the only executive outside of Caitlin who reported directly to Big Jake. As for the big man himself, he called every few hours, but from what Simon could deduce from the one-sided conversations, Jake only cared about his daughter and was perfectly content to let Caitlin run his empire.

Finally, after a long ten minutes, the progress bar completed its crawl and through the magic of cybertechnology, twelve new messages appeared in the laptop's IN-BOX. Simon scanned down the list, ignoring all but the last two: one from Lara and one from an unfamiliar Hotmail address. He double-clicked the Hotmail message, knowing from the SUBJECT header it came from VicThe-Quick.

Subject: VTQ
Date: Sunday, 9 November 08:54:13 EST
From: Ube Careful <ube-careful@hotmail.com>
To: Simon Leonidovich
<SimonL@WorldwideSD.com>

Received glass and picture disk.
Meeting friend tonight who works for the B.
Very discreet.
He will search files, including I.
Should know something within 48 hours.
Kisses . . . . Ube Careful

Kisses and advice, something no sane man would refuse from the brilliant and beautiful Victoria Halle. Her cryptic references to the Bureau and Interpol seemed slightly over the top, but when you worked for the NSA you probably assumed every email received a cursory computer scan, searching for key words or word strings that might prompt an investigation. Or maybe she *knew* it was happening. *Ugh, what a world*—he loved the convenience, hated the loss of privacy. He scrolled down to Lara's message and double-clicked.

Subject: Rynerson, re: background check
Date: Sunday, 9 November 11:11:24 EST
From: Lara Quinn <LaraQ@WorldwideSD.com>
To: Simon Leonidovich
<SimonL@WorldwideSD.com>

While you're in LV partying with the rich and famous, I'm working. Why is that, Boris? Don't bother to answer, I'll remind you when bonus time rolls around.

I did the best I could with the background checks (see attachment), I'm not a detective you know, and it would help if I knew what the hell you were looking for, but don't concern yourself, I'm ONLY your sister.

I'll resume my digging tomorrow, but want to spend a little time with the kids (you remember them???, Jack and Allie, your nephew and niece) before my weekend is totally ruined.

Пока L

Women, Lara in particular, they had such a fine talent for globbing on the guilt. He moved his cursor over to the Adobe attachment, opened it, and began to read.

Rynerson—Background Chk   Page 1
         Charles Case (aka: Hos), (43),
   Head of Security, Rynerson Enterprises, Inc.

- Recruited out of college directly into FBI.
  No way to penetrate their files, but through
  a contact in Washington determined that CC
  was well liked and left under good circum-
  stances. Supposedly, BJR made an offer he
  couldn't refuse.
- Loves his job and is good at it. A workaholic.
- Owns a townhouse in Henderson.
    (Provided by Rynerson as part of
    employment package.)
- Never married, but lives with long-term
  partner: Dawn Maro, an agent with the US
  Marshals Office, who transferred from New
  York to Las Vegas when CC moved to LV. (A
  step down, so it must be serious.)
- According to NV Gaming records, he pulls
  down over 250 a year.
- Drinks only at social events. Doesn't gamble—
  ever.
[The guy's squeaky clean. Whatever his faults
(and he's a man, so of course he has some),
they're well hidden.]

A Boy Scout. Not much Simon didn't already know or
suspect.

Leo Geske (63), K&R Specialist, EDK Insurance
             Company, Los Angeles.

- Has worked for EDK twenty-nine years. Perfect record. Set to retire at EOY.
- Well thought of, though considered a "loner," and doesn't socialize with coworkers.
- Described as "nerdish" and "timid."
- Widower. Wife (Helen) of thirty-two years passed away in '96. No children.
- Home in Pasadena. Paid for. No other debt.
- Doesn't drink. Doesn't gamble. Doesn't take drugs. (Boring!!) (Simon, K&R, in case you didn't know, stands for kidnapping and ransom! What the hell have you gotten yourself involved in? You do remember EJ?)

Mr. Milquetoast. No surprises, but he should have realized Lara would pick up on the K&R thing. No, sweetheart, I have not forgotten Eth Jäger.

Tammi Rynerson (29), wife (#4) of BJR

- Attended Fresno State (2 yrs. only)
- Ms. Citrus 1995
- Worked as an "Account Facilitator" for LV Advertising, the company that handles local advertising for the Sand Castle.
    Met BJR and facilitated wife #3 out the door.
- A health nut. Doesn't drink.
- Home in Pasadena. Paid for. No other debt.
- Likes clothes. Likes being Mrs. Jake Rynerson.

(Apparently BJR has learned his lesson. Prenup is said to be "bulletproof.")

Little Miss Honeybee, what you see is what you get. He clicked over to the second page, and the two people he was most interested in.

Anthony (Tony) Saladino (35), Attorney
Managing Director of Here-to-Help Legal Aid

* Husband of Kyra Rynerson
* Joined a big DC firm directly out of law school, gave it six years, hated it, and opened Here-to-Help, a nonprofit storefront operation that provides pro bono legal services to the indigent.
* Moderate home, with moderate mortgage, in moderate area of DC.
* Two car payments, plus a substantial payment on a 1983 Beechcraft Baron B-55. (Apparently they don't receive any financial help from BJR. What's with that?)
* Social drinker. Wine only. No other vices.
* Loves animals and kids, but doesn't have any (kids).
* Supposedly faithful and committed to his wife.
(Damn, he sounds like a good one. I could even contribute the kids.)

Tony certainly looked like one of the good guys. Loved animals and kids and provided free legal services to the poor. Not the type obsessed with money. Either Jake was wrong about his son-in-law, or Tony had a dark side that didn't show on paper.

Caitlin Wells (41), Administrative Assistant to
BJR, Rynerson Enterprises, Inc.

* Grew up in Odessa, Texas (same as BJR)
* Attended Midland Junior College (didn't
  start until the age of 21)
* Transferred to Stanford and graduated, cum
  laude, with a degree in business.
* Went to work for BJR directly out of college.
* Owns a small condo in Summerlin, TPC Canyons
  course.
* According to NV Gaming records, she pulls
  down over 500 a year. (I need a raise!!)
* Never married. No children. Works 14–16
  hours a day, never takes a vacation.
* Social drinker. Never gambles.

(Superwoman, no doubt about it, but there was
something missing from her background, a hole
between the time she graduated HS and started
at MJC.)

Caitlin certainly didn't need money—*$500,000 a year!*—
that was a shocker. The woman certainly didn't flaunt her
success. The *something missing* from her background
didn't especially bother him. She was a teenager back
then—probably got into trouble, did her penance, and had
her record expunged. Happened all the time.

When he looked up, the object of his thoughts was
standing in the doorway of her bedroom—no makeup, no
jewelry, no shoes, and not much in the way of clothing.
She looked more like a teenager than a forty-one-year-old
business executive. Dressed for comfort in a beige sum-

mer dress that hit her mid-thigh, with spaghetti shoulder straps, he could almost see her jumping out of bed, slipping on a pair of bikini panties and dropping the dress over her head—ten seconds, good to go. She offered a smile, the result dampened by the strain of waiting. "You hungry, Simon Leonidovich?"

He wasn't—unusual for his physicality—and a phenomenon he didn't care to tempt. "No. You?"

She slouched against the door frame. "Not really. But I'm depressed. I eat when I'm depressed."

"Obviously you don't get depressed often."

That brought a smile—undampened. "I'm a psychological abnormality."

A psychological abnormality? It might have just popped out, but was clearly one of those subconscious utterances that meant something. "Oh?"

She took a deep breath and straightened, as if physically trying to fight off the melancholy. "Forget I said anything. I'm just blabbering."

He knew better. "Give it up, Wells." He gave her what Lara called his *irresistible boyish grin*, as if he were only trying to lighten the mood. "I'm *especially* interested in your *abnormalities.*"

She shrugged, padded across the room, and plopped down into a chair across from him. "It's nothing. Really."

He forced himself to concentrate on her face, not to think about that flash of white when she folded her feet up beneath her tight little butt. He hadn't been with a woman since Pilár Montez—hadn't wanted to be—but that absence of desire had suddenly become past tense. "I demand to know your secrets, Wells. What exactly is this *psychological abnormality* with which you're afflicted?" He just hoped it didn't involve kidnapping and an uncontrollable desire for wealth. On the other hand, an unnatural desire to get naked and play hide-and-seek with a middle-aged, slightly overweight, suddenly horny suitemate would be a very acceptable psychic aberration. Are you listening, God? *Pray for us sinners now at the time of our lust.*

"What are you grinning about, Leonidovich?"

Uh-oh. "Was I grinning?"

"You were. A very nasty grin, I might add."

"Nasty?"

"Lascivious."

"Lascivious? Are you sure?"

"Downright dirty."

Damn, his defensive line was crumbling fast, time to go on offense. "Then I must have been thinking about you, Ms. Wells."

"Oh? And what exactly—" She hesitated, scrutinizing him with those gray dazzlers, then shook her head and laughed. "I don't think I'll ask that question."

Bad decision, just when things were beginning to bubble. "Good decision. So . . . you were about to explain this psychological abnormality."

"I told you, it's nothing."

He sat back, crossed his arms, and waited.

And she waited, a good two minutes, then with a good-natured shrug gave up the battle. "Okay, okay. I took a battery of tests once. IQ, Rorschach, MMPI. You know what I'm talking about."

Indeed, though what she referred to as a *battery of tests* sounded more like a full-blown psychological evaluation. *But why?* He suspected it had something, or everything, to do with that *something missing* from her background. "Sure, I know exactly what you're talking about."

"I was allowed to read the evaluation. Very impressive. Nailed me perfectly. But there was one statement that struck me as odd. Something I've never forgotten. 'Depression and anxiety are conspicuously absent in this individual.' That just blew me away."

"Why, you think it was wrong?"

"No, not at all, I think it was dead-on. I hardly ever get depressed. Or euphoric, for that matter. Not too high, not too low."

"I don't understand, so why were you surprised?"

"It was the way they wrote it—*conspicuously absent*—as if that were a bad thing. What's wrong with even-tempered? Isn't that better than moody?" She lifted her hands from her lap and gave them a little ironic toss. "Maybe not. Maybe I'm just a cyborg. Dull and boring."

Though he had to believe a little manic exuberance—such as throwing off one's clothes and having a little un-inhibited sex—would not have been a bad thing, he could hardly think of Caitlin Wells as a cyborg. "I think you're misinterpreting the statement."

"How's that?"

"You're being measured against—" He threw up some quotation marks with his fingers. "The norm."

"And?"

"And you *don't fit* the norm. Which you should not assume to be a bad thing. In this case, *conspicuously absent* is a good thing."

She cocked her head, unconvinced.

"And then of course there's the flawed evaluation factor?"

She smiled, just a little, suspecting that he was feeding her a line. "I'm listening."

"The people who evaluate those tests are all psychiatrists and psychologists."

"So?"

He hesitated, trying out different words in his head. "I've never met one who wasn't psychoneurotic."

"Psychoneurotic?"

"That's a clinical term. Loosely translated it means fucked-up."

There was an empty heartbeat, then a chuckle. "So

that's the flawed evaluation factor—that the doctors are sicker than the patients?"

"Absolutely, who else but some half-crazy shrink could come up with 'depression and anxiety are conspicuously absent in this individual.' That's about the dumbest thing I ever heard."

She laughed. "It is kind of stupid when you think about it."

Good, she felt better, he felt better, but he still didn't know why she had undergone the evaluation. *Something missing.* He wanted to know, but had a strong feeling that asking would not get him the answer or advance his chances into either the heart or the bed of Ms. Caitlin Wells. "Completely stupid. You don't seem the least depressed to me."

"See, that's the thing, even when I'm feeling bad I don't tumble off the cliff. My depression is more like a mild case of PMS."

"And you're depressed because . . . ?" Of course he knew what the answer should be, but he still wanted to hear it.

She looked as if he'd slapped her, the muscles in her jaw flexing. "What the hell do you think? It's been . . . ?

"Thirty-nine hours."

"Right. Thirty-nine hours. They promised to release her within twelve. How much longer are we going to sit around here hoping she's going to walk through that door?" Tears crept into the corners of her eyes and she blinked them away. "Kyra's dead and you know it."

He reached over and took her hands. "We don't know that."

"But you believe it."

He could have, it certainly made sense, but for no logical reason he refused to accept the possibility. "I really don't. I think we're going to find her."

Some out-of-sync vibration pulsed between her fingers

and his. "What do you mean, *find her*? We're not even *looking* for her."

"I didn't mean it like that." He wasn't prepared, not yet, to tell her about the fingerprints and his hopes of identifying the Duckman. "I meant, I think we're still going to find her *alive.*"

"Oh." She sat back, gently removing her hands from his. "Of course that's what—" The distinctive chirp of her cell phone interrupted. "Damn." She jumped to her feet and disappeared back into the bedroom.

Though he couldn't make out the words, he could tell from her voice it was Jake. She was back in less than five minutes, her expression a mixture of surprise and disbelief. "There's been a development." She took a chair at the end of the table.

Development, that word again, but judging from her expression it didn't qualify as a catastrophe. Maybe another body part—but not a body. "What's happened?"

"To start with, Jake gave Tammi the boot."

"What!"

"She told her personal trainer about Kyra. Jake found out and went ballistic. He called in the lawyers and five hours later Number Four was out the door."

"You make it sound like a country-western, stomp-on-your-heart tearjerker: 'Number Four was out the door.' So that's it? No second chance? Marriage over?"

"Exactly. Jake has marital dissolution down to a science."

"Unbelievable." So much so that he suspected Jake had used Tammi's indiscretion, as serious as it was, as an excuse to clear his path to Billie, who might be more receptive to his attentions once Tammi had vacated the premises. "Okay, so who did the trainer tell?"

"Nobody. He was smart enough to go to Charles with the story. He now has a permanent management job in the Castle spa. He'll keep his mouth shut."

"And what about little Miss Honeybee, what's to keep her from selling her story to the tabloids?"

Caitlin's mouth went a bit slack, as if caught between expressions. "Little Miss Honeybee?"

Whoops. "What can I say, the first time I saw her she came buzzing in like a bee, wearing gold sneakers and a gold lamé workout suit."

Caitlin nodded slowly, as if recalling the image. "And what cute little nickname do you have for me?"

"Who said it was cute?"

"Touché. You are quick, Leonidovich."

Quick enough to know it was time to change the subject. "So . . . what's to prevent the late Number Four from blabbing."

"The settlement. Jake is always generous with his exes. He's being especially so with Tammi."

"Salve for a guilty conscience."

"Of course. He never should have married her and he knows it. Even so, there would be no nostalgic forgiveness for a second indiscretion. That would violate the terms of their settlement and Tammi would lose everything."

"That should do it, all right. You said *to start with.* I assume there's more?"

"There's been a second demand for money."

Simon wasn't sure what to expect, but that wasn't it, and for a few seconds he couldn't decide what it meant: good or bad. Kyra hadn't been released, that was bad, but the kidnappers had to know any additional payment would require another proof-of-life, which meant she was still alive, and that was good. *Very good.* "How much?"

"Seven million."

Damn. She made it sound like pocket change. "Leo warned us that this could happen if Jake appeared too anxious to pay."

"Yes, but that's not why they're demanding more." She hesitated as if looking for the right words, then seemed to give up the search and just spit it out. "They found out the money was worthless."

Simon tried to restrain his feelings of shock and betrayal, but couldn't. "Worthless! Are you telling me I was risking my neck for play money and no one bothered to mention it?"

Caitlin held up her hands, as if to ward off an attack. "It wasn't play money, and I didn't know."

He took a breath and counted to five, forcing his temper back into its cage. "I'm listening."

"Charles convinced Jake that the bills should be photographed and recorded. If the kidnappers reneged on their promise to release Kyra, the information would be released to every bank, casino, and large money-handling operation in the world."

"I'm missing something here." He made a quick calculation. "That's over fifteen thousand out-of-sequence bills. What good would that do?"

"Except they *weren't* out of sequence. There were actually fifty different sequential groups. The bills were randomly sorted and banded. Charles figured a person would have to record the numbers and sort them on a computer before it became apparent the money was divided into sequential batches."

Clever. "Okay, I'm with you."

"If the kidnappers failed to release Kyra it was Jake's intention to offer a million-dollar reward for any information leading to their capture. Anyone who handles large bills would be watching for those numbers. A person might be able to pass one or two, here and there, but even that would be a risk. No fence in the world would dare touch the stuff. The money would be virtually worthless."

"Sounds like a pretty good plan. So what happened?"

"The kidnappers claim to have discovered the sequential numbering. Now they want another five million, plus two more in *penalties.*"

"They sound like bankers. You said *claim to.*"

"It would have been virtually impossible without a computer. So unless they had some reason to check, why go to the trouble? That's one helluva big job, entering over fifteen thousand serial numbers."

Simon didn't like where this was leading, though he wasn't completely surprised. "You're saying someone gave them the information."

"Yes."

"Who exactly knew about this scheme?"

"Initially, only Jake and Charles and Billie. And Arnel Dittmar; he helped Charles photograph and band the money."

"Initially . . . ?"

"When Kyra hadn't been released after twenty-four hours Jake wanted to distribute the list of bills. Charles thought he should wait. Once the list went out, the world would know. Billie agreed with Charles, so Jake called me, wanting my opinion."

"Which was?"

"I couldn't decide. I didn't have a lot of faith that Kyra was still alive, but if she was, I knew that sending out the list would be like signing her death certificate. At the same time Jake told me, he told Leo Geske. His company was on the hook for two of the five million."

"And what did Leo advise?"

"He couldn't. It was up to his company, but before he could get an answer he received a call from one of the kidnappers."

The Duckman, Simon would have bet his life. "Same guy, I assume."

"No, someone new, according to Leo. Younger. More sophisticated. Very angry."

It was all Simon could do not to show his surprise, though it completely blew the wheels off his two-person theory. "I'd like to hear that tape."

"No tape. The call came in early this morning, directly to Leo's cellular."

"How the hell did they get that number?"

She spread her hands in a helpless gesture. "Another leak? I don't know. We've all got his number."

"What about Tammi? Did she know about any of this?"

"No. Only the six I mentioned. You're number seven."

Mentally, Simon crossed Tammi's name off his list and added the name of Arnel Dittmar. "And anyone they told."

"Everyone knows better."

He wanted to believe that, but experience told him that most people liked being *on the inside*, a satisfaction that could only be enjoyed by sharing their *inside* secrets. All it would take would be one person whispering their big secret to someone else and the information would expand exponentially through the backrooms of the Sand Castle. "Is Arnel Dittmar married?"

Her answer came back slow and cautious. "Yes."

"And you don't think he and his wife engage in pillow talk?"

"For all I know they sleep in separate rooms, but I don't see how something Arnel *might* have said to his wife could get back to the kidnappers."

Right, not very likely. "What about Dawn Maro? You don't think Charles would tell his girlfriend about his clever idea to track the money? You don't think she would want to share her boyfriend's brilliance with her buddies over at the U.S. Marshal's office?"

A look of suspicion flashed across Caitlin's face, quick as a shuffle of cards. "How would you know about Dawn Maro?"

He glanced away, feigning embarrassment, though he had purposely let the name slip. "I must have heard Charles mention her."

"No. Charles *never* talks about his personal life." She

leaned forward, boring in with her gray eyes. "What are you up to, Leonidovich?"

"Look, I've never been comfortable with the *inadvertent leak* scenario." He frowned and shook his head, as if disgusted with himself. "I thought maybe I should check out the people who had the information to leak."

"Check out?" Her nostrils flared, as though she'd just caught the scent of something nasty. "Just how did you go about that, Leonidovich?"

Ouch, the way she snapped his name, she might as well have said *pond scum*. "Don't get your panties in a twist, Wells. I didn't go rummaging through anyone's garbage if that's what you think. I just had someone run a little background check. Nothing more."

"Meaning you divulged to *someone* outside the group what's going on."

"Absolutely not! My office manager ran the check. She doesn't know why."

Caitlin extended her hand, palm up. "Show me."

Exactly what he wanted to do. "Of course." He pulled up Lara's email and printed both the message and the first page of the background document. He handed her the message first. "As you can see, she doesn't even know I'm in Colombia. It's obvious she has no idea why I requested the information."

Caitlin read the email carefully, her anger visibly melting away. "This is your sister, the woman I talked to on the phone when I first called you?"

"Yes."

"What's this funny word at the end? With the squared-off, upside-down U?"

"It's Russian. It means *so long*."

She seemed to think about that, then nodded. "Okay, let's see the report."

He handed her the page, carefully watching her face as she read. Her lips curled when she came to Lara's comment about Charles's hidden faults. "I like your sister."

"She reminds me of you."

"Oh?" She continued to read. "How so?"

"Brass balls."

That brought her head up. "You think I have brass balls?"

"Sorry, I misspoke. Titanium."

She smiled and resumed reading. "That's more like it." She paused again when she finished with Leo Geske. "Who's EJ?"

"Eth Jäger." *May his name be tattooed forever on the buttocks of Satan.* "He's the guy who kidnapped Lara during the Mira-loss thing."

"In prison, right?"

"Right."

"Has Lara, uh—" She glanced up. "—gotten over it?"

"Not completely," he admitted, "but she's working on it."

"Good for her. I'd like to meet her someday."

That was all he needed, tag-team female abuse. "Handling one of you is hard enough. The two of you . . . I don't even want to think about that."

"You think you *handle* me?"

"Don't twist my words, Wells."

"I'm not twisting your words, Leonidovich. You said—" She made a face, that expression that only a woman can make—*Men!*—and turned back to the document. "Forget it."

Amen and hallelujah, stamp my tongue OUT OF ORDER and seal my lips with Krazy Glue. "With pleasure."

She finished with Tammi Rynerson and handed back the sheet. "Nothing there I didn't already know. Where's the rest?"

"The rest?"

"What about Kyra? You probably think she set this up to get back at her father."

"I considered the possibility. Something you've obviously thought about yourself."

"Of course," she answered, "we've all considered it. And I don't believe it. No matter how Kyra feels about Jake, she would never put Tony or her mother through something like this."

He had reached the same conclusion, for different reasons. "I agree. The whole thing with the Luis Acosta impostor was too elaborate and well planned for a hoax."

"Yes, I've thought about that too. Now where's the rest, Leonidovich, and don't give me any of that 'ah shucks, what are you talking about' routine. I work for Big Jake Rynerson, the master of that good-ol'-boy game."

He laughed, couldn't help himself. "Ah shucks, you caught me there, darlin'. I didn't think you'd want to read about yourself."

"Ah, but I do."

Which, of course, was the object of the exercise—reading and hopefully filling in the *something missing* from her background. He printed the last sheet of Lara's report and handed it over. "That's all of it."

She read slowly, not commenting until she finished the entire document. "That's Tony all right. Like Lara says, he's one of the good ones."

"What about that Wells broad? She makes one hell of a salary for an administrative assistant."

She smiled, just a little, her expression one of sly amusement, as if she understood the punch line to a joke he didn't get. "Would it upset your male ego if I told you her annual bonus exceeded her salary?"

"You make over a million a year! Are you kidding me?"

"Am I laughing?"

"Well, damn, I guess I was wrong about you, Wells. Your balls aren't titanium, they're gold."

She let loose with a rib-scraping laugh, her gray eyes dancing. "Believe me, I earn it." She tapped her finger on the report. "You read that? I'm on call twenty-four, seven. No husband. No children. *No fucking life!*"

Was she simply making a good-natured point, or was there some genuine resentment hidden beneath the words? "Sounds like you need a man, Wells."

"You know any good ones, Leonidovich?"

"You did say you made over a million a year?"

"I did."

Trying his best to imitate the suavity of 007, Simon slid off his chair and onto a knee. "Ms. Caitlin Wells, will you marry me?"

She tilted her head at him, a small grin curling the edge of her lips. "What about that *something missing* in my background? You want to marry a woman without knowing her secrets?"

"I didn't ask."

"No, but that's what this was all about. That's why you showed me the report, hoping I'd fill in the gaps."

Damn, brains and balls—a dangerous combination. "I'm down here on one knee, Wells. Are you accusing me of disingenuous intent?"

"I'm accusing you of acting like an idiot."

He slipped back into his chair, giving her his best hang-dog look. "You're a real heartbreaker, Wells."

"And you should be ashamed of yourself for trying to steal a poor woman's money."

"Now there's a contradiction in terms if I ever heard one." He gave her a wolfish grin. "But I have to admit, I do admire your assets."

She rolled her eyes. "Do women actually fall for that innocent charm of yours, Leonidovich?"

Innocent charm—a good time for a little flanking maneuver. "So what exactly is your role in the fiefdom of Rynerson?"

"It's simple. Everyone reports to me, I report to Jake."

"I didn't realize you had that much responsibility. That's a much bigger job than . . . uh—"

"Than my title would indicate?"

"Exactly. No wonder you earn those big bucks."

"Jake is a visionary and builder but he doesn't like to deal with the day-to-day stuff. He looks to the future, I take care of the present."

Power without title, was she bitter about that? "Very impressive."

She shrugged, as if it were no big deal. "It's what Jake hoped Kyra would do. I'm the daughter substitute."

Substitute daughter. Power without title. Daughter's secret friend. He felt like a chimp trying to make sense of the alphabet; there were too many complications to be logical. And, he had a feeling, there was one more complication yet to be added to the mix: some messed-up past relationship with the big man himself. "So"—*the big so*—"how did you meet Jake?"

"I don't know you well enough for that story, Leonidovich."

"Fair enough," though he felt certain it would explain that *something missing* from her background. "I wouldn't mind getting to know you better, Wells."

"I thought you might—" She shook her head deliberately, as if erasing the possibility. "But that's not going to happen."

It took an effort, but he managed to hide his disappointment. "Oh, why's that?"

"Jake wants me back. I've already notified the crew."

When it came to female rejections, that was one he could live with. "And me?"

"You wait here. Leo is negotiating a time and place for the second payment."

"What about another proof-of-life?"

"It's been requested."

Requested—it sounded more like a bow and a scrape

than a demand. "I won't make the payment without it."

"You're singing to the choir, Leonidovich. It's Jake's money and his daughter; he's the one you have to convince."

"I'll call him."

"Don't bother." She smiled. "He'll be here tomorrow."

CHAPTER TWENTY-TWO

Somewhere in South America

Sunday, 9 November 15:36:46 GMT −0500

At first Kyra thought she might be imagining things, that she was only suffering from irrational paranoia, but now she was sure; the pit bull hadn't moved its eyes in ten minutes, staring right at her tiny pinhole, its eyes to hers, as hard and straight as a bar of steel. It couldn't *really* see her, as a zoologist she knew that—a dog's crepuscular vision was less attuned to detail than a human's—but it could sense her, could calibrate the exact spot she was standing. As if to prove it, every couple of minutes the beast would emit one of its low, vibrating growls, barely loud enough to be heard, but enough to raise the hair on her arms.

El Pato grunted and rolled onto his back, his naked body damp with oily perspiration. It was the first time he had slept during the day and she had a feeling that something extremely bad would happen when he recovered from the liquor. After the bad-news call, he just sat there, naked, drinking *Aguardiente Antioqueño*—a clear fiery liquor distilled from sugar cane—and staring angrily at his pile of money, as if it were worthless.

Over the next two hours there had been three more calls, El Pato becoming more belligerent and drunk with each one. Twice, he screamed into his phone, assuring his partner that the "Rynerson bitch *todavía está viviendo.*" Both times, in two separate calls, he had used the same words: *todavía está viviendo. Still alive.* The final call had been the most disturbing. Though she hadn't been able to follow much of the conversation—El Pato's speech having digressed into outbursts of slurred Spanish—she understood enough to know he wanted to send her back in *pedacitos*. Small pieces.

One thing she now knew with absolute certainty, there was no reason to fantasize about being released. He intended to kill her—always had—it was only a matter of time. She needed to do something, no matter how desperate, and she needed to do it now. *But how?* She would never have a chance to finish the wall and that left only the door.

She closed her eyes, reviewing the exact sequence of the exchange. It was always the same. Exactly. Never once had he opened the door until she had placed her waste bucket near the door and returned to the cot. Then he would slide the pass-through closed, open the door, place an empty bucket and food tray on the floor, pick up the used bucket, and close the door. Seven, maybe eight seconds. Always the same. But, there was a moment, a few seconds, when he couldn't see her—between the time he closed the slot and opened the door. Enough time for her to scramble up next to the wall, ready to bolt through the opening. If she could get past him, she could outrun him, she was sure of that, but how could she get past him? The man was built like a tank and never stepped beyond the door. She would have to lure him in, make him believe she was sick or dying.

And now was the time, when the liquor had slowed his mind and reflexes. A long shot, but the only shot she had. Somehow she would have to avoid those quick hands.

She reviewed in her mind the vulnerable points: ears, eyes, nose, groin. But if she got close enough to poke or kick, he would be close enough to grab. She needed to catch him by surprise, make him blink, blind him if she could. She glanced around, but no magic weapon materialized out of the shadows. Only the . . .

. . . only the waste bucket.

El Pato grunted and rolled onto his side, starting to wake up. A wave of nausea welled up from the pit of her stomach, coating the back of her throat with the bitter, coppery taste of fear. Now that the time had come, she was having second thoughts.

Serious second thoughts.

Second thoughts for the millionth time.

Maybe she should wait. If he left again it would take only a few more hours to finish off the last toeholds. Why take the risk now? Why antagonize him? Maybe she was wrong, not thinking straight, maybe he didn't intend to kill her.

She shifted her focus to the dog, staked next to her grave. *Yeah, right.* Who was she kidding? Of course he intended to kill her. Or let the dog do it, so he could watch. He would like that, probably jack himself into sexual nirvana watching the beast rip her guts apart and kill her baby. *No,* she couldn't wait, she had to do it now, before he noticed the dog's attention and discovered her wall of holes, while his brain was struggling to metabolize the liquor, his quick hands not so quick.

She glanced at the window. Twenty, maybe thirty minutes of daylight. Running naked through the jungle at night was less than appealing; she would probably filet half the skin off her body, but the darkness would offer as much protection as it did risk.

What if he released the dog? *No,* it was a killer, not a hunter, and would turn on El Pato before it even thought to come after her. If she made it past those quick hands. If she made it out the door. If she made it into the trees before he shot her. *If—if—if. Lots of ifs.*

El Pato grunted again and pushed himself into a sitting

position. He sat there, on the edge of his narrow bed, elbows to knees, cradling his head in his hands, looking hungover and mean, his skin the color of wet clay. It was all she could do to control the fear working its way through her body, but she knew this was her opportunity and she had to try. He would get up, check on her, and then it would happen, he would come in, or not. It would be over in seconds—for good or bad. *Seconds.* She took a deep breath, trying to calm the butterflies fluttering through her stomach and reproducing at an exponential rate. *Seconds.*

Again, she measured the distance from her cell to the outside door. A straight shot, just beyond the reach of the dog—five, six steps at most. *Three seconds.* The door opened inward and had an old-fashioned slide bolt, but it would be open and she crossed it off her mental checklist. Pull open the door. *Two seconds.* Run, straight for the trees. *Four, maybe five seconds.* Ten seconds total. Ten seconds between her cell and freedom. Ten seconds between life and death. She glanced behind her. Everything was set, the waste bucket beneath the cot, the thin blanket draped over the side to conceal it. The stench was there, but it was always there, hanging in the humid air like a black fog.

El Pato leaned forward, coughed up a huge glob of phlegm, and spit it onto the dirt floor, between his feet. She took a deep breath and closed her eyes, trying to control her fear. Now that it was time, she wasn't sure she could do it. She could think about it, plan it, but when the moment came . . .

Of course you can do it! The harsh words came from somewhere deep in her memory, her father's voice, the first day she took flying lessons. *You can do any damn thing you want. The only question is whether you want it bad enough. You got the guts, little girl?* At the time she hated him for saying it—*You got the guts, little girl?*—but of course he was right. She saw that now, the way he pushed her to do things on her own—not to choose the easy way, to fall back on the Rynerson money or name.

When she opened her eyes El Pato was up, pulling on a pair of gaucho pants. He suddenly paused and looked over at the dog as it emitted another one of its low-humming growls, then he turned and looked directly at the spot where she was standing. *Jesus God*, she didn't dare blink, afraid he might see the movement. The moment seemed to last forever, then his gaze shifted back to the buttons on his pants and she quickly covered the hole with a small piece of dirt, slipped back onto her cot, and stretched out in exactly the same position. *You got the guts, little girl?"*

A moment later she heard the door open, the outside door, then the splatter of urine as he relieved himself in the underbrush. The wait—not knowing exactly what she would do, what he would do if she failed—seemed unbearable, like she was trapped in some kind of reverse vortex, the world stuck on its axis while her body spun wildly out of control. Her heart felt as if it might explode out of her chest, the sound of it pulsing up her spine and filling her head with a thunderous, white noise. Then the door slammed and everything went silent as she held her breath, listening, every moment stretching into infinity, every sound magnified: a *CLICK*, the scrape of his shuffling feet as he came across the room, another *CLICK* as he unsnapped the lock on the pass-through, the scrape of wood as he pushed it open, the sound of his snotty breath, and the pressure of his dark eyes as his gaze crawled across her pale skin.

"Eh!" He screamed the word, trying to wake her, but she expected it and managed not to flinch. *"Oiga!"*

She continued to hold her breath, not because she intended to play dead, but because she couldn't unlock her diaphragm, the fear paralyzing every muscle in her body.

"Oiga!" He screamed the word again, this time the tone

more concerned than angry. When she didn't respond, he shoved the pass-through closed and snapped the lock. *Time to move,* in that moment of blindness, before he unlocked and opened the door, scoop up the waste bucket, flatten herself against the wall, and when he stepped inside . . .

You got the guts, little girl?

No, she didn't. The most she could do was take a breath and wait. She heard the lock snap and the door open. She heard him take one step—stop—a long pause, perhaps waiting for his eyes to adjust—then two more steps. But not toward her. She wanted to look, a tiny peek, but didn't have the nerve. Then she heard the scrape of his hands, sliding over the wall—her climbing wall. Her ladder to freedom. In that instant she realized she was caught—she had missed her chance, squandered her opportunity—and knew the retribution would be swift and brutal. She forced herself to crack an eyelid. She could see his back, his hands moving back and forth across the wall, searching in the dim light. Everything from that moment seemed to happen in a haze, at half speed: swinging her legs over the edge of the cot, snatching up the waste bucket, his sudden awareness and turn . . .

She caught him square in the face, the smell of excrement and urine and rotten food exploding like a bomb.

Then she was running, through the first door—everything in slo-mo, just like her dream, feet buried in sand—conscious of his bellowing roar as he hit the empty bucket and fell. She could feel the dog off to her left, snarling and straining against its chain, but she never took her eyes off the door and the handle. *Almost there.* She reached out—just like she planned, not missing a beat, but aware of the seconds ticking by, the sound of El Pato as he scrambled to right himself from the slop—then she had the handle in her right hand, gave it a twist, and yanked. She nearly pulled her arm out of its socket, the door frozen in place, and in that moment remembered the *CLICK after* he shut the door and realized her mistake. She reached up and slammed the bolt aside—could hear El Pato closing the distance, a crazed bull in full charge. She twisted the handle again, yanked open the door, and leaped forward—only two steps and she'd be out the door, a dodge to the side and he would never catch her. *Going to make it.* She pushed forward off her back foot, accelerating as hard as she could through the open doorway. *One more step. Almost there . . .*

He landed on her with his entire body, and in that instant before she hit the ground and everything went black, she knew she was dead—the only question was how long it would take and how much she would need to suffer.

Consciousness, when it finally came, was like drifting upward through a deep pool of murky water, the sound of El Pato's voice muffled and indistinct. The landscape slowly solidified into a grainy patch of dark green and Kyra realized she was on her cot, on her stomach, staring at the canvas. She turned toward the dim light coming through the open doorway and could see the dog, staring at her like she was a burger and fries, its next Happy Meal. El Pato was somewhere beyond, on his cellular, his voice angry. She tried to move but couldn't, and realized she was tied down, spread-eagled, her hands and feet strapped to separate corners of the cot. Tilting her head, she could see the window and the darkness beyond, so knew she'd been unconscious for some time. She could feel a lump on her forehead, where she'd hit the ground, but other than a dull, fuzzy ache felt reasonably okay. As okay as one could feel lying naked and stretched like a piece of cowhide waiting to be skinned.

She couldn't stop herself from playing the mental video, as if in the replay she could magically alter the outcome—will herself one more step, one more second of time. *So close.* If only she had paid more attention, remembered that extra *CLICK,* gone for the lock first, but no matter how many times she ran through the images, the outcome was always the same, and no amount of what-ifs would ever change it.

She needed a new plan. A how-to-die-gracefully plan. If she could have held her breath and killed herself, she would have, but all she could do was lie there, engulfed in the smell of her own waste, and wait, wondering what kind of gruesome torture El Pato had chosen to gratify his sick mind. She could scream and cry, but knew that would only excite him and prolong the torture. Beg? *No,* that too would amuse him.

Had she believed in God, she would have prayed. Isn't that what most people did at the moment of death? Unable to face the inevitable, they succumbed to the desperate hope they would survive in another, more perfect dimension. But she didn't believe, never had, and wasn't about to add hypocrisy to her list of sins. *Forgive me, Daddy.* Somehow, she knew he would. Anthony too. She hoped he found someone—someone who would give him the love and children he deserved.

It wasn't until El Pato stepped through the door, momentarily blocking the light, that she realized the Grim Reaper had arrived. He had changed clothes and taken some kind of bath, his hair still wet. He stood there, holding her waste bucket, looking down at her with his dark eyes, his expression a mixture of contempt and restrained anger, like a schoolyard bully who'd just been told to "play by the rules." *Rules,* she had a feeling, laid down by his partner. Then he hoisted the bucket above her and emptied it across her back. She closed her eyes, thinking *acid,* but almost immediately realized it was water. River water, from the smell. For whatever reason he wanted her clean—perhaps thinking she didn't make a suitable appetizer for the dog. Two more buckets quickly followed.

When he returned the fourth time he had a lantern in one hand and what looked like pruning shears in the other. She immediately flashed on his threat to send her back in small pieces—*pedacitos*—and had to struggle not to let him hear the panic that threatened to send her heart into arrhythmic failure. "You don't have to do that. I won't try to run again. I give you my word." Even to herself, the words sounded hollow and foolish.

He laughed, a kind of mirthless bark. "No, *princesa*, you will not run again."

He sat down on the edge of the cot, facing her feet. She couldn't twist her head far enough to see, but assumed he meant to start with her toes, to make her suffer through the *small pieces,* before letting his canine alter ego finish the job. Despite her determination not to struggle—what was the use—she couldn't stop herself when she saw the shears, but could do nothing but curl her toes. Then she felt the cool steel of the shears close over the Achilles tendon of her left foot and realized it wasn't her toes that he wanted. "Please don't." Despite her determination to hide it, she could hear the fear. "Let me call my father. He'll give you anything you ask."

El Pato chuckled softly, the sound gruesome, the purr of a lunatic as he slowly closed the blades. She felt the skin separate and pull back, and in her mind could see the thick tendon exposed. Then she was screaming—not in pain, she felt only a tingling sensation—but to block out the very thought of what was happening. She actually heard the crunch of the blades as they started through the tendon, the sound traveling up the back of her legs and along her spine before exploding in her head. Then, when she thought it couldn't get worse, she heard the pop, like a large rubber band, as the tendon snapped back into her calf.

CHAPTER TWENTY-THREE

Cali, Colombia

Monday, 10 November 07:08:18 GMT –0500

Simon had just finished breakfast and was watching *CNN Headline News*—the only program available in English—when his cellular began to buzz, the vibrations moving it across the smooth granite counter that separated the kitchen from the dining room. He snatched it up just before it took a fatal dive into a sink of hot water. The number on the display was not one he recognized. "Hello."

"Buenos días, Bagman." Vic's familiar voice bounced through the stratosphere with a faint, distant echo. "I see you're still in Cali."

"Hey there, VicTheQuick. I feel like you've got a satellite strapped to my butt."

There was a moment of silence, the typical intercontinental delay, then the sound of Vic's amused chuckle. "Almost. As long as you're walking around with that cellular your ass is mine."

"What's up?"

"I've got your man."

The news was so unexpected it took him a moment to respond, as if his tongue had suddenly atrophied. "You found him! Really?"

"Whoa down there, Bagman. Identified—yes. Found—no."

"Of course. I just can't believe you *identified* him so fast."

"I'd like to tell you it was brilliance and diligence and a lot of hard work, but the computers did all the grunting and grinding. I ran the picture through our photo database and came up with nothing, but my friend at the Bureau was luckier. He was able to pull a full set of prints off that beer glass. We started with a very restricted search, South America only, and got a hit almost instantly."

"So the guy has a record?"

"No, that's why we didn't have a picture. But he's been on the International Wanted List for years."

"Wanted for what?" Not that he didn't have a good idea, *murder and mayhem* being high on the list of possibilities.

"The guy's a mercenary, you name it, he's done it. We know he's done some work for the cartels and he's been linked with FARC on a number of cases. I suspect that's what you're interested in . . . ?"

Simon ignored the probe, though of course he recognized the name as one of the pseudopolitical factions Geske had mentioned in connection with the Colombian kidnapping game. "FARC, what's that?"

"Don't play Simple Simon with me, Bagman, you know damn well who they are."

He wasn't going to lie, not to Vic, but he wasn't going to confirm what she suspected either. "What else can you tell me?"

She exhaled loudly, letting him know she wasn't fooled by his avoidance. "The guy's no genius, but he's good at what he does."

"Which is?"

"Whatever he's told to do. The guy's a fixer—works for the highest bidder."

No surprise. "So not the leader type?"

"I doubt if he's ever had an original thought in his life, but he's smart enough not to get caught."

"Can you send me the file?"

There was a long pause, then an unequivocal one-word answer. "No."

He didn't push, not wanting to compromise her position. "Okay, what's his name?"

"We don't have a name, that's one of the reason's he's never been picked up. All we have is his street name. El Pato."

The Duck, now that was a nickname that made sense. "You said one of the reasons."

"He never leaves any witnesses. You tangle with this guy, you end up dead."

"I'll keep that in mind."

"I'm serious, Simon, this is one bad dude. Don't go near the guy."

"I'll try not to get up close and personal," though that was exactly what he had in mind. "That's not much to go on. How can I find him?"

"Goddammit, Simon, did you just go deaf and dopey? Trust me, you don't *want* to find this guy. Now that we have a picture it's only a matter of time before he's picked up."

Unfortunately, time was not on the side of Kyra Rynerson. Even worse, if they picked up El Pato before they found her, they probably never would. "Can you sit on that picture for a few days? It's important, Vic. Really important."

"You idiot, you're going after him, aren't you?"

"I want to know where he is, yes, but I have no intention of messing with the guy. If I find him I'll let you know and you can be the hero."

"Okay," she answered after a slight pause. "I'll hold the picture three days. But that's it. After that I'm putting it out there."

He wanted a week, but before he could say anything they were interrupted by a sharp two-tone beep, indicating an incoming call. "Hold on a minute, let me see who that is."

"No, I won't hold on," she snapped back. "You're going to bitch about the three days and I don't want to hear it."

He could almost see her heels digging into the floor and knew better than to argue. "I'll call you the minute I know something."

"You better. Say hello to Big Jake for me."

"Damn, you even know who's calling me."

"I know everything, Bagman."

He started to say good-bye but she was already gone, her euphonic voice replaced by the gravelly twang of Big Jake's accent. "That you, Simon?"

"Good morning, Jake."

"You up and kickin' there, boy?"

"Up and dressed, anyway."

"Even better. I try to avoid naked men."

"Good policy. You here—already?"

"Just got in. Caught a little bunk time on the way down but I could sure use a big dark Colombian to get my heart started."

Assuming Jake wasn't looking for an aboriginal Amazon to be his next wife, Simon glanced over at the coffee machine—the pot was still half full. "Ready and waiting."

"Great, we'll be there . . . hold on a minute." There was the muffled sound of conversation, then Jake again. "Forget the coffee. Charles wants to keep moving. Meet you out front in five minutes."

"Of my hotel?"

"You can't miss us, we're in the fucking parade."

Parade? But before he could ask, Jake had disconnected.

Five minutes later Simon was at the curb, the street full of early-morning traffic—tiny European and Brazilian cars, a few big American models, motor scooters and taxis, buses and bikes—the worker bees heading off to do their thing. Nothing resembling a parade. Then he saw it, coming around the corner—*had to be*—a convoy of shiny black Humvees, three to be exact, the center one remodeled and stretched into some kind of hybrid limousine, the glass thick and dark. Though he didn't really expect Jake to be alone—the title of *Rich and Famous* came with baggage—the entourage of security did seem somewhat over the top. Before the wheels stopped moving all four doors on the lead and trail vehicles popped open and a detail of silent young men surrounded the center Hummer. The fact that they were all dressed in identical and bulky tan jackets only seemed to highlight the fact that they were heavily armed and wearing bulletproof vests. As the young men assumed defensive positions, the side door of the vehicle popped open and Charles poked his head out and smiled, his teeth white as chalk against his black skin. "Hey stranger, looking for a lift?"

"Good morning, Charles." Simon ducked inside and the door closed behind him—the solid *thunk* of reinforced steel. The street sounds instantly dampened to an indistinct murmur. Jake was sitting in a leather swivel chair facing forward, Charles in another facing back. Simon dropped into a third, creating a triangle. "What's with the army? Something happen I don't know about?"

Clearly perturbed, Jake aimed his prominent jaw at Charles. "Talk to Hos, I think he's been watchin' too many movies."

Charles shook his head slightly, as if the effort to explain was hardly worth the exertion. "It's bad enough he insists on coming down here, now he's bitching about the way I do my job."

"Even the President doesn't have this much damn security. It's embarrassin'."

"The President," Charles snapped, "isn't worth a few billion dollars." He looked at Simon, clearly seeking support. "I hired the best protection firm in the country. If they think this is what it takes to keep him safe in this damn city, who am I to argue?"

Relieved that the private army had nothing to do with

some negative turn of events, Simon tried to play mediator. "Charles is right, Jake, most businessmen down here don't go anywhere without a team of bodyguards."

The big man snorted, unconvinced. "You've only seen some of 'em. There's another Hummer-load guarding the puddle jumper."

"Puddle jumper?"

"That's Jake's *little* plane," Charles answered. "He doesn't like the whale."

"The puddle jumper is inconspicuous," Jake explained. "Nobody'd even know I's here if it wasn't for all this damn security."

A week earlier Simon might have agreed, but not now, not after witnessing how easily Vic could track a person's movements. And Big Jake Rynerson—not exactly popular with the current president—would certainly be on the administration's watch list. "Trust me, Jake, with or without the security, there are people who know where you are."

Charles threw up his hands. "Amen and hallelujah."

Jake glanced back and forth between Simon and his Head of Security. "What the hell is that supposed to mean?"

"It means," Charles snapped, losing patience with the argument, "that you're too damn big and rich and ugly not to be noticed."

There was a moment of hushed silence, then the lines around Jake's sad eyes crinkled with amusement. "Well, damn, I may be dumb as Gump, but I think ya won that battle, Hos."

Charles gave Simon a conspiratorial wink. "I'm taking lessons from Billie. Abuse the man and he folds up like a wet tortilla."

"Damned if ain't true," Jake admitted. "I got so many people kissing my ass I don't know what to do when someone puts up a fight." The furrow between his eyebrows deepened. "But if I don't get some coffee soon . . ."

"Take a left on Colombia Avenue," Simon suggested. "We can stop at one of the coffee stands along the river." Jake pressed the intercom button next to his chair, issued the order, and a moment later the mini caravan pulled into traffic.

Charles handed Simon a thin manila binder. "That's the forensic report on the Annie Hall note. Long and short, Kyra's thumbprint, no doubt about that, but they couldn't give us anything definitive on the dirt. It could have come from almost anywhere."

Simon nodded, not surprised.

"And here's the latest installment," Charles said, pushing a black duffel over next to Simon's feet, "seven million divided equally between U.S. and Swiss. Comes to forty-seven pounds, plus the pack. All yours."

Simon ignored the money, knowing that wasn't the real reason for Jake's impromptu visit to Colombia. "What are you doing here, Jake?"

"What? Well I . . . I just wanted to be here when Kyra's released, of course."

"That's it, nothing else I should know about?"

Not accustomed to someone questioning his motives, Big Jake's face darkened to the color of old bronze. "Now what kind of a tightfart question is that?"

"You didn't tell me about the sequential numbering—" Jake opened his mouth but Simon continued before the big man could defend himself. "And that's okay, I understand your reasoning. But if I'm stepping into a pile of shit, I'd sure appreciate a heads-up."

"What, it's not enough I wanna be here for my daughter?"

No, it wasn't, Simon knew there was more, but how did you accuse Big Jake Rynerson of holding back? "I just thought—"

Charles, who seemed amused at Jake's equivocation, shook his head, as though giving up on a stubborn child.

"Oh for God sake, Jake, the man's not stupid." He turned to Simon and grinned. "Billie threw his ass out."

The color in Jake's cheeks mottled from bronze to pink. "Now, Hos, you know that's not right, she didn't throw me out. Not exactly. It's just that . . . well—" Embarrassment tangled his tongue. "Well, she's upset about Tammi, that's all. Thinks it looks bad with just the two of us being there together at the hotel—like she had something to do with the breakup. I thought it might be a good idea if I skedaddled for a while."

Though the image of Billie tossing the big man out of his own hotel conjured up a rather humorous vision, Simon managed not to smile. "Okay. So I'm up to date. No more secrets?"

"Well now, there is one little thing—"

Simon waited; there was always one more *little thing*.

"—about that sequential numbering business. We didn't do that with the idea of tracing the money. No, sir, that was secondary. Believe me, Simon, I would never do anything to jeopardize my little girl's life. But after the FBI thing, we couldn't ignore the possibility of someone leaking inside information. And we knew if Kyra had overheard something, or even learned who that person was, she would never be released to tell her story. So, the numbering really had two purposes. If they didn't release her, we would then have a way to trace the money and find them. But more important, it was an insurance policy in case of a leak."

"You just lost me."

Charles picked up the explanation. "If there *was* a leak, and they found out the money was worthless, they would have no choice but to pretend they discovered the numbering on their own and demand a second payment."

Like a long-distance camera lens coming into focus, Simon could finally see the hidden details of their plan. "In which case you demand another proof-of-life."

"Exactly."

"Leaving them no choice but to keep Kyra alive."

Charles smiled, a small grin of satisfaction. "And we would know for sure that information was leaking out."

Leaking out. The words sounded far too passive, far too coincidental, for Simon's comfort. "I don't think we're dealing with some low-on-the-totem-pole tipster here. I think the main guy—or woman—" He let that hang for a second. "—is in Vegas. Someone close to you, Jake."

Jake started shaking his head before the last sentence cleared Simon's mouth. "Caity told me you've been narrowing down the list. And you might even be right about someone in Vegas pulling on the reins. But not someone close to me." His head shake ended with a final and resolute back-and-forth. "No way. I know my people."

Simon wasn't so sure. He had tried to discount the leaks as inadvertent, the timing as coincidence, but whenever he considered who knew what and when they knew it, the more everything pointed toward inside information. And more specifically, toward two people on the inside: Leo Geske and Caitlin Wells. "Then how do you explain these leaks?"

"Electronic surveillance," Jake answered quickly, as if anxious to defend his theory and discount the possibility of disloyalty within his inner circle. "Which fits perfectly with your theory of a Vegas connection. I'm convinced someone's been listening in on our plans."

"I thought your office got swept on a regular basis."

"Every week," Charles answered, "the entire floor. But that doesn't guarantee anything. If a network is shut down during a sweep it's likely to go undetected. It's even possible someone could be targeting the Fishbowl with a parabolic dish from another building."

"Those things can pick up conversation through glass?"

"Modern technology. Anything's possible."

It sounded more like science fiction, but when Simon thought about how easily Vic had tracked and recorded El Pato's phone conversations, he couldn't discount the possibility. "And you think it's okay to talk in here?" He nodded toward the driver and guard sitting beyond the privacy glass.

"That's a Cyrolon and glass laminate, over thirty millimeters thick, no way anyone can hear through that." He reached down and flipped open the cover of a burnished aluminum case. "And this is the best TSCM equipment available."

The case contained two small radar-type sweep displays and enough buttons, knobs, lights, and switches to send most techies into orgasmic shock. "TSCM?"

"Technical surveillance countermeasures. This little goodie will detect and scramble bugs, taps, and microwave transmissions. Check your phone."

Simon pulled his cellular. The display looked like a hieroglyphic crossword puzzle. "Charles, if you wiped out my phonebook—"

"Your phonebook is fine, the signal is scrambled, that's all. I guarantee you, what we say here stays here."

"Good, because I just heard from my friend in New York and we don't want this information to leak out." He exchanged a look with both men, making sure they understood the implication. "She—" *Damn,* he hadn't meant to divulge even that much about VicTheQuick. "I should say *they,* were able to identify the man who picked up the money."

Charles cocked his head suspiciously. "That's awful fast work. Just who does your friend work for?"

"Interpol has been looking for the guy for years," Simon answered, purposely ignoring the question. "He's a mercenary."

There was a jolt as traffic came to an abrupt halt. Guards from both the lead and chase vehicles began to form a defensive perimeter around the car, but almost immediately the traffic began to edge forward. Jake didn't seem to notice the interruption, his eyes never leaving Simon's face. "What do you mean by mercenary? A professional soldier?"

Simon shook his head, thinking a poke of reality might be exactly what was needed. "He's a professional killer. That's why they've never been able to catch him—he never leaves anyone alive who could identify him."

The big man seemed to deflate, like a huge balloon leaking air but trying desperately to hold on. "But we don't even know he's the one holding Kyra. Maybe he really was hired to pick up the money."

"Maybe," Simon agreed, though he didn't believe it. "But that's not the kind of work he does. If it were my daughter, and I had that kind of information, I'd want to do more than pay and pray." But as he said it, he realized that making such a decision could not be easy for someone like Big Jake Rynerson, accustomed to paying for and getting whatever he wanted, a habit not easily broken.

"What do you mean, *more?*" Jake demanded.

"He's saying we should grab the guy when he picks up the money," Charles answered.

Simon hated it when people tried to explain what he meant. "No, that's *not* what I'm saying. If he *is* just a go-between, they'll have someone watching, just to make sure he doesn't get picked up."

Charles edged forward in his chair. "So what *are* you suggesting?"

"We follow him."

"That would take a lot of men. Hard to keep an operation of that size quiet."

"And risky," Simon agreed. "He ran me all over the place, making sure I wasn't being followed. He'll be even more careful once he has the money. We need to track him electronically."

"It's the money we would need to track, and he'll check that, any fool would."

"No question about it, but we could sew a microtransmitter into the pack."

Charles hesitated, thinking about it, then shook his head. "He'll dump the pack."

"Probably, but if I could get a transmitter on him . . ."

"On him . . ." Charles sat back, his words trailing away as he considered the problem.

"I can think of a couple ways," Simon continued. "The last time I was able to get him to sit down and have a beer. Given the same scenario I could plant a small adhesive transmitter on the chair. Something that would stick to his clothes."

"That's assuming the same situation. Assuming he'll sit down. Assuming he won't notice he sat on something. That's a hell of a lot of assuming."

"I agree, it's a long shot. I could also have something on me that has a transmitter. Something he'd be tempted to take."

"Such as?"

"Such as my security case. He wanted it the last time. If he tries again I'll let him have the damn thing."

"Good idea," Jake said in what sounded like a major understatement. "Very clever. I think we should do it."

Simon concentrated on convincing Charles, goading him gently with a challenge. "Of course, we couldn't do anything unless you're able to come up with the equipment. State-of-the-art transmitters with good range and long battery life." He suspected Vic could supply the hardware, but knew she would demand details.

Charles smiled—a tiny, you're-not-fooling-me-for-a-minute smile—and nodded. "That shouldn't be a problem, I've still got my contacts at the Bureau. And we've got a day or two, until they provide another proof-of-life."

For the first time Simon felt like they were about to do something proactive rather than reactive, but he also realized if their plan leaked out the odds of finding Kyra in one piece would be somewhat less than finding Jimmy Hoffa buried in the garden. "We need to keep this between us. No one in Vegas needs to know." He gave Big Jake a meaningful look. "I know you trust your people, Jake, but this is your daughter we're talking about. We can't risk any more leaks."

Jake nodded, taking no offense at the warning. "We'll have to tell Tony, he's the only one."

For an instant Simon didn't believe what he heard, that Jake had said it. "I agree, he has a right to know, but if you're right about the electronic surveillance—"

"You don't have to worry about that, he's here."

"In Cali?"

"On the puddle jumper. Customs threatened to throw Brownie into quarantine if we took him off the plane. Tony volunteered to stay behind until Charles could find someone to bribe."

"But I thought—"

"He insisted on coming, what could I do? He *is* Kyra's husband."

"I remember what you said the last time he insisted." *Put up the money and you can do any damn thing you want.*

Jake made a face, as if to dismiss any suggestion of a problem. "That's water under the bridge. Things are different now. He wasn't in the loop on the numbering scheme, so it couldn't have been him. Fact is, I may have misjudged the boy. Billie's sure of it."

"Sure of him, or sure you misjudged him?"

"Both."

That sounded like Billie, sure of everything and not afraid to express it. If only, Simon thought, he felt that confident about his next meeting with El Pato. *If only,* but he knew the best-made plans did not always work— sometimes they unraveled like a Stephen King novel, all blood and guts.

CHAPTER TWENTY-FOUR

Somewhere in South America

Wednesday, 12 November 11:56:18 GMT –0500

Kyra woke up feeling like a collection of disjointed bones and ligaments. She had been fading in and out of consciousness for some time—darkness and shadowy light—but how many days she wasn't sure. Two or three. *Maybe four.*

As always, even before she opened her eyes, she listened for him—the monster—but could hear nothing, the hot air humid and eerily silent. Still, not until she was absolutely sure he was gone, not lurking at his voyeur window, would she allow herself the luxury of thought; it was too unpleasant, the weight of her situation almost more than her ability to hold inside. She tried to tell herself it was a dream, that no human being could be so cruel to another, but that wake-up fantasy was getting old and she could no longer make herself believe it, not for a moment. She took a deep breath, opened her eyes, and looked down at her feet. *No dream.*

The back of her legs were sore where the tendons had snapped up into her calves, but the pain across her ankles had disappeared completely; which only made it worse, the fact that her feet were so lifeless and dead. They looked the same, still pink beneath the dirt, and she could wiggle her toes, but beyond that they were useless bricks attached to her legs. Her stomach turned over and she closed her eyes, fighting off a wave of nausea. She drifted off, for how long she wasn't sure, but when she woke again she felt better, her mind clear, and she started to remember. . . .

The picture. A picture of her holding a newspaper.

A box of food. Water bottles. He was leaving again. *"Hola!"* she yelled the word as loud she could, but it came out thin and weak. "Anyone there? *Hola."*

There was a squawk beyond the window as a bird fluttered to life, then silence. *Already gone.* The dog too.

It was coming to an end. *One way or the other . . .*

He would get his money, then kill her. That had always been his plan and there wasn't a damn thing she could do. Nothing her father could do.

Escape was no longer an option. She couldn't climb and could barely walk. He could have left the door open and all she could have done was hobble into the jungle and died. A better choice, on her own terms, and better than letting him or his mad dog do the job. But he hadn't left the door open. There were no options, all she could do was clean her wounds and try to stay alive. It wasn't much, but as long as she was alive there was hope. Not much, but something.

CHAPTER TWENTY-FIVE

Cali, Colombia

Thursday, 13 November 14:07:08 GMT −0500

As a security measure, Charles had managed to procure the entire wing of the ninth floor. All resident guests had been quietly moved, their anger mollified by the hotel's generous offer to comp their stay, an amount immediately added to the account of B. J. Rynerson. The arrangement allowed most of the security detail to remain out of sight and sequestered in their own rooms, with only a few men stationed at the end of each corridor and at the elevators. No one—not the hotel staff or the security detail—had any idea why Big Jake Rynerson was in Cali, though the rumor that he had a proprietary interest in the hotel property was not discouraged.

After a bribe and a bureaucratic battle, the security men had finally managed to rescue Brownie and smuggle him into Jake's suite, which had evolved into command-central for what Charles referred to as *El Liberté*, a pidginization of Spanish and French that expressed perfectly what they hoped to accomplish. After three days, the tracking paraphernalia had finally arrived and everyone gathered around the dining-room table to watch Charles open his *special package*. Whatever the source—everyone suspected the FBI lab in Quantico, though Charles refused to confirm it—the equipment was clearly state-of-the-art.

"These things are even smaller than I expected," Charles said, as he carefully unwrapped and laid out twelve feather-light, dime-size alloy disks. "We could double-strap one of the money packets and hide one of these between the bands."

Jake, who had become more despondent and pessimistic with each passing day, shook his head slowly, as if the effort were almost too much. "No way, Hos, not after what happened last time. You know damn well they're gonna be checking every one of those bills. They find out we're tracking that money, my little girl's as good as dead." He turned to Tony, who in the course of a week had gone from estranged son-in-law to new best buddy. "You agree?"

"Absolutely, we can't take the chance. If we catch these guys, great, but we can't lose sight of—"

Charles interrupted. "Don't worry, Tony, I wouldn't do anything I thought might jeopardize bringing Kyra home. A reliable trace on the money might help, but if you think it's too risky, we won't do it."

"I understand the risk–reward ratio," Tony answered, "it's a judgment call. And yeah, I think it's too risky."

"Good enough. Your wife—your call."

Tony nodded and picked up one of the disks, inspecting it carefully. Because he wanted to contribute, and because Jake had supported his desire, it would be his job to track the movement of each disk and direct Charles and his assault team to the target. "How does this thing work?"

"It's a miniature GPS transmitter," Charles explained. "Accurate to within one meter."

"Power?"

"Each disk has a built-in, nuclear-powered battery. It will transmit until the chip starts to dissolve."

Tony rolled the disk over in his hand. "Dissolve?"

Charles smiled, unable to mask his enthusiasm for the high-tech paraphernalia. "It wouldn't be a good thing to have these little babies fall into the wrong hands. They're designed for exactly this kind of task. One mission. Very short-term. The chip starts to deteriorate the minute the battery is inserted and the disk sealed. It's got an effective life of six days. Within ten days the chip is electronic garbage."

"You're saying the clock is ticking?"

"As we speak."

"Damn, that's not good." He turned to Jake. "Maybe you better call Leo, see if he's heard anything more about that proof-of-life photo."

"Talked to the little pissant this morning. He was positive we'd have something before the end of the day." He scowled, as if he'd just discovered cow dung on his favorite pair of boots. "Much as I dislike that man, I gotta admit he's been right so far."

A fact Simon found less than comforting. Leo and Caitlin *always* seemed to be right. Or to know *too much*. But that was an odd little phenomenon Big Jake didn't care to consider. "What's the range on these units, Charles?"

"Unlimited over normal terrain."

"What do you mean normal terrain?" Tony asked. "I thought GPS worked anywhere on earth, that's why so many hikers and mountain climbers used it."

"That's true, but Global Positioning works by triangulation, needing three line-of-sight satellites to get an accurate fix." Charles spread his hands, a classic *what-can-I-say* gesture. "You get into an area of hills and canyons you can lose contact."

"Well now," Jake growled, his tone a sarcastic drawl, "ain't that a break, though. This damn country ain't got no hills—it's nothin' but mountains, one end ta the other."

Charles, who clearly understood the stress Jake was under, ignored the sarcasm. "If we get into the mountains we'll need to stay close." He reached back into the box and pulled out six beeper-size units. "These are the transponders my assault team will carry. It will give every man the location and distance to the target. They only have an effective range of twenty-five miles, but that shouldn't be a factor as we want to stay close enough to move in fast." He glanced over at Jake. "Once they check the money and know it's clean, they have less incentive to keep Kyra alive."

He reached back into the box and extracted a very thin, very lightweight notebook computer from the box and handed it to Tony. "This is a self-contained, wireless laptop scanner. Each disk has a numeric identifier and will show up on the screen as a different color, so you'll know exactly who's where at any given moment."

"How will I be able to identify the locations?"

"The program is literally a map of the world. You can zoom down to street level. Every view will include a grid overlay, allowing you to quickly measure the distance between GPS units and identify their exact longitude–latitude location."

"Sounds easy enough."

"It gets better. Whenever you hover your pointer over a disk, a balloon will appear giving you the disk number and exact location. Boot it up, I'll give you a demo."

While Tony booted the laptop, Charles finished unpacking his high-tech toys. In addition to the scanner and transmitters, the box included six Nightstalker binoculars and a complete two-way wireless audio system for communication. Charles and his assault team would wear the latest in surveillance headgear: earplug speakers and tiny bud microphones. Simon's ability to communicate would be limited—in case El Pato checked him for a wire—but he would carry a small wireless transmitter, camouflaged as a Bic disposable pen that would allow everyone to hear him.

The scanner bloomed to life and automatically located

the transmitters, the view from twelve thousand feet. Tony stared at the screen, as if a virus had suddenly made an assault on his computer. "That's not great."

Charles leaned over his shoulder. "What's wrong?"

"Well, look at that." He pointed to the cluster of colored dots. "How the hell am I supposed to keep everything straight?"

"Well, first of all, they're all sitting right here. It'll be easier to keep everything straight once they're spread out."

Tony gave Charles an "oh, yeah" look, clearly not convinced. "Or harder. Why do we need so many disks anyway?"

"One for the money bag, one for Simon, one for me, and four for my crew." Charles had chosen his assault team from an independent security service, unassociated with Jake's security detail. The men were all young, ex-military, in prime physical condition, and spoke English. Aside from knowing they were hired to make an armed assault, none of the men knew the target or the objective, but the money was good and they didn't ask questions. "Then we need one for Simon to carry, just in case he gets a chance to plant it on this El Pato character." Judging from his *just-in-case* tone, Charles didn't have much faith in that part of the plan. "And we have one for Simon's security case. The others are backup, in case of a malfunction. We can mask the transmission on those so they won't show up on the screen."

Tony tried to smile, but it congealed in the middle of his face, revealing his anxiety. "That still leaves nine people and or objects that need to be tracked. That I can do—I'm not concerned about that." His expression implied otherwise. "But to coordinate the movements of five people, making sure they don't lose contact or get too close, that worries me. What if—"

"Here," Charles interrupted, "take a look at this." He

leaned in, right-clicked the mouse, and began renaming the disks, changing their numeric identifiers to more descriptive names so that whenever the pointer hovered over a dot the name popped up. "We'll make Simon red." He clicked and typed. "The security case silver." Within minutes he had all the disks renamed. "There, now you'll be able to tell who's where and what's what without having to think about who's number four, or what number eight stands for."

Tony acknowledged the improvement by releasing a lungful of air. "Aaah. That's better."

Charles made a note of his changes in a small leather-bound notebook. "You play chess, Tony?"

"I played in college. Why?"

"This is similar, moving pieces around the board, trying to hide your intentions from your opponent. We'll do a run-through after dark. Everyone can take a disk, I'll be the target, and you can practice following me around the city. You'll want to keep me surrounded without letting anyone close enough for me to spot."

"What's too close?"

"Well, obviously I know everyone, so—"

"No, I mean for real," Tony clarified, "with El Pato."

"Good question. I'd say two hundred meters in the city, five hundred in the open."

"And how will I know if the target moves into the open? I can't see buildings on the screen."

"No, but you'll be in voice communication with everyone on the team but Simon. These men are all experienced trackers and will act as your eyes on the ground. They'll let you know if the terrain changes."

Tony opened his mouth to respond, but was interrupted by a beep on the tiny two-way attached to Charles's belt, followed immediately by the now-familiar voice of Raul, the head honcho on Jake's security detail, a man in his mid-thirties who took great pride in his *per-*

fecto inglés. Except for Jake—who had learned a raw version of conversational Spanish while working the oil fields—none of them understood half of what he said, but no one had the heart to burst the bubble of his linguistic illusion. "A package for Señor Leonidovich."

Charles looked over at Simon. "You expecting something?"

It was one of those still moments, everyone holding their breath, wondering if this was it. Simon was sure of it, and also sure that Leo Geske had been right. *Again.* "Nope."

Charles slipped on a pair of latex gloves and opened the door. Raul, also wearing latex gloves, extended a padded, manila envelope. *"Depositar el portero."* He glanced at a small notebook in his left hand. *"Son las dos y quince."*

Charles glanced over his shoulder, seeking help, and Jake stepped forward, Brownie at his heels. "It was delivered to the concierge—a quarter after two."

"Thanks. Did his men see who dropped it off?"

Raul—who understood English much better than he used it—didn't wait for the translation, erupting into a convoluted combination of English and Spanish and pantomime, ending with an expressive duck waddle that left no doubt as to the person's identity.

"Was he driving or on foot?"

Raul made a little walking gesture with his fingers. *"Rápidamente."*

"You followed?" Charles asked.

"As you instructed, *Señor.* No too close." It was an instruction, judging from the man's expression, he didn't like or understand.

Charles ignored the questioning look, unable to explain his interest in El Pato or why they couldn't risk letting the man spot a tail. "Good. And?"

Raul sprayed his fingers into the air. "Poof."

Charles nodded, the word requiring no translation. *"Gracias."*

"De nada, Señor!" Raul backed away, pulling the door closed behind him.

Everyone followed Charles to the table, watching anxiously as he studied the package under the light before carefully slicing open one edge. The first thing out of the package was another cellular phone, the exact same brand and model Simon had received the previous time. Charles held it up to the light, turning it from side to side at an oblique angle, then brought it to his nose. "Clean. Wiped with alcohol. This guy's careful."

None of which surprised Simon. *The guy's no genius, but he's good at what he does.*

Jake circled the table, a caged bear ready to explode. "Come on, Hos, is it in there or not?"

"There's something." Charles reached back into the package and extracted a small photograph—a Polaroid— and held it out so everyone could see. "Looks clean, but don't touch, I want to have it checked."

The image was straight out of a B movie: the kidnap victim—aka: Kyra Rynerson-Saladino—holding a current newspaper to prove her current state of existence, which, if the picture was any indication, was alive but not well. Her eyes appeared vacant and unfocused, her skin damp with perspiration, her hair swirling around her head in a greasy, tangled mass, hiding the reality of her missing ear.

Jake took one glance and turned away. Tony drew in a hissing mouthful of air, like he'd taken a gut punch. "Those bastards . . ."

Simon leaned in close, looking for some clue to her location, but there wasn't much to see: her head, the newspaper clutched beneath her chin, a few feet of rough plank wall. What everyone saw, and no one mentioned, was her obvious state of undress, her bare shoulders exposed around the edge of the paper.

CHAPTER TWENTY-SIX

Cali, Colombia

Saturday, 15 November 16:14:41 GMT −0500

Charles circled the table, the general laying out his battle plan. "Okay, let's go over it one more time."

Tony gave Simon a look—*Oh, Christ, not again!*—but didn't argue. Simon felt the same; they'd gone over it a dozen times, step by step, until he could have found his way through the alleys of Cali at midnight with one eye closed and the other fogged over. Tony would be at the airport, directing the assault team from the puddle jumper; while Jake would remain at the hotel, surrounded by his security detail, just in case anyone was monitoring their movements.

"I know you're tired," Charles continued, "but there's nothing we can do but wait, so why not keep working?" He wasn't looking for an answer and didn't wait for one. "Let's say he heads west into the Cordillera Occidental." He leaned over and tapped the main route out of the city, toward the port of Buenaventura. "If you see that happening, Tony, you need to . . ."

Simon zoned out. It wasn't the work or the repetition that bothered him, it was knowing the chances of anything going as planned were virtually nonexistent. That was the way of war—and this was very much a military campaign. Something *always* went sideways. Besides, by the time anything happened Simon Leonidovich's part would be over.

Hand over the money . . . go back to the hotel . . . wait.

Sounded easy enough. *Anticlimactic. Boring.*

Who was he kidding? Just the thought of meeting El Pato again was enough to turn his stomach into a cauldron of acid. *He never leaves any witnesses.* Not to worry, he was just the bagman, witness to nothing. *You tangle with this guy, you end up dead.* He certainly had no intentions of *tangling* with the guy.

"Knock-knock, earth to Simon."

"Sorry, Jake, I didn't hear you come in. What's up?"

Big Jake held up his cellular. "It's Caity. She wants to talk to you."

He took the phone, happy for the distraction, and wandered casually toward the far side of the suite, hoping for a bit of privacy without appearing to have anything private to say. "Hi there, Wells, what's up?"

"Miss me?" Her voice sounded teasing and sexy at the same time.

He lowered himself into a comfortable wingback overlooking the city, well beyond the ears of his roommates. The afternoon light was growing thin, the sky the color of hammered pewter. "I'm stuck here with three other guys, what do you think?"

"I think you miss me really bad."

And of course he did, but that was something he didn't want to admit—even to himself. Not before he knew about that *something missing* from her background. Until Kyra was safe, and he knew who was behind it, he couldn't allow himself the fantasy that Caitlin Wells might actually find him attractive. "It's hard to think about you when I've got Chiquita on one knee and Rosita on the other."

She barked out a one-note laugh. "Ha. I should have known. Turn my back for a second and you replace me with the Ita sisters."

"Don't be disrespectful, Wells. The sisters are very famous in this part of the world."

"Yeah, right. So when you're not peeling Chiquitas what are you guys doing down there?"

Slick segue. "Not much." He could think of no way to avoid the lie. "Just sitting around waiting for the call."

"Like hell. You bad boys are up to something, I can smell it."

"Then you need a nose job, Wells."

"And you're a lousy liar, Leonidovich."

"I resent that, I'm a very good liar." In truth he was the worst—Lara *always* caught him when he tried to wiggle around the truth.

"Bullshit!"

"I'm good at that too."

"Stop defending yourself, Leonidovich. I like the fact that you're bad at being bad."

"So there's still hope for a boring schmuck like me?"

"You are not boring and you are not a schmuck. And if it makes you feel any better, I don't give a damn what you boys are up to. In fact, I don't *want* to know. All I want is for you to bring Kyra home. Safe. You do that, Leonidovich, and you'll make my heart go pitty-pat."

Oh God, how he wanted that to be true. He swallowed back all his insecurities and jumped. "Simon says: dinner—as soon as I get back." By that time, Kyra would be alive or not, and he would know what he needed to know about Ms. Caitlin Wells.

"It's a date." She sounded almost chirpy, excited at the prospect.

"Good." *Very good.*

"You are coming back?" Suddenly she was the one who sounded insecure. "You're not going to do your bagman thing and run back to New York?"

No. He had made a promise to Billie, one he intended to keep. "I'm like MacArthur, I *shall* return."

"You be careful, Simon Leonidovich, it's dangerous out there."

Her words hung in the air like a cold breath of air. An innocent warning—*look both ways before crossing the street*—or did she know something he didn't?

For two days El Pato had done nothing but watch, sleeping only when the lights dimmed in the ninth-floor suite. He sat quietly, hunched down in his sarape and staring straight ahead—no different than any other homeless peasant. But he saw everything, his senses alert, clear and sharp, and he could smell blood, could almost taste the kill, but something held him back—the disquieting thought that he was the one being hunted. And now, when he needed good solid information, the *norteamericano* had little to share.

"*I can't ask too much, they're already suspicious.*"

"*Tú?*"

"*No, not me. The phones, the airwaves, their own shadows. Rynerson's convinced the place is bugged, that's why he's down there. It doesn't matter, I'm careful, we're okay.*"

El Pato was not so sure. "*Why so many men?*"

"*That's for Rynerson. His security. Cali is a dangerous city.*"

"*And the money? No more games?*"

"*You can be sure of that. They wouldn't dare try anything again.*"

But El Pato was no longer confident the *norteamericano* had the ear of the rich *yanqui*. "*I am not so sure.*"

"*Trust me, everything is fine. Just do what you're told. Wait for my call. Follow the plan.*"

The *norteamericano* had a smart mouth, but El Pato decided to let it pass—for now. "*Sí, of course.*" But he never trusted anyone and wasn't about to start—not with seven million *dólares* at stake.

"*In a few hours you'll have enough money to live anywhere, do anything.*"

But the money would be nothing if he had to spend his

time hiding from the rich yanquí and his army of mercenary hunters. "Sí, I try only to be careful." And being careful meant the courier as well as the yanquí princesa must die. No witnesses.

Simon slipped quietly back into the war council, hoping to avoid any *Caitlin questions* from his three new fraternity brothers. Charles, still hammering away at Tony, looked up from his map of the city. "So what's the scoop, Simon?"

Uh-oh. "Nothing to tell, she just wanted to see how we're doing."

"That's my Caity," Jake said, his teeth flashing.

Charles nodded. "Righteous."

"Extremely righteous," Tony agreed.

Simon could tell from their expressions the boys were just warming up, obviously enjoying a momentary hiatus from the pressure. He was more than willing to take a little ribbing, was actually flattered that they thought Caitlin Wells might have some interest in their intrepid bagman, but before they could stick him with another needle he was saved by an unexpected chirp. For two days he had carried *the Kyra phone* everywhere—to the dinner table, the bathroom, the shower, and into bed—but when it suddenly erupted to life all he could do was stare at the damn thing, sitting there in the middle of the table chirping like an underfed pullet.

Charles reached out, quickly linked the tiny unit to a microrecorder using a suction-cup attachment, then shoved it across the table. Simon picked up the phone and pressed the TALK button. "This is Leonidovich."

"You have the package?"

Simon recognized the voice immediately. "I do."

"You are alone, yes?"

"No." He had the feeling El Pato knew exactly who was there. "Mr. Rynerson and Mr. Saladino are with me.

They wanted to be here when Ms. Saladino was released."

"So the rich *yanquí* has come for his *princesa,* eh?" He didn't really sound surprised. "No one else?"

"Mr. Saladino." He purposely avoided mentioning Charles, hoping to find out how much El Pato knew.

"Only those two? No one else?"

"Mr. Case just came into the room."

"And who is this?" The question sounded perfunctory, as if he already knew.

"He's in charge of Mr. Rynerson's security."

"Security?"

"Mr. Case hired a local firm to assist in Mr. Rynerson's protection. They're not involved in this matter, nor do they know the reason for Mr. Rynerson's presence here in Colombia."

There was a short pause, as if the man needed to consider this information. "We have many men. Many eyes. Anyone follows, the woman will die."

"I understand." He just hoped the four men Charles had picked for his assault team understood.

"You will follow my directives *exactamente.*"

Simon recognized the language, exactly as he had said it before, as if the man were reading from a script. "Of course." He wrote the directions on a small pad, picturing the route in his mind as he took down the information. And exactly as before, the line went dead before he could ask questions.

"You think that was a good idea," Jake asked, "telling him we're all here?"

"He was testing me. He already knew."

Charles nodded. "Simon's right, he knew."

Tony began circling the table, like a leopard in a cage at the zoo. "Oh Jesus, what else do they know? What if they spot one of your men, Charles?"

"Won't happen, these guys are pros. Besides, you'll make sure we don't get that close. Not until it's time to move in."

"How will you know when it's the right time?"

"We'll wait for the money to stop moving. Then, I'll scout the location and—"

"What if you wait too long?" Tony interrupted, his eyes glassy with panic. "What if I screw up? What if—"

Jake reached out and grabbed his son-in-law's arm. "Relax, boy, you're gonna do just fine."

Simon smiled to himself, pleased that at least one good thing had come out of the ordeal. It was clear that as much as Jake missed his daughter, Tony loved his wife, and for that reason the two men had at last found some common ground. "Jake's right, Tony, you're going to do fine."

Charles threw in his own vote of confidence. "Absolutely, you're ready." He reached down, pulled his backup piece—a Mauser M2—and slid it across the table to Simon. "You sure this is a good idea?"

No, he wasn't sure at all. "Blanks, right?"

Charles nodded. "Right, nothing to worry about."

Right. When the general said there was nothing to worry about it, it was time to strap on the Kevlar.

CHAPTER TWENTY-SEVEN

Cali, Colombia

Saturday, 15 November 21:57:21 GMT –0500

After another back-and-forth and around-the-*Centre* tour, Simon felt like an actor trapped in some weird *déjà vu* movie. He half expected to end up at El Gusano, which, despite the neighborhood and fearsome clientele, would not have made him unhappy. He at least survived that experience and would have some expectation of walking away with all his body parts. More important, it would give him the opportunity to set the scene and plant a tracking disk. Then, if he was lucky—*I might need a little help here, God*—he'd get the Duckman to sit down. *Simple.*

But after an hour of contradictory instructions and double-backs and switches, Simon found himself alone on an overlook jutting out over the Rio Cali. The area was pitch black, the water approximately fifty feet below judging from the sound. Shielded from the street traffic by a thick hedge, the surrounding area was wide open, making it impossible for anyone to approach on foot without notice. It was, Simon realized, a perfect spot. *Perfect for El Pato.*

For a good five minutes nothing happened, though Simon knew Charles and his assault team would be moving forward. Tony would be monitoring everything from the puddle jumper, watching the colored dots on his computer screen converge around the promontory, then stop and hold at four hundred meters. Simon fingered the dime-size disk hidden between his index and middle finger, knowing his chances of planting the device on El Pato had just gone from difficult to dangerous. He took a deep breath of the damp night air, trying to calm his nerves. *It's possible there's a tad bit of danger involved.* No shit.

A lone figure suddenly cut through the hedges, angling toward the overlook. Though dressed like a country peasant, his hands hidden beneath a sarape, Simon recognized the man's distinctive waddling gait. He stopped about six feet away, his dark eyes moving from side to side. Apparently satisfied, he wagged his fingers, as in *gimmie.*

Simon removed the titanium wrist cuff and quickly dialed through the locks on his security case. As he extracted the money pack he purposely brushed the edge of his jacket to one side, exposing the Mauser. El Pato leaped forward, the movement shockingly fast, pinning Simon against the rail and ripping the gun from his belt. "What you do with this, Bagman?"

"Protection," Simon snapped, trying to sound indignant as he pushed back, pressing the adhesive side of the disk to the underside of the sarape. "I'm toting a bit of money here."

El Pato stepped back, looked at the gun, and slipped it into his belt. "No more *dinero.* No more need."

"Hey, that thing cost me over four hundred dollars."

"You pay too much. It cost El Pato *nada.*"

"What, you can't afford it?" Simon glanced at the money pack, trying to goad the man into an admission. "They're not paying you enough to play delivery boy?"

"You are right, *gringo—*" He leaned down and picked up the pack. "Half is not enough."

Though Simon suspected there were only two people involved, the fact that the Duckman admitted it—in a somewhat oblique way—came as a surprise. A disturbing, foreboding surprise.

"Adiós, gringo."

The finality of the words, the way El Pato said them,

confirmed the ominous feeling. A gun seemed to materialize in the Duckman's right hand. Not the Mauser with its load of blanks, but something else, big and black with a thick extrusion attached to the barrel. "Wait!"

The man smiled, exposing his gold tooth in a ghoulish grin, and pulled the trigger.

Simon felt the impact more than heard the shots, three quick pops, hitting him center chest and knocking him over the rail. The drop seemed endless, everything black, no up or down, his diaphragm paralyzed from the impact of the bullets, his chest on fire. He hit the river head over ass and sideways, and went straight down. He tried to gain control but his arms felt like they'd been yanked from their sockets, and the only thing that seemed to work was his brain, and all it did was confirm the worst: *Holy Jesus, I'm going to die!*

His chest felt like it was about to explode, and he fought the urge to open his mouth, knowing one gulp and it would be over. Then the current grabbed him, pulling him downstream and for a moment back to the surface. He opened his mouth but got more water than air before the current rolled him over and pulled him under again. *Sweet Jesus.* For what seemed a lifetime, it was up and down, rolling and tumbling, forward and backward, a few seconds of air and coughing followed by another plunge. Finally he found some rhythm to the current, riding it instead of fighting it, and managed to break the surface for more than a few seconds. He gulped a large mouthful of air, the effort burning through his lungs like hot gas. Under again. The Kevlar might have saved his life, but the vest was now a water-logged straitjacket, threatening to finish what the bullets started. He spun around, getting his feet out front, pointing downstream, and tried to strip off his shirt, but couldn't, rolling over whenever he tried to free an arm. Surface again. This time he laid back, stretching out his legs, arms to the side, letting the current carry him along, face and toes out of the water. *Go with it.*

A few dozen yards and a lung full of air and he started to feel better. His arms still burned like they'd been dipped in acid but they weren't broken, and if the bullets had made it through the Kevlar they hadn't gotten to his heart. *Might make it.* Aside from feeling like he'd just taken a four-hour ride in a commercial-grade washer, floating along on his back through the middle of Cali wasn't all that bad. The night was clear, the air warm, the water cool, a gazillion stars twinkling overhead. *E-ticket at Disneyland.* Suddenly the current picked up speed as the river narrowed and curled toward the north. *Time to abandon ship.*

As the current pulled him around the bend and swept him closer to the bank, he grabbed a lungful of air, flipped over onto his stomach, and tried to dog-paddle. The distance couldn't have been more than fifteen feet, but with his thick-soled walkers and the Kevlar weighing him down it was all he could do to make land and pull himself into the weeds before his arms gave out. *Jesus God, what a ride.* He felt like a beached whale, gasping for air, with two useless flippers.

He needed to contact Tony, but all he could do was lie there and cough up water, with not enough strength to pull off the Kevlar and ascertain the damage. He rolled onto his back, staring up at the embankment and the glow of lights beyond. *Ugh,* Everest couldn't have looked more insurmountable. Then he saw the light, a small but intense flash moving from side to side, moving quickly toward him as someone worked their way down the slope. Had El Pato seen him surface? Was that possible? He needed to hide, crawl into the brush, but the cliff was too steep. For an instant, he considered going back into the water, but realized he didn't have the strength left to fight the current.

In less than a minute a man was standing over him, a

stranger: medium height, with hard, angular features, toffee-colored skin, and dressed in black. "You are hurt?" He spoke in clear but heavily accented English.

Hurt! Jesus-God, yes, I'm hurt! Every damn ligament and bone in his body hurt. But was he injured? "I'm not sure. I don't think so."

The man reached down, grabbed the front of Simon's shirt, and with surprising strength pulled him to his feet. It was then Simon noticed the bud microphone dangling from the man's ear and realized he was part of Charles's assault team, directed to the location by Tony, who apparently witnessed the entire ride on his computer. *Hooray for electronics.* "Thank you."

The man nodded, pulled a black stiletto from his boot, and before Simon could flinch had sliced open the front of his shirt. The tiny beam of light centered over the three bullet holes, clustered in a small triangle over Simon's solar plexus, all three slugs embedded in the fabric. "You lucky, *Señor.*"

"Yes, very lucky." *God loves me.*

The man reached down and pressed one of six colored buttons on the beeper-size unit attached to his belt. "*Señor—*" He looked at Simon, that universal who-the-hell-are-you expression.

"Leonidovich."

"*Señor* Le-on-o-vich, up and standing." He released the button and waited, listening to a response through his earplug. "*Sí.*" He reached into his pocket, pulled a small cellular, touched and held the 1 button, then handed the phone to Simon.

"Hello."

Tony's voice came snapping back. "You okay?"

"A little shaky, but *up and standing* as the man says."

"Holy shit, that was some ride. I thought you were a goner."

"The possibility crossed my mind."

"I'll bet." He chuckled, more in relief than amusement. "Charles was on the building across the street—saw everything clear as day through his Nightstalkers."

"Did he take the security case?"

"Sure did, I'm tracking it as we speak."

"Well, don't let that sonofabitch out of your crosshairs. He's the one who's got Kyra."

"How do you know that?" Tony asked, clearly surprised.

"You didn't hear?"

"Couldn't hear much, the river was too loud. He actually said he had her?"

"Not in so many words, but he said enough."

"I better patch you through to Charles." There was a series of clicks, a few seconds of dead air, then Charles was on the line. "Glad to hear you're okay."

"Thanks. Nothing like a late-night swim to wake a person up."

"What's this about Kyra?"

"He's the one who's got her, I'm sure of it."

"Tell me what he said."

"I poked him a little, about what he was getting paid to do the dirty work, and he claimed half the money was his."

"So?"

"That means there are only two people involved." Of course it didn't necessarily mean that, but it's what he believed. "One here, one in Vegas."

"Come on, Simon, that's overstretching. It sounds more like he was just bragging and you bought it."

It was useless to argue, it could have been that way, but in his heart Simon knew better. "Just don't lose him."

"Not likely, we've got three buttons on him. The pack, the security case, and you must have laid that third one somewhere."

"I stuck it to the underside of his sarape."

"Nice work. I didn't think you could pull it off."

"Just don't let that sonofabitch get away."

"Don't intend to. Your work is done, you might as well join Jake at the hotel. I'm sure you could use a shower and I need my man back on station."

"Yeah, okay." But there was no way he was going to do nothing but sit in the hotel as part of Big Jake's do-nothing diversionary team.

"Good evening, Raul. I didn't expect to find you here." *Here* being a far corner of Alfonso Bonilla Aragon International Airport, standing guard duty outside Big Jake's puddle jumper. Though nowhere near the size of the whale taxi, the sleek Gulfstream G550 was no less impressive, sleek and classy with only the Sand Castle logo on its tail to identify ownership.

Raul gave Simon a serious head-to-toe, clearly shocked at his appearance. *"Buenas tardes, Señor.* I am told to accommodate *Señor* Anthony."

"Accompany."

"Perdón?"

"It's not important. *Señor* Anthony is inside?"

"Sí."

It didn't take a genius to realize that unlike the bigger plane—used primarily to ferry high rollers to and from the Sand Castle—the Gulf 5 was Big Jake's personal toy, everything solid and masculine: the walls covered in a thick but soft suedelike material to absorb the sound; the colors muted in shades of brown from tan to café au lait; the trim done in dark, Santo Domingo mahogany. The bulkhead lights had been muted, casting a yellowish, sunset glow over the main cabin. He found Tony in one of the snug but plush *conversational boutiques,* hunched over the screen of his laptop. "So this is what Jake calls a puddle jumper."

Tony jerked upright. "Holy Mother—"

"Sorry, didn't mean to startle you. How's it going?"

He ignored the question. "Charles said you were going back to the hotel."

"Taxi driver screwed up. Thought I said *aeropuerto* instead of hotelo."

"Very funny. You look like shit."

"If it makes you feel better, I feel worse than I look." He leaned down, checking the monitor. "What's happening?"

"Not much. He's been on the move since he dumped your ass in the river. A lot of doubling back and forth." He pointed to a cluster of three brightly lit dots near San Antonio Plaza, near the outskirts of the *Centre* area. "That's your buddy." He moved his finger up and to the right a couple inches, toward the Calima Museum—450 meters according to the grid overlay—to a black dot. "That's Charles." He swirled his finger in a circular motion. "You can see the others."

The others being the assault team—identified by blue dots, numbers 1–4—all circling the El Pato cluster, all maintaining a four-to five-hundred-meter distance. "He's checking for a tail."

"No question about it." Tony moved his finger to the very edge of the screen, twenty kilometers to the northeast of the city. "That's the *aeropuerto*." He dropped his finger down on a glowing red dot. "And that's you."

"And I appreciate you finding me. Seriously. If you hadn't sent that guy I might still be lying in the weeds gargling river water."

Tony shrugged, as if it were no big thing. "Glad I could help." His eyes crinkled with amusement. "Speaking of gargling, did I mention you stink?"

"Don't sugarcoat it, Saladino, say what you mean."

"If you don't back off I'm going to vomit."

"Clear enough. There wouldn't happen to be a shower . . . ?"

Tony jerked a thumb toward the back of the cabin. "About the size of a pigmy telephone booth. Don't see how Jake could ever fit into the thing."

"Clothes?"

"There's a closet. You should be able to find something."

Tony wasn't exaggerating when it came to the size of the shower, and the water flow wasn't exactly zippy, but there was a full assortment of shampoos, conditioners, body scrubs, and moisturizers, and Simon felt seriously better by the time he toweled off. Standing in front of the mirror, he looked like a training target for abused women, with blotches and scrapes from neck to ankles, including three serious welts over his heart. *Very lucky.*

In one of the drawers he found an assortment of still-in-the-package, light-weight Zegna workout suits, his size in a gray T-shirt and pants with a cobalt-blue zip-up-the-front jacket: *très chic* for those long overnight flights to Bali. There was also an assortment of cotton booties, but he passed on those, opting instead to dry his nylon walkers with a hair dryer. Fifteen minutes: *Good to go.*

Tony gave him a quick once-over before turning back to his computer. "Looks like you'll live."

"Yeah, I feel swell." *Swollen,* to be exact, like an overripe and bruised peach. "What's going on?"

"He stopped," Tony answered, pointing to the monitor. "Went into some fleabag hotel. Been there about ten minutes. Charles brought up the cars, just in case."

Simon leaned down, checking the location. "I know that area, it's near one of my favorite cantinas."

"Yeah?"

"Yeah. El Gusano, you should try it. Very upscale. Very select clientele."

"I'll remem—" Tony reached up and covered his ear with the palm of his hand, listening, then reached down and pressed the black button on the transmission unit attached to his belt. "Okay, sounds good." He released the button. "Charles thinks this might be it. That El Pato's passing the money off to whoever's behind this thing."

Simon knew better. "Trust me, Duckboy is not playing bagman to some kidnapping-for-profit faction. He's not giving that money to anyone."

"How can you be so sure?"

That was the problem, he couldn't, not absolutely, and it wasn't his life or his wife hanging by the thread. "If El Pato was just the bagman you think he would have put three bullets in my chest?"

"I'm not sure . . ." his words trailing away as he considered the possibility.

"I'm convinced there are only two people involved," Simon continued. "One here in Colombia and one in Vegas. If I'm right, El Pato's the one here, and he's the one holding your wife."

"What about the new guy Leo's been negotiating with? We know it wasn't El Pato. Sounds like more than one person down here to me."

"We never got a trace or a recording of those calls. We don't know where they came from."

"No, but Leo said he spoke with a heavy accent."

One of many things that didn't make sense, and Simon realized he needed to back off. If he was wrong and Kyra ended up dead, he didn't want to be the one responsible. "I don't have an answer for that, Tony. Let's just keep El Pato in the crosshairs and see where he takes us."

"Sounds good—" He held up a finger, indicating he was listening, then reached down and pressed the black transmit button, toggling back and forth between listening and speaking. "Yeah, he's here . . . nothing . . . sure . . . okay, give me a minute to set it up." He cranked his head around toward Simon. "Charles would like to have a word."

That much Simon had guessed. "You got another audio pack?"

Tony rotated his chair ninety degrees, opened his travel bag, and pulled an audio pack: earplug speaker, bud microphone, battery pack, and transmission control. While Simon got everything hooked up and adjusted, Tony patched the additional unit into the network. "You're good to go. Just press the black button and you'll be whispering in Charles's ear. Release the button to listen."

"Roger-wilco." Simon pressed the black button on his control unit. "You looking for me, Charles?" He released the button, automatically triggering a confirmation signal.

"I thought you were going back to the hotel."

"Changed my mind—thought it would be more interesting to watch everything from here."

"Don't start messing with my operation, Leonidovich. You did your job, now it's time to let the professionals do theirs."

Though he didn't appreciate the tone, Simon could hear the stress and decided to let it go. "It's your show, Charles, I just wanted to watch you guys in action."

"Okay, fine." The edge in his voice softened noticeably. "I'm sure Tony appreciates the company."

"Ten-four. We're at your service."

Tony leaned back in his chair, a hint of amusement in his eyes. "What's 'ten-four' mean, anyway? I never actually knew."

"Not a clue, but it seemed appropriate."

"I know how you feel. I could actually enjoy all this Op Center shit if I wasn't so worried about Kyra."

Simon remembered vividly being under Eth Jäger's knife, and had a pretty clear idea what Kyra was going through. It was not something Tony needed to think about. "There's nothing to worry about." They both knew that was a lie, but a lie Tony needed to hear. "Charles knows what he's doing."

Suddenly Tony rocked forward and pressed his NETWORK button, opening the channel to everyone. "Heads

up, target is on the move." But before the wo. . .
his mouth the cluster of colored dots stopped. . . .
have a visual?"

"I've got him," Charles answered. "He's standing out . .
front of the place. Like he's waiting for someone. He's still
got the money pack and the security case . . . what looks
like a grocery bag, and—" There was a pause, a few moments of dead air. "Some kind of crate. He's turning . . . I
can see it now . . . it's one of those pet carriers. Big one. I
can't see . . . wait, it's a dog. A mean-looking—"

There were two sharp *beeps* as Blue-3 interrupted the
transmission. "Two taxi vehicles have passed my position."

"You get a visual on passengers?" Charles asked.

"Negative."

"Okay, I see them. Both cars stopping out front. Target
approaching first car. Getting in . . . no . . . scratch that.
He's putting the security case and the sack . . . and the dog
crate in the car . . . now he's walking back to the second
car . . . leaning in . . . talking to someone . . . can't see who,
windows too dark. Bingo, there it goes, he just handed
over the money pack . . . now he's going back to the first
car . . . climbing in . . ."

A moment later the three-dot cluster began to separate,
the silver and yellow dots leaving the green behind as the
taxi with El Pato began to move, heading east. Tony
glanced over at Simon. "Looks like you were wrong—he
was just the delivery guy."

Just a delivery guy. Just. Exactly how people thought of
him, Simon realized. "I'm seeing it but I'm not believing
it."

"No question. The yellow is the bug on his sarape, the
security case is silver, the money green."

"I understand the color scheme, Tony, but the disk was
sewn into the pack. How do we know the money is still
in there?"

"Well, we don't but—"

There was a soft *BEEP* as Charles came back on the air. "Everyone hold their positions. We'll follow the money."

Simon felt his insides roll over with the sick realization that El Pato was about to get away—with both the money and any hope they had of finding Kyra. He reached down and jabbed the black transmission button. "Charles, how do you know he didn't put the money back in the security case?"

"It was too light, I could tell by the way he handled it."

"I still don't think—"

The communication was broken by a double *BEEP* as Charles broke in, a warning in his tone. "Cut the chatter. Second taxi moving out . . . heading same direction. We're going mobile."

Simon resisted the impulse to argue, hoping the second taxi might actually follow the first, though he didn't really expect that to happen. The four blue dots were moving quickly now, two joining Charles in one car, the other two in another. In less than a minute both chase cars were on the road. A few seconds later the second taxi turned north, then west on the main road heading toward the port city of Buenaventura. "He's heading for the mountains," Charles said, "let's back off to three kilometers. We don't want him to see our lights."

Simon watched El Pato's car moving away from the others and couldn't restrain himself, though he tried not to sound confrontational. "Charles, I think you're following the wrong car."

"Look, Simon, I know you hate the guy. I understand that, he tried to load your heart up with lead, but getting El Pato is not the object of this exercise. The money always leads to the bad guys. That's the weakness in the kidnapping game; eventually someone has to stick their nose out and grab the money. That's the way these things work. Follow the money, find the bad guys, find the victim."

From the corner of his eye, Simon saw Tony blanch at the word *victim.* "I don't disagree with you, Charles, you're exactly right, but I don't think it's the money you're following."

Charles came snapping back. "Of course it's the money. That grocery bag was too small and the pack went in the second car, I saw it with my own eyes."

"You saw the pack, not the money."

"Think about it, Leonidovich, if he pulled the money that pack wouldn't be moving across town—it'd be laying back there in some garbage can."

"Unless it's a diversion. He might have discovered the disk and figured out what we were doing."

"No way. It would have taken a X-ray machine to find that disk. Trust me, that fleabag joint *did not* have an X-ray machine."

A point Simon couldn't argue, so he played the only card he had left. "Maybe there's been another leak."

There was a momentary pause as Charles considered the possibility. "No, I don't buy it. We've been too careful."

Simon watched the gap between El Pato and the other cars widen, knew he was beaten, knew he should let it go. It wasn't his fight. He had, as Charles said, done his job. But looking at Tony, he couldn't stop thinking about how it felt when Jäger had Lara. "I've got an idea."

"It better be good," Charles snapped. *Damn good,* judging from the edge in his voice.

"Wait until you hit the mountains, there won't be any traffic this time of night, then send the lead car out ahead a few miles."

"You mean pass him?"

"Right. Go by—"

"Too risky," Charles interrupted. "We can't take the chance of tipping them off."

Simon took a deep breath, determined to be calm and

convincing. "Just hear me out. Go by him fast, like you're in a hurry to reach the coast. Then when you're out a few miles, fake a breakdown and try to wave the guy down. If he stops you know he's not our guy."

"And if he doesn't stop, what's that prove?"

"Nothing, but what have you lost?" He gave Tony a hopeless shrug, knowing the idea was about to be rejected. Charles Case was a good man, but like most generals couldn't bring himself to alter his battle plan once the action started.

"The problem—"

"Piss on your problem," Tony interrupted, "it's a hell of a good idea and we're going to do it." It wasn't a question.

Though thankful for the support, the outburst caught Simon completely by surprise. Charles too, judging by the silence. And then with perfect timing, Tony added one final and deadly rapier thrust. "She *is* my wife."

"Okay," Charles answered after a long moment. "Soon as we hit the mountains I'll send the other car up ahead."

Tony gave Simon a conspiratorial wink. "Meanwhile, just in case Simon's right, we'll keep an eye on the Duckman."

"Right," Charles answered. "Keep me informed."

Tony leaned forward and tapped his finger over the glowing silver and yellow cluster. "You see where he's heading? Right toward us."

Simon nodded, he'd been watching the movement carefully and didn't like what he saw or what it might mean. "I noticed."

"That's what convinced me we should go with your plan. We need to find out who's got the money before that bastard gets on a plane and disappears."

"Right."

From the look on his face, it suddenly occurred to Tony what such a development could mean. "You really think he's got the money? All of it?"

"Yes."

"Which means—" He faltered, a slight quiver in his voice. "Kyra is already dead." The last words escaped his mouth in a rush, like the final breath of air leaving a balloon.

Maybe, Simon admitted silently, but he didn't think so—not yet. "We don't know that. It could mean a lot of things."

"Such as?"

"Such as Kyra's not being held near Cali."

"You don't believe that."

No, he didn't. "I'm just saying it's a possibility." But realized it was more likely Charles was right, El Pato was *just a delivery guy.* "They might still intend to release her."

"You don't believe that either. Not after that sonofabitch tried to kill you."

No, he knew the moment El Pato pulled the trigger that Kyra had been given a death sentence. "But I don't think they'd kill her before they've had a chance to inspect the money and make sure they're in the clear."

Tony nodded slowly, a glimmer of hope coming into his eyes. "They waited last time, I guess."

Simon tried to sound upbeat. "Sure did." But he had a feeling the moment they determined the money was good, Kyra *would* be dead. "We just need to be sure we're following the right guy."

"And what do we do if El Pato jumps a plane?"

That was a question Simon had been asking himself for the last five minutes. In a perfect world Charles would find out who really had the money and follow—land or sea, it didn't matter—but Charles and his team were heading into the mountains and nothing in the world was perfect. Not even close. *Sorry, God, you screwed up somewhere.* "I guess we better be ready."

"You mean what I think you mean?"

Simon pointed to the green dot and the chase cars behind. "Find out what's going on. If the guy pulls over, Charles may still have time to make it back here."

Tony pressed the black button on his control pad. "Charles, what's your status?"

"Just cleared the outskirts of the city and heading into the mountains. We're maintaining a three kilometer distance, but I guess you can see that."

"I can, but I might lose you when you start cutting through those passes."

"Right. And radio contact. What's happening with the Duckman?"

"That's why I called. He's heading this way and we're thinking he might have a flight booked."

"Doesn't surprise me," Charles answered. "He did his job, probably has a pocket full of cash and heading off somewhere to celebrate."

Simon gave Tony a *let-me* signal and cut in. "Charles, Simon here. I'm sure you're right, but on the off chance El Pato *is* the one with the money, we're a little nervous about letting him slip away."

There was a pause, a good fifteen seconds of dead air before Charles came back. "Traffic is thinning out. Almost nothing. I intended to wait awhile, but I'll send the other car up ahead now. Maybe we'll get lucky, the guy stops and we're able to make it back there in time."

In a perfect world. "Sounds great. Thanks. We'll be standing by."

"You don't really think we should just sit around and wait for him?" Tony asked, glancing at his watch.

"No, we need to be ready."

"Sounds like you've got a plan."

"Just the obvious," Simon answered. "I'll take Raul and head over to the terminal. If El Pato checks in we'll try and find out where he's going."

"If he sees you it's all over."

"I know that, but with you in my ear I don't have to get close. Raul can ask the questions."

"Okay, that sounds reasonable." Tony stood up, rolling his head and shoulders, like an athlete warming up before a competition. "What can I do?"

"First, call the pilots for this little jalopy and get them over here. Just in case. Then call Jake, let him know what's going on. The guy is probably bouncing off the walls by now."

"I called him while you were in the shower, but I'll call him again, give him an update. What should I tell the pilots?"

"Don't tell them anything. Not yet. Just have them do the preflight and be ready to go. We may not have much time."

Tony frowned, obviously worried, and dropped back into his chair. "If this El Pato character ends up being the guy, I hope to hell Charles and his boys have enough time to get back here."

"Yeah, me too." Which at that moment had to be the world's greatest understatement; the very last thing he wanted in life was another face-to-face with the Duckman.

CHAPTER TWENTY-EIGHT

Alfonso Bonilla Aragon International Airport— Cali, Colombia

Saturday, 15 November 23:49:35 GMT –0500

The driver glanced over his shoulder. *"Aerolínea qué?"*

El Pato ignored the question, not taking his eyes off the black Humvee parked near the end of the terminal, then circled his finger in the air, letting the driver know he wanted to go around again.

The man frowned—it was their third trip around the circle and he wanted nothing more than to dump this *espantoso hombre* and his *espantoso* dog—but didn't have the nerve to complain. *"Sí, Señor."*

El Pato knew he needed to make a decision soon or he would miss his flight. He also knew he was being overcautious. There were many black Humvees in Cali. The vehicle had become the transportation of choice for both the cartels and the politicians—an amusing irony.

No one had followed, that he was sure of.

No one knew when he would leave, that he was sure of.

The Humvee was there when he arrived, that he was sure of.

The seven million was making him crazy, that he was sure of.

No, he would go tonight, make sure he was last on the plane so no one could follow. He reached forward and banged the Plexiglas shield. "Avianca Airlines. *Pronto!*"

Simon pulled his hat lower over his forehead and slumped forward in his seat. Just another weary traveler reading the paper. Though he knew the chances of El Pato seeing or recognizing him were next to nothing, he still felt conspicuous and exposed in the nearly empty terminal.

"Going around again," Tony said, his voice clear and sharp in Simon's ear.

Was the Duckman just being cautious, or did he see something? Another leak? It didn't seem possible. *It's the money.* Walking around with seven million would make anyone paranoid. *If*—and Simon was now having serious doubts—El Pato had the money. He adjusted the newspaper, making sure it covered his mouth, and pressed the gray transmit button. "We're running out of time. What's going on with Charles?"

"They're close. They've got the lead car sitting all caddywampus, one wheel off the highway. We should know something soon."

Not soon enough, Simon had a feeling.

"Hold on," Tony whispered, as if suddenly afraid he might be overheard. "Here comes our boy again . . . looks like they're pulling over this time. Yup. He's getting out . . . should be coming through the main doors in about ten seconds."

"Gotcha." Simon nudged Raul with his elbow. "Take a look." He motioned with his chin toward the terminal's main doors. "Anyone you recognize?"

A second later Raul emitted a sound of surprise. "Aaahee. It is the *hombre* who left the envelope. The one who walks like a duck."

Though the identification was undeniable, Simon couldn't resist a quick peek. *El Pato, all right,* dressed the same, lugging the security case, a rolled-over grocery bag, and a pet carrier big enough to hold a large-breed dog. The perfect place, Simon realized, to stash the money and guns. "You know what to do."

Raul nodded. *"Sí."*

"I'll wait in the car."

Tony was back in Simon's ear before he reached the Humvee. "This is interesting."

"What?"

"The two buttons just separated. They're going in opposite directions."

Simon wasn't surprised. "He must have checked the case. It's going into the baggage compartment. Hear anything from Charles?"

"That's a negative."

"What about the pilots?"

"Should be here soon. They insisted on clearing everything through Jake. He told 'em I was his son-in-law and whatever I said had his approval. You know, I think that's the first time Jake's ever acknowledged me as part of the family."

Though somewhat muted by the earplug, Simon could hear the excitement and pride in Tony's voice. "That's really great." But he couldn't help wonder how long *the family* would hold together if they lost Kyra. A thought that conjured up his own feelings of familial guilt. Lara still believed he was in Vegas—living the good life at Big Jake's expense. Explaining would not be easy. His sister never made that sort of thing *easy*, but that was part of their relationship—worrying about each other—and making the other pay for it. Oh yes, penance would be particularly severe this time.

"Simon, hang tight a minute, I've got a call coming in from Charles."

"I'm not going anywhere," but in fact, had a feeling he was. He couldn't seem to extract himself from the quagmire, as if every force in the universe was pushing him toward some inevitable, predestined conclusion: *Leonidovich, this is your fate.*

"Simon, okay to talk?"

"Go ahead, I'm in the Humvee waiting for Raul."

"Good news-bad news. The taxi stopped. The driver

didn't hesitate for a second, got right out, ready to help."

"Let me guess, the pack was full of paper?"

"You got it," Tony answered. "The driver was paid to deliver it to some address in Buenaventura. Bogus, no doubt."

"I'm sure. So what's the good news?"

Tony hesitated, as if trying to figure that out himself. "That was the good news. We now know El Pato's our guy. He must have the money somewhere. The dog carrier, I suppose."

"Okay, what's the bad news?" As if he didn't already know.

"Charles and his team may not make it back in time. Depending on when El Pato takes off."

Surprise—Surprise. "So where's our leader now?"

"Already heading this way, driving like hell. ETA approximately forty minutes. He might make it." He didn't sound overly optimistic.

"Okay. Guess we hover and hope."

"Uh-oh."

Two words that never brought good news. "What do you mean, uh-oh?"

"The Duckman's moving toward your end of the terminal."

Simon felt a sudden chill, then realized he was overreacting. "The guy's careful. Probably checking the perimeter, making sure no one's on his tail."

"What about Raul?"

"I warned him. Watch, get the flight information, *don't* follow."

"Okay, good."

"Keep me posted."

"Still coming your way. Must be getting close to the door."

For a brief moment Simon considered making a run for it, but the terminal doors were glass and El Pato would very likely see a very undead courier trying desperately to remain that way. And that would be the end of it, the end of Kyra. *Be cool.* Better to lie down—the glass in the Humvee was nearly opaque—and let the guy do his perimeter check. "Let me know when he's gone."

"Okay." But even before the word faded, Tony was back, his voice almost hysterical. "Holy shit, he's moving really fast now. Almost on you."

Before Simon could move the driver's door snapped open, and he knew he was dead, this time for sure, this time El Pato would put a bullet in his head.

"*Señor?* You are sick?"

Though he recognized Raul's voice, Simon felt like he'd been in a Jacuzzi for hours, his body a collection of soft bones and stretched-out ligaments. He took a deep breath and pushed himself upright. "Must have been something I ate." He could feel the perspiration running off his face. "I'll be okay."

Raul looked unconvinced, though he said nothing as he climbed behind the wheel and dropped a brown paper bag on the seat between them. The same bag El Pato had carried into the terminal. Without looking, Simon knew it contained El Pato's sarape. "He changed clothes?"

"In *el baño*. This he throw in trash."

"Simon," Tony whispered, "you there? You okay?"

He felt better than okay, he felt magically refreshed—nothing like cheating death twice in two hours to make a person appreciate that next big lungful of air. "Yeah, I'm fine. It was Raul. El Pato changed clothes in the restroom. Raul pulled them out of the trash."

"Christ Almighty." Tony's voice echoed with relief. "I thought that waddling bastard had you."

"Me too. Hold on, I'll get back to you in a minute." He turned to Raul. "So what's the skinny?"

"Skinny, Señor?"

"Sorry, that's American slang. What did you find out?"

"Ahh, that is skinny." Raul bobbed his head, pleased to have learned a new word. "The *aeroplano* will go first to Quito. Then to Lago Agrio. His ticket is for Lago Agrio."

"Lago Agrio? That's in Ecuador, right?"

"Sí."

"Departure time?"

Raul frowned—the English numeric system not his forte—and pointed to the number 7 on his watch. *"Doce treinta y cinco."*

"Twelve thirty-five?"

"Sí."

Simon glanced at his watch—*twenty-two minutes*—then reached down and pressed the Network button on his controller. "Okay, guys, here's the deal. El Pato has a ticket to Lago Agrio, scheduled to leave at twelve thirty-five."

"I'll never make it," Charles answered.

"No, but the plane stops in Quito. We'll have the Gulf 5 ready for you. You can beat him to Lago Agrio."

Charles came back instantly. "That's no good. If he's smart he'll have booked a destination beyond where he intends to get off. Oldest trick in the book. He's probably planning to jump ship in Quito."

Simon doubted the Duckman was smart in that way, but he was certainly careful and couldn't be underestimated. "Good point. You have a suggestion?" As if he wanted to hear it.

"You'll have to follow him. I'll charter a plane and catch up."

Right, catch up—sounded easy enough. *Leonidovich, this is your fate.*

They had been in the air only forty minutes, a quick hop over the border before the pilot started his descent into Quito. The Avianca jetliner with El Pato would be on the ground a good ten minutes before they landed, a circumstance that had Tony in a near state of panic. "Shouldn't we have seen it by now?" He was staring at his computer screen, waiting for the silver disk to reappear.

Simon fanned the pages of his passport, decided it wasn't going to get any better, and snapped off the hair dryer. "We're still twenty minutes out. We won't be within range until we're almost on the ground."

"He'll have a ten minute lead. Maybe more."

"Relax, we're not going to lose him." It was the third time he'd said it. "We're not even sure he's getting off in Quito."

Tony shook his head, refusing to accept any possibility other than the worst. "Charles thinks he will."

"Well, I don't." It came out harsher than Simon intended. Quito made perfect sense, smack in the middle of the Cordillera Central range, with a thousand good places to hide someone—a thousand places where Kyra would never be found. But Lago Agrio also made sense. It was near the Amazon Basin, the last place they had a fix on Kyra's plane, and Simon had a feeling that's where they were heading. "You get those rental cars lined up?"

Tony ignored the question, refusing to back off his worst-case scenario. "But what if he *does* get off here?"

"You know what, we've been over this. I'll follow him until Charles and his team can catch up."

"I should be the one, she's my wife."

"Don't start with that, Tony. You'll need to reprogram their transponders before they can follow." It was a weak argument; Charles could do each unit in less than a minute, but Tony was too emotionally involved and Simon was afraid he might do something rash to save his wife before the assault team caught up. "This is the best way."

"You think I'll do something crazy."

Yes! "Of course not. But I'd feel better with you in my ear, making sure I don't get too close." Something he had no intention of doing.

Tony hesitated, took a deep breath, then expelled a reluctant sigh of acceptance. "Okay, but if he leaves the city we'll probably lose the radio anyway."

"Then we'll go cellular." Though Simon had serious doubts about getting any kind of reception in such a remote area. "I'll borrow the pilot's, mine ended up in the river. Now what about the rental cars?"

"Two here, two in Lago Agrio," Tony answered. "We're set, either way."

"Good. The extra transponder?"

Tony reached down, detached the USB interlink, and slid the beeper-size unit across the table. "All set." Then he leaned forward, eyes serious. "So what happens if Charles doesn't get there in time?"

"He will." He snapped on the hair dryer, more to stop Tony from asking any more questions than to finish drying his wallet. Looking forward, beyond the cabin windows, the lights of Quito were just coming into view, leaking through the darkness from north to south.

Tony reached over and plucked a photograph—the only photograph Simon carried—from the row of documents drying on the table. "Who's this?"

"My sister and her kids."

"Nice looking family. Your sister's divorced?"

Simon gave up the battle and switched off the dryer. "Widowed."

Tony flinched, the word hitting an exposed part of his psyche. "Oh. That's too bad." He looked away, his voice wistful. "At least she's got the kids."

"How is it you and Kyra never had children? If you don't mind me asking."

He shrugged. "Kyra wasn't ready."

Simon was instantly sorry he asked the question. "You still have time. Maybe she'll feel different now."

Tony shook his head. "Truth is, things haven't been going so well."

"It's none of my business."

Tony ignored the hint, wanting to talk—needing to. "It's never been easy for us . . . we got married for all the wrong reasons. Or she did. I'm not blaming her, I don't mean that . . . I kinda knew she was trying to get back at her father for leaving Billie." He shook his head, as if he couldn't believe his own stupidity. "I should have known better, but . . . well, you know, I was in love and stupid enough to think it wouldn't matter . . . that eventually she'd learn to love me. All I cared about was her, didn't give a damn who her old man was."

Not sure how to respond, Simon let him talk.

"Stupid me, how do you compete with Big Jake Rynerson?" He took a deep breath and answered his own question. "You can't. No way. And I'm tired of fighting the battle."

Though he preferred not to, Simon felt compelled to respond. "I don't understand. Why should you *have* to compete with him?"

"But you do, all husbands have to compete against Daddy. It's a law of nature. And how can anyone compete against someone like that? You can't! You open the paper, there he is, you turn on the television, he's staring back at you, always doing something great. Something bigger than life. Nothing I ever did could measure up." He took a breath, let it go in a huff. "All I ever wanted was to be her hero."

Ugh, he felt like Father Simon in a confessional. "Tony, for an educated man you sure are a dummy."

His head came up a notch. "What do you mean?"

"You get her and Jake back together, you *will be* her hero."

Tony cocked his head to one side, thinking about it. "Never thought of that." He nodded slowly. "You might be right. I sure hope so."

Me too, Simon thought, as the laptop gave a sharp *BEEP* and two words flashed onto the screen: TARGET ACQUIRED.

CHAPTER TWENTY-NINE

Mariscal Airport—
Quito, Ecuador

Sunday, 16 November 00:42:19 GMT –0500

El Pato leaned against the Plexi window, watching the baggage handlers work. As was his custom, he had taken a window seat in the last row, giving himself a good view of anyone who boarded or left the plane. Most important, it gave him a good view of the luggage ramp. The pet carrier had made it onboard in Cali, he made certain of that, and he wanted to be equally certain some idiot baggage handler didn't unload it here in Quito. He tried to tell himself it was over, that everything had gone exactly as planned, that he could relax, but his mind refused to accept it. Too many times the *grande* masters had taken advantage of his skills. *Not this time*—this time El Pato would drink from the golden cup.

Off to his left, a sleek *aerojet* broke through the darkness and settled gently onto the runway. He tried to read the logo on the tail before it disappeared down the tarmac, but the distance was too far and then it was gone.

Tony hadn't taken his eyes off the monitor since the disk in Simon's security case came into range. Charles and his assault team were still on the ground in Cali, well beyond coverage, so there were only two disks visible: the silver one in the case, and the red one inside Simon's left shoe. Tony moved his cursor over the silver dot, illuminating the location balloon.

S CASE
Latitude: 0°8' South
Longitude: 78°30' West

"That thing hasn't moved an inch. You think there's any chance he left the case behind?"

Simon finished squeezing everything back into his damp wallet. "No, if he didn't want it, he wouldn't have taken it. Either they haven't finished unloading the baggage, or he's not getting off. I'm guessing the latter."

"But you're going in, right? Just in case."

"Unless that disk moves there's no reason to leave the plane. I'd like to beat him to Lago Agrio—just in case."

"In case of what?"

"In case Charles doesn't get there in time." Something Simon preferred not to think about, but in fact could think of little else. "I want to be prepared."

"Prepared how?"

"I need to clear Customs before he's on the ground, otherwise I'll have to wait until he's out of there."

"Good point. And . . . ?"

Simon ticked off the other items on his mental checklist. "I'd like to pick up the rental car and some maps. And if there's time, a few bottles of water, a good flashlight, some snacks . . ."

Tony studied Simon's face, reading his hesitancy. "And . . . ?"

"And a very big gun."

"Just in case."

"Exactly." *Just in case I get a chance to blow the bastard into history.* "How much cash you have?"

Tony pulled his billfold. "About two-fifty American. And—" He paused, counting his Colombian currency. "Three hundred thousand pesos."

"That's about three-fifty, and I've got a couple hundred. A little damp, but it'll spend."

"That's five-fifty, enough to get a bazooka down here. What were you thinking about?"

"A rifle with a scope sounds about right to me," Simon answered. "I don't think I care to get any closer to that bastard."

"I assume you're familiar with guns?"

How hard could it be? *Point and pull.* "Absolutely." He pressed the flight-deck intercom button. "Captain, Simon Leonidovich here. Can you beat that Avianca flight to Lago Agrio?"

The captain's voice came back slow and methodical, a man who liked to be precise. "Well, let me see now . . . that's a Boeing MD-80 . . . she'll be cruising somewhere between Mach .75 and .78, depending on the winds. Our bird can do Mach .90, but it's only about one hundred nautical, so that means . . ."

Simon had already done the math and realized there wasn't enough distance to create any significant time gap. "Don't worry about it, Captain. We're talking minutes—I was hoping for more."

"Ten, twelve minutes if we're lucky. And that's if we get off the ground first."

"When they push back from the gate, you hit the gas, okay?"

"Yessir, the minute we have clearance."

"Then get clearance a couple minutes before their scheduled departure. If they don't push away on time, claim some sort of minor mechanical and have the controllers drop you back a couple minutes. Keep doing it until we see that Avianca start to move."

"Ground control wouldn't appreciate that, Mr. Leonidovich." From his tone, it sounded more like the captain was the one with a problem. "Not a good idea."

Tony flashed an annoyed expression. "Ex-military, goes by the book."

Hides behind it, Simon thought, as he pressed the intercom button. "Captain, as I'm sure you know—" The man, of course, knew nothing about what they were doing. "Mr. Rynerson expects this job to be completed on time. Expects *us* to make that happen. You can be sure I won't forget to mention *any* effort you make"—*or fail to make*— "in that regard."

There was a very brief moment of silence as the Captain considered the not-too-subtle threat, who he worked for and how much he enjoyed the pay, the perks, and the prestige. "Yessir, we'll beat that Avianca off the ground if I have to fly around it."

"Thank you, Captain."

Tony's dark eyes glinted with amusement. "Nice play."

But meaningless. "It still won't give me enough time."

"It won't matter," Tony said, as if trying to convince himself. "Charles will make it."

"I hope so." Surprisingly, a tiny part of his psyche hoped otherwise. It made no sense; the logical part of his brain told him to put as much distance between himself and El Pato as humanly possible—that this was a job for Charles and his commandos—but that tiny nugget of neurons left over from the snakes and snails wanted to face the devil one more time—wanted payback for those three bullets intended for his heart.

CHAPTER THIRTY

Somewhere in South America

Sunday, 16 November 02:03:51 GMT –0500

Kyra watched her son—a beautiful child with platinum hair and big intelligent eyes—peek out from behind the couch and giggle. Anthony, down on all fours, began to circle around behind, his favorite flanking maneuver. Feigning oblivion, Junior scanned the room, apparently unaware of his father's presence until the last possible moment when he spun around and screamed, "Peekaboo! Peekaboo!" Anthony reeled back and collapsed onto the floor, mortally wounded. Neither of them ever tired of the game.

On the couch, seemingly oblivious to the drama taking place around them, Billie and Jake sat curled up together, rifling through the Sunday paper and squabbling in a good-natured way, playing their own adult game of peekaboo.

With his father dispatched and apparently down for the count, Junior leveled his big blues on his mother. "Mommy!" It came out *Maw-mee!* "You play! You play!"

Kyra smiled back at her son. "You know Mommy can't walk." *Can't walk? Why couldn't she walk?* She looked down, saw her feet dangling like two wooden shoes off a puppet and realized instantly she was dreaming. *Again.* She kept her eyes closed, holding on to the vision for as long as possible. That's all she had now, sleep and dreams. Imaginary images. Her father looked so young, the way she remembered him in Odessa. And in her dreams they were always together. *The perfect family.*

She could still see the smile on her son's face . . .

On her husband's face . . .

The way they would have been together. *Perfect.*

The images faded and she opened her eyes. Still dark. Everything the same. Then she heard something, soft and muted, but definitely something. She held her breath, straining to hear, afraid it was him. Then she heard it again, soft as a sigh, and realized it was only the wind.

The black shapes of the branches began to stir as the wind picked up and the first drops of rain hit the ground. The cool air felt good as it washed over her body, and she could imagine herself lying naked next to Anthony and whispering in his ear: *We're going to have a baby.* Maybe that's the way she would die, drifting away on some sweet dream.

The wind suddenly picked up, the tree branches parting high overhead, and she caught a glimpse of one lone star. It winked down at her—a magical moment—and then was gone.

> *When you wish upon a star, makes no*
> *difference who you are . . .*

The song her father sang to her as a child, every time he tucked her into bed and kissed her good night. For the first time she understood why he repeated it night after night. She was Kyra Rynerson, Big Jake Rynerson's daughter, and could do anything she set her mind to. What opportunities she had been given! What a failure she had been!

She would die having squandered the love of two good men: one because he ended up being human, the other because of her selfishness. Even as a parent she had failed—failed to provide her baby with nourishment and life. Even her father had done better than that.

*When you wish upon a star, makes no
difference who you are . . .*

But wishes only came true for those who believed. She rolled onto her side and sat up. *Mommy can't walk.* But she could, not well, but some, and she hadn't given up. She reached down, found her water bottle, drank what she could—two or three ounces before her stomach felt bloated—then stood. It took a moment to find her center, then with measured practice she started forward, dragging her toes in the dirt, one step, two steps, until she was at the wall. She knelt, running her fingers over the scratch marks and counting. *Fourteen.* She might have missed a day or two, might have double-marked a day in confusion, but it was close. *Two weeks.* It felt like years.

How long could she live without food? How long before the baby started to suffer and shrink? A while yet, she was sure of that—it was the perfect parasite, feeding off whatever nourishment she had left—until it killed her. *Justifiable parricide.*

CHAPTER THIRTY-ONE

Lago Agrio, Ecuador

Sunday, 16 November 02:51:44 GMT –0500

"Simon, you awake?"

No, but he was now. "Absolutely." He reached down, gritting his teeth against the fiery burn that pulsated from the bruises over his heart, found the seat's power button, and pushed it forward, bringing the lounger to a sitting position. "What's up."

"We just received landing instructions," Tony answered, "should be on the ground in about ten minutes."

"What's the status?"

"We've got about an eight-minute lead on the Avianca flight. By the time the Duckman gets his pouch and clears Customs you should be out of there."

"What about Charles?"

"He finally found a plane but it took some time to round up the pilots. They just took off."

Not good. "So that means what, they're two hours behind?"

Tony nodded. "At least. Probably more like three by the time they clear Customs and get their visas."

Not good at all, more than enough time for El Pato to check the money and do whatever he intended with Kyra. "That's, uh—"

"Bad," Tony said, acknowledging the obvious. "Very bad."

"Maybe he'll get hung up in Customs." But as Simon said it, he realized that would be just as bad. *Or worse.* If they caught El Pato with either his gun or the money, the chances of finding Kyra alive would be somewhat less than hitting the Super Lotto.

Tony's stonelike expression said as much. "I've got an idea."

Good, they needed one, so why was he thinking *uh-oh?* "I'm listening."

"We both go. If we're lucky, we pick up some weapons along the way. If not, it's two against one."

Lucky, they hadn't gotten lucky yet. Nothing about the idea sounded good. *Two against one,* that sounded more like two VW bugs taking on an Abrams tank. "Forget it, we've been through this. You need to reprogram the other transponders when Charles and his guys get here, and you can check out the cars and have them ready to roll. They'll catch up."

"And if they don't?"

"If I see any indication"—he tried to think of some gentle way of saying *your wife's about to be killed*—"that Charles won't make it in time, I'll call in the local police."

"And Kyra ends up dead in the crossfire."

"What, you think she prefers you get killed trying to save her?"

A sharp look of anger flashed through Tony's eyes. "Maybe *I* would."

That, Simon believed: *All I ever wanted was to be her hero.* But that was the last thing they needed, some kamikaze rush of heroics that would get everyone killed. "This isn't about you."

Tony hesitated, as if searching for a good response, then unexpectedly gave up the battle. "I guess you're right. It was just an idea."

Simon tried to mask his relief. "Don't worry, we'll get her back."

Tony smiled, but the effort looked forced. "Guaranteed, right?"

"Absolutely, my lips to your ears. The Bagman always delivers." *The Bagman always delivers.* Where the hell did that horseshit line come from? As if things weren't bad enough, he'd now gone and promised two people he'd bring Kyra home.

El Pato tried to sleep—once they landed, the drive would take several hours—but he couldn't seem to turn off his mind. Never before had this been a problem—he did his work and never looked back—but the ransom money complicated things in ways he never imagined. He never thought past what it would buy; but now that he had it, and planned to keep it—*every solo centavo*—the problems led one into another, into another, with no end in sight.

Seven million dólares, where does one hide such a sum? Not the banks, those he could not trust.

How did one cash such grande bills and not be noticed? He suspected Rynerson would have *mucho* spies watching for such a thing.

And the original five million? The *norteamericano* wanted it buried along with the woman, but that would be *estúpido,* there had to be some way to spend it.

Twelve million dólares! He struggled through the conversion. *Thirty-four billion pesos!*

AIEEEE, so much money, it was going to make him *loco.*

The plane hit the runway hard and bounced. El Pato blinked and looked around, trying to clear his mind as the jet settled back on the tarmac with a final thud. He glanced at his watch—3:15—then out the window at the small terminal. Off to one side a fuel tanker pulled up alongside a small business aerojet, the windows glowing with yellow light. *Jesu Cristo,* his imagination must be playing tricks, the aerojet looked *muy* similar to the one he'd seen in Quito.

• • •

"Simon?" Tony's voice reverberated off Simon's eardrum. "You there?"

Simon dialed down the volume on his earplug. "Still here." Here being directly across from the tiny terminal in a silent and dimly lit parking lot.

"How's the car?"

"Good." The car was actually a four-wheel-drive Defender—Land Rover's ultimate off-road machine—with a slightly abused body and a well-tuned engine. "If the map is any indication, it's the perfect vehicle."

"What do you mean?"

"Most of the roads are gravel or dirt, and since this is the rainy season, I guess that means mud."

"Maybe he won't leave the city."

City, that was a generous description of Lago Agrio—*Sour Lake*—a rough and rugged frontier town that existed only because of the oil hidden beneath its wet, tropical soil. "Maybe," but he knew better—*not if Kyra was alive*—El Pato would never leave her anywhere near other people, where she might be able to attract attention. "But I wouldn't count on it."

"You didn't happen to notice if they sold any nice big guns in the gift shop?"

"We should be so lucky. I was happy to find a few bottles of water."

"Great, if Charles doesn't get here in time you can always piss on the bastard."

At least Tony was making an effort to stay upbeat. "My thoughts exactly."

"Heads up." Tony whispered, his tone suddenly tight with anticipation. "Looks like he finally made it through."

Simon picked up the transponder. The arrow pointed directly toward the terminal, the digital readout automatically adjusting downward as the distance to the target disk narrowed. The small screen, which provided only a direction arrow and text information—distance, location coordinates, and elevation—did not, Simon realized, give him the same feeling of detached safety as the visual overview displayed on the laptop. "Looks that way." *Thank you, God.* El Pato had been in Customs for over thirty minutes and Simon was starting to think they might have found his gun. Or the money. Or both. If that happened the operation was blown and Jake would have no choice but to swallow his personal dislike for all things Potomac and call the President, who *might*—for some hinted-at pound of political patronage—turn the screws on the Ecuadoran President, who *might*—for some hinted-at offer of foreign aid—turn the screws on El Pato, who *might*—for some hinted-at sweetheart deal—be convinced to reveal Kyra's location. *Long odds. Killer odds.*

"He's heading straight for the door," Tony reported, "must have his own car."

"Or someone's picking him up." Which would instantly shatter the El Pato-is-the-one-holding-Kyra theory. Using his Nightstalkers, he scanned the few vehicles parked along the curb. Everyone looked tired and dispirited, the last place anyone wanted to be at four in the morning. "We'll know soon enough."

"You should see him any second."

Simon swung his binoculars back toward the main doors just as the Duckman emerged, listing awkwardly toward the animal carrier in his right hand. "Got him."

El Pato paused at the curb, his eyes working slowly down the line of cars, as if looking for someone, then his focus abruptly moved forward and out, scanning the parking lot. Though the digital readout registered eight to nine meters, Simon hunkered lower in his seat, not about to test the Duckman's nocturnal instincts. The man was like a wild animal, wary and watchful, always on guard.

Apparently satisfied, he started forward, crossing the street into the parking lot. When the distance narrowed to fifty meters Simon flattened himself out across the bucket seats. He felt a bit foolish—*twice in one night!*—but couldn't stop himself from thinking the worst, that somehow the Duckman had found him. At thirty meters his heart rate began to skyrocket. *Holy Mother, who's tracking whom?* Then at twenty-five meters El Pato angled away, the distance increasing to thirty-six meters before stopping.

"What's going on?" Tony whispered, as if afraid El Pato might hear him.

Simon sucked down a deep breath of the heavy air, forcing his heart rate out of the red zone, and pushed himself up, just enough to see out the window, in the direction indicated on the transponder. "He's standing by one of those old VW buses."

"A hippie van?"

"Exactly. You don't see many around anymore—not in the States anyway. Okay . . . it's his . . . he just opened the side door . . . putting the dog inside . . . shutting the door . . . going around to the opposite side . . . getting in—"

"You see anyone else?"

Simon refocused his binoculars. "Nope, not in front anyway. The back windows look like they've been painted over."

Tony came back instantly, his voice edgy with excitement. "Maybe he's got Kyra in the van."

Not alive. "No, he wouldn't have left her anywhere she could attract attention."

There was a slight pause before Tony came back. "Yeah, right. Of course. Now what's he doing?"

What he was doing was enough to make Simon duck back beneath the window. "He's just sitting there, smoking a cigarette and looking around."

"What the hell's he looking for at four in the morning?"

"Us."

"What are you talking about? You think he's on to us?"

"Not *us* specifically. He thinks I'm dead."

"So what *do* you mean—*specifically?*"

"The guy's a shark, not very bright, but he's dangerous and cunning and can smell danger."

"And you think he smells something?"

"That or the money's made him paranoid. Lugging around a few million bucks can do that to a person."

"I'll take your word for it."

"Trust me, I'm an expert."

Two cigarettes and ten minutes later, El Pato started the van and slowly made his way toward the exit. Simon watched him go, in no hurry to follow. When the distance reached eight thousand meters, Tony began to panic. "You're going to lose him."

"How am I going lose him? He's less than five miles away and the transponders have an effective range of twenty-five miles—minimum."

"You might get hung up in traffic."

"Traffic? This town has a population of thirty thousand, and most of them can't afford a car."

"You could have a flat tire."

"Tony, relax. What's the worst thing that could happen?"

"You lose him."

"Okay, second worst?"

"He spots you."

"Right. There's no reason to take any chances, especially at night, when there is no traffic and he could see my headlights."

"Okay, you're right. Listen—" Tony paused, expelling what sounded like an exhausted sigh. "Unless you need me I think I'll get a little sleep before Charles gets here. You good with that?"

Though surprised—in seconds Tony had apparently gone from worried to weary—Simon was more than happy to have a little time to think without someone chattering in his ear. "Sure, go for it. I'm pulling out now."

"Call me if anything dramatic happens."

Anything more dramatic and he'd be on the hotline to Jesus. "Will do."

For the next ninety minutes El Pato skirted around the edges of the small city, through dark neighborhoods without street signs or paved roads, stopping twice for at least ten minutes before cutting back over the same route in an obvious attempt to see if he was being followed. Simon easily avoided the possibility, maintaining a ten-thousand-meter separation, much of the time just sitting, watching the Duckman weave his way back and forth over the same roads. Finally, as the sky mutated from black to charcoal to gray, and the town began to stir, El Pato turned onto a wide, well-maintained gravel highway and headed west. Except for a few oil tankers and trucks, the roadway was deserted. Simon snapped off his headlights and closed to within eight thousand meters. Stretched across the southern horizon, eerie in the early-morning light, hundreds of oil derricks stretched upward into the gray sky, centurions standing guard over their slaves, the pumpers, moving up and down with monotonous repetition, unrelenting in their quest to suck the earth dry.

Within an hour the derricks and tankers had disappeared, and the gravel highway had deteriorated into a narrow gravel road, barely wide enough for two small vehicles. Though Simon had read countless articles about the burning of the rain forest and its potential effects on the environment, this was his first up-close encounter. The sight and scale of devastation far exceeded anything he imagined. The land had been stripped of all vegetation, the rain forest cut and burned and turned over to cattle for grazing. There were no towns or cities, only an occasional village—unmarked on the map—with a few small houses and little else: no TV antennas, no electrical lines, no schools, no soccer fields.

None of the necessities—no Starbucks, no 24-hour GunsAreUs.

By seven o'clock the air was hot and steamy, the sun shining directly into his eyes. With every mile he felt more isolated and alone—the villages getting smaller and farther in-between, the elevation reading on his transponder dropping toward sea level.

"Simon!"

Tony's sudden bark came like a phone call in the middle of the night, sudden and disconcerting. "What? I'm here."

"You realize he's stopped?"

Simon glanced at his transponder, startled to see that the distance had gone from eight to less than four thousand meters, and slammed on the brakes. *Way to go, Leonidovich!* "No, I didn't. Thanks."

"You see a house or something?" Tony asked, his voice rising with anticipation. "This could be it."

Not likely, Simon thought, unless the Duckman had a place right on the road, the direction the arrow on the transponder was indicating. He switched the Nightstalkers to DAY view, and pointed them toward a small rise about two miles ahead. Even with the binoculars he almost missed it, the rusty green van blending into the vegetation like a chameleon, invisible except for El Pato sitting cross-legged on the roof, his pale gaucho shirt standing out like a sore pimple. "No house, but I see him. He's sitting on the roof of his van, watching the road."

"Oh shit! You think he sees you?"

That was the million-dollar, bet-your-life-on-it question, but one Simon was sure he knew the answer to. "No, he doesn't see me." *Almost sure.*

Tony expelled a whistling sigh. "Thank God! How do you know?"

"Because he's not doing anything. If he saw me he'd be hightailing it down the road, looking for someplace to surprise me." *Made sense.* He just hoped it was true.

"I hope to hell you're right."

Me too. Simon checked his watch. 7:40. "You get some sleep?"

"Not really."

Not surprising, but what did surprise him was that the audio link still worked—*perfectly,* clear as crystal—no cutouts, drops, or fades. "I expected you to call on cellular, didn't think I'd get reception this far out." He glanced at the odometer—one hundred and twelve kilometers—and made a quick conversion. "I've driven about seventy miles."

Tony hesitated a good ten seconds before answering. "But you're out only forty as the crow flies. I'll probably lose you soon, I'm getting a little static on this end."

Something about the explanation sounded wrong, but Simon couldn't think what it might be. "Yeah, you're right. I guess I should be happy whenever the government makes something that exceeds my expectations."

Tony chuckled, though it sounded forced. "Right, so I won't remind you that all this good stuff was manufactured by the lowest bidder."

"Thanks, I appreciate your not mentioning it." He adjusted the focus on the binoculars, hoping to confirm his invisibility, but the Duckman was far too distant to read his facial expressions. "What's the word on Charles?"

There was a another short delay before Tony came back. "Say again. Getting some static here."

"I asked about Charles. What's the status?"

"Okay, got that," Tony answered. "Not here yet."

"That's not good, we need to close this time gap. Why don't you lease a helicopter and—"

Tony cut into the transmission. "Where the hell am I'm supposed to find a helicopter out here?"

Out here? "Lago Agrio's in the middle of an oil field. They use choppers all the time on those rigs. I'm sure if you—"

"Those would be private," Tony interrupted again. "No one's going to lease me one."

Why the resistance? "Tony, I don't have a weapon. Nothing. I couldn't do anything for Kyra if—" He took a breath, swallowing his frustration, sure that Tony was only reacting to the stress. "Look, it's stupid for us to argue about this, it's your wife we're talking about here. Call Jake if necessary, he'll pay whatever it takes. Hell, he'll buy a chopper if he has to."

"You're right," Tony answered, his resistance evaporating. "I'll try."

Try! Try wasn't good enough. "Do whatever it takes. We really need Charles and his team up here. If they chopper in, they can take my car and I'll go back with the pilot." But as he said it, he knew he wouldn't go back; he wanted to be there when they found Kyra, and in that dark shadowy place beneath the bruises that covered his heart, he wanted to be there when they took down the Duckman.

"Okay, I'll get right on it," Tony answered. "Ten-four, over and out."

Simon played the conversation over in his mind—trying to justify Tony's curious resistance to the helicopter, then his sudden acquiescence and sign-off, as though he couldn't wait to end their conversation—but the true reason kept floating away, teasing the edge of his brain.

El Pato shifted positions, his shirt soaked with sweat. The sun, still low in the sky, shimmered off the vast green landscape in misty, caloric waves, diffusing his view beyond a few kilometers. *Nada,* not a single vehicle in thirty minutes. *Imposible,* he felt certain, that anyone could have followed, but the memory of the small aerojet continued to gnaw at his psyche. He waited another ten minutes, then refilled the water bottle attached to El Diablo's cage. No food, *muchacho,* better you are hungry. Soon enough you will eat—a last meal, but a good one.

● ● ●

Simon let the gap reach ten thousand meters before following. *No more lapses,* another mistake and someone would have to dig the bullet out of his ear. He waited thirty minutes—not wanting to push Tony too hard— then tried to reach him on the audio link. As expected, there was no response—the distance back to Lago Agrio well beyond the range of the equipment—leaving the telephone as the only means of communication. *Not good.* Simon couldn't remember seeing a single utility line since the oil fields, and the display on the tiny cellular he borrowed from the pilot indicated a similar problem: NO SERVICE.

Out of choices, he shifted into four-wheel and headed overland toward a small rise about a half mile to the south. The moment he reached the crest the signal indicator on the cellular jumped two notches and the NO SERVICE message disappeared. *Thank you, God.* But the gratitude was premature, the momentary relief dissolving in the echoing silence of twelve unanswered rings. Desperate, he tried to reach Charles. It rang once, followed by a recorded message: *This is Charles, you've reached my private voice mail. Leave a name and number, I'll get back to you.*

"Charles, Simon here. Can't reach Tony. It's zero eight-thirty. El Pato is now at—" He glanced down at the transponder.

> Latitude: 0°10' North
> Longitude: 76°13' West

"—zero degrees, ten minutes, north latitude. Seventy-six degrees, thirteen minutes west longitude. I'm behind him approximately fourteen thousand meters. He's continuing to head west at about forty miles an hour, directly into the Amazon Basin. I'll continue to follow and will call in whenever I get a signal. Tony is trying to—" There was a faint hum as the signal dropped into the NO SERVICE range and disconnected. *Damn!* Still, he got out most of what he needed to say, and felt certain Charles would get the message when he reached Lago Agrio. He waited another five minutes, hoping the signal would come back, but when the gap increased to seventeen thousand meters—over ten miles—he gave up the wait and returned to the road.

Slowly, over the next hour, he narrowed the distance back to ten thousand meters, the road becoming worse with each mile. Shortly before midday he topped a small ridge and the earth seemed to slip away into a vast sea of green— the great Amazon Basin—the world's largest drainage system, rivers and tributaries circling and twisting back on themselves, going nowhere, flooding into stagnant dark pools; over two million square miles of jungle and marshland. An area large enough to swallow Texas and never belch. Never in his life could he remember feeling so isolated and small. In the distance he could see the beginning of the rain forest; a place, he had a feeling, where the Duckman would feel very much at home.

Deep in his gut Simon had the feeling he had gone far enough, maybe too far—*you did your job, now it's time to let the professionals do theirs*—but the professionals were nowhere around, and if he let El Pato get away . . . they would never find him again, and they would never find Kyra.

No, he could never live with that. *Leonidovich, this is your fate.* As he started down into the Basin the sky began to darken and within minutes the first drops of rain splattered against his windshield. Big, heavy drops. In seconds the drops had turned into a downpour, which quickly became a deluge, the rain coming in sheets, turning the dirt and gravel roadbed into a skating rink and cutting his visibility to less than ten feet. By the time he reached the rain forest the rain had stopped, the road a dark trench between dense jungle walls, the high trees turning day into a gray twilight of heat and haze and humidity.

He stopped and rolled down the windows, the air so hot and dense it felt like he was breathing through a dishrag. He glanced at his cellular, the hundredth time in the last few hours: NO SERVICE. *Electronically naked in an electronic world.* Combining the precise information on his transponder

Latitude: 0°4' North
Longitude: 75°56' West

with the sketchy overview of his rudimentary map, he was now sitting at the heart of Drug Dreamland: less then ten miles from the Rio Putumayo, a substantial river dividing Ecuador from Colombia, and only a few miles north of Peru; a tri-country area infamous for its cocaine and cannabis. The Duckman, Simon had a feeling, was close to home. *Very close*—a fact his transponder seemed to confirm. Despite the fact that he had stopped, the separation number:

9,542 meters

hadn't changed in over a minute. Was this it, or was the man out peeing in the weeds? A minute passed, then two, then finally the number began to change, but slower than before, much slower, the meters clicking off one at a time rather than jumping forward in spurts. Either the van was bogged down in mud, or the Duckman was on foot. Simon waited, watching the numbers slowly increase, not sure what he should do. After five minutes there seemed to be a slight shift in the arrow. Another five minutes and he was sure of it, and equally sure the Duckman had left the road and was on foot. Then the numbers stopped, holding steady at 9,994 meters. *Okay, Leonidovich, now what?*

He could sneak up on the location, try to confirm that Kyra was still alive, then go for help. He could continue on, the Putumayo couldn't be more than a few miles; hopefully with some kind of town or crossing, and a phone. He could even go back, until he was able to reestablish cellular contact. Option one would be risky, he had no weapon and no way to help Kyra even if he found her. Going back would be the safest, but Kyra could be dead before he made contact. Option two was clearly the best choice, the smart move.

He started forward, holding his speed below fifteen miles an hour, one eye on the road, one eye on the transponder. As the separation number clicked lower and the gap narrowed, the arrow began to shift southward, away from the road. Thirty minutes later, at 500 meters it pointed due south, but within a minute, as the separation number began to climb and the arrow edged past the perpendicular, Simon realized he had missed the spot where the van left the road. *Didn't matter,* he had the exact coordinates of the disk. *No reason to stop. You did your job, now it's time to let the professionals do theirs. No reason at all.* He edged over toward the trees and stopped. Just a quick peek, that's all, nothing more, then he'd find a phone and call Charles.

Walking, he found the spot easily, the van no more than a few meters into the trees. The place was eerily silent, which for some reason made him feel exposed and vulnerable, but he shrugged it off, knowing he couldn't be more alone. That's when it hit him—*too quiet*—no birds in the trees, the hush unnaturally deep. He froze in his tracks, straining to pick up any sounds or movement, but saw nothing, heard nothing . . . only? . . . a smell . . . something familiar and out of place . . . something acrid and musky. And then recognized it—sweat. Someone close.

Behind him.

CHAPTER THIRTY-TWO

Putumayo Region, Ecuador

Sunday, 16 November 14:29:27 GMT –0500

When Simon regained consciousness he was on the ground, his shirt open, his hands and feet tied together behind his back. The top of his head felt like it was about to split open. It took a few seconds to figure out where he was and what happened, about half a second more to realize he'd just won the annual Darwin Award for Stupidity. How could someone who waddled like a duck move so quietly? The Land Rover had been moved, parked up next to the van, so he'd been out for a while—at least ten minutes. He turned his head and a fresh stab of pain burned through his skull, temple to temple. "Aaah!"

El Pato, sitting cross-legged on the ground, his attention on the transponder, looked up. "You die hard, *gringo.*"

Was that a comment or a promise? *Probably both.* "Lucky, I guess." His voice sounded far away, like it was lost somewhere deep in his trachea.

El Pato nodded and patted the gun in his belt. "You lucky, I kill you quick."

Answered that question.

"You lie—" El Pato ran a finger across his neck. *"Comprende?"*

He understood all right, but suspected he was going to die slow and hard no matter what he said. *"Sí, I comprende* very well." *Asshole.*

El Pato held up the transponder.

"It's a tracking device," Simon answered, knowing it

would be useless to claim otherwise. "To my security case."

"Where are your *compadres?*"

"My *compadres?*" Simon tried to look confused without overdoing it. "What *compadres?*"

El Pato fixed him with a glare hot enough to melt asbestos. "Don't lie to me, *gringo*. You would not come for the woman alone."

"The woman? What do I care about the woman?" He tried to make the question sound foolish. "I'm a professional courier, my security case has a built-in homing device. When you took it I saw an opportunity."

El Pato stared back, his expression one of expectation, as if waiting for the punch line to a long-winded joke.

"The money, you idiot!" Simon hoped his histrionic outburst didn't get his throat slit before he had a chance to think of something. "I came for the goddamned money!" Something apparently registered in the man's brain because he didn't react to the insult and was still listening. "You think if I was here for the woman I would have come alone? I'm a businessman, same as you. I don't even have a gun." The circumstances were so absurd—the fact that he was there, alone, unarmed, that it actually sounded plausible.

El Pato nodded slowly, apparently thinking the same. He stood up, pulled a stiletto switchblade from his pocket—*CLICK*—and stepped forward.

"Wait! Don't—"

El Pato smiled, his lips stretching back over his uneven teeth in a ghoulish caricature of evil, then leaned down and cut the rope between Simon's feet and hands. "You will show me this *homing device.*"

Simon tried to hide his relief, but failed, could see it in the Duckman's eyes, the enjoyment the man got from inflicting fear. He motioned toward a twenty-liter can of gasoline sitting next to the van. *"Llévesela."*

Simon didn't understand the words but understood the message well enough: *you carry*. He also realized the gasoline was the reason the Duckman had returned to the van. The reason for the gas he didn't care to imagine. He pushed himself upright, the movement setting off a fresh lightning storm in his head, his thighs going pins and needles with the surge of blood. All things considered, this was turning into a really shitty day, and he had a feeling things were about to get worse.

The hike took about fifteen minutes but felt like an hour, Simon leading the way with the heavy container, the light so diffused by vegetation and high trees he could barely see the trail. Every time he slowed down to shift the can from one hand to the other the Duckman would prick him with the stiletto and laugh. A real jokester. They were almost on top of the crude shack before Simon even noticed it was there. Impossible, he realized, to see from above, the only hope he had: that Tony had found a helicopter, that Charles had gotten the message and would follow the road west and spot them from the air. *Cavalry to the rescue.* It wasn't going to happen.

The inside of the small structure was no less primitive. He tried to see everything, absorb all the details—no windows, a second door, newer, with a heavy inside bolt, camp kitchen, a shallow hole in the dirt floor, and a large pit bull chained and lying unconscious near a narrow bed—but no sign of Kyra Rynerson. The Duckman motioned with his knife toward a plank table, empty except for Simon's security case, a satellite phone, and the seven million in currency. *"Rápido, gringo."*

Simon laid the case on its side, turning the top toward El Pato. *One quick move*—the dye bomb would explode and activate the siren—but both measures were designed only to draw attention, and he hesitated, afraid it would do nothing but turn the Duckman into a glow-in-the-dark homicidal maniac. *Too risky.* He pointed to the tiny bump along the bottom edge, near a seam in the leather. "It's there."

El Pato motioned for Simon to step away, then leaned down, slit the seam, and extracted the disk. He turned it over in his hand, then dropped it on the floor and ground it into the dirt with his heel. Reaching into his pocket, he pulled the transponder, glanced down at the display, smiled, and turned his dark eyes on Simon. "Okay, *gringo*—"

Simon waited for the *now what* to be answered when a muted female voice broke the silence. "H-e-l-p me."

Simon tried to hide his surprise but El Pato looked delighted, his gold tooth flashing, as if the soft cry had given him an amusing idea. He pointed his stiletto at the locked door. "You want to see, eh?"

Simon shrugged, trying to maintain the illusion that he had no interest in the woman. The Duckman pulled his automatic and motioned toward the door. *"Abierto."*

Simon slid the bolt aside and pulled open the door. El Pato shoved him forward and slammed the door, the bolt sliding into place. The fetid odor of human waste stopped him dead, burning his nostrils; so strong he could taste it in his mouth and feel it behind his eyeballs. He took a thin breath of the hot muggy air, pulling it in between his teeth, trying not to gag. The room was minuscule, a dungeonlike cell, five or six feet wide, eleven or twelve long, one window, bamboo bars, a rusty pail in the corner and a steel cot. Nothing else but a waiflike figure standing frozen in the dim light. She just stood there, like a wooden Indian, her skin dark and dirty. Her shoulder-length blond hair looked like sewage foam, hanging around her head in damp, greasy strands, her body thin as a ballerina. She made no effort to cover herself, her expression more curious than afraid. "Hello, Kyra."

"Who are you?" Even her voice sounded thin and lost.

He placed a finger to his lips, not wanting to say anything until he was sure El Pato couldn't hear. She nodded and took two awkward steps forward, her toes dragging in the dirt, and pressed her face against the wall. Then she stepped aside and gestured for him to look. He stepped in beside her and found the hole. El Pato was at the table, about ten feet away, carefully packing the money into the security case. When Simon stepped back Kyra turned away, as if conscious of her nudity for the first time. He stripped off the light cotton jacket he'd found on the plane and held it out. She slipped her hands through the armholes, the fabric barely covering her bottom, and zipped it up, a dirty mannequin in a baggy negligee.

He leaned close, keeping his voice low. "I'm glad you spoke up when you did. You may have saved my life."

She nodded. "I was watching. I thought you were with him until—" She hesitated, eyes wary. "Who are you?"

"My name is Simon Leonidovich. I was hired by your father to—" He suddenly realized he was whispering into an ear that wasn't supposed to be there. *What the hell?* He stepped back—thinking he must have gone punchy from the head blow—but saw that she had both ears.

She gave him another puzzled look. "What's wrong?"

"Your ear—"

She reached up and touched the left side of her head. "Is it disfigured? He really gave me a crack, broke my eardrum. It bled for two days."

"No, it looks fine. It's just that—" But he couldn't say it, not when her father and good friend, Ms. Caitlin Wells, had been so confident in their identification. *I gave her the earrings myself. Caity picked them out.* "It's uh—" He felt like a parrot struggling to learn words. "It's nothing. It's just that someone told me you wore diamond studs." *Lame, Leonidovich, really lame.*

She looked at him like he had suddenly sprouted stupid horns, not understanding why something so trivial could be important. "He took them."

"Right. I just wanted to be sure you were Kyra Rynerson."

"Believe me—"

"I do, of course I do." And he did. Whatever game Big Jake and Caitlin might be playing—and he would have to think about that—it was obvious Kyra Rynerson-Saladino had nothing to do with it. He motioned toward the cot, which he noticed was bolted to the wall with heavy steel lugs. "Let's sit, it'll be easier to talk." He was still trying to ignore the stench, to get it out of his nostrils and the back of his throat.

She half-stumbled the two steps and he realized something was seriously wrong. "What happened? Your feet?"

She leaned close, her mouth next to his ear. "I tried to escape. He cut my Achilles tendons."

The very thought of it rendered him momentarily mute.

"The only thing he *didn't do* was rape me," she added, as if anticipating the question.

"I'm sorry. *Really* sorry. I can't even imagine." He didn't want to. "The guy's an animal."

"Oh no." Though barely a whisper, her voice echoed with hate. "Even the *lowest* animal strives to realize its limited purpose. He's scum. Nothing but *fucking* scum." Then she chuckled, very softly, as if amused at her own vehemence. "And that's a professional opinion, Mr. Leonidovich. You may quote me."

Despite the circumstances, she could still find some humor in life, and he liked her immediately. "We'll tell it to the world, together, when we get out of here."

"Are we going to get out of here?"

He couldn't imagine how. "No question about it."

"How?"

Wrong question. He leaned closer, until his lips were almost touching her ear. "I have a GPS tracking unit in my shoe. Tony was—"

She jolted back. "My Tony? Anthony?"

"Yes. He's in Lago Agrio. He w—"

"We're going to have a baby."

Her response seemed so out of the moment Simon wasn't sure how to respond, though he knew how Tony would feel. "That will make him very happy."

Her eyes gleamed with pride. "Yes, it will. I can't wait to tell him."

What could he say to that? The whole conversation was surreal, both of them ignoring the fact that they could be dead at any moment. "You don't look—"

"I'm only into my second month."

"Are you getting enough to eat? You look a little thin." Anorexic would be more accurate.

"It's been a few days." Her gaze slid away, as if trying to recall how many. "I've been drinking rainwater."

THUNK. The dull sound reverberated through the wall. *THUNK*.

"What the hell is that?"

It was obvious from her expression that she knew. "He's digging again."

"Digging what?" But he knew—should have realized it the minute he saw the hole. "A grave?"

She nodded. "Guess he expects us to share space."

He took her hand and gave it a gentle squeeze. "It's not going to happen."

"Where is Lago Agrio? What did you say Anthony was doing?"

"It's about seventy-five miles east of here." *By helicopter.* "He was tracking my movements"—no reason to mention the fact that they were now sitting fifty long miles beyond the range of his GPS unit—"and was supposed to direct the rescue team to our location once I found you."

"Was?"

"Is. I meant *is.*"

Her eyes augured in, searching for the truth. "Will they make it in time?"

"Absolutely." *With a helicopter and God at the stick.* "But Mr. Scum does seem to be in quite a hurry to spend his money—" *Bags packed, gasoline ready.* "It wouldn't hurt to have a backup plan."

"He won't do it until he gets the call."

Simon didn't need to ask what she meant by *it*, and had a pretty fair idea about *the call* as well. "Call?"

"He never does anything without approval."

His heart was suddenly beating like a bird in distress. "Any idea who it is making the calls?"

She shook her head. "But it sounded like someone close to my father. Someone in Vegas. They seemed to know a lot."

He wasn't surprised, but the thought that it might be Caitlin cut deep, a physical pain in the center of his chest. He took a breath and tried to keep his voice calm, the question sounding casual. "Who in Vegas knew you were going to the Galápagos?"

She stared straight ahead, searching her memory. "No one I can think of—" Her voice came slow, thinking about it. "I don't really talk to anyone but Caitlin." She came back from the memory, avoiding his eyes, embarrassed. "My father and I—"

"I know."

"I really want to change that. I know he loves me."

"Very much, still calls you 'his little girl.' He's worried sick. So's your mother, of course."

"You've met my mother?"

He nodded. "She's in Vegas. I promised her I'd bring you home." He gave her hand another soft squeeze. "It's a promise I intend to keep."

She smiled faintly, with her eyes. "You seem like a really nice man, not someone just paid to find me."

Right, sweet as honey and telling more lies than a politician. "Thanks, there's a lot of people out there who care about you."

"That's nice to hear."

"You mentioned Caitlin. Did you discuss your trip with her?"

"I could have. Probably."

Not what he wanted to hear. "But you're not sure?"

"Not really. Why? You think someone might have overheard her say something?"

No, that wasn't at all what he was thinking. "It's possible. Do these calls come on a regular basis?"

"Almost every day. He gets a beeper message first, then he makes the call."

"Any special time?"

"Early in the morning or late at night," she answered. "Almost never during the day."

Good, they still had time, but to do what? He looked down at his wrist, then realized El Pato had taken his watch along with everything in his pockets.

Kyra glanced back over her shoulder, at the window. "Two, maybe three more hours of daylight." She pointed at the corrugated tin sheets overhead. "You might be able to push through if you stood on my shoulders."

He almost laughed, the thought of Dumbo the elephant standing on the shoulders of Minnie Mouse. "Good idea, but you'd have to be the one to stand on my shoulders."

"I wouldn't have the strength to pull myself up. Even if I could, it would be hard for me to climb down. I can barely walk."

"Well, I don't see how you could hold me. I weigh over two hundred."

"Don't be too sure about that," she answered forcefully, the familiar stubbornness of Jake Rynerson coming into her voice. "If I wedged myself in the corner and you climbed over me."

He didn't believe it—she was too fragile, probably weaker than she realized—but she had her father's determination and there was no reason to quash her hopes. "Okay, no reason not to try."

"Except that he'll hear us."

"He'll go to his car, probably sometime in the next couple of hours. We can try then."

She gave him a questioning look. "What makes you think he'll go to his car?"

"It's obvious he wants to get out of here fast, that's why he's out there playing gravedigger. And the only reason he would dig inside is—"

"I figured that out," she interrupted. "He's going to burn the place down."

"Right. Which means he'll want his car loaded and ready to go before he does it. I doubt if he'll want to lug his stuff through the jungle after dark."

"Makes sense." A bewildered frown slowly creased her forehead. "But won't the rescue team be here before then?"

"I hope so, but they were following another lead. It will take them a while to get here after Tony pinpoints our location. Like I said, it doesn't hurt to have a backup plan."

"And what if he decides to kill us before he loads the car?"

The very question Simon was asking himself. "I'm working on it."

There was a sudden scrape of wood and then the eyes of El Pato looking at them through a small window-slot in the door. He didn't say a word, just stared at them like a couple of specimens in a petri dish—as if his silence carried some kind of lesson he wanted them to learn—then he laughed, a chilling low-in-the-throat chuckle, and closed the window. They sat there, silent, waiting for the next scrape of the shovel, but heard nothing, everything eerily quiet.

Simon leaned close to Kyra's ear. "Creepy."

"You have no idea."

But he did, or could imagine, and that was more than

enough. He motioned for her to stay, then stepped quietly to the wall and pressed his eye against the tiny hole. El Pato was sitting on the edge of his bed, bare-chested and sweaty from digging, head back, drinking *Aguardiente Antioqueno* from a liter bottle, the satellite phone lying next to him. The pit bull appeared to be recovering from its drug-induced sleep: head up, eyes struggling to focus. The table was now empty, except for the miscellaneous items El Pato had taken from Simon's pockets: wallet, passport, a few coins, his keys, and the antique gold compass Caitlin had given him for his birthday. His security case and a blue duffel were stacked near the door.

"What's happening?" Kyra whispered as Simon returned to the cot.

"Looks like he's ready to go. Just waiting for the call, I guess."

She looked up at the roof. "If he goes to the car, how much time will we have?"

"Twenty, maybe twenty-five minutes." But *time* wasn't the issue—it would only take a couple minutes to bust through, a few more to climb down, release her, and disappear into the jungle—all of which depended on her supporting his weight. *Not likely.* "Listen, so you know—" He reached over and took her hand. "Just in case the rescue team doesn't make it in time. When he opens that door I'm going to rush him."

"He always has a gun."

"And I'm going right for it. Maybe I'll get lucky and catch him by surprise."

She gave him an evaluating stare. "That's suicide."

"A lot of people survive gunshot wounds. You just do whatever you can to get away. Don't stop. Don't think about it. Just go."

"No." Determined.

"It wasn't looking for a vote, Kyra. That's what I intend—"

"Not *no,* don't do it. If it comes to that, it's probably the best thing to do. But *no,* I won't try to get away. With my feet that would be impossible. If you're going to rush the bastard I'll try to help. I can still gouge and bite and kick."

He didn't especially like the idea—she seemed too frail to offer much assistance—but she was probably right, it would be useless for her to try and run. "Okay. I'll go for the gun, you go for his eyes."

She gave his hand a squeeze. "Good. Let's bury that bastard in his own grave."

"I'd like to—" He hesitated, thinking he heard something, a faint vibration across the back of his neck. "You hear that?"

She cocked her head, listening, then nodded. "I know that sound. He's asleep."

Now Simon heard it, the low, gurgling snore, but that was not the echo that lingered in his memory. Then he heard it again, a low warning *shhhhhhh* at the window.

CHAPTER THIRTY-THREE

Putumayo Region, Ecuador

Sunday, 16 November 15:52:13 GMT –0500

Despite her injuries Kyra leaped off the cot, the sheer joy of seeing her husband's face propelling her to the window. For Simon, the moment of elation evaporated in the sudden realization of what it meant—and what it meant was not good.

It meant Tony had followed, unable to resist the opportunity: *All I ever wanted was to be her hero.*

It meant he purposely severed the audio link to hide the fact. *I'll probably lose you soon, I'm getting a little static on this end.* But digital didn't produce static.

It explained his resistance to leasing the helicopter. He wasn't in Lago Agrio.

It all added up to *no helicopter, no Charles, and no rescue team.* All of which Tony admitted in a glance; then Simon turned away, feeling like a voyeur at a reunion between long-lost lovers. But he couldn't ignore the tender whisper of Kyra's first words. "We're going to have a baby."

Trying to suppress his anger, Simon stepped to the wall and pressed his eye over the tiny pinhole. El Pato was on his back, his rattling snore vibrating the air. The automatic was still in his belt, the satellite phone beside him. Simon shifted his focus toward the dog, staked and chained between the table and narrow bed. If the hate in its dark eyes meant anything, the beast appeared to have regained most of its mental faculties, a limited catalog that included *ATTACK* and *KILL.* Simon tried to block out the soft whispers from behind and focus on what they should do. Unless Tony had a weapon—which seemed unlikely—they were still in trouble. El Pato could kill three as easily as two. *Okay, Leonidovich, what are the options?*

"Pssst." Kyra's soft interjection forced its way through his mental logjam. "We have a plan."

He listened silently, as she explained, not believing they actually thought Tony could simply walk in and bash El Pato over the head with a tire iron. "Are you crazy, he'll wake up."

She shook her head. "Listen."

He listened to El Pato's snore vibrating through the wall. "So?"

"I've been listening to that for—" She flashed her husband a look, a shorthand glance that required no explanation.

"Fifteen days," Tony answered.

She nodded slowly, as if that confirmed her own calculations. "Believe me, I know that monster's sleep patterns. He's not going to wake up, not if we're careful. He's at the beginning of a sleep apnea cycle. In a few minutes he'll get into his rhythm, crescendo snoring followed by periods of silence, sometimes up to a minute, ending with a big snort as his body fights for oxygen. Eventually he'll go too long without a breath and wake up. That's why we have to do it now, before he gets too deep into his cycle."

"It won't matter if we're careful," Simon argued. "The dog's between him and the door."

"Oh—" The hopeful enthusiasm in her voice evaporated. "It's usually on the other side."

Tony leaned in, his face against the bars. "I can still open your door. We could be at the car before he ever wakes up."

"Forget it. That dog will go ballistic the second you crack the door."

Kyra shook her head deliberately. "No, the most he'll

do is growl a little. He doesn't want to scare you away. He's a killer—he *wants* to meet you up close and personal."

"You hope."

"I'm a zoologist, trust me."

But it wasn't a matter of trust, it was about making the right decision, the smart decision, and it was hard to believe this was the best they could conjure up. "We could wait until he goes to the car."

"And what if he doesn't go to the car?" she argued. "What if he decides to kill us first?"

Two what-if questions Simon couldn't answer.

"It's risky," Tony admitted, "but unless you have a better idea . . ."

That was the problem, he didn't. "I assume Charles doesn't know . . . ?"

"Sorry."

But it was too late for *sorry* and too late for recriminations. "I understand." *All I ever wanted was to be her hero.*

"We need to do this now," Kyra whispered impatiently.

The need to rush made Simon all the more uncomfortable. He was missing something, could feel it, but couldn't quite connect the warning dots in his head. "Okay, but—" He gave Tony a meaningful look, trying to send a message without embarrassing him in front of his wife. "Don't try anything heroic. Just unlock the door."

"Of course. If you can carry Kyra out of the house and across the clearing, I can take her from there."

"No problem."

"We'll take my Jeep, it's about fifty yards to the east of the other cars. I grabbed his phone charger and pulled the distributor caps off both the van and Land Rover so he won't be able to follow us."

"Good." At least he was thinking. "But if that bastard starts to wake up, I'm going to yell. You get the hell out of here and find a phone."

"Ten-four." Tony leaned forward, kissed his wife through the bamboo bars, then disappeared around the side of the shack.

"You get on the bed," Simon whispered, "when I stoop down climb on my back."

She nodded and hobbled the two steps back to the cot while Simon planted himself in front of the peephole. El Pato's nocturnal volume seemed to be growing, rotating back and forth between a vibrating rattle and a snotty gurgle. Simon found himself breathing to the same irregular rhythm. *Five minutes,* it would all be over. They would be free—or dead.

Even before Tony reached the outside door the dog emitted a low humming growl, barely audible above El Pato's vocal thunder. Slowly . . . one centimeter at a time . . . one soft squeak after another . . . Tony edged the door forward . . . until it was finally wide enough to poke his head through. He carefully checked everything with his eyes, then resumed the effort, taking his time, until the door was wide enough to step inside. The dog now had its legs under him, straining at the chain, its lips pulled back to expose a nasty array of yellow teeth, its soft growl as unrelenting as its desire to kill. Tony switched the tire iron from his left hand to his right and stepped forward. One step, then two . . . he paused . . . looked at the dog . . . looked at El Pato. Simon could almost read his mind: measuring the steps, wondering if he could kill the dog and get to El Pato before he woke up. Simple enough, in the abstract, but to do it, to crush a man's skull, not an easy thing. Considering the dog and the speed of El Pato's hands—nearly impossible. *Don't do it!*

Finally, after a good thirty seconds, Tony turned and resumed his silent trek across the room, one slow step after another. Then the room went silent, El Pato's chest still as stone, his mouth open but no air moving back and forth. Tony froze in midstep, one foot hovering above the floor. Simon held his breath, sweat pouring off his face. The moment seemed to last forever . . . thirty seconds . . . forty . . . then El Pato gave a sharp snort, sucked in a huge mouthful of air, and the thunder resumed.

Relieved, Simon forced himself to breathe as Tony lowered his foot and started forward. He was now only a couple steps from their cell, at his most vulnerable should El Pato wake up. Moving quickly, Simon stepped back and squatted, letting Kyra climb onto his back. Like a little girl getting a piggyback ride, she wrapped her arms around his neck. He pulled her knees up close and stood up just as Tony pushed the door open, the scrape of wood buried beneath a crescendo of nasal thunder.

Simon didn't hesitate, moving quickly into the room . . . one step . . . then another . . . he glanced at El Pato . . . still into his rhythm . . . and veered toward the table. *Two extra steps.* Kyra instinctively understood, and as he paused between one step and the next she reached down and silently scooped up his billfold, passport, keys, and compass. *Good girl.* Three more steps and he was at the door. *Going to make it.*

Then he was outside . . . moving faster now . . . across the small clearing . . . toward the trees and the trail leading back to the road . . . then realized the only nonjungle sounds were those of his own feet. He glanced back just as Tony appeared in the doorway, the blue duffel in one hand, the security case in the other. The temptation to play the ultimate hero had been too great. He was still in the doorway when a faint but distinctive *BEEP-BEEP-BEEP* ruined his perfect fantasy.

"That's his beeper," Kyra shouted, "run!"

But Simon was already running as hard as he could. Only a few more feet to the trees. He looked back, one quick glance before ducking into the thick vegetation. Tony was catching up fast . . . almost across the clearing . . . still lugging the case and duffel . . . still playing hero . . . then El Pato was at the door, gun in hand. He shouted something, but it was muffled by the undergrowth and the roar of the Duckman's automatic—*BANGBANGBANGBANGBANG*—nine quick shots, one on top of another. The bullets sliced through the vegetation, slamming into trees with a hard *THUNK*, or ricocheting away, whining like a band saw.

"Keep going!" Tony screamed, as he came up behind. "We can still make it!"

Simon knew better. Kyra suddenly felt like an elephant and his legs were starting to give out. They had only one chance. *Hide.* He picked his spot, darting right as the trail veered left . . . plunging into the trees, the branches and vines slicing into his arms and cutting his face . . . plowing straight ahead . . . thirty yards . . . lungs burning . . . forty. He cut back toward the road . . . ran until his legs threatened to buckle, then collapsed against a tree. Kyra slid off his back, her bare legs ribboned with cuts and scratches, but still clutching the items she had snatched off the table. Tony staggered in behind them, panting hard, still toting the security case and duffel.

Kyra stared at her husband, her expression a mixture of anger and confusion. "Why?"

He shrugged. "I didn't want"—He paused, gulping air—"those bastards to have it."

Simon held up a hand, warning them. "*Shhhh.* He's coming."

And coming fast, a mad bull at full charge. For a few seconds it sounded like he was heading straight for them, then the sound began to recede as he missed the spot where they had left the trail. "It won't take him long," Simon whispered, "to figure out he missed us. We need to keep moving."

Tony nodded. "I'll take Kyra, you take the money."

"Leave it. Jake wants his daughter back, he doesn't give a damn about the money."

Tony hesitated, but only a second. "Okay, I'll hide it."

"Come on," Kyra whispered, her tone pleading, "Mr. Leonidovich is right; my father doesn't care about the money."

But Tony had made up his mind and was already on his knees, pushing Simon's case under a thick layer of vegetation. "This will only take a minute."

Simon realized it wasn't worth the argument, not until some minutes later when it was too late to go back. Taking the money had not only been foolish, it guaranteed El Pato wouldn't give up until he found them. *Not good.* He checked his compass, trying to keep them on course, a difficult task when he had to keep altering direction to avoid the more impenetrable areas. He pushed through a layer of swamp grass rising two feet over his head, then glanced back over his shoulder. Tony looked as if he had just taken a dip in a stagnant pond: his clothes soaked and covered in pollen and mulch and flies, his boots encrusted with mud, rivers of sweat dripping off each side of his chin. Kyra looked worse, struggling just to stay on her husband's back, her eyes dull and unfocused. Simon wasn't surprised; she hadn't eaten in days and was operating on pure adrenaline. Adrenaline that apparently had run out. "You okay? I can take her."

"No sweat," Tony answered, his words coming between breaths, "just got . . . second wind."

"Let me know."

He nodded. "You sure . . . we're heading . . . right direction?"

Simon held up his compass. "Due north. We'll hit the road eventually."

"I didn't think . . . it was . . . this far."

A feeling Simon shared, though the first time he had a crude trail to follow and didn't have to weave his way through a quagmire of trees and vines and a thousand varieties of plants he didn't know existed. "We should be close."

He had heard people talk about the rain forest—how beautiful it was, how important it was to preserve—but at the moment he was having trouble appreciating the so-called *jungle experience.*

Admit it, Leonidovich, you're just a city boy. Not that city life didn't have its dangers. *But this shit* . . . everything about the place seemed dangerous and ominous and anti–Homo sapiens. It was hot and humid and sticky and swarming with a gazillion flies, fleas, and mosquitoes—and God knew what other kind of creepy crawlers—all intent on setting up housekeeping in his eyes and nostrils and ears. Despite what the gung-ho adventurers had to say, it was *not* a place for any creature with less than six legs.

He broke through another wall of high grass and suddenly found himself on the edge of the road. He stepped back, knowing El Pato would be searching for another vehicle and watching.

"What's up?" Tony whispered, as he came up behind. Kyra's head bounced and then settled on his shoulder. She was either asleep or unconscious, her arms locked around her husband's neck, her bare bottom exposed beneath the warm-up, a nice target for the swarming flies and mosquitoes.

"The road," Simon answered.

Tony hooked his jaw toward the right. "Should be that way."

"You said you were parked east of the other cars."

"Right."

"Then it should be to our left. We went to the right off the trail."

Tony hesitated, thinking. "You're right. Unless we came out between them."

A possibility Simon hadn't considered. He tried to estimate how far they had moved east, but with all the detours and backtracking it was impossible; which meant the Jeep could be in either direction. And if they went the wrong direction they would probably stumble right into El Pato, who could, Simon remembered, move very quietly when he wanted.

"So what do you think," Tony whispered impatiently, "right or left?"

Simon didn't have a clue, but before he could say it, the silence was shattered by four quick shots—*BANGBANG-BANGBANG*—somewhere off to their right. *Close,* maybe fifty yards, but with the vegetation sucking up the sound it was hard to be sure.

Kyra jerked awake, her eyes white with fear. "What's that?"

"He shot something," Tony whispered. "No idea what."

But Simon had a very good idea. "Stay here, I'll check it out."

As usual, Tony wanted to argue the point. "I should do it."

Right, one more heroic stunt and they'd all be dead. "You take care of Kyra, she needs you." Something Tony-the-husband-and-father-to-be couldn't argue against. "I suggest you coat her skin with mud, she's being eaten alive by the bugs."

"Okay, good idea."

"But whatever you do," Simon warned, "don't leave this spot, I'd never find you."

He took his time, edging forward one slow step at a time, staying low, skirting around anything that might make a sound, not about to let the Duckman catch him off guard a second time. An unnecessary precaution, Simon realized, as a muffled but rising clamor of sound penetrated the vegetation. He crawled the last ten yards, slithering between the branches of two fallen trees, until he had a perfect view of El Pato beating the shit out of Tony's Jeep.

The hood was up, the ground littered with small engine parts. The tires were flat, the windows broken, the doors and fenders bashed and dented. El Pato was now working on the interior, screaming Spanish profanities as he hacked away at the seats with his machete. He finally emerged with Tony's laptop, which he slammed to the ground before drawing his gun and emptying an entire clip into the defenseless black box.

Having seen enough, Simon scooted back until he was well into the brush, then quickly retraced his steps over the soft ground. When he emerged through the grass Tony's eyes bulged like organ stops. "Jesus man, we heard the shots. Thought he got you."

"He never saw me." He squatted down next to Kyra, who was sitting on the ground, back against a tree, her legs and arms and face covered in mud. "How you doing?"

She shook her head, as if lacking the strength to verbalize what he could already see.

"I like your makeup. Very avant-garde."

She cracked a tiny smile, her teeth a white slash in the mudpack.

Tony knelt down beside them. "So what was he shooting?"

"Symbolically speaking: You."

"Huh?"

"Your laptop. Your Jeep was already dead at the scene." He meant to sound funny, to boost their spirits, but could see the hope drain from their eyes. "Don't worry, Charles will find us. I've still got that tracking disk in my shoe."

Tony cocked his head. "But—"

Simon interrupted before he could completely destroy what little hope Kyra might still have. "I left a message on his cellular. He doesn't know exactly where we are, but he'll be looking in this direction."

Tony nodded, getting the message, though he knew none of the transponders were programmed to that disk.

"Okay, good. That's great." He gave Simon a quick, cut-the-bullshit glance. "So, uh . . . in the meantime, uh, what-daya think? Head for the river?"

The obvious choice, Simon thought, as obvious to El Pato as it was to them. "He's between us and the river. And you know he'll be watching the road."

"It'll be dark in an hour, we could sneak by him."

Kyra took a deep breath, as if to gather her strength. "Too hard."

"No, we can do it. Right, Simon?"

He wasn't sure, and even less sure they could *sneak* past El Pato, but tried to sound confident. "Absolutely, no problem."

She took another deep breath. "In a few minutes . . . that road—" Another breath. "—will be a foot deep in mud."

Through the dense canopy of trees, Simon couldn't even see the sky. "You sure?"

She nodded and closed her eyes.

A minute later it started to rain. Hard.

Four hours later it was still coming down hard, but before it got dark they had managed to find a semisheltered place a couple hundred yards back from the road. Kyra was asleep, sitting up against a tree, beneath a makeshift canopy Tony had constructed from his shirt.

The jungle experience. Simon couldn't imagine any sane person paying good money to have such *fun*—thunder, lightning, and unrelenting rain. At least it was warm, and the torrent had temporarily driven the bugs underground. If only he could stop thinking about the snakes—God, how he hated snakes—he could see them in his mind, circling.

"You asleep?" Tony whispered.

Simon leaned toward the voice, less than three feet away, but in the absolute darkness could see nothing. "No."

"We can't move fast carrying Kyra. We'd stand a better chance if one of us made a run for the river."

Though he hated the thought of splitting up, Simon couldn't deny the obvious. "As soon as it's light I'll go. If I'm lucky I'll be back with help before nightfall."

"I should do it," Tony argued. "She's my wife." His voice dropped another notch. "And I'm younger."

"Don't worry about me, I'll be fine. You just take care of Kyra. She needs you." He waited, expecting an argument, but none came. A few minutes later he heard the sound of deep breathing and realized Tony had drifted off. Simon leaned back and closed his eyes, hoping to do the same, hoping some giant python didn't get him.

When he woke up the rain had stopped and Tony was gone.

CHAPTER THIRTY-FOUR

Cali, Colombia

Monday, 17 November 07:03:19 GMT –0500

Jake tried to control his frustration. "What do you mean, disappeared?"

There was a momentary pause as the scrambler filtered and reconstituted Charles' response. "The plane is here, but Simon and Tony are gone."

"They left together?"

"No, they rented two cars, a Jeep and a Land Rover. From what I could find out, Tony left shortly after Simon."

"But why? Tony knew you were on your way, didn't he?"

"Talked to him myself before we left Cali." He paused, as if groping for the right words. "Jake, we have to consider that Tony might be the one behind this. If that's the case we'll never see him again."

Meaning, Jake knew, he would never see his daughter again. "No, I don't buy it." But as he said it, he realized that a week earlier he would have been the first to jump on the Tony's-the-one bandwagon. "He cares too much for Kyra."

"I agree with you," Charles answered, "but we can't dismiss the possibility."

"So what's the status?" He had a good idea, but needed to hear it.

"We're blind. All our transponders were programmed to follow the money."

"So why can't you reprogram the damn things?"

"The hardware and software are integrated and Tony took the laptop. By the time I could get a replacement the disks will be dead. They've only got a six-day life."

"You're telling me we have no idea where they are?"

"It's not quite that bad," Charles answered. "Simon left me a message with his location and the direction he was heading. He was trying to tell me something when he lost the connection."

"Then he'll call again."

"Maybe," Charles answered, "but I wouldn't hold my breath. Simon lost his satellite phone in the river. He had to borrow the pilot's cellular. He was heading into the Amazon Basin—I doubt there's much coverage out there."

"So what's the bottom line? Can you find them?"

"It's not going to be easy, Jake. I've got my guys organizing an air search. We'll start from Simon's last known location and head west. Maybe we'll get lucky."

Lucky. Big Jake Rynerson, billionaire and businessman, luckiest sonofabitch to ever punch a hole in the Permian. But Jake knew better. He'd never been lucky. He'd worked harder, taken chances, and put it all on the line a thousand times. And now he was supposed to rely on *luck* to find his daughter? It wasn't enough. "I'm coming down there."

"Jake, there's nothing you can do here that I can't. Go back to Vegas; you don't want to give Billie this kind of news over the phone."

No, he couldn't do that, but he couldn't face her either. Not yet. The thought of breaking her heart a second time was more than he cared to imagine. "You let me worry about Billie. Send the puddle jumper back here. I'm coming down."

CHAPTER THIRTY-FIVE

Putumayo Region, Ecuador

Monday, 17 November 10:54:68 GMT –0500

"Mr. Leonidovich."

Simon jerked around, startled and a little embarrassed to be seen in only his boxers. "I didn't know you were awake." She was curled into a ball on her mattress of fern leaves, naked except for a fresh coat of mud. He knelt down, keeping his voice low. "How you feel?"

She hesitated a moment, as if asking herself the same question. "Better. Where's Anthony?"

"He went for help."

She pushed herself into a sitting position. "When?"

"Five, maybe six hours ago."

She nodded slowly, didn't seem surprised. "He didn't say good-bye."

"He did, but you were pretty much out of it." A white lie, but a good one. "He said to tell you he loved you."

"How long have I been out?"

"Twelve hours, maybe more." He placed his palm over her mud-caked forehead. "Your temperature has dropped."

"Good." She looked around, as if seeing their hideaway for the first time, then down at her thick cushion of leaves and fronds. "Nice bed."

"Best I could do. I'm not much of a Boy Scout."

"Looks like you're pretty handy with the mud."

Though foolish—he only did what he had to—he felt like a schoolboy caught beneath the stairs, trying to catch a peek up the girls' skirts. "I hope you don't mind, the bugs are ferocious." He realized he was talking too fast and forced himself to slow down, to keep his voice to a whisper. "I swear, some of the mosquitoes are big as vultures."

"It's okay." She smiled, as if amused by his embarrassment. "I'm way beyond modesty. I appreciate the help."

Still feeling a need to explain, he pointed to their clothes stretched over low-hanging limbs and plants. "Thought I should dry our stuff while I had the chance."

"You better get used to wet clothes, nothing ever gets dry in this climate. Not this time of the year."

Not what he wanted to hear. "I thought—"

"Trust me, I did a three-month internship in the rain forest. Three months of damp and dew, living with the spiders and snakes and—"

"Don't tell me about snakes. I'm a wimp when it comes to reptiles."

"It's not the snakes you need to worry about. You avoid them, they'll avoid you. Usually."

Usually. Now why did she have to add that little caveat? "So, what is it we need to worry about?" As if El Pato wasn't enough.

"The bugs, no question. They kill more people in the Amazon than anything else."

"I'm not especially fond of bugs, either." He waved a hand through the swarm of flies that circled constantly around his head. "But the mud helps."

"A lot. It absorbs much of the poison from the bites we've already gotten."

"Good to know. Anything else we need to worry about?"

"Well . . . there's the two-footed jungle palmate. That's our most immediate danger."

"I've never heard of a palmate."

"A palmate is an animal with webbed feet."

He tried to picture a dangerous animal with webbed

feet, but when he thought of webbed feet he thought of friendly little animals: beavers and otters and . . . *ducks*. "You're right, that's what we need to worry about."

She smiled, a flicker that vanished almost instantly. "How long will it take Anthony to bring help?"

A question Simon had been asking himself all morning. "I don't think the river is that far. Ten miles at the most. Assuming that's true . . . and assuming there's some kind of village or crossing . . . assuming there's a phone and that Charles is standing by with his team . . . " *And assuming he made it past the Duckman.*

"That's a lot of assuming, Mr. Leonidovich."

"Please, call me Simon."

"Okay, that's a lot of assuming, Simon."

"But they're reasonable assumptions. And so, the answer is"—he didn't want her to lose faith—"late afternoon. Tomorrow morning at the latest."

"Really?" Her voice lifted in doubt. "I assume you're familiar with Murphy's Law?"

Uh-oh, trapped in his own web of verbal optimism. " 'If something can go wrong, it probably will.' "

"Exactly. With that in mind, I think we should *assume* we might be stuck here for a day or two."

Jesus—just the thought of another night in absolute darkness, in the rain, surrounded by snakes and lizards and other creepy crawlers—it made his insides go cold. He took a deep breath, trying not to let his anxiety leak into his voice. "That could be a problem. I checked the neighborhood this morning—no golden arches."

"Very funny. You always turn everything into a joke?"

He didn't feel funny, but humor had always been his defense mechanism whenever he got into trouble. "Only when I'm running like hell from reality."

"And what reality is that?

"That I'm a city boy, lost in the fucking jungle . . . sorry, pardon my—"

"I've heard the word."

"—with a pregnant woman who can't walk, with no food, no fresh water, and being hunted by a psychotic killer who waddles like a duck. How's that for reality?"

She didn't seem surprised. "That's your reality. Want to hear mine?"

Why not? He couldn't imagine anything worse than his own. "I'm listening."

"You may be a city boy, but I've lived out here and I know what it takes to survive. Yes, I'm pregnant and I don't walk so well, but I'm not helpless. If you want to try and make it out on your own, just go for—"

"Hey, wait a minute! I didn't mean it like that. I'd never leave you."

Her eyes sparked with amusement. "I know that. I just wanted to make you feel bad for saying it."

Female attack. "Mission accomplished."

"Good." She batted at the flies swarming between them, a momentary improvement. "Water is not a problem. It'll probably rain three or four times today. I'll show you how to collect and save it. We're surrounded by food—"

She let that revelation hang, wanting him to bite, so he did. "Okay, Jane of the Jungle, what food?"

"We're surrounded by edible plants. Tropical yams, tubers, tree ferns—" She pointed to a small plant with yellow and green spiky leaves. "You see that?"

"Lunch?"

"That's exactly what it is. It's yellow nutsedge. The tubers are really quite sweet."

*Yams, tubers, ferns—*YUCK! "Did I mention that I was on a serious diet?"

She gave his body a quick up and down. "Now that you mention it—"

Uh-oh.

"—you could afford to lose a couple pounds."

"Thanks. And you could stand to gain a few."

"*And* I've got a baby to feed. So here's what we do . . ."

She talked for nearly an hour—a quick education on survival in the jungle—exactly the kind of information that would fire the mind of a student; but Simon was no student and he realized it wasn't simply a matter of food and water and waiting for help. El Pato wanted his money, knew the clock was ticking, and would be coming—sooner rather than later.

CHAPTER THIRTY-SIX

Lago Agrio, Ecuador

Thursday, 20 November 11:27:36 GMT –0500

"Jake, are you listening?"

"Sorry, Caity, my mind drifted." A condition that seemed to grow exponentially worse with every passing second. *Four days,* one second at a time. Never in his life had Jake felt so utterly powerless. He wanted to get out there, trudge every square inch of the Amazon until he found his daughter; but that was ridiculous. In that damned jungle, a hundred thousand men couldn't have found Yankee Stadium. How could he have let this happen? How could he have been so stupid? Every move and countermove—*wrong.* He should have called in the FBI. He should have let the professionals handle things. He moved the phone to his other ear. "What were you saying, something about the new tower?"

"We buried that subject ten minutes ago. I was telling you about Billie."

"Billie?" The word fused a connection between ear and brain. "What about Billie?"

"I said she was coming down there."

"No, you can't let her." He couldn't bear the thought of facing her, of admitting he had lost their daughter. "For one thing, there's no decent place to stay." He glanced around at his room—modest, sparsely furnished, clean—no worse than half the motels along the great American Interstate. "It's nothing but an oil town on the frontier."

"Get a grip, Jake, that's where you and Billie started—Odessa, oil pit of the Permian. Billie can handle anything you can."

"It's not that. It's just that . . ."

"I understand, Jake, I really do, but you know Billie, *no one* is going to tell her what to do."

"Let me talk to her."

"Jake, she's fed up with your bullshit. She wants to find out what's going on and nothing you say is going to stop her."

It was true. Billie had always been the one woman who stood up to him. "Okay, but make her take the whale."

"She'll never agree. That plane is too ostentatious for Billie."

"Yes she will. She doesn't want to waste two days flying commercial. It'll take less than twelve hours in that beast."

"You're right. I'll convince her."

"Thanks, Caity. What else?"

"Nothing you're interested in. Is there something you want to tell *me*?"

Every day she asked him that—so did Leo Geske—and every day he refused. *No leaks.* "I want you to get me everything you can about Simon's family. Telephone numbers, etcetera."

She came back instantly, her voice piping with concern. "Why? Has something happened to Simon?"

It didn't take a degree in psychology to realize she liked the guy. "Absolutely not." *Not that I'm aware of.* "I just want—"

"Don't bullshit me, Jake."

He ignored the warning. "I want the same information on Tony."

"What the hell's going on?"

There was a familiar double rap at the door, then the sound of a key. "Charles is here, gotta run. Call me when you know Billie's arrival time." He disconnected before she could argue.

Charles stepped inside, a large rolled-up map under one arm. Unshaven, his bush clothes wrinkled and damp with sweat, he looked like someone who hadn't slept in days— a man with bad news. "Am I interrupting?"

Jake shook his head, trying to prepare himself for the worst. "What's happened?"

"This is going to sound bad, but I don't want you to jump to the wrong conclusion."

"Okay, Hos, no jumping." Though that's exactly how he felt: teetering on the edge, just waiting for the nudge.

Charles unrolled his map on the Formica dinette. "We found *Babe*, Kyra's plane." He pointed to a spot west of Pantoja, a border town on the Río Napo, between Ecuador and Peru. "Right there. Just a little strip in the jungle. Probably used by drug traffickers."

Jake waited for the news that would finally push him over the edge.

"The plane had been burned but we did find a few personal items. Watch, wedding ring, shoes—"

"That's it, just . . . personal items?"

"There was a body," Charles answered, "but not Kyra's. I'm sure of it. Almost sure. Ninety-nine percent."

Jake forced himself to breathe. "What do you mean, *almost sure?*"

"Like I said, the plane was burned. Not much left."

Jake tried not to visualize the scene, his beautiful daughter incinerated. "So why don't you think it's Kyra?"

"It looked like the plane was torched a couple of weeks ago and we know Kyra was alive on the twelfth."

But did they know? The photograph could have been altered. "So how *can* we be sure? Dental records?"

Charles glanced away, evasive. "It won't be that easy."

"Will you quit with all this stalling, Hos? What is it you're not telling me?"

Charles nodded, took a breath. "We didn't find a head."

Jake felt the words as much as heard them, a physical pain in the center of his chest. "What's that mean?"

"My guess, someone didn't want us to make the ID."

Was that good or bad? Did it mean Kyra was alive, that some other person was lying dead in her plane; or did it mean she was already dead and they wanted to cover it up? "How will I ever explain this to Billie?"

"Don't," Charles answered. "She'll do just what you're doing—assume the worst. There's no reason to say anything until we're sure."

"She's on her way down here."

"Oh, shit. You can't stop her?"

"What do you suggest?" He couldn't keep the sarcasm from his voice. "A cruise missile?"

"You should have gone back to Vegas, Jake."

"Maybe." But he couldn't see how that would have made things better. "So, what do we do now?"

"The plane was on the southern edge of our search grid. I'm moving everyone south." Charles pulled a yellow marker from one of the smaller pockets of his bush jacket. "We'll use the plane as the center point—" He made an *X* over the spot and drew a circle around the area. "And expand our search outward from there."

Jake lowered himself into one of the cheap Naugahyde armchairs, suddenly feeling tired and old. "Sounds right." It took an effort just to speak. "Anything else?"

Charles nodded. "Funny thing." He looked Jake straight in the eye. "We found Kyra's diamond earrings. Both of them."

CHAPTER THIRTY-SEVEN

Putumayo Region, Ecuador

Friday, 21 November 12:27:36 GMT –0500

Careful not to make any noise, Simon reached up, got a good grip on a limb big enough to hold his weight, and pulled himself upright. Once standing, he slowly began working the stiffness out of his neck and legs. Though better than the wet ground with all the leeches and fire ants, tree-house living was not exactly Swiss Family Robinson-comfortable, nor was it free of flies, mosquitoes, and a thousand other multilegged creatures. He leaned out toward the edge of the platform—a crude, interwoven layer of branches and vines barely twelve feet above the ground—trying to gauge the time by the intensity and angle of light filtering through the canopy. *Midday, maybe one o'clock.* Every hour felt like a week.

Five days. Five miserable, all-the-same days: hot and humid, like a steam iron coming down on a wet shirt, the air ripe with the fecund scent of earth and rain and unrestrained vegetation. Even the routine had become routine: scavenge for food at first light, then hunker down for the day, sleep when he could, never for more than an hour. Kyra, whose fever always peaked during the day and receded at night, slept through the heat, oblivious to their hell. Remarkably, aside from her jungle fever, she appeared to be getting stronger.

At night, when it rained, they huddled together and talked. Mostly, she talked, he listened. He didn't mind, she had things she needed to express: regrets and sorrows from the past, hopes and dreams for the future. Despite her injuries and the ordeal, she never gave up hope—not when Tony failed to return, not when the planes came and left. "My father won't give up."

That Simon believed, but he also knew the search had passed them by. "No, I'm sure he won't."

"I don't deserve it, you know."

He'd heard it before, didn't want to hear it again, but what are friends for? And he now considered her a friend. Five days trapped in the jungle had a way of bonding people together. "Of course you do, you're his *little girl.*"

"I gave up on him." She tried to blink away the tears that suddenly welled into her eyes.

"Stop beating yourself up. Kids do that to parents, it's a law of nature. Even big kids like you."

"I should have listened to my mother. She was the one he hurt the most and she forgave him."

"Your mother's a real broad." He held up a hand, as if to ward off a blow. "Don't attack, I use the term affectionately. She's the only woman I know who could boot your father out of his own hotel."

"What?"

Damn, he hadn't meant to open that wormy box. "Your mother didn't think it would look right, the two of them staying in the same hotel after Tammi left."

"Tammi left? You didn't tell me that."

"She's gone, that's all I know."

"Permanently gone?"

"Yes, and your mother thought it would look bad if—"

"Uh-oh."

He knew he shouldn't ask, but couldn't stop himself. "What do you mean, *uh-oh?*"

"Mom doesn't care what anyone thinks."

He hadn't thought about that, but realized it was true. "What are you saying?"

"She still loves him. I've always known it."

"So . . . ?"

"She's afraid of herself. Afraid of what will happen if she spends any time alone with the old buzzard." She held up a hand, mimicking his earlier response. "I use the term affectionately."

"Interesting theory. And convenient."

She gave him a puzzled look. "Convenient?"

"Caitlin believes Jake wants to get back with your mother."

Kyra's eyes popped, a pair of white umbrellas unfolding from the black mudpack. "No!"

"Yes."

"Wouldn't that be something." She grinned, a small, catlike expression. "Mrs. Rynerson the First becomes Mrs. Rynerson the Fifth."

"How would you feel about that?" As if he didn't know, as if every child of divorce didn't secretly wish their parents might someday reunite.

"When it comes to my father and marriage—" She shrugged evasively. "What about you? Never married?"

That was one nightmare memory he didn't care to revisit. "Once—a long time ago. Don't ask."

"Okay, so what's with you and Caitlin?"

"Caitlin? What do you mean?"

"Your voice changes every time you mention her name."

"You're imagining things."

"Am I?" It was obvious from her expression she knew better.

"That woman is way out of my league. Not someone I dare think about." But in truth he had spent a great deal of the last five days thinking about Caitlin Wells and about the *something missing*. Was she loyal to Kyra, or a jealous want-to-be daughter? Was she loyal to Big Jake, or a discarded lover intent on revenge? Why did she so vehemently oppose the FBI? Was it to protect Jake, or herself?

And why, if she truly cared about Tony, was she so against him knowing about the ear? Because he would have recognized the fraud—a body part belonging to someone else?

Maybe, but he had doubts.

But he also had doubts about Leo Geske. The man had spent years in South America, dealing with scum; and scum had a way of sticking to those who got close. Did he get too close? Did he get tired of handing out money and decide to get some for himself? It would explain so much:

His stilted conversation with the Duckman.

Why there was no tape of a *third* kidnapper.

His confident and correct predictions about when the kidnappers would call.

And why the man was always right. *About everything.* One thing for sure, he was not as meek and unassuming as he first appeared.

It was even possible, Simon realized, that Tony might had fooled them all and pulled off the perfect crime. It would explain why he ditched the rescue team, why he took the money and hid it, why El Pato had missed him with all those shots, and why he didn't return. Was it all coincidence, Tony playing out his heroic fantasy, or was it payback for a marriage of unrequited love?

Possible, but not something Simon wanted to believe. Still, it had to be one of them—Leo Geske, Caitlin Wells, Anthony Saladino—that he was sure of. *Almost sure.*

Kyra suddenly sat up, her head cocked to one side, listening. "Plane?"

Simon leaned over, mouth to ear, the way they always talked. "No." It had been at least forty-eight hours since the last one. "Must be another dream." She woke frequently, five or six times a day with fever dreams.

The hopeful expression in her eyes turned remote. "Oh. Any sign of birds?"

Birds, their euphemism for the Duckman and his flock:

four teams of hunters, two men each. "No, nothing." They hadn't seen or heard El Pato in four days, a fact Simon found more worrisome than comforting. The men he hired were less stealthy—peasant farmers from the river town a few miles down the road—loudly hacking their way through the undergrowth with machetes, talking boisterously about what they would do with their thousand *yanquí dólares* when they caught the *norteamericanos*.

"If we stay here much longer they'll find us," she whispered.

He couldn't argue with that; despite their boisterous nature, the hunters were determined in their pursuit, cutting down everything in their path, working a grid from all four directions, slowly narrowing the search area. "You know I'm ready." The problem was how? They couldn't take the road toward the river, not with a bounty on their heads, and he couldn't piggyback Kyra all the way to Lago Agrio. "You think of something?"

"Yes," she answered, a determined edge coming into her voice, "but you won't like it."

He suspected she would encourage him to hike out on his own, something he couldn't suggest, but had come to believe offered their best chance. "I'm listening."

"We fly." It rolled off her tongue, almost as though she couldn't wait to say it. "It's the only way."

"You're kidding?" Though she obviously wasn't, her eyes serious as ice picks.

"You've heard it yourself, every other day, about an hour before dark. That plane lands no more than a mile south of here."

He had a bad feeling about where this conversation was heading. "Yeah, drug traffickers."

"Probably. But there may be a farming operation near here."

Right, a marijuana or coca farm. "You don't really believe that?"

"No," she admitted, "but it's possible."

"So what are you saying? You think some friendly drug smuggler is going to fly us out?"

"I'm not that naive. We'll steal the plane, and I'll fly us out."

He hardly dared blink for fear he would miss some nuance of expression—a tiny grin, a spark in the eye—some clue that she was joking, yet he somehow knew that she wasn't. "You can't be serious. You can hardly walk, let alone fly a plane."

"I'm dead serious. There'll be dual controls, if you can handle the rudder pedals, I can do everything else."

"Are you crazy?" It took an effort not to raise his voice. "I don't know anything about flying a plane."

"You don't need to know anything, I'll talk you through it. I'm a good pilot, you can trust me."

"It's not a matter of trust. It's just too risky. Forget it."

"Okay." She shrugged, as if it were no big deal. "Let me know when you come up with something better."

But there was no *better;* they both knew it. "You sure you could do it? You think you're strong enough?"

"I'm sure."

He wasn't. "You don't even know what kind of plane it is."

"It's a small single-engine, I can tell from the sound. No problem."

He hesitated, but the idea was addictive: the possibility that they could just fly away, that it could be over so quickly. "Okay, I don't see any reason why we couldn't at least check it out. Maybe there is a farm." *A legitimate farm.* "With a phone." *Maybe,* but he wasn't holding his breath.

"There's one more thing."

He wasn't surprised, with women there was always *one more thing.* "I'm listening."

"I know Anthony. He can be stubborn. He would

never give up the location of that money without a terrible fight."

"What are you saying?" Though he had a pretty good idea where she was heading.

"If El Pato caught him, he might still be alive, refusing to talk."

Still playing hero. "Are you suggesting we go back there?"

"Why not? There won't be anyone around during the day, not while they're out here searching for us. Besides, the airfield's in that direction. We should check it out—just in case."

CHAPTER THIRTY-EIGHT

Putumayo Region, Ecuador

Saturday, 22 November 05:49:12 GMT –0500

In minutes the night sky—what little Simon could glimpse through the trees—had faded from black to navy to charcoal. "Ready?"

"If you can see," Kyra whispered, "I can ride."

He couldn't see much, but the next thirty minutes were crucial if they hoped to make it past the hunters before the ground fog burned away. He squatted down, taking her weight across his back and shoulders, pulled her legs in tight to his sides, aligned himself toward the south, then stepped off into the damp clouds.

Kyra leaned forward, her voice a soft whisper. "You do realize how easy it would be to get lost out here?"

"I've got my compass."

"Which only means we'd be lost walking in a straight line."

"Right." But he wasn't really depending on his compass. He walked with his shoulders hunched, sticking to the trees where there was less vegetation but more exposure, staying low, not stopping until his legs threatened to give out and the smell of the hunters' campfires had passed behind them.

Kyra slid off his back, supporting herself against a tree. "That wasn't so bad."

He shook his head, too winded to even whisper—something, he had come to realize, that took more effort than normal conversation—and collapsed onto the wet ground. She lowered herself down beside him. "Sorry, guess it was a little more difficult for you."

He nodded, surprised at how much strength he'd lost in five days. Clearly, tropical yams and tubers did not qualify as a high-energy food. "I'll be fine in a minute."

"Any idea where we are?" She tried to sound casual but failed, her voice edgy with concern.

"No," he whispered back, "but I'm about to find out." He rolled onto his side, fished his key ring from his pocket, and held it up. "Our last link to a civilized world."

An expression of confusion mirrored in her eyes. "A car door opener?"

"It just looks like a car door opener. It's actually a re-mote link to the antitheft measures hidden in the lining of my security case. Here, take a look—" He removed the re-mote activator from the key ring and snapped off the cover, exposing three tiny buttons—red, green, yellow—and a small liquid crystal display. He pointed to the green button. "That sets off a nice little ear-splitting siren." He moved his finger over the red button. "That's the bomb detonator—"

"Bomb detonator!"

"A very small bomb—big boom, lots of pink dye."

"Oh."

"But this is the one we're interested in." He pressed and held the yellow button, illuminating the display and a small arrow alongside a digital readout. "It's a homing de-vice. We're exactly 732 meters from where Tony hid the money." He pointed in the direction of the arrow. "That-away, Kemosabe."

She nodded, a look of understanding coming into her eyes. "And once you find the money you can find the trail, and from there—"

"You've got it." At least the part he wanted her to un-derstand. What he didn't say was that if the money was gone, then Tony was dirty, in which case Simon had no intention of going anywhere near El Pato's little shack of horrors. "Ready to mount up?" She nodded and he handed her the activator. "You point, I'll play horsey."

Though less than half a mile, there were no straight lines through the jungle undergrowth. By the time they found the spot, nearly an hour later, Simon felt like a worn-down pack mule. A very worried pack mule. If it was that difficult finding their way with a homing device, what chance did they have of finding a small airstrip? "We may have a problem."

Kyra was already digging under the vegetation. "Just a sec." She pulled out the blue duffel. "That's one." A second later she had the security case. "That's both of them."

Simon nodded, mentally crossing Tony off his list of possible bad guys. That left Geske and Wells, but unless they caught El Pato and made him talk, finding out which seemed about as likely as finding the airstrip.

"You said something about a problem?"

"You're pretty sure that strip is within a mile?"

"Yes," she answered, "maybe closer."

"Which means the pilot's on final approach?"

"Yes."

"Which means he's already lined up with the field."

She nodded in the affirmative, very slowly, thinking about it. "Yes."

"Which means the strip is running in the same direction we'll be heading. Even if we knew the exact location, the chances of finding it are—" He couldn't even imagine the odds.

She finished his thought. "A thousand to one."

"At least. We could be off one degree, walk right by it and never know. And if we get lost out there—" He motioned toward the south. "We won't last long."

She lay back, resting her head on the duffel. "There has to be a way."

"Good, and while you're trying to think what it is, I'll get ready."

"Ready?"

"I have a plan." *Not a very good plan,* but something was always better than nothing. "Just in case things turn to shit." *If something can go wrong, it probably will.* While she watched, he removed the money from the security case, stacking it up alongside the duffel. "Okay, now I need your pillow."

She sat up. "Are you going to tell me about this plan?"

"I'm leaving you here."

"So far I don't like it."

"I didn't think you would." She opened her mouth but he cut her off. "Just hear me out."

She nodded, not speaking again until he finished. "I still don't like it."

"It's nonnegotiable."

"You're not giving me much of a choice."

"Nope." He gave her a wink, trying to keep it light. "Not as long as I'm the mule on this here team."

She forced a reluctant smile. "How long will you be gone?"

"An hour." He said it with more confidence than he felt. "Two at the most."

Stretched out in a patch of high weeds just beyond the tree line that surrounded El Pato's shack, Simon tried to ignore the spiders and centipedes and other crawlers. As long as nothing slithered into his space he could handle it. *No snakes—you hear me, God?—no snakes!*

The silence lengthened into minutes. Rivers of sweat ran down his face and stung his eyes. *Twenty minutes— had to be.* He knew Kyra would be counting down the minutes in her head, afraid she might never see him again. What kind of ironic twist would that be? The daughter of Big Jake Rynerson, surrounded by millions in cold cash, dying helpless and alone.

Twenty-five minutes—maybe thirty. It felt as if he hadn't moved in hours—the air so hot and heavy he could feel the weight of it across his back, pushing him into the earth. *At least thirty.* He forced himself to wait longer, to be absolutely sure El Pato was gone.

Forty. Not a sound. No Tony. No El Pato. Satisfied, he pushed himself to his feet, retrieved the security case and duffel, and stepped into the clearing.

He heard the dog's low humming growl before he even reached the door. *Quick and easy—in and out.* He cracked the door, just enough to be sure the beast was still on its chain, then pushed it open. Two things struck him instantly: the open door to Kyra's cell, and the grave, now partially filled and partially covered with dirt. What remained uncovered was the stump of Tony's left arm, the hand eaten away by the pit bull staked alongside. Simon felt his insides going soft, like he was folding in on himself, his body momentarily overcome with a sense of sadness and horror. He wanted to run, to put as much distance as possible between himself and what he saw, but he couldn't; couldn't let that stupid animal go on devouring his friend. He would have to kill the beast—Tony deserved that much at least.

He turned, looking for something to do the job when he sensed a movement from behind. He spun around, knowing his mistake even before he saw El Pato looming in the doorway of his little dungeon, gun in hand. "I knew you would come, *gringo.*"

Simon took a breath, forcing himself to focus on a plan he never expected to use. One he didn't expect to work.

El Pato stepped forward, only a couple feet, eyes cautious. "Where is the woman?"

"Dead."

"That is most unfortunate." He glanced over his shoulder at the dog. "I promised El Diablo his last meal would be *muy delicioso.*" He laughed, the sound anything but humorous.

"You let me walk out of here, I'll tell you where to find the money."

El Pato snorted, his eyes auguring in on the security case and duffel. *"Qué,* you think El Pato is blind?"

"No," Simon answered quickly, hoping to sound desperate. "These are empty. I was going to fill them with food."

"I think you are full of stories, *gringo.* They do not look so empty to me."

"No, really." Simon dropped the duffel and leaned forward over the security case, as if eager to open it. "Let me show you."

"Oye!" El Pato motioned with his gun. "Not so quick." He wagged the index finger of his free hand, *gimmie.*

Simon frowned, just a little, not wanting to overdo it, and shoved the case forward with his foot, not too far, hoping to draw the Duckman a little farther into the room, between himself and the dog. El Pato stepped forward, picked up the case, then backed off a step, not taking the gun or his eyes off Simon for even a second. He knelt down on one knee, snapped open the latch, and pulled back the flap.

There are moments in life when all the stars align, and Simon was ready, instantly pushing the red button on the remote activator hidden in his hand. The explosion erupted upward—a loud *WHUUUMPF*—all the twigs and sticks Simon had stuffed into the case hitting El Pato in the face, enveloping him in a cloud of pink dye. As he struggled to regain his balance—his face cut and bleeding, a stick protruding from his left eye—Simon lunged forward, hitting the man square in the chest. He staggered back, stumbled over a pile of loose dirt next to the grave, and fell, the dog on him the moment he hit the ground. Blind and bellowing with rage, El Pato tried to fight the animal off, the two of them rolling in the dirt, raising a tornado of dust, El Pato pummeling the animal with his fists and trying to kick it away, the dog snapping and snarling, looking for an opening. Twice El Pato managed to get his feet under him and both times the dog brought him down with its powerful jaws, the second time ripping into the Duckman's exposed neck. Simon snatched up the gun and fired, hitting the dog in the chest and killing him instantly, but not before the beast had extracted its revenge.

Simon knelt down, hoping to somehow pry the name of El Pato's partner from the man's torn esophagus, but it was too late, blood gurgling in his throat. Within a minute he was dead, the secret with him. Simon started to turn away, anxious to get away from the horror of it all, when something shiny in the dirt caught his eye.

"Oh my God." From her relieved look he must have looked like Moses coming out of the wilderness. "I thought something happened to you."

"No, I'm fine," he answered. "Everything's fine." But of course *everything* wasn't fine, Tony was dead and they were still stuck in Jungle Hell. He dropped the duffel and lowered himself down beside her. "I grabbed a few things."

He reached into the bag. "A gun. A very useful item when it comes to stealing planes. A machete . . . a few cans of food . . . can opener . . . water . . . satellite phone . . . unfortunately the battery's dead. And finally . . . *ta-da—*" He pulled a T-shirt and a pair of baggy shorts. "The latest in female fashion. Might not be much of a fit, but . . ."

She nodded, not taking her eyes off his. "Anthony?"

Until that moment he hadn't decided if he should tell her now or wait to see if they survived the day, but after five days she had come to expect the worst and deserved to know. He reached into his pocket for the treasure he had found in the dirt—Tony's wedding band—and laid it in the palm of her hand. "I'm sorry."

He could see the air go out of her, the tears welling in her eyes. "Did he suffer?"

"I don't think so," he lied. "Not from what I could see." He reached out and took her hands. "You okay?"

She took a deep breath, gathering herself, drawing on that deep inner pool of Rynerson strength. "No, but I can't think about that now. Tell me what happened."

She listened quietly while he related the story—a sanitized version—and looked visibly relieved when she learned El Pato was dead. "I hope the bastard rots in Hell for all eternity."

Though Simon didn't buy into the literal concept of Heaven and Hell, it did seem fitting that the executioner happened to be the devil himself: El Diablo. "I think that's a safe bet."

She gave his hands a squeeze. "I'm really glad you're safe." She glanced around, as if suddenly remembering something. "Where's your case?"

"I left it behind. It's covered in pink dye—not too good for playing the nondescript bagman."

"You think the homing mechanism still works?"

He dug the remote activator out of his pocket and pressed the yellow button. "Still working. Why?"

"I have an idea how we can find that airstrip and not get ourselves hopelessly lost."

"You have my attention."

"We use the case as a beacon. The same way a pilot uses the outer marker to line up on a runway. It will tell us exactly how far we've traveled and keep us directionally aligned."

"But we're not sure of the exact direction."

"Right, so we head south a mile and stop. If we don't find the airstrip we just wait for the plane and see where it lands."

"And if we can't see it through the trees?"

"We should be close enough to tell if it's right or left. And if we can't find it"—she gave a little shrug—"we can use the beacon to find our way back."

Back being El Pato's shack, not a place Simon wanted her to see. "It's a good idea. We'll find it." *Or die trying.*

"Okay, then—" She reached for the clothes. "Let's go steal a plane."

While she dressed, Simon began stuffing the money into the duffel. "We may have to buy that plane."

She frowned in disbelief. "You don't really believe some drug dealer is going to sell us his plane?"

No, of course he didn't, they would kill him and take the money, but that was only an excuse. It was a matter of professional pride, a sense of responsibility. The man who could deliver anything, anywhere, didn't leave twelve million dollars of his client's money behind.

CHAPTER THIRTY-NINE

Putumayo Region, Ecuador

Saturday, 22 November 16:44:08 GMT –0500

Simon leaned close to Kyra's ear. Though hidden in the trees, they were less than forty yards from the plane, where two bare-chested men were unloading boxes of supplies—mostly beer. "You sure you can fly that thing?"

She nodded. "Piece of cake. It's a Cessna 182. Good plane, lots of power, no problem."

That's what he wanted to hear—*no problem*—because the plane, tucked back into a pocket of the trees just beyond the end of the dirt runway, looked scarred, scraped, and incredibly small. "That thing could fit in the main cabin of your father's whale taxi."

"Whale taxi? What are you talking about?"

He shook his head; it was hard enough to carry on a whispered conversation without getting into unnecessary explanations. "Tell you later." He crawled forward a couple feet, for a better view of the runway—a narrow strip cut out of the trees, no more than two thousand feet in length—and a tiny shack set back in the trees about halfway down, where the pilot had disappeared.

Kyra edged up alongside. "You hear that?"

He glanced at the men. They were now sitting on the tailgate of their battered pickup, drinking beer and talking loudly. "I don't speak Spanish."

"The ugly one is complaining that the shipment won't be here until after dark."

The ugly one? They both looked mean enough to scare a rattlesnake. "That's good news."

"Yes."

"So we've got—" He glanced up at the sky. "About an hour to snatch this thing and skedaddle?"

"At least. You want to go over those rudder controls again?"

"No." The more she told him, the more nervous he got. "I understand everything. Whether I can do it, that's another story."

She gave his forearm a squeeze. "You'll do fine."

"What's going to happen when you fire this thing up?"

"What do you mean?"

"I don't think these boys are going to be real happy about us taking their plane."

"Those two are just grunts, hired for their brawn, and not too quick on the upload. The pilot won't want to damage his plane. I'm hoping he'll hesitate."

"But what about a warm-up? Don't you have to—"

"No," she interrupted, her breath hot against his ear. "The engine will still be warm. I'm hoping we can get past them before they start shooting."

Lots of *hoping*. "And when they *do* start shooting?"

"It's not like the movies," she whispered. "These things are harder to stop than most people think. Unless they have automatic weapons, then we're in trouble."

"In the movies they *always* have automatic weapons."

"This isn't the movies."

No, this was scarier. *Much scarier*.

She nodded toward the pickup. "They're leaving. Let's do this now, before we lose the light."

Before, Simon thought, he came to his senses and chickened out. "Climb on."

He circled around, keeping to the trees until the plane was between them and the shack, where the men were now unloading their supplies. Kyra slid off his back, reached up, and pulled the latch on the pilot's door. "It's locked, we'll have to use the door on the copilot's side."

She ducked under the fuselage. By the time Simon pulled the duffel bag through and stood up she had the door open and was staring into the cockpit. "Uh-oh."

Uh-oh was not what he needed to hear. Then he saw it too, the interior stripped bare to make room for cargo. The moment seemed to last forever, both of them staring at the empty spot where the copilot's seat and controls should have been. *If something can go wrong, it probably will.* "Simon says, plan B."

"We don't have a plan B."

"But we have a lot of money."

"You saw those guys, you really think they're the type to play *Let's Make a Deal?*"

No, of course he didn't, but what choice did they have? "I can be very charming."

"I'm sure of it, but you don't speak Spanish, so unless you want to be sodomized by a couple of big ugly tattooed—"

"Whoa, you just convinced me."

"Besides—" She glanced back at the plane. "I think we can do this."

"Don't be crazy, you're in no condition to fly this thing. You can hardly move your feet."

"You're right, I can't do it myself, but the two of us could."

He felt the skin prickle along the back of his neck, the warning whisper of bad news. "What are you talking about? There's only one set of controls."

"You already know how to use the rudder pedals. If you can handle the yoke I can do everything else."

"You *telling* me how to use the rudder pedals is a long way from *knowing how.* There is absolutely no way I can fly this plane."

"Normally I'd agree with you, but we're in a bit of a jam right now." She placed her hand where the copilot's seat should have been. "I'll sit right here. Close enough to handle the throttle and trim. All you have to do is keep us heading straight down the runway."

Right, straight into the trees. "I had no idea flying was so simple."

"You're lucky it's not a tail-dragger, they're much harder to keep straight."

"Now I'm really thrilled."

"This tricycle gear is very stable," she continued, ignoring his sarcasm. "You won't have any problem."

Of course he wasn't going to have a problem, he wasn't going to do it. "Let's talk about Plan C."

"Just climb in, things will seem different when you're in the seat. It feels just like a car."

Just like a car! What kind of bullshit was that? He tried to ignore her but she was pushing and shoving him toward the door so he climbed in, just to placate her—*just for a minute.*

"How does it feel?"

"How do you think it feels? I've been living in a damn tree! I think I'll just sit here until they shoot me, my butt is already in heaven." He glanced down the runway, which from an elevated position looked longer, though the trees at the end looked considerably higher. The men had disappeared into the shack. When he turned back Kyra was in the plane, sitting on the duffel of money, between him and the door and escape, still droning on about how simple it was to fly.

"The important thing to remember . . ."

She was trying to make everything sound simple and easy, but he was staring at all the dials and switches and knobs, and knew better. "Forget it. It's not happening. No way, José."

"Don't let the panel intimidate you," she went on. "I'll

worry about all that, you just concentrate on keeping the aircraft straight."

Why was she talking as if this was going to happen? "Even if we were lucky enough to make it off the ground, I could never land this thing."

"Landing is easy. This plane could float down on its own."

"That's great, now let me out of here."

She pretended not to hear, her voice like running molasses, thick and slow and unrelenting—pointing out various switches and dials, instructing him as to what he should and shouldn't do, the commands she would give—talking to herself as much as to him. "Switches off . . . prop full forward . . . one-quarter throttle . . . elevator trim to neutral . . . flaps set for takeoff." He wanted to ignore her, but was afraid not to listen. She tapped a gauge directly in front of him. "That's your speed indicator."

"Excuse me, I have a terrific need to urinate."

"Just remember, small corrections. Everything smooth and slow." She leaned over and pointed to a red switch on the lower left side of the panel. "That's the master power switch. When I say, flip it to ON."

Why am I listening to this? "Let me out of here."

"You of course know what those are." She pointed at the floorboard beneath his feet. "Rudder controls with toe brakes. When I fire this thing up you'll need to be on the brakes. Don't release them until I say." She looked at him and smiled. "Any questions?"

Questions! "Yeah, just one, where are the air sickness bags?"

"Okay, so much for preflight, guess we're ready to go."

Ready to go! "Don't be crazy, I'm not doing this. Period. End of story."

"Remember what I said about landing? I should have said landing in *daylight* was easy."

"I forgive you. Now let me out of here."

"If we leave now we should reach Lago Agrio well before dark. That would make things much simpler." She smiled, as if amused at her own words. "Okay, time to buckle up."

JesusMotherofGod, she sounded like a flight attendant: *tray tables and seat backs in their upright position.* "I can't do this. There has to be a better way." He struggled to think of one, knew he was missing something, but couldn't concentrate, her instructions and warnings and commands flying through his mind like a harried bird.

She reached across, found the other side of his belt, and cinched it tight. "Ready?"

Ready! Was she nuts? "No, I'm not ready, I'm not doing it."

"Okay, step on the brakes."

"No!"

"Have it your way." She leaned over and flipped the power switch to ON. "But I'm about to crank this thing up and we're going to be in a real mess unless your feet are on those brakes."

HolyMother, she was doing it. *Leonidovich, this is your fate.* He stepped on the brakes, afraid not to. "Wait a minute . . . let's go over this one more time . . . I'm not ready."

"Talking about it won't help. Just remember what I told you—"

Remember what? He couldn't remember one single thing.

"Smooth and slow. Small corrections." She reached out, turned the ignition key, and held it. The engine coughed once, then caught and settled into a steady purr loud enough to attract lions in Africa. "Okay, sounds good. Stay on those brakes." She started to push the throttle. "Okay, release the brakes."

He realized it was too late to argue. *Keep it straight.* They were moving, not fast, everything happening in slow motion, the sound turned off. *Small corrections.* Off to his left the three men burst out of the shack and stopped, goggle-eyed, as startled as Simon was scared, then started to sprint toward the plane. *Smooth and slow.* The pilot suddenly stopped, turned, and darted back into the shack. For a gun, Simon was sure, but there was nothing he could do about it, nothing he could do about anything.

As the two grunts closed the distance, Kyra increased the power, the torque pulling the nose of the plane to the left, just as she had warned him it would. He eased down on the right pedal—*smooth and slow*—and the nose came back into alignment. *Small corrections.* The two men were almost on them . . . and then they were . . . one fell as he tried to grab and hold the wing but the other caught the strut and held on, pulling the plane toward the edge of the runway. Simon tried to hold the line, pressing the right rudder pedal to the floor, but the drag was too much. *Not going to make it.* Kyra leaned over, pulled the automatic from his belt, snapped open a small window vent, and fired. The shot missed but was close enough to scare the man into letting go. Instantly the plane jerked to the right and Simon eased the nose back toward the center of the strip. *Small corrections.* From the corner of his eye he saw the pilot come charging out of the shack, a revolver in his right hand . . . *not good* . . . he heard the shots, one after another, but it seemed irrelevant, the least of his problems . . . they were moving faster now . . . *too fast* . . . bouncing and skipping over the dirt strip . . . *keep it straight* . . . the trees at the end of the runway were rushing toward them at a frightening rate but Kyra seemed unperturbed, her voice slow and steady and unrelenting, like a mother to a child.

"Doing good, Simon . . . that's it . . . right rudder . . . keep it steady."

He could feel the sweat pouring off his face. *Too fast* . . .

can't control it. The plane suddenly felt lighter, seemed to take on a life of its own, holding the line.

"Okay, that's eighty-five knots, ease back on the yoke."

He eased back . . . *smooth and slow* . . . and suddenly they were airborne . . . but too late . . . the wall of trees rising up to meet them . . .

"A little more, Simon . . . a little more . . . left rudder, just a touch . . . that's it . . . a little more on the yoke . . . ease it back . . . ease it back." She was talking faster now, a touch of desperation in her voice. "Back. More. More!"

A ripple of vibration passed through the fuselage, the plane caught in that vacuum between climb and stall. Simon nudged the yolk forward just a hair, felt the prop dig in, but too late . . . *going into the trees.* And then the wall of green suddenly disappeared and there was nothing but gray sky. Kyra reached over, pushed the yolk forward and retracted the flaps. "Nose down, just a bit."

"Did we make it?"

She laughed, full of pleasure and relief. "I think we did." She twisted around, checking the underside of the right wing. "No damage here. How's your side?"

He couldn't look, didn't dare take his eyes off the horizon. "I don't know."

"How does she feel?"

"How is she supposed to feel?"

And then they were both hooting and howling, like a couple of stoners on a laughing jag. She reached over and gave his shoulder a little attaboy punch. "You did well, Leonidovich. You're a natural flyer."

Whatever he did, he couldn't remember it, not one damn thing. He took a deep breath, forcing his pulse out of the red zone. "Okay, now what?"

"Level off at four thousand feet." She pointed to a dial on the instrument panel. "That's your altimeter. I want to practice some gentle maneuvering, let you get a feel for the aircraft in a landing configuration, flaps down and prop at increased rpms."

"Landing is easy, right? You weren't shitting me about that?"

"Very easy, we're going to make a power landing, fly this thing straight into the runway."

Straight in, what could be easier?—one big ball of flame to announce their arrival.

She reached forward and began flipping switches. "I'll call in, make sure they're ready for us."

The minute she said *call in* he realized the *better way.* "Why didn't we just use the radio to call for help?"

She stared at him, a look of genuine astonishment, then grinned sheepishly. "I might have rushed things a bit."

"You think?"

"You were nervous enough about the rudder controls, I wanted to get us out of there before you had time to think about it."

"I was *not* nervous. Anxious . . . tense . . . concerned . . . maybe a bit apprehensive . . . but *not* nervous. Nervous is a female condition."

"What about petrified?"

"Petrified works, I was definitely petrified."

"Well, you can relax now. It's almost over."

"Right, almost over." *Almost,* but not quite, there was still one question yet to be answered: Geske or Wells? It would take some finesse, a little luck, a bit of misdirection, but it was a question he intended to answer. While he mentally worked through the finer points of his plan, Kyra did what real pilots did in an emergency:

Inexperienced pilot at controls . . .

Emergency vehicles . . .

I'll talk him down . . .

but he wasn't listening, didn't want to hear it, didn't want to think about it. She had him do a few simple maneuvers, which he performed without thought or memory. He didn't even notice she had lined them up for the final approach into Lago Agrio.

"Copilot to pilot, you there, Simon?"

"Sorry." He forced his thoughts back to the here and now. "I was thinking about something."

"Anything you want to share?"

"Actually, I need a favor. A big favor."

She cocked her head, a knowing expression coming into her eyes. "Put in a good word for you with Caitlin, I suppose?"

Hardly, since her good friend might be spending the rest of her life in a federal prison. "Thanks, but what I want is for you to forget that little side trip I made this morning."

"I don't understand."

"Aside from your parents, I don't want anyone to know about El Pato or Tony."

She hesitated, thinking about it. "You're going to try and trap the person behind all this?"

"Yes."

"And you think it's someone close to my father?"

"Yes, but my plan won't work if anyone knows El Pato or Tony are dead."

"Explain that."

"We have to assume that before his battery gave out, El Pato told his partner he had Tony. Something we would have no way of knowing, unless—"

"I understand."

"I know it's a lot to ask, but if you could just limit your story to everything but that one hour of time. Then we escaped and have no idea what happened to Tony. Simple as that." Of course it wasn't simple, asking a woman to keep silent about the death of her husband, but necessary if his plan had any chance of success.

"How long?"

"Forty-eight hours."

She nodded slowly. "Okay, forty-eight hours."

"Thanks. I really appreciate it."

"Then we're even." She took a breath, let it go. "What do you say we land this thing?"

"I'm ready."

"That's good, because we're almost there." She pointed straight ahead. "That's the runway."

Though the sun wouldn't disappear for another thirty minutes, the runway lights were on, a double strip of white dots that faded into the distance. Compared to the strip they had taken off from, it looked like a superhighway. *Smooth and easy.* "Do I pull it back before we touch?"

"No. I'll control the rate of descent and speed. You just fly her straight in, the aircraft will flare on its own. The second we touch down I'll kill the power."

From the corner of his eye he could see the oil derricks and houses, the ground rising toward them . . . *straight in* . . . he could see Kyra adjusting the trim, manipulating the throttle, talking on the radio, but he blocked it all out . . . *smooth and easy* . . . and then they were over the end of the runway, almost floating, the nose rising slightly as the wheels touched.

Kyra leaned over, reaching for the power switch, but he caught her arm. "If I could get this thing up and down in one piece, I can taxi her in."

She hesitated, then smiled in an understanding sort of way. "They won't like it, but I think you've earned the right." She pointed to a spot off to the left, away from the terminal. "Pull in there. Forget the rudder, just ease down on your left brake."

He readjusted his feet, was about to turn, when a large jet with a familiar crest on its tail caught his eye. Without thinking, he pressed the right pedal.

"Hey—" She stared at him, eyes wide with surprise. "What are you doing?"

"You see that?" He pointed toward the jet. "That's a whale taxi."

As he said it Big Jake and Billie emerged from the forward door, leaping down the stairs in an exuberant rush. They reached the plane even before the propeller stopped moving, Big Jake yanking open the cockpit door and scooping his daughter into his arms.

"Hello, Daddy." She wrapped her arms around his neck. "I've missed you."

CHAPTER FORTY

Somewhere over Arizona

Sunday, 23 November 22:07:25 GMT –0700

Vicki, the flight hostess, poked her head around the partition. "There you are."

Glancing up from his book, Simon forced a smile. "Here I am." Here being one of the whale's semiprivate conversational areas, where he'd been trying to hide. "What's up?"

"Ms. Wells is on the phone. I told her I'd see if you were awake." She waited, the unspoken question—*Yes, No, Tell her I died*—hanging between them.

No, he didn't want to talk, didn't want to relate one more time his version of *the great escape*. Most of all, he didn't want to talk to Caitlin Wells, not until he knew for sure which team she was on—but this was her third call in twenty-four hours and to put her off again would only make her suspicions. "Sure, I'll talk to her."

Vicki smiled, obviously relieved, and pointed to the communications panel on the bulkhead. "Line three."

"Thanks." He stopped her before she could turn away. "How soon will we be landing?"

She glanced at her watch. "Just after midnight, Vegas time. About an hour from now."

He reached over, pressed line three, and picked up the phone. "Hello there, Caitlin Wells. You never call. You never send flowers."

"Don't you give me that bullshit, Simon Leonidovich, you know damn well I've called."

"You're right, now I see your name, way down here at the bottom of my list."

"Is that where I am, Leonidovich, at the bottom of your list?"

Ah, Wells, if only you knew—first in my heart, first on my list of suspects. "I *was* in jail, you know?" A slight exaggeration, though the police did question him for more than four hours. "That should count for something in the excuse department."

"That should teach you not to go around stealing airplanes."

He suspected she knew every detail, but played along. "No, no, no, that's the problem, everyone gets the story wrong. It was *previously stolen*, we were simply trying to return it to its rightful owner."

"I'm surprised the police didn't give you a reward."

"My sentiments exactly."

"So how did you escape this hellhole of a jail?"

Now he was sure she knew everything. "A damn miracle, that's how. We discovered Jake actually spoke their language."

"He bribed them."

"We're calling it a donation."

"But seriously—" Her voice took on a businesslike tone. "That was one hell of a thing you did. You should be proud."

"Thanks, but Kyra did most of it. She's a very special lady."

"Yes, she is. So when are you getting in?"

He had a feeling she knew that too. "A little after midnight."

"I'll meet you. I want to hear everything."

But she was the last person he wanted to know everything. "I appreciate the offer, but I really need some sleep."

There was a slight hesitation, his negative response

obviously catching her by surprise. "We have some things we need to talk about."

Sure do. "Absolutely. Tomorrow, okay?"

"I understand. See you then."

It was obvious from her tone she didn't understand at all. "Looking forward to it."

"Oh, Simon, one more thing. Your sister arrived a couple hours ago. I put her in the Shōgun Suite."

"Thanks. She'll enjoy that."

He no sooner put down the phone when Charles slid into the opposite seat. "How you feel? Get some sleep?"

"A little. How's Kyra?"

"You mean other than having her Achilles severed, being half starved, losing her husband, and seeing her parents together after twenty years?"

"Yeah, other than that."

"Remarkably well. She'll bounce back, it'll just take a while."

Simon leaned forward, keeping his voice to a whisper. "You understand no one is to know about Tony?"

Charles nodded. "Jake made that clear enough. Forty-eight hours."

"Right, after that you can send someone in to get his body."

"Understood. I just don't understand why you—"

Simon interrupted, not yet ready to explain why. "How do you feel about turning everything over to the FBI?"

"I feel like I missed the party, but—" He shrugged, clearly not happy about the way things turned out. "We don't really have much choice."

"What if I told you I know how we could trap El Pato's partner? You interested?"

Charles leaned forward, his voice dropping to a whisper. "What have you got in mind?"

Simon pulled the satellite phone from his new travel bag. "The Duckman's phone. No one knows I have it, and there's only one person we know of who has the number."

"His partner?"

"Right. The trick, of course, is to get that person to make the call. Then we'd have him." *Or her,* but he didn't want to say it.

Charles began rubbing his hands together, as if the fun was just about to start. "You have my full and undivided attention."

"Great, here's what I need you to do."

CHAPTER FORTY-ONE

Las Vegas

Monday, 24 November 09:12:42 GMT −0800

Simon had just finished breakfast and was catching up on the news when the phone interrupted. He expected Lara, but was surprised by the gravelly growl of Big Jake's West Texas accent. "You up and kickin' there, boy?"

"I'm upright, don't feel much like dancing yet."

"Understood. Mind if I stop by your room?"

"Of course not." It was, after all, Big Jake's hotel—*his room*—especially this particular suite—**GIANT**—named after Edna Ferber's big, bawdy Texas novel. In contrast to most hotel accommodations, this slice of ranch life forty-nine floors above The Strip was designed and decorated for the male species, with leather sofas and chairs, a stone fireplace, brass lamps, Western art, and bookshelves crammed with leather-bound rarities—all blending into a warm and comfortable haven of cowboy maleness, so emblematic of Big Jake himself. "Any time."

"Be there in five."

Simon barely had time to start a fresh pot of coffee before the buzzer sounded. The television automatically switched to a view of the suite's entry foyer, Big Jake alone except for Brownie—no family, no staff, no security. Simon pulled open the wide door, its surface a carved landscape of Edna Ferber's fictional ranch. "Welcome to Little Reata."

Big Jake flashed a smile. "You've read the book?"

"Who hasn't?"

"Most people. But they saw the movie so they think that qualifies."

Simon was tempted to quote a line from the book—*Against the brassy sky there rose like a mirage a vast edifice all towers and domes and balconies and porticoes and iron fretwork*—just to prove he wasn't *most people*, but let it go. He didn't need to prove himself to anyone, including Big Jake Rynerson. "Coffee?"

"Black. Biggest mug you got."

Brownie went straight for the living area, stretching out between two over-size club chairs, as if she'd been to the suite many times and knew her spot. Big Jake took a chair next to his canine buddy, stretched his long legs over the leather ottoman, and settled back, looking comfortable and pleased with life. The minute Simon sat down, Brownie thumped her tail, lowered her head, and fell instantly asleep. Jake took a long sip of coffee and leaned back, apparently in no hurry to begin the conversation.

"How's Kyra?"

The big man's eyes glittered with happiness. "Great, I talked to her doc just an hour ago. Says there's a good chance she'll be walking normally in a matter of months."

"And the baby?"

"They're still doing tests, but so far everything looks fine—thanks to you."

"Not me. Tony's the one who saved the day. If he hadn't shown up, I'd be sharing a grave with your daughter."

Jake nodded slowly, his expression suddenly regretful. "He was a good man and he loved my little girl." He pushed himself out of his chair and began to pace, Brownie instantly awake, her eyes following Jake's movements like a spectator at a tennis match.

"If it makes you feel any better, he died doing what he wanted."

Jake paused in front of the stone fireplace, the six flags

of Texas—the Spanish, the French, the Mexican, the Republic of Texas, the Confederacy, and the United States of America—hanging in a colorful rainbow over his head. "How's that?"

"Tony told me all he ever wanted was to be Kyra's hero. He got his wish."

"Well, damn, isn't that something." He returned to his chair. "A dying wish fulfilled. Most people ain't so lucky."

They sat there, silent, thoughts of Tony hanging heavily about them. Then Jake shook his head, as if to force away the memory. "Guess we better talk about that ear thing."

That ear thing, interesting way to put it. "I guess we should."

Jake picked up his coffee mug but didn't drink, holding it in both hands and staring at it, avoiding Simon's eyes. "I needed some way to convince you to take the job. My methods might have been misconceived, but the results speak for themselves. You brought my little girl home. Simple as that."

But it wasn't *simple as that.* Billionaire or not, Jake was just a good ol' Texas boy at heart, not the type to conceptualize such a devious plan. "Nice of you to fall on the sword, Jake, but it wasn't your idea. It was Caitlin's."

Jake jerked around, ready as always to defend his indispensable right arm. "Now don't you go trying to blame Caity. This is my responsibility. Mine alone."

But Simon wasn't worried about responsibility or blame or pointing fingers; he was thinking of the grand manipulator and who he could trust. "But it *was* her idea."

Jake glanced away, unable to lie. "Well, maybe it was, but I was putting a lot a pressure on her to bring you around. She feels terrible—sick as a puppy dog about doing it."

Not good enough. "That ear didn't fall off the cadaver truck, Jake."

The big man rolled his eyes, embarrassed. "Actually, it did. I've made a few contributions to the medical school over here at the university. Caity told the dean we were playing a little joke on someone."

Yeah, someone by the name of Simon Leonidovich.

Jake lowered his eyes, a puppy-dog look that could have made old Brownie cry. "I'm sorry we had to do it."

And maybe, Simon realized, he should have just taken the job and not forced the man into such a corner. "Let's just forget it." But of course he wouldn't. Couldn't. Not until he knew who was behind Kyra's abduction and the one ultimately responsible for Tony's death.

"Good, I'm glad that's settled." The big man looked relieved, the way a person looks when they finish a difficult job they've been dreading. "Speaking of settlements—" He drew an envelope from the inside pocket of his tweed jacket. "For services above and beyond."

But not done, Simon thought. "Thanks." He laid the envelope down next to his mug. "It was interesting, I'll say that."

"You're not going to look?" Jake asked, his voice rising in disbelief.

Not that Simon wasn't curious, but he didn't have a clue how much it might be, or even how much it should be. "I'm sure it's fine."

"I wouldn't want you to walk away disappointed."

"I know you're a fair guy."

Jake frowned. "Everyone seems to have their own idea about *fair.* You take a little peek, make sure you're satisfied. I insist."

Simon really didn't want to—didn't want to show any disappointment if the amount wasn't large enough to justify all the business Lara had referred to other companies over the past twenty days, but Jake wasn't about to take *no* for an answer. "Okay, sure." He picked up the envelope and pulled out the check, determined not to show any emotion. He failed, his eyes blinking like a Brownie camera trying to record the image before it disappeared:

Blink—Simon Leonidovich.

Blink—$2,000,000.00.

Compared to many of the treasures he transported around the world, two million was a relatively small amount, but this was different, this had his name on it. "I can't accept this."

Jake looked as if he thought Simon had just taken leave of his senses. "What are you talking about? Of course you can, you earned it."

"Not two million." Simon leaned forward and laid the check down next to Jake's cup. "That's too much."

Jake grunted three times, as if to say, "Now I've heard it all." "And here I was worried you'd think I was cheap."

"Cheap?"

"Well, besides my daughter, you did manage to save my twelve million."

"That was your money, Jake, not mine."

The big man pushed the check back across the table. "And that's yours. Enjoy it."

"What the hell am I going to do with two million dollars?" But his mind had already seized on a few ideas: a college fund for his niece and nephew; a snazzy, just-for-the-fun-of-it sports car for Lara; flying lessons for himself.

Jake rocked back in his chair and laughed, clearly enjoying his benevolence. "Any damn thing you want. You could retire."

But Simon knew instantly he wouldn't, and he could see in Jake's expression that he knew it too—that the big man had something else in mind.

"You could even open an office here in Vegas."

That was the last thing Simon would have thought to consider. "And why would I want to do that, Jake?"

"I had a little chat with your sister—"

Uh-oh. A little chat with the infamous Big Jake Rynerson. No wonder she had been acting so sweet.

"She tells me you have more business than you can handle. That you live in a hotel—" He smiled, as if the idea amused him. "Not that I can figure out what's so terrible about that. And that you never have time to do anything for yourself."

"That's just my little sister being Mom. Wants me to cut back on clients, wants me to—" Simon threw up some quotation marks with his fingers. "Get a life."

"Well, you've got yourself a little pocket change now, why not go the other way—expand?"

A little pocket change, only Big Jake Rynerson would refer to two million as pocket change. "I think you better just come out and say whatever it is you're promoting here, Jake."

"I've got a little space here in the Castle. Nothing big, just enough for a small office. Of course you'd have all my business. No reason you couldn't hire an employee or two, take a little time for yourself."

Simon had the feeling Jake was still talking around the edges of something, avoiding it like a steaming pile of manure he was trying hard not to get his boots in. "And?"

A tiny smile flickered across the big man's face. "And I know Caity would like it."

Simon hesitated, not sure how to respond, not sure how he felt, his personal feeling so convoluted with the idea she might be involved in Kyra's abduction. "This was her idea?"

"Absolutely not. Nope, this here is my own little idea. I know she likes you, even an old fart like me can see that. And I kinda suspect you like her."

Simon couldn't deny that, but *like* had nothing to do with it—it was a matter of trust. A matter of finding out who Caitlin Wells really was, and what that *something missing* from her background was all about. "I'm not sure taking romantic advice from Jake Rynerson is the best idea I've ever heard."

Jake roared like an old lion, laughing until his eyes filled with tears. "By God, it's hard to argue with that. But I do know my Caity. Yessir, I do know a bit about that woman."

Simon wasn't so sure, but if everything went according to plan he would know soon.

Very soon.

CHAPTER FORTY-TWO

The Fishbowl

Monday, 24 November 11:08:13 GMT –0800

Charles had scheduled the meeting for eleven o'clock, but Simon waited until everyone was in the room before making his appearance. He felt nervous enough about seeing Caitlin and what might happen, without engaging in disingenuous small talk. He just wanted it to be over.

Everyone was already seated around the large board table: Jake and Billie on one side, their backs to the wall, Leo and Caitlin opposite, Charles at one end, impatient to get started. "Nice of you to join us," he snapped, not bothering to hide his irritation.

Simon just hoped the three actors in the drama—Billie, Jake, and Charles—didn't overplay their roles. "Sorry, the phone rang as I was walking out the door."

Caitlin gave him a little wink as he slid into the chair opposite Charles, but it wasn't the same, she obviously didn't know where she stood after his gentle but firm refusal to see her the previous night.

"Okay," Charles began, "let's get this over with. First of all, I want to tell you that Kyra is doing very well, considering her ordeal—" Jake reached over and covered both of Billie's hands with one of his giant meatgrinders. "And we're hoping for a full recovery. She has a slight case of malaria, but all tests indicate the baby is fine."

"Has she been able," Geske asked, "to provide any information about how many people were involved in her abduction and who they might be?"

"No, the only one she saw was this person known as El Pato. We're not even sure of his real name."

"But she must have heard *something*," Geske pressed. "Something that would help us?"

"Well, she did overhear a couple of phone calls, but not enough to help us identify anyone."

Geske bore in, somewhat atypical of his timid nature. "Nothing? I need to tell my company more than *nothing*."

"Only that she got the feeling that there was only one other person involved. Someone here in Vegas."

Geske bobbed his head emphatically, as if that confirmed his suspicions exactly. "And I guess we all know who that is."

Billie gave the man a look, so straight and hard it could have punched a hole in the man's forehead. "And just who would that be, Mr. Geske?"

Geske seemed to shrink a bit under the glare. "I'm sorry, Mrs. Rynerson, but I think it's pretty obvious."

"Well it's not obvious to me. Explain."

"Well, if I understand the sequence of events, this El Pato character disappeared the same time as Tony, along with the money. That seems pretty clear to me."

Billie looked ready to explode. "No, I don't believe it! Tony would never have done anything to harm Kyra."

"I don't believe it either," Caitlin quickly added, "and I think it's pretty damn lousy of you to suggest it."

Leo dissolved deeper into his chair.

"Now Caity," Jake cut in, "don't pick on Leo. I'm afraid he's got a point."

Billie turned on her ex. "You never liked him, Jake."

"Well, maybe I didn't," Jake admitted, "but the facts speak for themselves."

"Okay, okay," Charles interjected, before things got out of hand. "It doesn't matter what *we* think. The FBI will be taking over the investigation. That's the reason I asked you all to be here."

Simon tried to gauge how everyone accepted the news, but if it made anyone nervous they didn't show it. Jake and Billie, of course, knew what was going on. Geske looked a bit curious, nothing more, and Caitlin continued to seethe silently over the attack on Tony.

"There will be a team of agents here tomorrow," Charles continued, "and they would like you all to stick around for a—"

"That's impossible," Simon interrupted, "I've got a business to run. I need to get back to New York."

Charles held up a hand. "Hold on, just hear me out. I anticipated that. And I know Leo wants to file his report and start enjoying his retirement. So, I pulled a few strings." He gave them all a look, letting them know it was no easy task. "The Bureau's agreed to let me conduct the initial interviews."

"What's that mean," Billie asked, "initial interview?"

Charles thumped a stack of papers lying on the table. "It's nothing more than a compilation of information. Who you are, your relationship to the parties involved, everything you know, everything you did, the whole enchilada. There's even a section for what you *believe*." He looked directly at Caitlin. "So that's the place to express your opinion."

She looked right back at him. "That could take hours."

"Yes, and since you're not to discuss the facts among yourselves or form any consensus, you need to complete the forms with me in the room. This information will provide the investigators with an overview of the situation prior to any formal interview. It's not something you have to do, but I guarantee it will save you lots of hours in the long run. It's up to you."

"Of course we'll do it," Jake snapped, "why wouldn't we?" For Caitlin, such words amounted to a direct order; for everyone else, a challenge none would dare argue against.

"Good," Charles continued, as if that settled the matter. "If anyone needs to make a call or use the bathroom—" He hooked a thumb toward Jake's private dressing room and shower. "That place is quiet as a tomb." He circled the table, handing each of them one of the multilayer forms. "By the way, I received a call a few minutes ago from Colonel Mendoz, who's in charge of the search. He thinks they've found the location where Kyra was held. They're just waiting for additional troops before moving in. If El Pato or Tony are still there, he'll have them within the next hour or two. We may get those bastards yet."

"I assure you," Billie snapped, "my son-in-law is *not* one of those bastards."

"Yes, ma'am, I hope you're right."

The clock, Simon thought, was now ticking, so whoever the bastard was—Geske or Wells—they would have to make a move soon or risk being caught. He forced his hand to move over the paper, to keep up the charade as everyone began working on their forms, but now that the moment had arrived he couldn't look at Caitlin for fear she might see the truth. Worse, he wasn't sure he could ever look himself in the mirror; what kind of man falls in love with a woman and then tries to send her away for life? *Love,* was that possible? *No,* too soon for love. But serious *like.*

The object of his thoughts was suddenly on her feet. "Excuse me, I need to make a call."

Those were the exact words Simon didn't want to hear. He exchanged a quick glance with Charles, who looked stunned. The problem for Simon was not the lack of belief, but the fact that he did believe—he just didn't want to. He found himself counting off the minutes, almost afraid to breathe for fear El Pato's phone would start to vibrate.

But five minutes later she was back, and whatever call she made, it was not the one he was both dreading and expecting. Another twenty minutes crept by, enough time to conjure up fresh doubts as to his analytical ability. If not Caitlin or Geske, who? Lost in thought, he hardly paid attention when Leo disappeared into the bathroom, an act, Simon reminded himself, that did not exactly qualify as criminal behavior. Then he felt the vibration.

He hesitated, not quite believing it was happening, then the adrenaline kicked in and he felt an amazing sense of calm and clarity, his body reacting before he consciously issued the command. He reached down, unclipped the phone from his belt, activated the microrecorder, and started across the room. Charles stepped past him, his passkey out. Simon took a breath, covered the mouthpiece with a thin piece of perforated foam, and tried to imitate El Pato's grunting tone. "Hola."

There was a slight hiccup in time—a virtual lifetime in Simon's mind—followed by Leo's tentative response. "You know who this is?"

Simon nodded, Charles turned the key and snapped open the door.

"Yes, Leo, I know exactly who this is."

Stunned, Geske looked like a man caught with his pants down. Charles plucked the condemning instrument from his hand. "Leo Geske, you're under arrest for kidnapping, extortion, conspiracy, and just a whole bunch of nasty shit—including murder."

"But I—"

"Save your breath, Leo. There's a federal agent in my office who can't wait to hear what you have to say."

It was now, Simon had a feeling, time to fall on the sword. The confused look on Caitlin's face confirmed it.

"What just happened here?"

He tried to think of some good way to explain, but there was no *good way*. "What Charles said earlier about closing in on El Pato—that wasn't exactly true."

"Oh?" The wheels behind her gray eyes were starting to spin.

"El Pato is dead. I had his phone. We knew whoever called had to be his partner. Leo Geske just confirmed that link."

"But—" She shook her head, struggling to sort out the pieces. "What did Charles mean, *murder?*"

"I'm sorry to have to tell you like this, but Tony is dead."

She spun around, her eyes moving from Jake to Billie and back to Jake. "I . . . you knew." A statement, not a question.

"Caity, honey—"

She cut him off, turning back to Simon. "So this was all a charade, to see who would—" The wheels were slowing down, the answers falling into place; that besides Geske, she was the only person in the room who didn't know what was going on, that she was the only other possible *who*. She glared at him, started toward the door, then spun back, lashing his face with a blistering slap. "You sonofabitch." Then she turned and stomped out of the room.

"She'll get over it," Jake said. "I'll talk to her."

"No you won't," Billie said, her voice soft but decisive. "I'll talk to her."

But Simon had a feeling that all the talk in the world wouldn't put Simon and Caitlin together again. No one wanted to be suspected of kidnapping and murder. She needed to lash out at someone, and though he didn't like it, she had found the right person.

Las Vegas

Monday, 24 November 05:53:09 GMT –0800

"I didn't know you were a player."

Without turning, Simon held up a finger. "Just a sec." Buried in the middle of a green-felt sea, he knew Caitlin's sudden appearance at the blackjack tables was not by happenstance. She wanted to *settle things*, to deliver her it-was-nice-knowing-you, now-go-to-hell speech. He dropped another twenty-five-dollar chip alongside his original bet, split his eights, and motioned for a hit. He caught a queen, for a total of eighteen, motioned to stay, and pointed to the second eight.

The dealer pulled a four. *Twelve.*

Simon scratched again and caught another four. *Ugh. Sixteen,* but the dealer was showing nine and Simon had no choice—not if you knew the odds—and scratched again.

A deuce—*eighteen*. Not great, two losing hands more than likely.

As the dealer moved on to the next player, Simon took a deep breath and swiveled around, ready to face the bad news with a smile. Dressed in her usual Kate Hepburn attire—slacks and a mannish shirt with an up-turned collar—Caitlin somehow managed to look seductive, understated, and unattainable, all at the same time. "No, I wouldn't really consider myself a *player*," he answered, "but I've been known to hit the tables from time to time."

"It looks like you know what you're doing."

"If I knew what I was doing I wouldn't be sitting here, right?"

She leaned forward, near his ear, her voice low. "I think you've earned a little recreation." Then she gave him a knowing wink. "You can afford it."

"Oh God, don't tell me everyone knows."

"No, but Jake wanted my opinion before he wrote the check. Wanted to know if I thought the amount was appropriate."

Though he knew better, Simon couldn't resist. "And?"

She smiled, just a little, but the smile was not conveyed solely by the curve of her lips—her eyes were a part of it, their blue-gray color filled with what seemed to be genuine affection. "I told him I thought you were worth twice that amount." She nodded toward the table. "The dealer had an eight in the hole. You won both hands."

He reached back, pulled his money, and motioned to the chair alongside. "Lara just left, she's having dinner with Billie and Jake. You want to play?" He knew she wouldn't, knew she had an agenda that didn't include the dealer and four other people at the table.

"I was hoping to buy you a drink—" She hesitated, just long enough to convey a measure of self-doubt. "If you're interested."

Of course he was interested; until that moment of hesitation he was almost certain his suspicions had ruined any chance he might have with the bodacious Caitlin Wells. "Sure." He shoved his chips toward the dealer, waited for the young woman to convert his quarters into hundreds, tipped her twenty-five, and stood up. "You have someplace in mind?" *Your room or mine? Get real, Leonidovich, not until the Gods of Serendipity and Fair Play give you a Tom Selleck body.*

She smiled knowingly, as if reading his mind. "I do. Follow me."

He fell in behind as she began weaving her way between tables, toward the back of the casino. "Looks like you did okay, Leonidovich."

"Picked up a couple hundred. I'm satisfied."

She glanced back over her shoulder. "So what's your system?"

He shrugged; he didn't really have a *system,* it was more a *method* of play, not much more than common sense. "I do a number of things, try to read the bias of the cards, bet high when the deck's running in my favor, bet the minimum when it's not. Most important, I don't get greedy. Quit when I'm ahead."

"That's a pretty good set of rules." She smiled, a tiny curl of the upper lip. "Guess I won't have to boot your butt out of here?"

"Don't even think about it, Wells, I happen to be a very good friend of the owner." He meant it in jest, of course, but realized that was exactly how he felt.

"I'll keep that in mind." She skirted past an open but cordoned-off high-stakes Baccarat area—open to anyone willing to bet at least a thousand a hand—turned into a nondescript service hallway and then around another blind corner to the Cigar Bar, a subdued, intimate watering hole with plush carpeting, small pedestal tables, and deep comfortable chairs. The lights were muted, the furnishings red mahogany, the carpet hunter green. Simon paused in the doorway, waiting for his eyes to adjust. There were rows of bottles and crystal decanters, beer pumps with ivory handles, and a glassed-in wall of cigars. Except for the bartender—a man with silver-gray hair, who looked to be almost seventy—the room was empty. "This is great, but I don't know how anyone could find the place without a map."

"That's the idea." She led the way to a corner table, well away from the bar.

The bartender arrived within seconds. "Good evening, Ms. Wells."

"Good evening, Jerry. Happy birthday, plus a day."

"Thanks. I'm glad you stopped by, I wanted to thank you personal for the check and the flowers—" He nodded toward a mixed bouquet near the end of the bar. "That's a first for me."

"Eighty years too late, then. I hope you like them."

"Just as long as I'm not pushing 'em up from below." He chuckled, amused by his own little joke. "I've been telling everyone I've got an admirer."

Caitlin reached out and squeezed the man's hand. "And you do."

Jerry grinned like a schoolboy, his face turning pink as a new sunburn. "What can I get you two?"

Caitlin turned to Simon. "I think we should celebrate. Would you share a bottle of champagne?"

He nodded, not sure what they were celebrating: past, present, or the long good-bye. She turned back to the bartender. "A bottle of the Louis Roederer, Jerry. The Cristal Rose 95."

"Yes, ma'am. Coming right up."

"I think *you're* the one who has an admirer," Simon whispered as Jerry disappeared behind the bar. "I can't believe the guy's eighty."

"We offered him a nice retirement package but he didn't want to hear it. His wife died a few years back and we're about the only family he has. As long as he can do the job, Jerry's got a place at the Sand Castle."

"I have the feeling he has a place here whether he can do the job or not."

"You're probably right," she agreed. "I'd find something for him."

"What did you mean about not wanting people to find this place?"

"This room is primarily for celebrities and whales—a place for them to relax away from the crowds."

"And if Joe Public happens to wander in?"

"We show them a menu. Everything is top of the line and the prices reflect that."

"So most people bail out before they order?"

"Or they have one drink and skedaddle. If any of our *special* clients are here, we just say the room has been reserved and give them a drink coupon for one of the other bars." She gave Jerry a wink as he arrived with the cooler and two crystal, coupe-style champagne glasses. "Believe me, Jerry knows how to handle the situation without embarrassing anyone."

"Anything to eat?" Jerry asked as he extracted the cork, the PFSSST barely audible above the soft vocals of Billie Holiday. "Maybe some beluga to go with the champagne."

Caitlin looked at Simon.

"Maybe later," he answered, though he wasn't sure if there would a *later.*

Jerry nodded, filled their glasses, and withdrew to his spot behind the bar.

Simon raised his glass. "So what are we celebrating?"

"It seems we have a lot to celebrate. Kyra's safe return. And yours. Not to mention your well-earned financial reward."

"Nothing there I can't drink to. And we can't forget Tony. He deserves first salute." He extended his glass. "To Anthony Saladino. *Kotory nye poytyi na risk, nikogda nye vipit shampanska.*"

They clinked glasses and drank, each of them draining their glasses, as if needing to slake some emotional thirst. Caitlin sighed and laid her glass back on the table. "Okay, now tell me what you just said."

"It's an old Russian toast: 'He who doesn't risk never gets to drink champagne.' "

She nodded approvingly. "Good one. Most appropriate."

Simon refilled the glasses. "This is really good. Don't think I've ever seen a clear champagne bottle before."

"Only Louis Roederer makes one. It was created in 1876 for Tsar Alexander II. He wanted to *see* the champagne, to better enjoy its elegance and purity."

Simon raised his glass a second time. "To Alex, a man of good taste."

They touched glasses and drank again, this time taking only a sip. "And," Simon continued, "Marie Antoinette, a woman of fantasy and form."

"Oh no," Caitlin snapped back. "I'm not drinking to some other woman's grand tetons."

Simon pondered his glass, twisting it around in the soft light. "Hardly grand in size, but quite perfect in shape if I do say so." A shape, he thought, very similar to that of Caitlin Wells.

"That's nothing but a myth," she argued. "The champagne glass was not designed from a mold of Marie Antoinette's breast."

"I did say fantasy, Wells."

She cocked her head, as if trying to read his thoughts, her lips slowly curling into a mischievous smile. "Okay, Leonidovich, I'll drink to your fantasies." This time she drained her glass. "Just because you're half right."

"Oh?"

"It is the perfect shape."

"I think so." He refilled their glasses again, knowing she was stalling, working up the courage to say whatever it was she intended. They had nearly finished the bottle before she was finally ready. "I was really pissed at you this morning."

Was—past tense, at least that was positive. He reached

up and touched his cheek, still tender from the sting of her hand. "You made that clear enough."

"I just couldn't believe you really thought I might be involved."

"It's not what I *wanted* to believe. It's just that—"

"I know, I know, I've thought about it. It had to be Geske or me."

"Right."

"About the ear. I—"

"Forget the ear. Jake explained all that." Not that it didn't bother him, the fact that she would go that far for her employer, which made no sense unless there was something going on between them.

"And you thought I was hiding something."

Something missing. "Yes."

"You thought I might be angry at Jake over some past relationship? That he dumped me and I might be trying to even the score?"

That was one scenario. "It was obvious you two had a history."

She hesitated, let that percolate a good half minute, then met his eyes with an unflinching steadiness. "Yes, we have a history."

"It's none of my business." Yet he knew if there was ever the chance of anything between them, even a strong friendship, it would have to come out.

"Are you seriously considering Jake's idea, to open an office here in Vegas?"

He knew exactly why she was asking and where it would lead. "That depends."

"On what?"

There was no reason to avoid the truth; she already suspected and would never open up if he couldn't admit to it. "On you."

She smiled, clearly not surprised. "Oh hell, I guess it's going to come out eventually."

As much as he wanted to hear the truth, he realized he was forcing her. "You don't have to tell me."

But she had made up her mind and was now determined to tell the story, her voice going soft and distant, as far away as the memory. "My family came from Odessa, same as Jake's. Both my parents were alcoholics." She shook her head, as if that was the understatement of the century. "Things were pretty rough. By the time I was sixteen I had dropped out of school and was into drugs. One night three roustabouts picked me up outside a bar. They took me out to their rig—"

This was not what Simon expected. "Forget it. This is none of my business."

She ignored the interruption, her voice lost in the memory. "They got me into the logging trailer . . . that's where they bunked . . . and began taking turns. Then the rig boss walked in and the guys invited him to *join the party*. I was stoned and drunk, but I remember that, the first time I laid eyes on Big Jake Rynerson." A painful smile flickered across her face—there and gone. "Well, he joined in all right, but not the way those boys expected. He beat all three of them to within an inch of their lives." She paused, took a deep breath. "To make a long story short, I became Jake's cause. He made sure all my problems got wiped off the books—"

Something missing.

"—got me off the drugs, off the streets, and back into school. I rebelled of course, told him to go to hell, but he just ignored me. The minute I graduated high school he forced me into college. And he didn't just pay my tuition and forget me. Oh no, not Jake, he was there all the time, checking on me, demanding I do better, acting like a father. After a while I got tired of the fight and just went along. Then somewhere along the line I discovered I was smarter than ninety-nine percent of my classmates. It felt good being good at something and I began to demand more of myself. By the time I finished college I was at the top of my class. By then Jake had made it big in the oil business, and naturally I went to work for him. Hell, by that time I thought the guy was God."

Simon knew there was more, but had already heard more than he needed to—more than he had a right to. "Okay, I get the picture. That's enough."

She shook her head, refusing to stop, silent tears dripping onto the table. "About five years ago, when Jake was between wife three and four, we finally had our fling. One night. One terrible night. It felt incestuous, dirty, like I was going to bed with my father. Jake felt the same, maybe worse."

"Okay, that's enough."

She stared at the table, avoiding his eyes. "That was it, that one night, and believe me, neither of us has any interest in going down that ugly road again. Not that I don't love the guy, I do, like a father, and would do just about anything for him." Her eyes came up. "I guess you found that one out the hard way."

"I'm sorry, I had no idea."

She took a deep breath, gathering her reserves. "I feel so terrible about it. If Kyra ever found out I'd . . . I'd—"

"No one will ever hear it from me, you know that."

"Maybe I should have told you, made you understand, but you don't tell something like that to—" She hesitated, rubbing a sleeve across her eyes. "—to someone you really liked."

Like or liked—past or present? "No, of course you don't."

She let out a thin sigh. "You think maybe we could start over?"

He didn't really need to think about it; there were too many regrets in life, too many opportunities missed to pass up second chances. He reached out and took her hand. "It's nice to meet you, Caitlin Wells. My name is Simon Leonidovich."

"And it's very nice to meet you." She smiled, a wonderful, glowing smile that instantly buried the past. "What is it you do, Simon Leonidovich?"

"Nothing very exciting. I'm just a bagman."

Visit
❖ **Pocket Books** ❖
online at

....

www.SimonSays.com

....

Keep up on the latest new
releases from your favorite
authors, as well as author
appearances, news, chats,
special offers and more.

2381-01